Readers love *Valhalla* by ARI BACH

"…when it's not making you laugh, it'll make you think…."

—Lesbrary

"…it's well-written and very original for the right reader. I recommend it for science-fiction fans…"

—Hearts on Fire

"This is a very good book, full of action and intrigue."

—Glen Hates Books

By ARI BACH

VALHALLA
Valhalla
Ragnarök
Guðsríki

Published by HARMONY INK PRESS
http://www.harmonyinkpress.com

GUÐSRIKI

ARI BACH

Harmony Ink

Published by
HARMONY INK PRESS

5032 Capital Circle SW, Suite 2, PMB# 279, Tallahassee, FL 32305-7886 USA
publisher@harmonyinkpress.com • harmonyinkpress.com

This is a work of fiction. Names, characters, places, and incidents either are the product of author imagination or are used fictitiously, and any resemblance to actual persons, living or dead, business establishments, events, or locales is entirely coincidental.

Guðsríki
© 2015 Ari Bach.

Cover Art
© 2015 Ari Bach.
Cover Design
© 2015 Paul Richmond
Cover content is for illustrative purposes only and any person depicted on the cover is a model.

ISBN: 978-1-62380-110-6
Digital ISBN: 978-1-62380-735-1
Library of Congress Control Number: 2015912450
First Edition October 2015

Printed in the United States of America
∞
This paper meets the requirements of
ANSI/NISO Z39.48-1992 (Permanence of Paper).

Chapter I: Caithness

THERE WERE crosses everywhere in those days, all across America. They hung on people's walls. They covered Bibles, which you could buy at any bookstore. They stood tall on churches, for there were hundreds of churches in every big city. Even Jessica had a small silver cross on her necklace.

As she sat watching her son, a knock came at the door.

Jessica pushed herself up out of the chair. Her back hurt. She'd given birth days ago, but her back still hurt like hell. She opened the lock and saw a handsome man of about forty with brown curly hair.

"Hello, ma'am, I came over to see the miracle."

"Oh, yes," she said cheerfully, "come on in."

She led him past the couch to Andy Jr.'s crib. He gazed down in adoration.

"Just look at that, a little baby… boy?"

"Yes. His name is Andrew, after his father."

"And where is Andy Jr.'s daddy today?"

"Afghanistan. Gets back soon. He was supposed to get a phone call this morning, but—I'm sorry, please, have a seat."

He sat on the couch.

"Well, it's a shame he couldn't be here. My goodness, I haven't even introduced myself; I'm Ryan Sparks. My father, Pastor Sparks, will be here any minute now. He heads the little white church just down the road. I just wanted to welcome Andy Jr. to the neighborhood myself," he said, looking over and calling to Andy Jr. in his crib. "Your grandmommy told me all about you in church!"

Jessica smiled. "Oh! Of course."

"And forgive me for being forward, but I gotta say we'd be happy to see you in church every Sunday."

"Oh, yeah, I—I've been meaning to make a return to church. Especially now that Andy Jr. is here."

"We do encourage children of every age to come and hear the word! Children from conception and up."

She sat down in the chair beside the crib.

"So are you… nondenominational?"

"Well, it's Christianity that's nondenominational. You see, trying to divide up the church is simply against the church; there's only one true church, and all that talk about Baptist and Lutheran and all that nonsense is just that—nonsense. At my father's church, we accept anyone of any faith, as long as they believe," he said, counting on his fingers, "one, that Jesus Christ is our savior; two, one must be baptized to be saved; and three, the Lord hears prayers spoken in tongues. That's the one language that's pure, that the devil can't understand."

"So…. You take Catholics?"

"Well, we accept all faiths, but not heresy. See, that's a very wrong thing. There's a difference between acceptance and going too far. Are you…?"

"Oh no, only by technicality. Andrew's—my husband Andrew's father is strict Catholic, and they're not on speaking terms. His dad was very insistent we baptize Andrew Jr. Catholic and—"

"Say no more. Seen it a hundred times, and it's a sad, sad thing, but you're doing the right thing now. Yes, yes you are. I tell ya, I don't envy the world your son is going to grow up in. We're one of the last generations. All the signs are here, here for the end of days. Have you read the book of Revelations?"

"The whole Bible, even who begat who. But, you know, I think some in every generation believe they're the last, even in the Gospels—"

"Now that's getting into some technical mumbo jumbo my father can clear up. I myself don't like to read much. I'm all about a *personal* relationship with the Lord. Do you have that, Jessica?"

"I'd like to think so."

"Well, that's a start, but you need to know so."

"I do consider myself a Christian."

"That's good, Jessica. That's good. You should be very thankful for today, for ten fingers and ten toes."

Ryan looked over to Andrew.

"When was he born exactly?"

"At 5:30 a.m., two days ago. June sixth."

"That's what your mother said," he remarked cordially. "Any big birthmarks on his forehead, or his hands?"

"No, no, just the usual tiny spots."

"None that caught your attention?"

"No, why?"

"Oh, nothing, nothing. Just wondering. You're both American?"

"And proud of it."

"I saw a nice bright flag outside."

"Yep."

"We're lucky to live here, you know. When the end comes, there's no place I'd rather be."

"No, I suppose not," she replied, slightly amused at his apparent apocalyptic preoccupation. They both watched Andy Jr. stir in his crib for a moment. Jessica found the silence a bit awkward and spoke.

"So tell me about your dad."

"Well, ma'am, he's the most noble man I ever saw, and a good father to boot. He's also a first-rate pastor, and exorcist."

"Exorcist?"

"Absolutely. Why just this week there was an afflicted man in our congregation, and my father, he put that man on the floor, he grabbed ahold of that demon and told him in the name of Jesus Christ that he would hurt that man no more. And that demon, through the man, he shouted"—Ryan shifted to a mock demonic voice—"'*You cannot face me, for we are many, our name is Legion, and we will not leave!*' But my father shouted," Ryan screamed, "'*In the name of Christ you—*'"

Andy Jr. started crying at Ryan's shout. Ryan stopped and stared at him. "Funny he started crying when I said 'Christ' there."

Jessica ran over and held him.

"I think it was just the volume of it all. You have quite a voice."

"Well, thank you. You know I used to be a musician."

"Really. So, your father—"

"Oh he cured the man, that's for sure. The man suffered a broken arm and some severe contusions, but he was all right after that, all right in his soul."

"He broke his arm?"

"An exorcism isn't a pretty matter. You'll see that when you come in."

"I suppose I will," she said, less enthusiastic about attending. The silence grew more awkward as Ryan stared at Andy Jr.

"Harry Potter. That's what lies in wait for your son. They're gonna tempt him with witchcraft starting today, and perversion tomorrow. And it won't end until he's in the Kingdom of Heaven. There are adversaries out there. Did you know that's what the devil's name means? The adversary?"

Jessica nodded. After a moment, five loud, slow knocks came at the door.

"That will be my father."

Jessica moved to stand up, but Ryan jogged to the door and let his father in. He was an older man with white hair, wearing a white linen suit. He walked to Jessica and shook her hand firmly. His voice was soft and warm.

"You must be Jessica. A pleasure to meet you! I'm Cody Sparks."

"Thank you. Ryan was just telling me about you."

"Oh boy, you must be evangelized out by now. I'm sorry, my son can be a bit forward when it comes to his old man."

Ryan looked a bit ashamed.

"And that must be our new friend. What a strapping young lad!"

"Thank you!"

She nodded again and set him down in the crib. "So Ryan tells me you're pastor at the little white church out that way?"

"Sure am, services and school Sundays, studies Saturdays. Ice cream on Wednesdays! I'm proud to say there's not a man, woman, or child in this little town that doesn't attend regularly. Only a true church can earn that kind of loyalty. And I tell you we would love to see you there Sunday."

"Yes, I think I will. Will I meet Mrs. Sparks there too?"

The pastor bowed his head. "I'm afraid she died some time ago."

"Oh, I'm so sorry."

Ryan interrupted. "Christ tells us that in the end days it will be parents against their own children, and my mother was a good example. She wasn't a believer; she was never born again. Sure, she went to church, but—"

"We don't need to go into that, Ryan—" said Cody, but Ryan continued.

"She was sinful. Plain sinful. She read books. Books about Islam and Judaism. One of those people who thought Jesus was a Jew, but the synagogues we know today, those are the synagogue of Satan. And he pulled her in like a hooked fish. She was a school teacher, mind you, and she had power over many a child's mind. And she used it to teach blasphemies. Evolution. That we came from apes, and what sickens me, this sickens me most of all, she knew Genesis. She read the Bible every week, but she taught lies. And she taught tolerance of the faggotry too. Tolerance."

"I'm sorry to—"

"You want to know why she died? Why my momma died? Because the avenging angel, the angel Samael, came to her. Whose name means 'The Poison of God.' On the night of my tenth birthday I saw—"

"Ryan, we've known this kind woman about one fourth of an hour."

"Our Lord is a Lord of fire," Ryan said, "and woe to she who forgets it."

Another awkward silence gripped the room.

"You know, Jessica," Cody began, "I prayed for you last night. I didn't know it was you that I prayed for, because I prayed in tongues, but it was. You see, you are a smart woman, and a good woman. And what's coming won't be easy for you, but you will survive, and you will survive because Jesus will help you. I want you to remember when things seem impossible, or rough, that he is watching over you. That he is there to help you if you'll only turn to him."

"I know it. And thank you for saying so."

The sun sat on the mountains. Cody went on.

"Do you know what evil is, Jessica? It's not a big red man with horns. It's not a Nazi or an Iraqi or even a democrat congressman. It's the apathy to do what's right. As a mother, you will determine the fate of your son. And the only thing that makes that responsibility possible is the example set by the Holy Bible. When God looked down and saw the evils of men, the sins of men.... He knew in his infinite wisdom that another flood, another Sodom and Gomorrah, another tenth plague, he knew none of that would teach us sheep the lesson. He knew he had to make a sacrifice, the ultimate sacrifice. He gave us his Son, Jessica. His only begotten Son."

The sun set.

"It is by his blood we are redeemed. And by his grace we live our lives. And by that sacrifice we may enter the Kingdom of Heaven. If the Lord could give his Son for us, then we must give our children to the Lord. So when I ask you if you know what evil is, I need to hear you reply that evil is when a good parent disobeys the Lord. When a good soul lets evil happen, because she is too afraid or too lazy or too self-centered to do a hard thing when she knows that thing is right."

"I agree, I agree absolutely."

"That's good, ma'am," said Ryan. "That's good. It will make this all a lot easier."

Jessica didn't understand. "I'm sorry, make what?"

"The Lord gives me warnings," said Cody. "He tells me about the dangers that come to my fine town, and into my church. I keep my neighborhood safe."

Ryan stirred. "Your son was born on June sixth, 2006."

Jessica didn't understand.

"Six, six, six," said Ryan.

Jessica spoke up. "Whoa, whoa, whoa. Let's not—"

"Look at how you react! You fear the words because you already know the truth of them!"

"Look, I'm a good Christian, but that shit is—"

"Shit? Shit!" shouted Cody, furious. "You will not speak again! You are the whore of Babylon, a bitch of the devil, and I will not tolerate such—"

Andy Jr. began to cry again.

"Hear his wail," Cody proclaimed, seemingly happy at being justified, "the voice of sin and profanity, enraged at the truth!"

Jessica ran to his crib and held him.

"Okay, you get out right now. You won't do an exorcism. Not on my baby, you'll hurt him. Now listen—"

"We won't. We won't do that. We didn't come to do that. It is clear, ma'am, that your son is the spawn of the devil's loins. And we are here to send him back to hell."

"Leave or I'll call the police!"

"Gee, I must have never introduced myself properly. Ryan Sparks, Chief of Police for this little village."

"Leave now!"

"We will, we will," said Cody quietly, subdued. "Son, let's go to the car."

In an instant they were gone. Andy Jr. stopped crying for a moment. Jessica held him close, breathing heavily. She was beyond scared. She did the only thing she knew to do. She grabbed Andy Jr. and prayed.

"Our father in heaven, I beg you. Protect my son. Protect my baby. Protect us from the men who wish us harm."

She began to stutter; Andy Jr. began to cry again.

"Please, just please protect him. Let them see he's just a child. Let them change their minds. Please, God, don't let them come back. Oh God," she pleaded, her voice quivering, "please save us from your followers."

She began to cry.

"God, let Andrew come home and protect us. Protect his baby. Those men are Christians, Lord. Remind them not to do us any harm. Please! Don't let them come back!"

Five loud, slow knocks came at the door. Jessica suddenly realized she'd not locked it. She left Andy Jr. in the crib and ran up to the door. She reached out to lock it just as it burst open, hitting her in the head and knocking her out.

When she awoke she was bound with rope. Cody and Ryan stood over the crib, against which one had rested a rifle. Ryan was holding the lamp she kept by the crib's side in his right hand. Cody saw her stir and spoke.

"We had higher hopes for you, ma'am, that when the time came, you would let us do what we had to do in peace."

"No, no, no, no—" She tried to get out of the rope.

"You'll be silent now," said Ryan. "I don't want you to shout. You know there's only one house close enough to hear, and you should know that Margaret lent us the rope."

"You're lying."

"She comes to our church, Jessica. She told us when he was born."

"No. No! You're lying, you're lying! She wouldn't."

"Jessica, your mother Margaret is a faithful woman. And I think you know the truth."

Jessica sobbed. She didn't have the strength to do anything else. Her head stung and ached worse than she'd ever felt before. The men turned back to Andy Jr.

"Come on, Dad, it's time. Let's do this here."

"Let us pray."

They closed their eyes. Ryan spoke.

"Lord, we have found thy enemy, and found the seed of the devil's loins."

Cody started speaking in tongues. Jessica was petrified. Ryan spoke, eyes closed.

"As you asked Abraham, as you asked Noah and your own son in Gethsemane, we do thy bidding here today."

Cody's voice grew louder, deeper as he shouted glossolalia.

"Praise Jesus!" shouted Ryan. "Praise the Lord God! Thy will be done!"

Ryan lifted up the lamp, hesitated, and brought it down on the baby's head. Cody stopped praying and picked up the rifle. Ryan struck the baby again.

"Praise Jesus!"

Cody crushed his ribs with the wooden stock.

"Praise Jesus! Praise the Lord!"

Ryan struck again and again, disfiguring the child into pulp. Cody erupted into tongues again as he grabbed the gruesome mess and crushed organs and bone.

"Praise Jesus!" Ryan shouted.

Jessica was screaming, but no sound came out. Ryan and Cody came out of their frenzy and nodded to each other. They held bloody hands.

"Amen."

"Amen, Lord, amen."

Cody and Ryan walked to the kitchen and washed their hands in the sink, dripping blood on her dishes and the baby's used bottles. Jessica stared across the room to the crib. She saw blood drip over the side. Ryan returned and knelt beside her.

"God will forgive you, Jessica. He will. Our God is a loving God, and he will hear you repent. He's gonna watch over you. As for us, we are watching you too."

He cut her ropes and left, but she couldn't move. She tried to cry but couldn't.

Cody departed, and Ryan moved to close the door behind them. "Of course you are still welcome at church next Sunday."

He left, and she heard their car drive away. She crawled to the bathroom and tried to throw up, but nothing came. She sat there, still and dazed, staring at the stray wet hairs and specks of grime on the side of the toilet bowl. She sat up against the bathroom wall and went numb, still and unmoving. Eventually she slept, shivering.

She awoke without any sense of denial. She knew what had happened. She knew it was real. In time she was able to stand. She looked in the mirror. She stared at herself. Tried to think clearly but couldn't. Then she spotted it. The cross on her neck.

She grabbed it and tore it off as if stung by it, threw it on the floor. It was dawn. She'd slept through the night. She absentmindedly looked to the clock on the counter. It read 7:59 a.m. She knew what was coming at 8:00. Andrew hadn't been able to call the day before as planned, to hear his son's voice. At 8:03 the phone rang.

It took all Jessica had to answer it. She didn't even think of how to tell him. She didn't think he'd believe her if she did. Thankfully he wasn't on the other end of the line. It was an operator.

"This is DSN. We have a call from Corporal Andrew Geki for Jessica Geki and son."

She held still for a moment, thinking of any way not to tell him. She knew she couldn't do it, there was no way. She hung up the phone. The call was for her and her son. And her son wasn't home.

OVER MOUNTAINS and frozen wastes, Vibeke trudged through the snow. It crunched with every step and built up before her, so deep that sometimes she had to sidestep the growing mass. She let it collect over and over out of apathy. She didn't feel it through her Thaco armor's fur, but she existed in those days in a constant state of frozen cold, body and mind.

She tried as hard as she could not to think. It was difficult in the near absolute silence, the muffling snow. She inevitably failed to clear her mind and focus on the vast unbroken surface, sparkling day and night even under the thick clouds.

The cloud cover was almost as bright at night as it was by day. After the sun set behind the dull gray sky, it began to glow like the fog atop a vast city. But there were no artificial lights. No city had lit up at night for weeks now. No net link had blinked. The power stations had been the first targets. Quark inversion plants, nuclear plants, geothermal wells, even solar intakes were annihilated.

Some batteries still held a charge. Anything plated in Valhalla gold was functional: her armor, her microwave, her Tikari, and the other Tikari. The Tikari that followed her like an unwanted puppy. With all the radiation in the air, it would never need to recharge. It would follow her for the rest of her life, and then…. The thought sickened her.

She thought about microwaving it a hundred times. Or sending her own to kill it, or smashing it with her boot the next time it landed on a rock. Sometimes she felt Violet's stare emanating from its eyes. The violating stare she was so averse to seeing from her. In those moments she was sure Violet was watching her through it. That only made her miss Violet more. She had craved another month of nothingness in which they could talk, link back and forth like the trip to Mars. Finally she had it, and Violet wasn't there. The link was offline.

She stopped under a dead tree where the snow was only half a meter deep and sloughed the icebox off her shoulders. She stretched her arms and rubbed her trapezius muscles. It was a damn heavy icebox. Hundreds of years old and made of hollow metal, courtesy of the Frasers. She opened it and dug out the old browning snow, then packed in fresh white matter from around her. Her only daily ritual in the last weeks. The snow didn't turn brown the way it did at first when it was full of blood. The blood was almost all gone. She closed the box and set it aside.

From her chest pockets she took another slug of radiophobic gel and slathered it on her hands and face, and through her hair, the only spots her suit didn't protect. Her training did her well; survival in a radioactive zone was second nature to any Valkyrie. She could do little about food and water, the water being snow from a radioactive blizzard, and the food being…. Well, the food was a bit radioactive too but never in short supply. Internal radiation tabs kept her healthy enough.

She reached into her food satchel and pulled out some jerky. It was one of her last pieces, so she'd be on the lookout for more. She wondered if eating nothing but real meat would give her gout. Her legs hurt enough already without acid crystals forming.

She didn't sleep. She wasn't tired. She wanted to keep moving, to get to Orkney and see Violet again. All other goals in her life were extinguished. There was nothing to distract her. She stood up and adjusted her scraps and satchels.

She was coming to the remains of Caithness, the radiation was growing worse, and the people were growing more frequent. She spotted them in the patches of snowless earth, around the houses and stray buildings. Fires grew more and more common, the tame kind in cans and pits along the road, the kind with animals roasting and people gathering for warmth. And the kind that devoured what buildings were still standing. Started by carelessness or by gangs, vandals for whom the world wasn't wrecked enough. A blaze in the northern sky suggested some of the massive fires from the bombs still burned.

She assumed gangs got the Frasers sometime after she left. Lairg wasn't a big town, but looting had already begun when she departed. She considered staying to protect them. After all, she thought, she had nowhere else to be. With the ravine vaporized and nearly everyone she knew dead, there was no rush to get anywhere. The snippet of link from Orkney hadn't come yet. Her only discernible will was to see Violet again, and even that was corroded and rotten.

She tried to think happier thoughts. She assigned the Frasers a pleasant death in her mind, freezing in their sleep, cuddled together and as happy as anyone would ever be again. Surely they and others had met with merciful fates. Many were simply vaporized painlessly. Nothing more merciful than that. Happy thoughts.

With the fires came wanderers. Most kept their distance. Most didn't want any confrontation—they were just walking, who knew to where. Not them. Many were just walking away from someplace worse. She knew from the tumors that some were from down south. Inverness had taken a wave bomb, or at least been in one's range.

The tumored people were no threat. Just hideous. Monstrous, really. They wandered sullen around the landscape, their deformities sloshing or bouncing gently as they walked. Their moans were always feeble and pained. The one she'd seen up close didn't even see her. Its eyes were gone, melted, mutating into fingers. It only caught her because she didn't care to hide the crunching of snow under her feet.

"Have you any arms?" it called.

"Two," Vibs muttered back.

"Weapons, I mean?"

"Plenty."

"Would you be so kind as to use them?"

It stood before her and held out its upper extremity stumps. She pulled her microwave and asked if it was ready.

"Can you tell me a joke? I'd love to die laughing," it begged.

Vibeke thought for a moment.

"So three guys were talking. The first said, 'My wife read *A Tale of Two Cities* when she was pregnant and she gave birth to twins.' 'What a coincidence,' says guy two. 'My wife was reading *The Three Musketeers*, and she gave birth to triplets.' Then the third guy gets up and runs home. They call after him, 'What's wrong?' And he shouts back, 'My wife is reading *Ali Baba and the Forty Thieves*!'"

The deformed creature chuckled. She fired and kept walking.

One more person, or former person, that she'd killed. She estimated her mistakes in the silo had killed about five billion and mutated five billion more. She knew it was optimistic to guess ten billion had survived the war unscathed, but she was in an optimistic mood. All she had to deal with were walking cancerous masses.

At first. As she approached Caithness her wilderness survival tactics were gradually getting replaced by her urban disaster tactics.

There were the healthier people, the survivors who got pushier with their demands for food. Uncharacteristically she gave them food when she had an excess; it was as easy a way to get rid of them as killing them. That marginal laziness had saved dozens of lives.

She killed the rude ones, of course, or the ones that posed any threat. But like any other low animal, they were most threatening in gangs, and closer to the city she found more and more gangs. Robber gangs, cannibal gangs, the common huddle for warmth gang, and the most aggressive— and Vibeke's personal favorite—the rape gang. As buildings grew common and fires could be spotted at every street corner, she found one.

She could see the gang long before they could see her. Five men, one captive. Female, about Vibeke's age and build, though without the muscle. They were letting her freeze naked on the ground. They were already finished with her.

She hated seeing victims. It was depressing, and there was enough depression in the air already. She tried to feel more for them but never managed it. As soon as the word "victim" crossed her consciousness, she felt nothing. The very notion of a victim was alien to her. She knew better rationally. Not everyone on earth could kill off a gang of men in a second. But she didn't feel it in the form of sympathy. Most of the time, she felt angry at them and didn't know why.

But victims aside, she had come to enjoy meeting rape gangs. They were in fact the highlight of her postwar life. She had to suppress a grin at seeing the latest.

She'd grown downright playful with them. The last she'd killed with completely unnecessary slowness, cutting off their feet in one swoop of her Tikari and letting them bleed, watching them crawl, cradle their legs, hope to survive. It was the hope that she relished, the darkest humor she found in their absurd expectation she would let them live. That they even wanted to live, or—if they were that far beyond stupid—that they deserved to.

Rapists tasted best of anything in the region. Most of the animals were long dead and their rotten flesh was hard to choke down. She hadn't bothered with any of the stringy, starving men or women; she wasn't some kind of sadistic cannibal, just a contingency cannibal, and there was no shortage of healthy bullies. They stole food from the weak and kept fat in their figures, necessary to digest their muscle. But there was something else in devouring rapists, a more psychological spice that came with ridding the world of them.

Five men, one captive. Valhalla training demanded she send her Tikari through their necks, killing the men before they had any chance to attack. That was the wise thing to do. But what had wisdom ever earned her? Wisdom had ended the damn world.

"Help! Please!" Vibeke whimpered.

The men spotted her. Laughed.

"I'm freezing," called Vibeke weakly. "I need food!"

Their victim tried to call out to warn her. Vibeke tried not to look at her. Pale, naked, scrawny. She might have been beautiful before she had starved.

A man kicked her to shut her up. Vibeke limped closer and slid her cloak back to reveal her suit, telling it to pull in its fiber. The men wouldn't recognize Thaco armor. They'd just see the tight mesh that clung to her skin between its metal slats.

"We can help you," one called out as the others giggled. She approached the man who had kicked the girl. Vibeke tried not to look at her. She was pathetic. They were all the same; they were all weak, and weakness demanded contempt, or so she told herself. But above all they were to be ignored in favor of the warmth to come. Blood was always warm. No matter how cold the climate or cruel the vanquished, their blood was always hot on her skin.

"Please, I just need some food."

"Yeah, we can get you food," he said, grinning widely. They always seemed so happy. They thought something was funny about what they planned to do. Vibs couldn't fathom it. At least her dad was ashamed of what he was. Violet was ashamed of what she did. But all the men in gangs were proud.

Two men grabbed her from behind and held her as the man before her tugged at her collar. She acted afraid.

"Don't be afraid! Don't run away," laughed one of the men.

"No, please don't!" she begged. "You don't have to, just stop."

"I… don't think so." More laughter. The laughter pissed her off to no end. She gave them a chance. She always did out of a perverse curiosity to see if any would ever take it. They never did.

"Are you sure?" she asked.

The men looked slightly bewildered. "Yeah. Yeah, we're sure. How do you take this thing off?"

She sloughed off her boxes and satchels and tried to sob. "You run your finger down the back."

One of the men holding her stepped up and pulled off her cloak, and put his finger right at the top of her neck, exactly where she needed it for Kata 17. It was so rare in real combat that she got to use a Kata exactly as she'd learned it. But two men holding her, one before her—it was the exact setup she needed.

Within two seconds she pulled her left arm free, held her hand over the right man's grip, keeping it in place, twisted her elbow back, and snapped his arm with a deafening crack. As he pulled away, she grabbed his finger behind her and bent it backward over the back of his hand, then pushed forward, flipping him by his disjointed digit.

Then a kick to the laughing man, a punch to the fellow on the left. It was as close as she got to dancing. The other two men attacked, clumsily. Rape gangs never seemed to have any training. She hadn't fought a person with training since she'd stunned the aus-guard at the silo.

The first oncoming idiot was quite buff and might have posed a minimal threat, so she snapped his neck up front before pummeling the last into the snow. They were all on the ground. About ten seconds from capture to victory. Not a record for her.

She knelt by the formerly laughing man, who stumbled back from her and up against a wall.

"Don't be afraid," she mimicked him. "Don't run away."

She gently brushed his legs open and unbuttoned his pants. She winked at him, and he grew confused. He didn't resist as she lowered his zipper and reached into his underwear.

He began to resist when she grabbed his balls and pulled as hard as she could, crushing a testicle and ripping the skin. He screamed a ridiculous scream, one of the funnier ones she'd heard.

"Shush shush shush, you don't need to scream."

He kept screaming.

"Shut the fuck up!"

He went silent, and she loosened her grip.

"Now what were you gonna do to me?" she asked. "Huh?"

She squeezed again. He screamed his monkey-like scream. The man to her left propped himself up to attack her. Her Tikari rocketed into his head and took him down.

"Come on, what were you gonna do?"

"Fuck you," he wept, "I was gonna fuck you."

"How?" She pulled again; he threw up from the pain. "Come on, be specific, you suck at pillow talk."

"I—I don't know maybe a—I don't know, just a blowjob?"

"You want to put this little thing in my mouth?"

"What?"

"That's what you had in mind, your dick in my mouth?"

"Yes, yes, I—I'm sorry!"

"Ohoho, you don't know the meaning of sorry yet."

She pulled again as hard as she could, ripping his genitals out by their roots. He screamed a much less funny scream. Two of the men were running away. She Tikaried their necks and recalled the blade to her shoulder.

"I'm happy to oblige, you know. Your oral fantasies."

As he watched she bit the skin around the bloody base of his penis and pulled some of his connective tissue out with her teeth. He fainted.

"Wimp."

She threw the genitals over her shoulder and had her Tikari slit his throat. She began to carve him up along with the others, gutting them like fish. Suddenly she caught sight of their victim, cowering in a corner of icy masonry. Vibs took some of the men's clothes and threw them her way. She began pulling them on.

"You have to act fast, you know. The trick is to get the guts out and pack the hole with snow so it brings the body temperature down quickly. That preserves the meat for a while."

The victim covered her mouth with her hands. Vibs was disappointed by her. At least some of the victims thanked her. Maybe she was hungry, she thought. She sent her Tikari to cut off a slice of meat from the castrated man and bring it to her. She drew her microwave and cooked it thoroughly, then tossed it to the woman.

"C'mon, eat up, you're all skin and bones."

The woman didn't even pick up the meat. Ungrateful bitch.

"Fine, more rapist for me."

She picked up the fillet and took a bite. It was good. The man wasn't too stringy nor too fat. It was much better than the last man, a lone wolf who was suitable only for jerky, which really took too long to make and wasn't a good route at all given the lack of flavorful marinade. She'd keep the new batch cold and only cook as she consumed, and she'd try lighting a fire and cooking them instead of using her microwave directly. The microwave cooked the meat thoroughly but sort of sucked the flavor out of it.

"You're missing out."

She offered it to the victim again, waving the floppy meat at her, but she was already half dressed and running away. South. Vibs shouted after her.

"There's nothing that way!"

She kept running.

"Have fun dying, ya dumb slut!"

She felt a pang of guilt for the last slur, but silenced it quickly. She was getting fed up with victims. She just didn't understand them. She had been one too once, but those times were so far in the past; she was under two decades old, but she felt a lifetime beyond her childhood. Whatever she had grown up to be, it simply had no taste for weakness.

But rapist ass meat, that she had a taste for. She butchered only the yummiest bits from each of the other men. It wasn't like she could drag their bodies all the way to Orkney.

She stood again, gave the laughing man's corpse one last kick, then set out eastward, gnawing on her last old slice of rapist jerky. Good riddance to it; a fine idea but too chewy. She was certain the new batch would taste better properly cooked. She cursed the lack of salt and vowed to check for the stuff in the remains of Caithness.

"I AM ready to relieve you, sir," said Lieutenant Pytten.

"Are we really doing this, Pytten?" asked Lieutenant Bax.

"I am ready to relieve you, sir."

Bax nodded, then looked angrily at the deck.

"I am ready to be relieved," replied Bax, annoyed. "Be aware we remain stationary at 61.400N 1.200E on the sea floor. Our ship remains dead in the water, our captain remains deceased, we're all going to die when the bulkhead collapses in an hour, and you're still fucking following protocol like a fucking *peräeva*. Does that report satisfy your needs, sir?"

"I relieve you, sir."

"I stand relieved," he said sarcastically. "Attention on the bridge, Lieutenant Pytten has the deck."

Bax saluted with mocking strength and pomp, then headed to walk out. "Glad we'll all die on your watch, you stuck-up freeloading oxygen-breathing guppy from—"

"This is Lieutenant Pytten, I have the deck. Ensign Hetulat," said Pytten, "please escort Lieutenant Bax to the brig."

Bax turned. "You fucking smeghead piece of—"

"Captain Turisas held a standing order that there would be no cursing on the bridge, Lieutenant."

"We're all about to bloody fucking die you *pompous motherfu—*"

"Now, Ensign Hetulat, if you please."

Hetulat shrugged and took Bax by the arm.

"The one good thing about death, Pytten, is that you're coming with me! You hear me, Pytten? You're dead too! Brig or bridge, we're all fucking—"

The hatch closed behind them. Pytten looked around to the bridge crew. All were staring. Finally Commander Drake broke the silence.

"Admirable, Pytten," he said, coughing. "Your composure is—is admira—"

He coughed again, blood staining his chest.

"Sir, your orders?"

"Last orders, Pytten. Last orders. The boat has an hour. I have less. You are hereby in command. Save us if you can."

Drake closed his eyes, then his land eyes. Pytten leaned forward on the back of the tactical display. Everyone stared.

There was no hope. The nuclear blast on the surface had vaporized most of the UKI fleet they were monitoring, sending debris from the rest raining down on them. The damage was catastrophic. For two days they'd watched as the captain and now the commander slowly died. Pytten was junior officer of the deck when the shockwave hit. Turisas herself had ordered Pytten to take over when the officer of the deck was killed in the first wave of debris. With Bax off-shift and jailed, Pytten was now in command of the entire sub, for at least the estimated single hour before it collapsed. It was hopeless, but Pytten thought at least the crew could be granted hope. All they needed was a plan that would seem to have potential, and then they could die in peace. And if the plan worked, well, they'd cross that bridge when they came to it.

"Pursimies, can we sound general quarters?"

"Yeah, the system's still online."

"Puuseppä, where is it likely we'll see the first full breach?"

"Deck ten aft; we've evacuated the area, but—"

"Pursimies, go ahead."

Boatswain's mate Pursimies sounded the call. Pytten spoke.

"This is Lieutenant Pytten in command of the VA Saukko. With all locks compromised, we are trapped in the boat, which is soon to be crushed. The first breach will form in deck ten aft. I am ordering all crew to that berth."

The crew looked to one another.

"We will remove all dangerous objects from that space and insert ourselves. When the breach forms, we will leave through it before the rest of the boat collapses on us. Your bodies were engineered for this. You will live."

Pytten spoke with certainty. Having none in reality, the illusion was most critical.

"Move!"

The crew started and headed aft. Pytten with them. By the time the bridge crew arrived, surviving personnel were emptying the berth of its cargo. Food supplies filled the hall, stacked along the sides and coating the floor like weak tile.

Once the area was empty, they filed in. The bulkhead was shaking, concave to the pressure outside. The crew was afraid. Pytten had no idea how much force would enter the berth when the water broke in. A Cetacean body is made to survive the depths and the pressure. Pytten was certain of that. But of the explosive force, of the metal bulkhead soon to shatter, of the hundreds of other things that could go wrong, there was no telling. In the end the idea was more about a swift painless death than an excruciating crushing end.

They stood in the berth, silent. The sound of the wrenching, horrible pressure on the weakening bulkhead grew louder and louder. If Pytten had anything to say, it had to happen before it grew any louder. And there was one thing left forgotten.

"All hands accounted for?"

"All hands!"

Pytten breathed out.

"Save for Lieutenant Bax," said Ensign Hetulat.

Pytten stopped breathing. The bulkhead burst. A jagged hole erupted in the metal and peeled open, disgorging the ocean into the room, filling it in seconds. Pytten looked around. Everyone seemed alive. Pytten shoved vocal cords aside in favor of underwater vocalization implants and called out in a series of shrieks, "Swim to the surface. I'm going back for Bax."

"This breach has compromised the superstructure! The Saukko will be crushed in seconds!"

"I'm in command. Skipper leaves last. Get out now!"

Pytten swam back for the door and took a deep breath of dirty saltwater, then opened the hatch.

Water carried Pytten fast back into the walls of food packaging, then down the hall away from the brig. The force was too strong to fight. Pytten could only wait until the area was flooded. The bulkhead was already twisting and crunching in on itself, space was growing thinner.

When the area was finally flooded, the corridor was only half a meter across, jagged and broken. Pytten swam.

Through section after section, Pytten swam as the bulkheads grew ever smaller and sharper. By the time the brig was in sight, the metal of the sub was warped and twisted beyond recognition. The hatches were all broken off their dogs. The brig was open and filled with water.

Bax's fist struck Pytten in their sea eye, collapsing it inward. Pytten was blind on the right side.

"I came back to save you!"

"You came back to die with me!"

"Bax, we can both escape if you come with me now!"

"I can escape without you."

Bax struck again, this time piercing Pytten's right sea eye completely. Bax swam out as Pytten struggled in pain. The bulkheads took another jarring stab inward and knocked Bax on the head, rendering him unconscious.

Pytten saw it happen. It meant only an easier tow of the belligerent bastard. Hands around Bax's flipper, Pytten drew him out of the brig chamber and toward the collapsing corridor. It was crushed completely. The water was growing hard to breathe, now filled with noxious debris and oil. Only the corridor forward was still swimmable. Without thinking, Pytten swam toward it with Bax in tow.

The bulkheads drew closer and closer. Only a quarter meter remained, slowly crushing inward as Pytten swam past. Finally they emerged into the sonar bay. It had held its shape fairly well. The rubber walls were closer than before but still intact. There was no way out.

Pytten's eye hurt worse and worse as the toxic water irritated it. There was blood loss, dizziness, pain. Pytten had no choice, though, and started to work, looking with one left eye, to spring the sonar release dogs.

One by one they gave way, some sticking badly, but Pytten forced them open; their lives were at stake. There was no choice. They opened.

Suddenly the sonar bulb rocketed off the front of the sub, towing them with it in its wake. Freezing water hit Pytten's eye and stung even worse. The pain was enough to pass out, but they were free, and Pytten swam, forcing through the current upward toward the light.

A hand grabbed Pytten's. Pursimies. He took Pytten's hand and towed them upward toward the surface. They broke the membrane of flotsam and inhaled the thin, radioactive air. Pytten changed back for vocal cords.

"Status!"

"All present and accounted for! And alive!" laughed Pursimies.

There was laughter all around. And hands, everyone was slapping Pytten with their fins, on the back, on the head, on the arms. Among them was Bax. Pytten tried to think of something to say, anything appropriate.

"Bax, you're still under arrest."

"Pytten, you're still an asshole."

The crew swam for Harlin Colony.

THERE WAS a vast red blur, dim but somehow too bright. It spread to every corner of his peripheral vision, farther to the right and left and top and bottom than he even knew he could see. He tried to close his eyes to it, but it remained, and his eyes hurt like hell. He tried to look away from it, but he only felt pain in his neck and heard a horrible grinding noise. But the visual… that was only a minor nuisance compared to the smell.

It was rot, a powerful rot of wet flesh. A hot stink that seeped deep into his head. He thought to pinch his nose, but he couldn't move his arm. Just grinding and more pain. He tried to at least wrinkle his nose, but he couldn't feel his nose, only more pain. Pain and red and rot and no body part working. He felt something heavy, an immense weight on his legs, which were similarly immobile and seemingly seized up trying to hold up the force upon them. Had he been crushed?

He replayed his last memories. Varg stabbing him in the heart and cutting off his face. Well, that explained most of it. He'd come to without a face and thus without the benefits of having a face. No eyes, or at least no lenses for them. He suspected he still had retinas; that would explain the blur. And the stink was forced raw into his nasal turbinates. Everything was exposed.

He tried to sit up. More grinding gears. More pain. Something else was very wrong. He called out.

"Varg?"

It didn't sound like he said Varg. It sounded like water bubbling up through gravel with a side order of retching. Veikko found himself dismayed and somewhat concerned.

"Morning, Veikko," said Skadi.

Thank fucking Odin, he thought. Skadi was there. Everything would be okay. He moved instinctively as if to hug her but suffered the grinding again.

"Don't try to move. Most of your body was burned off."

"Where am I?" he asked. The words were barely understandable.

"Don't try to talk either. I couldn't find your face."

He sat silently trying to feel his body. He couldn't help but try to move, if only to adjust himself. From what little he could feel beyond the pain, he was moving slightly but not the right way. It was as if he were miswired, as if the muscles pulled on the wrong bones. And that force—he was pinned under something heavy. Or more accurately, he was stuck holding it up. The weight was inconceivable. He didn't know how he was holding it at all, let alone injured.

"You're in Valhalla. What's left of it."

"But Valhalla was nuked!" he tried to belch out. It hurt to speak, cut through his tongue.

"Yeah, your plan didn't go so well. Nukes flew all right; wave bombs too. *A*s, *H*s, *N*s, a whole alphabet of missiles and bombs, but nothing hit here. Here's fine. The Ares is alive and well and active."

"No!"

"Yes, actually. Very yes."

"Pelamus?"

"I watched the detector logs. Looks like Varg killed him for you right before he died himself."

"Varg's dead?"

She looked over at the comm tower. "Unless he could survive a neurotoxic dart and a really nasty fall without Niide."

Veikko found himself hurt by the news. Varg had just killed him, but he couldn't hold a grudge for it. He'd wanted Varg on his side more than anything. He should have just explained it all better, more slowly. He hadn't thought Varg would be back from Mars so fast. He must have never even gone. He should be on Mars, he thought. He never should have died.

But there was hope in that sentence. Niide, she'd said.

"Get me to Niide."

"Oh, Niide already patched you up on Orkney. This is you fixed."

"I'm broken."

"No, you're just half-assembled. See, Niide put you in his latest body, that big experiment he's been wanting to try on us all. You're actually in the most advanced fighting body ever created; you should be honored."

"I can't—"

"No, you can't do much of anything. I made sure he left you immortal but immobile. And made sure he didn't give you a new face. I didn't want to see your face, ever again."

"Skadi—"

"Don't say my name either."

She sat in silence, looking over Veikko's horrific form. All the parts were there but in a puddle. A Gigeresque mass of organs and muscle and mechanics strewn about the rocks, and down into the hole she'd cut earlier.

"W team?" asked the horror.

"Varg killed 'em. He just came back and killed everyone, everyone you didn't. Good thing too, for you. I had to use their spare viscera to keep you alive till Dr. Niide. Bound your wounds with your own kids' intestines."

"Varg killed them all?"

"Yeah. You still win for mass murder. You know you got Balder and Alf. You missed Cato, he left with Wulfgar. But you killed Sigvald and Snot real good. You killed my brothers with that shot. You killed Vibs and

Violet, that's for sure. I assume they started this war on your orders, so you have another fifteen billion on your conscience. Your intel plant didn't work, your plan didn't work, you really failed in every way you possibly could. You fucked shit up, Veikko. You fucked up bad."

"But you saved me."

"Death is far too good for you. Far, far too good. A thousand deaths aren't enough. So you're not gonna die. That 'body' of yours is gonna keep you alive forever. Forever in pain. Breathing dead walrus with dead friends as your company."

Veikko didn't try to speak. The ravine shook, a deep rumble echoed through the caves. He felt something stinging from under his skin, from his open face. The pain grew and grew until he couldn't help but shout. Then suddenly the shaking ended, and the pain ceased.

"What was that?" Veikko choked.

"The Sigyn System. See, the Ares drips. Downright rains when there's a breeze. The drops never stray too far from the tree. They always get collected by the Sigyn System. Apparently that's what that big ring around the base was: Valfar's recycling system for the water. Fun bonus, since you're stuck under the thing, every time it drips on you the system will rip the water back out of you. Enjoy that part.

"But the Sigyn System was designed before the rampart, and before Wulfgar added a hundred bodies worth of meat to it. When it's active it pushes down on the rock, and most of the rock this ravine sits on is currently over its top. It's begging to collapse, and if it does...."

"If it does?"

"Ocean floods in, ocean expands."

"We have to stop it!" he barked.

"You are stopping it. Right now you're the only thing stopping it."

"What?"

"I destroyed the rampart system so it can never go back down. There's a pit under this place now, and the only thing keeping the ravine from collapsing when the Sigyn turns on is your lower half. I carved a hole under the power plant, right down to the rampart well. And crammed you in. Stuffed whatever part of you fit between the rocks and set it all to spasm."

"I can't be that strong."

"Oh, you're stronger than's good for you. Your legs can hold up a ravine. Your hands could crush diamond. Your lungs can blow down a jet. Try not to sneeze, by the way; that would be bad."

"My hands, I can't—"

"No, you can't move shit. You're exactly as formed as I want you. You get to live your life as a mess, a tangle. Still, you get to play Atlas now, for the next forever. Maybe you'll figure out how to move, maybe, but the Sigyn turns on every twenty minutes, and before you got here it did a real number on the rock. I give it one, maybe two more times before it breaks. If you're not there when it does, if you leave or die—then the fish win. Your brother wins."

Her mention of Risto hurt worse than the drips.

"What if I'm abducted, what if I'm killed?"

"Then Pelamus smiles from heaven. But you'll never die. Niide saw to that, even with the EMPs, even with the nukes and winter, the system you're in will keep you alive until the planet falls into the sun. Alive in agony—are you in agony? Can you feel pain where your face used to be? I hope you can, I hope it itches for ten thousand years. I hope the loneliness drives you insane. I hope old bitch misery discovers her finest plaything."

"Skadi—"

He was cut off by a buzzing sound, and into his nostrils were forced the particles of Skadi's burning skin. She had microwaved her chest into vapor, which mixed with the rotting air and tormented Veikko without his nose. Without his face. With eternity's tortures to come.

CAITHNESS WAS mostly crater, but between the blast zones a good deal of city remained. Radiation spiked, but not as much as Vibeke had expected. Likely a couple low-yield fission bombs. That didn't seem a great deal more fortuitous than the alternatives, judging by the piles of burnt, mutilated dead.

People milled about. A few half-melted or tumored but mostly just normal run-of-the-mill civilians in clothes they'd worn for months. Clothing was gradually changing to rags. It wasn't rags yet, not on anyone, but the grime was apparent. No more washing machines. Nobody had enough on for the cold. Nobody had any clothing for cold like this, not in Scotland. Most wore drapes upon drapes and robes around robes; others just wore too little, unaware how much damage the cold was doing beyond the pain.

The smell of the place was also unfamiliar. Nothing like it had graced the civilized world in centuries. The smell of sewage seeped out from the buildings that had been made into outhouses. The physical library with its abundance of paper seemed to be the commode of choice for most of the city and stank accordingly. But only in its immediate area. The sewer smell was less prominent around the corpse piles, where the smell of rotting meat took over and grew sharp despite the cold. Both smells were subdued by smoke in the vicinity of fires, and even smoke was negligible when it came to the salty garbage scent of the crowd itself.

Vibeke put her oxygen mask up and inhaled clean, manufactured air, assembled by her suit from the raw energy in the atmosphere. She still saw the miasma's effects on the populace—they coughed and hacked and threw up on the ground, and that was the healthy ones. The diseased lay dying in the gutters, rotting before they died. A fair number of melted, tumored wave victims had made it to the city, but they were all rejected by the merchants. A caste system had worked itself out with them as the untouchables. Not a class system, but a caste system based on superstition, the belief that seemed prevalent among the people that karma held its sway over the war. Karma, that they who lived unscathed were superior, that those hit by the wave bombs had been evil before the fall. Vibeke was so offended by the man who bragged of the new system that she microwaved him on the spot.

Nobody sought justice against her. A working microwave was such a rarity it marked her as the local goddess. Her health and pace backed it up. Veikko had been absolutely right in Håvamål: In a world at war, Valkyries were the lords of all they surveyed.

She found a quiet corner of a broken theater to lie down in for the night. The thoughts on society and humankind kept coming back, but they got old the first time she thought them. Prissy philosophy did nothing to keep her alive.

But Violet did. She lived, strange as it seemed, for Violet. For a dull thought that refused to fully form. She knew it was beyond logic and beyond sanity, but that's love for you. She loved someone who wasn't there. So she clung to what was.

And to her memories. Sweet, maudlin moments like getting her cheek bashed in or being violently stripped and molested. What she thought were the worst moments they had together suddenly had some form of demented charm.

Then the pain seeped in. The other memories of Violet. Of sex. Sex had existed once, long ago, as an act of love. Vibs had to laugh at the idea.

She had once had "loving" sex with a real live girl. She wondered if any couple had managed since the war. Spawning more children to live miserable lives. Even then sex was an act of cruelty.

She cursed Violet's name. Had she only held out a few more days, kept romance forbidden under a hundred hours, she'd have had no choice to make. No question of destroying the missiles. Ah, the worst joke of all. She stopped a few missiles. Wave bombs, bad missiles, very bad. Almost as bad as if they'd launched.

She hadn't known about the other dozen silos across the globe, hadn't considered what they'd do if a few bombs failed to launch. Any one wave bomb can cover the entire planet. They had several so they could target several small targets, not affect the population centers. Harm no innocents.

Unless some failed to make their targets. They had a great contingency plan: if some fail to launch, others expand their range to compensate. Though they have to take out population centers to do it. In the end, all Vibeke had managed was to mutate more civilians than would've been hit otherwise.

Not that it mattered given her choice. As soon as she saw Violet again she knew she'd chosen wrong.

As if it knew she were thinking about her, Violet's Tikari snuggled up to Vibeke's chest. It was so pathetic, it soured her guts to think about it. Like a dog that lurked on its owner's grave until it grew old and died alone. Vibeke's Tikari peeked out of her chest. It didn't know what to make of the other. Their travel companion. The thing was traumatized enough after seeing what she had done to Sal back in the silo, months ago.

Months ago.

"Vibeke, I know what you're planning," Sal had begged. "It serves no purpose."

She said nothing as she linked into the broadbrain and pinpointed Sal in the neural network. He had flown in through a vent and anchored himself in the cortex node for the heating systems.

"This serves no purpose."

"Killing you is the purpose, Sal."

"But think of Veikko."

"I'm just about ready to kill him too."

"You don't mean that, Vibeke. Vibs. May I call you Vibs?"

She found the node partly exposed with a Tikari cut in its dura mater. She wasted no time in firing a tractoring beam into it, smashing Sal into the cortex.

"Vibeke, this serves no purpose. Can we just talk for a moment?"

She pulled apart the dura and spotted Sal inside, paralyzed by the tractoring beam.

"Vibeke, Vibs. Veebee baby. Killing me won't solve anything. This serves no purpose."

"It'll make me feel a whole hell of a lot better."

She reached into the cortex and found Sal's anchor. It was securely welded in place. She cut open its plastic exterior and pulled out a meter of wire.

"I'm welded in, Vibeke. This serves no purpose."

"I'm making sure you stay welded in."

"Why, Vibeke? It serves—"

She reversed the beam for a single pulse and ripped Sal out of the cortex, where he slipped the beam and flew, restrained by the wire.

Violet's Tikari, Nelson, suddenly bolted for him. They locked legs and tried to slash each other with their wings, falling to the ground. Sal tried to break free with his rockets, and Vibeke had to back off to avoid the mayhem.

The two Tikaris bashed around the hall, slamming into walls and cutting pipes that bled red onto the floor. The mechanical catfight tugged on the wire but stayed connected to the wall. Sal's grunts echoed from the silo PA. But the Tikaris were in a violent stalemate; neither could possibly win they were so evenly matched.

Vibeke finally sent her own Tikari into the chaotic mass, striking Sal down to the floor. Both Tiks held him down until Vibeke tractored him up, smashing him up against the wall. She held him there in the beam, motionless.

"It means you can still feel pain, Sal. As long as you're tied in, your damage sensors are going to register as pain."

"I believe you're incorrect, Vibs."

She pulled off one of his legs. Every alarm system in the silo went off, deafening wails of electric agony.

"Okay, you were right! Please stop!"

"No, Sal, this is how you're going to die."

"This serves no purpose! Pain serves no purpose!"

"You... are so wrong...."

She pulled off another leg, and another. The cortex behind Sal grew inflamed and red.

"Vibeke, please, please stop!"

She pulled off his last leg. He tried to flutter his wings, to cut her as she ripped away his arms, but couldn't move under the tractor force. He tried to fire his internal rockets to no avail. He only inched along the wall.

"This serves no purpose!"

She pulled off one wing, then the other, dropping the pieces on the floor. Sal was now only a carcass with a wire running to the cortex. Alarms continued, doors opened and closed, the spent vacuum fire system tried to activate and only clicked in place. She turned off her microwave and let him fall to the floor.

"This serves no purpose!"

She crouched over the broken Tikari and pried off its armor plating with her bare hands, breaking off two of her own nails in the process. She exposed the inner mechanics and circuitry of each of its segments.

"Vibeke, please! It hurts so much. I don't deserve this! You can't do this! It serves—it serves no purpose!"

"I hope you're fucking watching, Veikko," she said as she stepped on Sal's abdomen, crushing it under her boot. Then his thorax, and finally his head. She dragged her foot down across the grated floor, smearing the twisted components of his AI into scrap metal. The alarms stopped. It stuttered out its last words.

"This serves... no... purpose."

How wrong it was. It was satisfying to hurt the small thing, to know she was causing it pain. She took the anchor and severed it, then stuffed a nociceptor tab into its open end. The alarms began again—the nervous system of the silo was in pain. She stuffed the wire into the dura mater and sealed up the access. It would live on in pain for a long time to come.

She vowed to do the same when she found Veikko. For having sent Sal in the first place, for his entire plan. Except of course for the idea of nuking Valhalla—that was for the best. Something in the back of her mind wouldn't let her think otherwise. That was a good idea. Surely the one good thing to come of it all was that the ravine was gone and the Ares with it.

The world was safe at last! Back in the present a woman dragging her child's body behind her passed out and fell in the street. Veikko's hack didn't stop Vibeke from wondering if it would've been better to flush it all away. *No,* she thought, *even after this, Earth will come back better than ever. Humanity will band together to fix the planet, survive the radiation and mutation and*—Vibeke laughed. She knew mankind better than that.

WULFGAR HAD just become the richest man in the world. And then the world was no more. Of course the economy survived, in some form. Earth's holiest constant was invincible. The fall of the nets merely delayed trading one morning. What little juice survived in the computer systems was devoted to brain and bulk transfers of information. For a time, the few people whose minds encapsulated the financial records were themselves the most expensive commodity.

But things sorted themselves out soon enough. They cracked open the vaults and gold became the medium of exchange. An ancient joke of sorts to those in the know, but families lined up by the millions to take their share, to prove their identities and trade their wasted homes for gelt.

The insurance companies fell; the relief organizations rose. The armies that could maintain their electric charges took control of their regions and implemented taxes within days of the day-long war they'd all missed fighting. All missiles, it was. And no certain results. GAUNE and UNEGA were both annihilated. It was their subsidiaries that survived, the companies small enough to communicate by speech.

The largest and most powerful of which was of course the YUP, owing to the genius of its new CEO, Wulfgar Kray. While other companies were scrounging together their surviving board members, Wulfgar was acting the warlord and seizing territory and assets. His underlings proved quite willing to follow any order. The cruelest manners in which he functioned as a mobster were simply expected from him as a politician. He could order deaths by the thousands without question, and he had the means. Only hours before the war began he'd inherited the rights to the biggest private army money could buy.

But he hadn't wanted to use it on old-fashioned battles over land and assets. He was lord on Earth, but lord of the flies. They were all that was left. And so Wulfgar took solace in what little he could manage, like his new home.

His new home he'd bartered with Sable Mouvant in the hours before the missiles flew. Mouvant had built quite a fortress on Elba. As the CEO of Dylath-Leen, she'd accrued several billion Euros and two of the largest construction forces in France. She put every bit of all the above into building her home. She owned Elba but UNEGA still had laws governing the place. None of the historical buildings could be touched. So she commissioned a structure to straddle Portoferraio.

It was infamous as the greatest eyesore ever created. A blocky bit of brutalism that cast Portoferraio into shadow from dawn till dusk. What it lacked in aesthetics it earned back in security. Reports of Hashima's demise made Wulfgar less interested in underground living. He wanted a home so secure that not even a fusion bomb would make a dent in the thing. Mouvant guaranteed that the structure was made from fusion grade Fiphp Steel, ten-meters thick around every segment, all TK chromed on its surface.

Mouvant even included her security staff, her array of drones, the ammo for the weapons systems, and more. She even offered Wulfgar her *nain aveuglant*, but some traditions were too grisly even for Wulfgar to enjoy. But she gave him the works in exchange for the YUP's utility rights. When the war began, she owned 1,076 power plants. Wulfgar was sorry to hear 439 of them were bombed with conventional ordinance, 329 of them were nuked, and 117 of them were caught in wave bomb ranges. Mouvant didn't mind, though; she was vaporized along with the quark inversion plant in Al-Ḥudaydah.

The only real problem with Mouvant's fortress was the powerful radiophobic field. It was a good thing in those postnuclear days, but Wulfgar's jaw was malfunctioning from the magnetized air. He brought doctor after doctor into his castle to look at it, and dismissed each of them upon failure. His men were still hunting for Dr. Mowat, but she'd been in the center of a wave zone. She was almost certainly melted. That was the worst of his problems.

The rest was heavenly. He'd thought that being transferred trillions of euros was the best thing that could happen to his gang. He was wrong— getting transferred trillions of euros a few hours before the world broke into war and the economic nets fell: That was the best thing that could have happened. Every record frozen in its last instant of use marked Wulfgar as the richest man alive. So the masses flocked to him seeking shelter and order. And he gave them both.

The YUP headquarters building in Yemen was hit with a couple fission bombs, eradicated. But Pelamus had already wiped it out and made it mobile. Wulfgar planted it in the Mouvant fortress along with his top wolves only an hour before the first missiles landed. From there he controlled the first emergency measures to protect all he could under the YUP banner, which he had quietly renamed the company and country of *Ulver* in his last linked sleep.

So he and his top wolves survived. When the masses came amassing, he hired them on, paid in *"Loups,"* the money he printed with the mints and printers he bought. He traded his new money for their gold at a somewhat unfair markup, but nobody complained. They had money again instead of shiny metal. It would be a historical oddity to anyone who knew Wulfgar's past, but the Orange Gang was already long forgotten in the year since its demise. Nobody knew, or if they knew they didn't care, that Wulfgar Kray was a mass murderer and crime lord. He was in fact unanimously considered the first genuine hero of the new era.

He still made sure the physical logs of his past were destroyed. He kept hackers on retainer in case the net survived, but it was becoming clearer and clearer that none of the server centers had gone unbombed. Earth's past had been erased as thoroughly as its future.

It only took Wulfgar weeks to take over Europe amid the chaos, and a couple more to take over enough of the old world to proclaim himself Emperor of the Globe. Then he didn't have to buy anything. He owned it all, or so he claimed. Some old armies disagreed, a minor problem.

He actually had about a quarter of a globe to run. His empire, despite his titles, really covered about half the hemisphere, ending around Mongol Uls to the east and at the UKI in the west. Progress was rapid in the east, but the isles were still owned by B&L, and he hadn't figured out how to convince them to sell. He tried a hostile takeover, but was wary of letting the war go nuclear again. He already regretted the frivolous bombs he allowed in the early days.

Ah, the nukes, he thought; why did the world have to offer itself at its crispiest? Of twenty billion souls, he could only claim the four that survived. And of those four he only had about one and a half billion in his extended employ. Indeed he still had work to do. So he gave up on his jaw for the day and barked orders to his top wolves. He had long since run out of boot related names.

"Spike, move the 4th Army to Norge, mass and prepare for a hostile takeover of Lindisfarne."

"Yes, sire."

"Mike, the 8th Army will join, subject to Spike's whim. Dagbog?"

"Sire?"

"How goes the siege of Orkney?"

"Not well, sire. UKI still has the coasts, and our troops are being shot from the sky before they can land."

Wulfgar checked the roster.

"Those men are from the Siberian fleet! How dare you waste them?"

"Sire, we have to take the beaches before we can—"

"Arrgh!" shouted Wulfgar.

"Yes, sire," said Arrgh.

"You have Orkney to deal with now. Take the beaches with cheap navies and only then use my Siberians for fine-tuning. Understood?"

"Yes, sire!"

Wulfgar grunted in anger. Had he known ruling the world would be such a pain, he might not have taken it over in the first place. Well, he thought, grinning a wide chainsaw grin, yes, he would.

Chapter II: Orkney

VIBEKE WOKE up and realized she'd slept—a rarity. She'd made it through nearly an entire night without having to kill someone. And in a city no less.

She stood and stretched and surveyed. There was nobody around. She followed the street toward the center of the city. It had been plowed somehow. The roads were only a couple centimeters thick with packed snow. There were even tread marks in places.

Beyond the largest crater, she spotted a market. The street was filled with vendors. In the burnt remains of buildings, commerce had persisted: merchants selling food and supplies, water they claimed was clean. All the lies and trifles of civilization, going strong. She had yet to see how people traded without monetary implants. But she had something to sell and ventured to find out. She headed for the smell of burning flesh and found something like a restaurant. She approached the maître d', a woman in a tattered suit.

"Table, dearie?"

"Selling, do you buy meat?"

"What did ye find?"

"Some wild pigs. Made pork."

"Live pigs? You found live, unmutated pigs?"

"Healthy ones too."

"Sliver a pound if it's good."

She pulled the choice cuts from her satchel, keeping only a few for herself. The vendor examined them. Vibeke was certain they were small enough bits to ensure they were unrecognizable, but the flavor could still give them away to anyone familiar with real pork or soylent goods.

"Very good," she said, weighing them. "Fourteen slivers for the lot?"

Vibeke nodded.

"One more if you point me to your hunting grounds."

"Due west in the outskirts. They were wandering around a blue house. Could I have a shaker of salt instead?"

The vendor jogged over to a table and gave her one. "Anything else you're buying?"

"Boats."

"Shore's nothing but debris. Some broken boats, hull of a big ship ashore a kilometer north of the pier, but I don't think you'll find anything seaworthy, or anyone selling if there is."

"Is there a medical vendor around here?"

"There's a doctor, Steven Shagrath. He's set up in the basement of the glass tower right there past the pissweed." She pointed.

"Pissweed?"

"You haven't come across—wow, you're lucky! Used to be asparagus until the wave bombs mutated it. Now it grows fast and far and oozes uric acid, or whatever it is makes pee smell like pee. You'll know it when you smell it."

"Thanks," said Vibeke. She walked the short way to the tower. Sure enough the smell of urine was overwhelming as she passed a grotesque outcropping of mutant shrubs, covered in odd seeds and dripping yellow.

The glass building was among the least damaged. It had a short line running into its lobby and down the stairs. Makeshift torches lit the way down. Vibeke walked alongside the line; nobody seemed to object to her passing them. In the basement she saw the doctor tending to a man's legs, which had been badly burned. A nurse spotted her.

"What can I do for you?"

"Buying med supply."

"Don't have many surpluses."

"I just need clamps."

"Clamps we've got."

The nurse led her past some beds toward a table with supplies. In the beds were diseased men and women, not from wave bombs or radiation but bacteria, infections. Without electronic antibiotics, superstrains had returned. The world saw plagues it hadn't seen since the post-antibiotic era.

From under the table, the nurse pulled out a box of clamps of varying sizes. Vibeke silently sorted through and found the largest of them, then paid the nurse four of her slivers.

"Oh my! Thank you!"

"Was that a lot?"

The nurse looked worried.

"Don't worry, keep it," said Vibeke as she took her clamps and left. She walked topside and headed for the coast. It was only a few blocks away.

The smell there was rot. Sea rot—thousands of dead fish clogged the water along with scattered debris and several corpses. Some nearly skeletonized, others fresh. She wandered the coast toward a distant pier.

The fish lasted out to the horizon, and when the wind blew toward her the smell was almost unbearable. She put up her oxygen mask again, but still the stink permeated. She spotted the big, broken hull. A fire in it marked some strange gathering that braved the smell for a secure spot. The men inside watched her hungrily. She wasn't in the mood to play with anyone, so she kept Bob, her own Tikari, on her shoulder, ready to kill them all without risk.

One began shouting. He started following her. She sent Bob to cut his head off. She wished to high hell that Violet was there with her. To kill people. Torture them, fight them, survive them. It would be so different with Violet. They'd talk on the long stretches of walking. About how things used to be, about how they could be. About whether the miserable present was truly any worse than the glowing, linked-in past. She felt like with Violet there, it wouldn't have been. Not for her at least. She often caught herself holding imagined conversations with Violet. She never spoke out loud but knew every word in her mind.

"Did you ever get to this part of Scotland?"

"No, I stuck to the west. The east was all artsy and pompous."

"Not your style?"

"My parents took me to a Shakespeare play once. I pounded on the seat in front of me the whole time. The poor man in it didn't know what to do. My parents had to keep apologizing and holding me back, but I bit their arms."

"You sound like you were a lovely child."

"Who said child? I was sixteen."

Vibs laughed, and then it soured and threatened tears. She tried not to think of it. The thoughts came unbidden every hour or more and stabbed into her. She could feel it in the back of her neck. The thoughts were destroying her. Making her act foolishly.

The battle to walk on and the battle to stay sane amid madness. The world had gone mad in days, but Vibs was a fighter, a Valkyrie. It would take weeks to drive her completely insane. Maybe even a whole month.

She almost smiled to herself at that estimate as she topped a mountain of rubble. This one held a view far better than most of the sorry remains of Scotland. She saw the waters of Pentland Firth, cold and junked at the shore, but beyond it was Orkney. Beyond it was her only chance of seeing Violet's face again.

INVESTIGATORS FROM the city worked quickly to piece together what had happened. Services had started at 8:30 a.m. as usual. At 8:42 during the opening sermon, a brown Chevy truck (identified by the security camera on Elm and Hanover) drove into the parking lot of the small white church. It paused for a few seconds then backed up into the front doors, obstructing them.

The assailants, both dressed in black cloaks, then took four Molotov cocktails from the truck and threw them through the glass windows of the nave, lighting fires across the interior. The Molotov cocktails were made with frozen orange juice and gasoline, producing napalm that stuck to several patrons. Most of the victims died of burns, a few of smoke inhalation.

With the front door obstructed, patrons ran for the side door by the pulpit, the only other door to the building. At this point the assailants took guns from the truck and positioned themselves outside the door. At least one 12-gauge shotgun and one 9mm weapon were used. The lab would rush results for the exact types. The assailants fired over forty-nine shots (counted on the first pass, likely more), most hitting their victims.

Many of the laity died on the scene of gunshot wounds. The clergy died… differently. Pastor Cody Sparks and his son Ryan Sparks, police chief of the town, were found burned to death, nailed to two of the three crosses standing out in front of the church. Backward, facing the wood. They had burned slowly, succumbing to the wick effect, likely without losing consciousness until they died. The third cross held the burnt remains of Margaret Clay.

The truck left at 8:59 a.m., only five minutes before first responders arrived at the scene. The security camera was unable to identify the license plate, but an APB was issued for all brown Chevy trucks in the county. The targeting of Margaret Clay proved the most critical information, as when officers went to inform Andrew Geki and his wife Jessica of her mother's death, they were missing, as was their brown Chevy truck.

Investigators swarmed the house and surrounding lot. In the lot they found a recently buried infant, severely mutilated. The biggest manhunt in the history of the state began. The Geki couple were branded terrorists, and the Department of Homeland Security became active in the hunt. But the trail was utterly cold. There was absolutely no sign of the couple until the next Sunday—when another church was attacked.

Thirty seven died in the attack, committed in much the same manner but almost a hundred miles northeast in the big city. The brown Chevy was found parked at the doors, and it took a day to ascertain which of the laity's cars was stolen. By then it had already been found in the neighboring state. Security at every church in both states was exceptional the following Sunday. The next church they attacked was all the way out in California.

By the time of the fourth attack in Texas, Homeland Security was shamed by their inability to catch the couple, who appeared and disappeared without a trace, as if by magic. Their reign of terror lasted three years and killed hundreds. Dozens of churches attacked.

But after their capture, after the famous revelation of their motive, after debate and anger and blame ran their course, after the copycats and after the creation of the House Of Worship Defense Infantry, what people remembered most was the tremendous fear the Geki couple had caused across the nation. The image of two black cloaks, for a time, was the very quintessence of fear in America.

Politicians adeptly played upon that fear to suit their agendas. In the following years, the first antiheresy laws were passed in violation of the First Amendment. Criticism of Protestant Christianity was classified as hate speech. Under the guise of persecution, practitioners of the religion were elected en masse and soon the country was effectively a Protestant theocracy, leading to the peaceful first Catholic uprising and its violent quashing.

The Protection Of Islam act of the EU functioned similarly. Sharia law had to be respected, criticism was prohibited, and the globe finally found itself split between Muslim rule in the eastern hemisphere and Christian in the west.

Politics stagnated for decades. The quality of living decreased slowly, marred by the prohibition of vaccinations, which led to widespread disease, the restriction of women's rights across the planet, the downfall of higher education, and more. It was in this age of decline that June Waystone, after her release from prison on heresy charges, posted the work she'd written inside, a work that put her right back in prison before she could say "injustice." But the work, *The Foolish Weaver*, was on the net and impossible to stop. It revealed to the public the first "World Cold War."

Christian America and Muslim Europe were at the brink of going hot. Intelligence in Europe had found Muslims in internment camps in the United States. Intel in the States had uncovered mass executions of Christians in Denmark. Both blocs were planning military intervention. Waystone didn't stop at these revelations. She also proved that the intel on both sides had been forged by Sadie Schrubb, the vehemently Christian arms manufacturer who had bought most of the US Senate.

As both sides of the globe weighed the nuclear option, *The Foolish Weaver* went viral in influenzal proportions. Tens of millions risked arrest by spreading the literature, and hundreds of millions found that they were not alone in their doubts about the religious nature of their countries.

The counterculture was soon ravenous, champing at the bit. The nonreligious majority was growing tired of the prospect of nuclear war. But the majority had little say. The orthodox elite that ran the country went on and instituted a draft to gather warriors of God.

For many that was the last straw. With nowhere to run from the draft, draft centers, many located in churches, were burned and bombed. When the masses were merciful, that is. When they were less so, the masters were burned alive or crucified backward, reminding a few historically savvy individuals of the Geki couple.

The revolution marked the end of the World Cold War. It quickly inspired an old world counterpart and all religion was banned for good. That inspired the less peaceful second Catholic uprising and a great number of similar events. What companies had bought up the governments of the world, as they began organizing into GAUNE and UNEGA, pursued means of controlling the uprisings while allowing religious extremists to believe they were still forces to be reckoned with, to believe they still had a say so long as they remained nonviolent.

They had to scare the religious groups into believing there was a force that could easily incinerate them all on a whim but did not. A force that allowed them to act within reason to gather and exercise the most extreme of individuals while maintaining control. Above all, a new force that could infiltrate any deviant group to frighten the holy hell out of them when they grew out of hand.

No such force had scared the religious community so since the Geki couple. Lacking any real creativity, the companies in power over the regions with the worst religious rumblings elected to resurrect the Geki.

With a few modifications of course. Instead of Molotov cocktails, Zaibatsu donated their experimental flame implants. Instead of plain black cloaks, Google donated their displacement satellites and the displacement fabric to warp across the air inside them. Pfizer donated a med chamber and Puma County donated land for a base of operations, coincidentally only seven kilometers from Andrew and Jessica Geki's old house. The icing on the cake came from RAND: the Farnesene Pulse. Pure weaponized fear.

Dozens of the highest military elite were subjected to the Farnesene Pulse. Five were able to function within it. The five trained under the pulse to use the implants and the satellite system, to learn advanced psychological warfare techniques, to learn psychiatry and politics and police work. In the end Michael Lederer and Richard Gregor were selected to don the cloaks.

The second Catholic uprising was well under way when they were selected. Fighting viciously against their oppression, the Order of St. David Roland Waters began by assassinating politicians and scientists, bombing community centers and clinics and other usual religious terrorism targets. Their headquarters in downtown Providence, Rhode Island, was identified by conventional intelligence, the fully automatic Geki intel web still being under construction.

The Geki prepared for their mission. They had both mastered the Farnesene Pulse; they had both mastered the fire. They knew the ultimatum they were to deliver. They jumped.

Fear struck the basement of the cathedral. Paul Perry was startled when they appeared, a feeling that didn't leave him once affected by the pulse.

"W-what—what are you?" he asked as bravely as he could muster.

"We are the Geki."

"What do you want?"

"You will stop your terrorist acts or we will incinerate you all."

"Yes!" The pulse forced him to agree. "Yes we will, anything!"

"We are watching you. We can see your every move."

"I believe you!"

"You will see that all in your command obey us."

"Yes!" He composed himself as best he could. "Can—can we still give the word?"

"What?"

"We'll become missionaries, anything you command!"

"Uh, yes. That's good."

"So we can practice? We can preach?"

"Just don't blow anything else up and you can preach to your heart's content."

"So we can do whatever we want?"

"We will not stop you unless you threaten the status quo with violence."

"So a mission to the people is okay by you two?"

Gregor grew frustrated.

"Just…. Don't fuck shit up."

And they were gone.

They arrived back in the citadel, concerned about the Farnesene Pulse.

"He didn't seem very scared. He seemed almost… unsurprised."

"Yes, it's as if he's used to living in fear of a vengeful omnipotent commanding force that's always watching him."

THERE WERE no boats visible on the shore, just flotsam or jetsam. She didn't remember which was which without the net to check. And there were the usual corpses. Everything bobbing in the water under a layer of snow. Everything filthy.

She hunted for anything she could sail in, hoping she'd not have to use the clamps. There was a suitable oar in the form of a burnt roofing shaft but nothing seaworthy, nothing that could hold her weight. She accepted the inevitable and began looking for a sturdy cadaver or two.

There were two shaggy cows amid the trash, one too torn up to use—presumably someone had tried to eat it. She examined the other. It was in good shape. It had only died recently, and the cold had preserved it, so far. She got to work skinning it with her Tikari. Nelson picked up on what she was doing and tried to sneak under the skin, but she shooed him away. She couldn't risk any holes in her new boat.

Shortly after she had it free, thawed and floppy. She began clamping all holes but the neck. Once airtight she threw in a smoke bomb and held the neck closed. She'd have to retrieve the bomb before the inflated skin burst, so she didn't clamp it. The skin neared its breaking point so she held the neck closed around her arm and retrieved the bomb, tossing it into the water. Sadly as she clamped off the creature's neck its natural grease slipped in her hands and sent the thing sputtering out to sea like a leaking balloon.

She sighed and got up to look for another corpse. There were no more animals, just their owners, an extended family of cherubic freckled Scots. No sense in letting them go to waste.

The sailboat, *The Sinclairs*, left port early the next day. She rowed toward a small speck she could identify on the horizon, hoping whatever was floating so far out would make a better boat than the unfortunate family. As she approached she found she was in luck: it was a real sailboat. She abandoned the *Sinclairs* and climbed up its ladder.

She could smell the boat's crew. Dead for quite some time, rotting from before the freeze. She found two men and one woman in the cabin, killed by microwave burns. Working microwaves were rare after the EMPs. She assumed pirates were at work and cleared the boat just in case. Once certain it was abandoned, she dropped the bodies overboard and tried the motor, also dead.

There was just enough buzzing radioactive wind, so she checked her Valhalla partitions for sailing and found a simple file with the basics. She still had to fumble with line and sail for an hour before she caught a breeze that sent her toward the Orkney Islands.

She stood at the bow and reapplied radiophobics to her head and hands. The wind was very cold on her wet skin. Nelson and Bob fluttered around, orbiting her slowly on the prowl for anything dangerous. But the sea was dead silent except for the sound of the boat cutting through the water and hitting the occasional rubbish or body.

The bodies were everywhere. Inescapable. She'd long since stopped telling herself they weren't all her fault. She tried at first to blame Veikko alone, or assure her conscience that GAUNE and UNEGA were on a path that wasn't dependent on their break-in or the Prešov nuke. But she suspected, accurately, that hacking the Ehren Plates kicked off the nuclear war.

She knew there was no point in dwelling on it. No matter how bad the results, she had to try to nuke the ravine. She simply had to. She wondered why the Geki hadn't killed her to stop it from happening. Had Veikko crippled them at the critical moment? Had he not killed one would she have been burned to a crisp before she could've launched the missile? Had he finally killed the other? That was her only guess. On the Geki scale of Fucked Up Shit, total global nuclear and wave war had to be an eleven, so why else wouldn't she be dead? Or perhaps there never was any Geki fire, nothing but tricks to keep Valhalla and its allies in order.

Those allies. She thought them through. Karpathos, Udachnaya, Vladivostok, Abu Simbel, Luna, Qosqo. She should be heading for one or another. Dr. Niide might be in one already, the last net whisper of Orkney was weeks ago, and she had only pried a few words out of it before the net went dead for good. Surely Karpathos or some other base was on top of things. Valhalla might be nuked, but the loose allied organization, the nameless amoeba, was still going strong. And hunting her if they knew what happened. The fact she wasn't dead likely meant the others had all been nuked by merit of their proximity to cities, to civilization. The destruction presumably knew no end. *Fuck it,* she thought.

It took only hours to reach Kirkwall at the center of the archipelago. It was something of a shock—it looked like a perfectly normal city. People wandered about in the snow, heading to a nearby bar or market or heading home. She saw families out in the open. It was as if she'd entered an alternate dimension where the war never happened. She linked into her Tikari and confirmed there was still no shortage of radiation in the air and the temperatures were in flux, but the buildings stood, not in ruins. And the people seemed almost happy. One approached her. She remained wary.

"Welcome to Kirkwall, young lady! Have ye come far?"

"From Lairg."

"My goodness! Ye must be freezin' years off if ye came by sea. Y'care for some beer?"

"Yes, thank you!" she exclaimed, more out of surprise than gratitude. She followed the man back to a small house a few blocks south where he showed her in. There was a fire burning and a small family lounging, reading paper books. Vibs felt like she'd entered one of her dreamscapes. One of the books she saw was *The Devil Drives*. Familiarity that seemed too perfect to be real. She grew somewhat suspicious.

The man introduced her to his wife and her other husband and all three of their children, seven, eight, and ten. He insisted on sharing some of their food. She wanted to respond in kind, but the idea of feeding the family butchered rapist seemed impure, as if it would taint them with the misery of the mainland.

"The peace won't last much longer," said the man. "There's fighting on Eday and Sanday, not far from here. North Ronaldsay's been taken by force. YUP army."

"YUP? They're here?"

"Comin' here. UKI's fighting the good fight, but they say the YUP is part of a new clan that's taken all Europe. The nation of Ulver."

The word sounded familiar to her. "Ulver?"

"Aye. They took the Shetlands last week. Rumor is they left it untouched mostly, except the blondes. Kidnapped all the blondes on the Isles. Insanity, if it's true."

"Does anyone know why?"

"Rumors about Ulver are wild, lassie. Some say it's run by the old man's child himself, that we're in the end times. Religious tomfoolery's been rampant since the war. Some say it's run by a man with a metal jaw."

Ulver meant "Wolves." Vibeke was haunted by the idea it could have something to do with Wulfgar's gang. How much had he made selling the Ares? If he captured Valhalla?

Two of the boys observed Violet's Tikari, which frolicked before them, careful not to cut them with its wings. They took it as being timid. They had no idea how dangerous a piece of equipment they were toying with.

"All we really know," he continued, "is they fight strong but fight fair. No chemical attacks, no more nukin', they take prisoners when they can avoid killin' and 'on't massacre the towns, so the escapees say."

"But they take blondes."

"Rumors abound, lassie. Rumors abound."

They let her sleep in the children's room, keeping their three boys in their own. Their naiveté was stunning. Tactically unsound. But these weren't people obsessed with tactics. They were altruists, creatures not to be trusted but taken advantage of in the extreme. Vibeke felt like she sullied their house, the things she'd done. The things she'd enjoyed doing. But shelter was not to be abandoned in such times. She got another full night's sleep and woke rested and ready to hunt. She thanked the family profusely, but offered them no supplies nor protection should the war come. She couldn't tie herself down or lose a single syrette. She left in the morning asking only one question.

"Have you heard of a doctor with a red beard coming to the islands?"

He had not. She began the search.

DIM GLIMPSES of the water flickered before Mishka's eyes. She was coming out of the cryo—if all went well, and she was alive, so it had—a week and a half after Balder's death. Not long enough for the ravine to forget her acts, but long enough they wouldn't be looking for her right under their nose.

She flexed and let the ice inside her muscles break apart and warm. She opened her eyes. A thin gap between the rocks let light in. The dim light of a winter sun, dimmer than she expected.

She began diagnostics. Radiation was higher than normal. Pollutants off the scale. She kicked the tank to dig out of its tomb. It shoved away the heavy rocks and deployed its periscope. She looked over the water. There was nobody to be seen. She assumed that if Valhalla had found her she'd not be alive, so she anticipated no traps. Valkyries didn't trap enemies like her. They killed them. She let the tank surface.

There was nothing around but virgin snow, covering all of Kvitøya. A giant bulge where the rampart was still up. And nothing else but an eerie calm. She set the tank as tall as it could go and still scraped the snow with its belly. She trotted over to the bulge in the snow. She waited. There were no alarms, no discernible links from the HMDLR. No links at all.

The net was gone. She felt around for anything, any sign of link traffic, but found nothing at all. Radiation and pollutants. A nuclear war had been fought as she slept.

And Valhalla wasn't attacking her. She slowly walked around the rampart. Scans showed nothing under the snow but the wreckage from Balder's Ice-CAV and a pogo. No sign of the chromatic drawbridge—it must have been off. But she spotted a depression in the snow. She fired at it with the tank's microwave, melting the area. It was a drill hole in the rampart. Wulfgar's access. She dismounted and walked down in, microwave ready.

The drill was still plugging the hole, but someone had cut through the back of it, offering a cramped but slick trapdoor down onto the edge of the pit. She took it and walked inside.

Mishka entered the ravine to find nothing like it was left. The power system was still glowing, but glowing red. Throbbing, living water stuck to it as if by design. Bloodred water striated with guts, as if Valhalla's heart had come alive, but come alive as an evil, seething core.

There were several walruses, most dead, some dying, some seemingly alive and well and unashamed of necrophagy. The place was overrun. The smell was terrible. She continued down the spiral wall, cautiously and keenly aware of the emptiness of the place. Except for one spot near the core. Something was moving, something clearly not a walrus.

It was a mechanical beast like nothing she had ever seen before. It was alive, that much was certain. It had once been a man. But now it was something else. It had no face, just a bare cross section of its original head. It still had human parts, scattered throughout its heavy mechanical frame. It had clothing distributed in pieces, affixed to what might have been its torso. Thaco armor. The color was familiar.

"Are you alive?" asked Mishka.

Veikko tried to stand up, but he only heard more grinding. He tried to say "help" but heard only his grisly rasp.

"What are you?" she spoke again.

He recognized her voice. "Mishka?"

"Who are you?"

"Veikko," he grunted.

"Veikko? Valknut team Veikko?"

"No, Veikko Jacobs, inventor of the automatic spatula. Mishka?"

"Well, fancy meeting you here. Or, what's left of you."

"What's left of me?"

"Not a great deal. Do you… do you know what you… are?"

"More or less."

"You have some retina left. Let me get you some adaptive lenses from the med bay."

She left; Veikko was about to tell her to wait, but the promise of sight was too great. He reclined, or at least let his body rest.

He'd spent the last week trying to find some way in which he could move, and not entirely without success. Though 99 percent of his nerves ran into dead ends of grinding and pain, the last percent were like the start of a puzzle box. Each opened nerve led to two more. He was almost able to crawl, though he feared tearing his organic components if he tried too hard. So he stayed cautious and worked slowly.

"This will hurt," said Mishka.

He felt pain in his eyes, more pain than he was in before. Something burned around them. He tried to blink, but he had no eyelids. Or eyes. But he could see something, shapes, blurry but growing sharper from tunnel vision half-faded to red.

And then he saw Mishka. She smiled at him.

"Good as new!"

She held up a mirror.

Veikko wasn't sure what he was seeing at first. It looked like a Rorschach test but red and raw. Blood encrusted tissue, nasal turbinates, two clear eyes—it was a cross section from a head.

Then he realized it was his own. Horror struck him as if a Geki had jumped into the ravine. It couldn't be him, but it was. He was reduced to a shingle of meat and bone, a grotesque visage like nothing he'd ever seen even among the Unspeakable Darkness. He was a horror.

"That's not the best part," said Mishka. "Look down."

He looked down and saw the mass of machinery and meat he'd been trying to master. It looked like a twist of jagged metal and mutilated flesh sinking into a hole in the ground. He was right beside the Ares, the YGDR S/L, his body propping up the heavy power plant and entire ravine atop the curved empty space of the rampart.

"I think you actually have arms and legs, but you're... not put together."

"Skadi...."

"She's to your left."

Veikko looked. His eyes were foggy. He had only lenses in front of his retinas but no sclera, no actual eye to keep the stray light out. He had half a sense of vision.

Skadi lay dead on the stone floor. Her chest was a hole, her suit burned up black around it. Veikko felt nothing at the sight. He couldn't even absorb her loss; too much had happened to him.

He was the ultimate victim of the great prank. He got all he wanted, but he got it wrong. He owned the ravine, but it was empty of everything but the Ares, to which he was now bound. The world was at war, but he couldn't rise up and play in it. And all the wrong people had died. Everyone who received his link dump. Everyone on his team. He might have cried if he still had tear ducts.

"Don't kill me," he said.

"Why would I do that?" asked Mishka.

"I'd kill you if I could."

"But you can't. You can't do much of anything, can you?"

"No."

"Poor little thing. How about you tell me where your sister is?"

"Dead."

"How?"

"I got her killed starting this war."

"Oh, this is your doing? Why start a war?"

"Was trying to nuke the Ares."

"The Ares?" She looked up at the throbbing mass. "Is that what this thing is? That's what this was all about? They brought it back from Mars? Ah! And you were the team sent to stop it. Good job, Valknut!"

"Fuck you too."

"Good thing the rampart's up! I'd hate to see the whole planet end thanks to you. Oh wait."

"What's it like up there?"

"Radioactive and quiet. Haven't been south yet. So you claim Vibeke is dead? How dead? All dead or only mostly dead?"

"I don't know. I hacked her to launch a nuclear missile. If it didn't land here something went wrong."

"You know a Valkyrie isn't dead until you see their liquefied brain. And Veikko, really? You hacked your own teammate? We hacked a hundred people a year in M team but not each other, silly fish."

Veikko might have looked ashamed if he had a face to show it. "Don't call me a fish."

"Okay, nudibranch. Where did you send my pet?"

"Dimmuborgir."

The ravine shook. Veikko screamed in pain. Mishka just looked around until it ended.

"What was that?"

"That's why you can't kill me. I'm the only thing keeping the ravine from collapsing. Only thing keeping the Ares from hitting ocean."

"That's... that's a pretty good reason."

"Just go away, Mishka."

"I'll kill your sister soon enough, or worse. Or I won't. If these are the end days, I best forgive her."

"Don't make me vomit. I don't know where it would come out."

"Some of us have been waiting, Veikko, waiting for the end. You see, the Bible tells us that—"

"Jesus fucking Christ, Mishka, give it up."

"Now's not a good time to blaspheme, Veikko. The apocalypse is upon us. This, this is all God's judgment."

"Spare me your religious bullshit."

"You're free to walk away." He ground gears again. "But what was I saying? Ah yes: the Bible predicted all of this, you see. This is the confirmation, the culmination of God's plan. 'The beast that ascendeth out of the bottomless pit shall make war against them, and shall overcome them, and kill them.' Good job, Veikko, you started the apocalypse. It's a good thing."

"You're full of shit."

"'And the angel, which I saw stand upon the sea and upon the earth, lifted up his hand to heaven—'"

"Please just shut the fuck up. I know I'm condemned to eternity in this pit, but you don't have to fucking preach at me through it."

"I'm just proud of my own role in the prophecy."

"Don't care, Mishka."

"The good souls of men must have already ascended to heaven in atomic rapture. We're the sinful remainder. You know how sinful we are. But Christ is a forgiving God, and I'll attain heaven too. I'll spread his word to those who remain and—"

Veikko tried to punch her and something moved, some semblance of an arm lifted up then fell back to the rock.

"Pull yourself together, Veikko. Then come find me when you come to your senses. Even you can be saved."

"I'm bound here, stuck to the Ares, the—"

"'He laid hold of the dragon, that serpent of old, who is the Devil and Satan, and *bound him* for a thousand years.'"

"She. Skadi did it. And I'm not fucking Satan!"

"No, no you're not. But your face would give him nightmares. Enjoy your time here, Veikko."

"Eat shit, Mishka."

She laughed and walked away. Veikko tried to move his arm again and metal ground against metal. He tried to look over his new body. It was a tangle. But some parts were open on top. He tried to move them. Slowly, very slowly, the pieces began to fit together.

BALLARD HEIGHTS stretched out for kilometers under the skyway. Through its transparent floor Hati could clearly see the entire arcology, tan baking to orange in the sunset light. It was one of the best-equipped places on earth for the disastrous war. There was food to last an eternity. There was geothermal power, still practically unlimited. There was a radiation screen for an emergency such as this. But best of all, nobody outside cared about Ballard Heights. It had no strategic value; really it had no value at all beyond the holdings of the company that ran it, and without the net, even those were deleted.

But the isolation was rotting the stable supports. Unable to leave the arcology, citizens were going stir-crazy. Arguments and petty fights were up 1,400 percent from before the war. Class disputes had begun to manifest. Floor 141 laid claim to an elevator and held it as their own. A group of neighbors on the 35th floor was trying to enforce their rights to the pool. The arcology's first ever instance of vandalism had cropped up when a band from 12 raided 178.

The war was a world away, the planet's darkest days evidenced only by the color and opacity of the clouds, but Hati knew something was brewing inside Ballard Heights that would become more of a threat than the radiation or troop movements. As head of the penthouse level homeowner's association she felt an obligation to fix it, or at least to keep it out, away from her tenants.

She reached the end of the skyway and entered the north ziggurat's observation deck. There she met with Épinard Quiche.

"Hati," he said with a brutally nasal voice.

"Quiche."

"Out with it, I don't have time for the pleasantries."

"Fine: your protest yesterday was way out of line. That swarm of—"

"Swarm? Are you comparing my tenants to ants?"

"You had over 150 at the Ristorante d'Oro. This mob mentality is unnecessary and—"

"Mob now. My people are a mob."

"Quiche, I think it's a reasonable request to—"

"Now you're giving orders."

"Quiche, you're blowing this up to proportions it—"

"I'm not the one dehumanizing our citizens and barking orders to keep out. This arcology has always kept every floor open to every tenant."

"And I'm not changing that nor issuing orders nor trying to dehumanize anyone. I'm only asking that you not lead your tenants to our establishments intending to disrupt their climate."

"I can't rule my tenants' lives, Hati. I have no say in what they choose to do."

"Quiche, you were standing on the salad bar shouting 'Eat the rich.'"

"Radicchio. I told them to try the radicchio and—"

"Bullshit all you want. The next time this happens, I'm going to the senate."

"Good luck. My brother—"

"Will bow out because this is a conflict of interest, and if he doesn't, I'll make sure the senate sees—"

Quiche held a poker face. "Are you threatening my family now?"

Hati sighed. She looked out the observation window to her ziggurat. The sun was going down behind a black cloud. In its last rays, she saw a pogo coming in for a landing on her tier. A militarized pogo.

"We have to cut this short, Quiche. Keep out of my floors."

"Storming out now!" he called after her. "I tried to negotiate with you in good faith, and you stormed out! The people will hear of this, Hati!"

As she crossed the midpoint of the skyway, she ran into Wyvern heading the opposite way, looking for her.

"Did you see? There's a military pogo on our—"

"I saw; I'm on my way."

"What do you think it is? How bad? Is this just a visit or like seriously the beginning of the end?" asked Wyvern.

"I don't think so," said Hati. "It's probably a deserter, someone with family here. It might not even be with a real military. And it came alone. Negotiations first. And those should go fine, we have nothing anybody wants."

"We have doctors, engineers, personnel to draft."

"So does everyone else. There's no reason for them to come here."

"Then why are they here?"

"I'm finding out."

They came out in the penthouse atrium. They could see officers standing around the pogo through the atrium roof.

"You hear Floor 79 just raided 80's museum? They're not even stealing essentials, just prizes. It's like gang warfare."

"It's like class warfare, and we house the highest class. They're gonna come for us sooner or later, the protests are just the beginning."

"What are we gonna do?"

"I have some ideas."

The elevator door opened. A soldier emerged. He stared directly at her; he recognized her.

"Hati?"

Hati stared at him. They'd finally come to take her.

"I don't have time for this," she told him flatly.

"Hati, I need you to come with me."

She still stood motionless.

"Hati, oh my God," said Wyvern. "Who is this?"

"A representative. For someone I've been avoiding," she explained.

"Hati, you need to come with me now."

"I have a life here. And I have an emergency brewing. The arcology is going downhill, and I need to protect my tenants."

"Not anymore."

"You can't take her against her will," said Wyvern.

"Yes he can," said Hati. She knew there was no possible resistance.

The man nodded in the affirmative.

"It's for him, isn't it?" asked Wyvern.

Hati looked at her. She knew Wyvern hated him. Hated that he had anything to do with her.

"Fuck off," Wyvern shouted at the soldier.

"Hati," said the man, "you know he won't take no for an answer."

"I know. But I can't just give up my life here. Not now."

"You must."

"Can I say good-bye to my friends? To my fiancé?"

"There's no time. Come. You'll be safe with us."

"Fuck him," said Wyvern. "He's done nothing but fuck up her life since the day she was born."

The man only stared. Hati looked down.

Wyvern continued to protest. "You go back and you tell him she doesn't answer to him. He has no power here. She can stay if she wants and—"

Hati put her hand on Wyvern's shoulder. She shook her head. Wyvern started to cry.

"Of course he has power here," Hati explained. "He sent it here to get me. And if he doesn't, he'll send more."

Wyvern shook her head no.

"Tell my friends he took me in. Tell Brendon I'll find him again."

"Hati—"

She hugged Wyvern hard, and Wyvern broke into sobs.

"I'll write to you too. He'll make sure you get every message. He's not a monster, Wyvern."

"He is a monster!"

"No, Wyvern. He's my dad."

Hati managed a faint smile and patted Wyvern on the shoulder, then turned and walked to the man with the rifle.

"Let's go," she said.

He escorted her to the pogo and they took off, leaving Ballard Heights and Texark behind them. Wyvern headed for the hospital to find Dr. Blacha. He only nodded solemnly when she gave him the news. Hati was gone and they both knew, though they couldn't say it, that she was never going to come back.

An alert sounded. Floor 30 had just captured raiders from 28 and planned to execute them publicly. Arcology police were on the way. Everything else was heading for lockdown.

NURSE TAAKE cauterized the soldier's legs while Nurse Kampfar held her down. She'd been hit by common shrapnel and triage put her on the list to fix fast and move on. They took the next soldier, and the next.

UKI was losing the war. They held their positions until they ran low on personnel, and then the survivors fell back to repeat the process a few kilometers away, a few kilometers less, lost to Ulver. They came to a soldier with nothing left below his ribs. Kampfar called for Dr. Niide.

Dr. Niide was frustrated. Years of working in Valhalla had spoiled him terribly. The finest equipment Valkyries could steal, reliable power, every tool for every job.

The front was the opposite. There was no reliable power, no predicting when the generators would work. The equipment was beyond limited. He found himself using electrical wire for tourniquets. Tape to build splints from sticks. Fire to seal wounds. He couldn't heal people. He could only delay their deaths long enough to let them heal themselves.

He still had everything from the pogo, of course. A couple advanced stasis chambers, an assortment of field generators, a supply of every drug he could possibly need but a shortage of means to deliver them. He had to use syringes to inject them; the only hyposprays gave out on the first day. A common hypospray only has fifty charges in it. They were disposable.

One was meant to bring them along for a mission in their armor, then throw them away before the next.

He had one medical standard microwave that could kill as efficiently as it could disinfect. He kept it on his side, clipped to his arm like the Valkyries did. He felt like a Valkyrie. He was in the field as they were, operating without support. An adventure, he thought. But he was never much for adventure. Adventure was hectic and unsterile. A courier burst into the medical tent.

"Eday is lost! We're bouncing to Shapinsay in ten!"

Medicine is not meant to be practiced on the bounce, he thought. He finished sealing up his patient and began packing. He detested packing.

The medical pogo lifted off and came back down in one hop. Shapinsay was clean and orderly. It held both regiments of the Orkney forces and would provide a break from the front line action. When Ulver came for this island, they'd have to take on the full base. The colonels spoke as if it were unquestionably the spot on which Ulver's advance would end. Though they spoke that way of each previous island too.

An alert sounded. Surely they couldn't be attacking already. Eday would've been a Pyrrhic victory for them. They had the island, but UKI had taken down a dozen of their pogos before getting routed.

The alert sounded in the open air. Niide missed the quiet linked warnings above all. The fight was noisy, blasts and commands shouted across the field. Here they shouted about a woman with knives.

From what Niide could gather, a single woman in a blue and green suit was tearing through the defenses, quite literally with a flying knife. That sounded awfully familiar. He stepped out of the medical tent to take a look.

He recognized a Valkyrie instantly. She hadn't killed a single man, she was simply walking in with an orbiting Tikari and the men were smart enough to keep their distance. Microwaves bounced off of her. Projectiles too. Dr. Niide shouted to let her in and put an end to it. The lieutenant heard him and, confused by the woman's invincibility, decided to order them to cease fire.

He recognized Vibeke as she drew near and walked out to her.

"Vibeke, yes? Mm, gutted Veikko on your first day before you got around to fighting. Mhmm"—he looked her over—"radiation burns, exhaustion, malnutrition, broken, yes, irreparable harm? Yes, imminent death. How have you been, Vibeke?"

"Good, and you?"

"Busy. Very busy. Too busy. Come into my tent. Gruesome fatality."

PYTTEN WAS happy with the promotion but not the delay before reaching the next post. After days there was some question if they'd forgotten the officer, buried all records in the paperwork. There were tales of it happening before, rumors of men, women, and others like Pytten getting promoted but never spotted again when the papers went missing.

So Pytten visited an old academy hangout, LeChuck's Groggery. Where there were always some humans singing chanties in the corner, where the grog was just toxic enough to ease any stress but not enough to kill you, where Tull used to hang out.

Pytten hadn't seen Tull since graduation. It was happy news that Tull of all people would be coming to explain the delay. When he arrived he met Pytten with a hug and a pat on the back. And a cringe.

"Your eye got fucked-up big time!"

Pytten was ashamed. There was no reason to be, of course. An eye lost saving a life was an eye well lost. One might even call the eye patch stylish.

"And you got more tattoos," Pytten observed.

Tull looked himself over. "From the Tonga Trench Tribe!"

"You won the *fe'auhi*?"

"I had so many points I could have left before the last round and still won."

"Well done, Tully!"

"Thank you, Pytten! Now, sit back down. You'll want to be sitting for the news from command."

Pytten was worried. Was there to be a hearing? Or a discharge?

"What's going on?"

"You impressed all the right people, of course. Saved your crew's lives and went back for the bastard Bax to boot. They called you a credit to the Valkohai. Wanted to make an example of you!"

"Vellamo no."

"No, no, no, you got a good one. The best I can imagine. You still want to use all those strategy and games courses you took at the academy?"

Pytten looked up. "I do, can you—"

"Already did my good friend, already did. You've been promoted to lieutenant commander and given a new post."

"Out with it, Tully! Where did they put me?"

"You'll be an administrative assistant!"

Pytten squinted with land eyes.

"They made me a secretary? Are you... are you kidding me? They made me a—"

"To Risto Turunen."

Pytten stopped talking. Tull smiled broadly.

"You're kidding."

"No joke, my friend. You'll be the right-hand of the Admiral of the Valkohai. My old captain from way back when."

Tull watched as it set in on Pytten's face.

"So.... When do I—"

"You sober?"

"Yes, I've only had half a grog."

"Then there's no time like the present. There's a limo waiting for you at the south docks."

"Vellamo!"

Tull laughed. "But we have time to catch up on the walk. The ride to Itämeri leaves whenever you wish. Come, come, you haven't even told me your grand hero story! The tale of Sävel Pytten, savior of the Saukko, rescuer of Bax the asshole, who's still awaiting charges for your eye by the way. Just think of all the clever names they'll have for you!"

They walked to the docks.

"Your boat was far from the worst incident. The war topside has killed at least two hundred Cetaceans. Debris, poison, radiation. Luckily the topsiders seem to have forgotten we exist at all as they annihilate each other. All collateral damage. But damage nonetheless. One hundred boats lost. Two small shore colonies damaged beyond repair, hundreds of families displaced. If ever we're to be called into duty, it will be soon."

"The Valkohai in action against humankind."

"Or our own. Piracy has octupled. The police forces have their hands full. Some of the larger organizations have grown more daring. The food bank off Yallahs was raided yesterday. The surplus is intact but diminished. But the food bank! The DPR is responsible, no doubt about it. This is far too daring for them. They'd never have tried before this nuclear business. Anyhow, you'll find out all about it. You'll find out everything now. Nothing will be classified to you. You will learn directly from the grand master."

"Did you have a hand in this?"

"None at all. It's by pure coincidence I was the one to inform you. I was starting my furlough in Pohjanlahti, so they gave me this last assignment."

"Then you won't be joining me in Itämeri?"

"The big city isn't for me, friend. I will drink and sleep and try to meet a compatible female with whom to have sexual intercourse, if you get my meaning."

"Yes, I get your meaning. You said it without the least bit of ambiguity."

"Hmmm, I do that, don't I?"

They reached the dock.

"Enjoy your limo ride, Pytten. Just don't turn on the television. Nothing but news. And you'll be dealing with plenty of news in the coming days."

"Thank you, Tully. It was good to see you again."

"You too, Pytten, you too. I hope we can meet again soon. Though somehow I don't think it's in the cards."

"I fear not as well. Unless you happen to have some top-level intel for my new boss."

"I'll see what I can dredge up for you," Tull laughed. They hugged again and butted heads. Then, with a pat on the back, Pytten was on the way.

VIBEKE DISARMED the last missile, boiling the wave bomb and deactivating it completely. Even if it could still launch, they'd see in GAUNE that it was unarmed. It would read no differently from a conventional rocket launch.

"You did the wrong thing, Vibeke," said Sal. The SSS robots shut down. Vibeke hopped down from the Ehren Plate and ran for Violet's position. Her link was still online, her Tikari still in the sky. She was still on the tarmac, but she must have outlasted the robots. Sal must have given up when he saw it was over.

She didn't see Violet in the darkness. She spotted a magnetic crane system and turned on her magnetic shield, then set her suit for full illumination. Still no sign of Violet, only glitter on the ground. SSS shells, she thought.

She linked out asking for Violet's position. There was no reply. She grew concerned. But the link was active. She was almost there.

There was more glitter on the ground, sparkling shards of metal and—flesh. Frozen flesh, shattered. Not necessarily Violet. She kept looking.

There were visible shards of organs. Definitely someone. If it was Violet, she wasn't lost yet.

The link lay severed on the ground. It was definitely Violet's. Frozen on. But there was minimal gray matter attached to it. Violet wouldn't be able to use her link again, but that didn't matter. Vibeke suddenly understood. Violet had missed the text warning and frozen in place with the SSS robots still on. She would have made it out if she could read.

Vibeke kept hunting. She just needed Violet's brain. She saw motion.

Nelson, Violet's Tikari, was fluttering around. It had gone ronin; that was okay. Vibs had lost her Tikari before. Violet wouldn't be able to link into hers once she was fixed. Not the end of the world.

The Tikari was fluttering about Violet's heart. Broken in three but only that, not shattered utterly. An organ had survived. Her brain could too.

She scoured the field of shattered Violet. Her brain would be around somewhere, frozen and ready for stasis. It would be problematic to regrow her, she'd be in serious trouble medically speaking, but if she could just find her brain, everything would sort itself out.

She found a shard of it. That was okay too, a few memories lost, a few personality traits altered. Another shard.

Vibeke began breathing harder. The Tikari fluttered behind her. It was hunting too. As if it knew they just needed a little more of her brain. Vibeke picked up a shard of it. The shard fell apart in her hands.

Violet had hit absolute zero. The SSS robots had stopped because she'd lost her shield and shattered completely. Vibeke didn't give up hope.

She scoured the field for another half hour, slowly realizing that Violet was completely, irreparably dead. It seemed impossible. Absolutely impossible. There was something missing, some piece of information, something she'd overlooked. She expanded her search perimeter. Violet would be there somewhere. She just had to look.

But she couldn't see. There were tears in her eyes. No, she told herself, she wasn't crying because Violet wasn't dead. She wiped away the tears and kept looking but found herself stumbling. Suddenly she was on her knees and bawling. Her fingers felt along the ground, finding frozen shards of her girlfriend. All that was left.

Not all that was left. In desperation she found the heart again. In three pieces but repairable. She ignored how useless that was. It wasn't useless. It was what she had to work with. She pulled her microwave and gently thawed the pieces before picking them up, making sure they weren't too brittle.

She put them on her arm clingers and stood up. She had what she could get. Violet was safe. It was time to kill Sal. She'd deal with the rest later.

On Orkney, Violet's heart grew pink and lively inside the stasis field. It was back to only 2 percent necrosis and in time, even that would fade as cells flourished and structures healed. The heart was fine, but as Dr. Niide pointed out, "It's a heart. Not a brain. Violet is dead. You've saved muscle tissue. Might as well have saved her gluteus maximus."

"It was all that was left of her."

"Sentimental, Vibeke. Since when have Valkyries been sentimental?"

"Since we fell in love."

"Uch, dreadful, Vibeke, utterly dreadful."

"I know," she said, ashamed.

"So…. Hmmm…. Saved the muscle tissue and found me. Preserved it, your final mission is fulfilled. Next? UKI could use you. If we had you a week ago we'd have three more islands."

"I suppose they can draft me if they like. But I don't think they like me."

"Slaughter an island of Ulver, mmm, they'll warm up."

"Maybe."

Vibeke thought. She really didn't have any plans after she got the heart to Niide. She tried to think of what she intended to do with it. Keep it preserved in a jar? Make out with it? Plastinate it and hang it from her ceiling lamp?

It was clearly time to move on. It was time to forget about her pipe dreams about seeing her dead lover again. She had to move on, or she'd drive herself insane or far, far worse. She had to leave the island, to get away from Dr. Niide.

She would leave immediately, leave the heart behind, leave the man behind, leave her foolish dreams behind. She left Niide's tent and trudged through the pissweed that grew around it. She headed straight for the boat on which she arrived. She made it in time to see it destroyed by the incoming Wolf attack.

Chapter III: Odobenusia

"SIRE, WE have news of a book burning in Birobidzhan."

"A book burning?"

"Yes, sire, the libraries were raided and thousands of volumes were destroyed."

"For the love of God send them some lamp oil. Next?"

"No, sire, it seems to have been an act of protest. A Buddhist sect destroyed canonical books to various other religions."

"Religionists?"

"Yes, sire, it appears so."

"Ulver will have none of this. Arrest the entire sect and make it known that vandalism will not be tolerated."

"Yes, sire, and other sects?"

"What have they done?"

"Nothing, sire, but they are appearing across Eastern Europe and Russia."

"If they've done nothing let them be."

"Sire, religion—"

"Is inevitable after the apocalypse. Inform me if any sects show a predilection toward violence."

"Yes, sire." Gerät bowed his head and left to make room for Temujin.

Temujin had already spoken not an hour ago, informing Wulfgar of the failure to take Khökh Khot. Wulfgar was surprised to see him back so soon.

"Temujin?"

"Sire, permission to speak frankly?"

It was the first time anyone under his command had asked.

"Granted!"

"Sire, Khökh Khot was not lost by the 9th; it was lost because we lacked proper intel."

"Granted. And if we had eighty-seven task forces, I assure you one would have been devoted to Khökh Khot. But we have eighty-six in operation and two in development. There aren't enough personnel to cover the entire globe, and Khökh Khot was eighty-seventh on the priority list. A priority list you composed, Temujin."

"Yes, sire, but I was not allowed to determine the top five allocations."

"Indeed you were not. You have an effective eighty-one forces to work with."

"Sire, if just one of those forces—"

"They may not."

"Sire…. May I ask—"

"You may not. They are on a mission far more important than Khökh Khot, more important than all of Mongol Uls."

"Yes, sire."

"Is there anything else?"

"No, sire."

"Then you may leave."

Temujin clicked his heels and marched out of the room.

Wulfgar was concerned that Temujin was correct about the allocations. He was using up five units, the most experienced, most clever units he had, in the search for Violet MacRae.

Unit Alpha had scoured the ravine and found only unstable ground and a biomechanical mass that could barely move. The mass luckily seemed to know Violet MacRae's last location. It belched out that she was likely dead, but seemed happy to explain her corpse would be in Dimmuborgir. If she survived, she'd likely be in Arcolochalsh.

Units Beta and Gamma headed to Dimmuborgir and found only a crater where the silo was to have been. Whatever was there, it was vaporized. Units Delta and Epsilon headed to Arcolochalsh and found it burned down.

All five teams continued the hunt, interviewed every witness, tracked every footstep. Given the uncertainty of her death, Wulfgar would not give up the search until they found her body, and if her body was vaporized, they would simply keep looking until the end of time. He had nothing to lose by continuing the search.

Except for Khökh Khot. He looked over the reports: 1,176 dead, 1,214 wounded, 113 missing in action, 81 tanks lost, 7 battlepogos, and numerous small arms. A bad day to be sure, but he felt only resolve. He simply didn't care about Khökh Khot.

He cared about Violet MacRae. He'd lost his duplicate action figure and grown all the more intent upon collecting the real thing. He had such plans for her, such torments and such pleasures. He threw the Mongolian log panel down on the table and walked to his bedroom antechamber.

The latest captives had been reviewed by Donatien. He'd thrown away the ugly ones, the diseased ones, those too close to nukes that got burned or broken. That left only twenty-eight, still too many to review personally. He had Donatien root out the platinum blondes, the dusty blondes, anything that wasn't just her tone.

That left seven in the antechamber. He surveyed them. Had them stripped and chained, and looked over those that reminded him of her most.

None looked like her. Their faces were all too round or too square. Violet's face was triangular more than anything. And she had angry eyes. None of these girls had angry eyes.

What he wouldn't give for a snip of her DNA. He could hit himself for not taking one while he had his toy. He'd failed to on Venus, under Hashima, and now the men he'd sent back to scrape the warehouse where they'd first met were coming back with nothing. And the ugly mass in the ravine had called her dead. Vaporized, if Unit Alpha was correct. He might never see her again. He didn't even have a partitioned snapshot of her. In time he'd forget how she looked. He simply couldn't allow it.

The task forces would stay on the job. It was as simple as that. He'd rather have lost all of Mongol Uls than lived with the knowledge he'd given up on his search.

VIBEKE DIDN'T know where she would go had the boat survived the first fusillade. As the debris rained down around her, she couldn't even bring herself to raise an arm to protect her head.

She turned to see the Wolf pogos, still painted with YUP colors, forming a line just off the coast, launching long range missiles to weaken the UKI rear. Her area was sure to be a landing zone for Wolf troops.

A tear streaked down her face. She didn't know what she'd expected to come of the heart. She felt shame, a shame unlike anything else that had hit her before. Shame for losing Violet, shame for needing her, shame for thinking she could have her back. She'd become so used to Violet dying that she simply couldn't accept that it could be permanent.

The Wolf line became mobile, heading toward her beach. She wanted to kill them all, certainly. Killing gave her a good perspective. Ending lives, aside from the pleasure, made her own seem more worthwhile. But she knew that pleasure would elude her with the incoming troops. She'd lost too much. The core of herself, she thought. She'd become soulless.

Seven UKI soldiers were approaching, targeting her.

"Leave the area, ma'am."

She went through the motions of a conversation. "I would, but my boat got blown up." She was headed for the boat. She forgot why. But it was as good a purpose as any she had left. "Can I have one of yours?"

"No, ma'am, just walk away or swim. We don't care."

She wasn't that useless. "I'll fight for you if you give me a boat."

"I'm not authorized to make that decision, ma'am."

"Then get someone who is."

"You need to leave this area! Now or we will arrest you!"

"Okay, fine, arrest me."

Seconds later all seven UKI soldiers were restrained on the ground in their own cuffs. The violence perked her up. Her sore fists reminded her of something good.

"Now if I let you go, will one of you get someone who can lend me a boat?"

"Yes, ma'am...."

Vibeke waited. Two Wolf cargopogos neared, drawing heavy fire from the UKI but keeping their distance just out of range until other pogos destroyed the artillery. Three platoons of soldiers from the UKI camp marched toward her, fronted by a very angry-looking officer.

"You have ten seconds to vacate before we open fire. Leave now!"

"I need a boat."

"I need twenty buck-naked slave girls and a king-sized bed, but nobody's getting what they damn please today, kid. Now move! Five seconds!"

"I'll fight for you."

"I have hundreds of men, I don't need one more girl. Two seconds."

"If I kill all the Wolves that come ashore by myself, will you reconsider?"

A blast echoed from the south.

"That was our last southwest artillery. That pogo's landing, kid. You want to stand here with your nifty little knife toys when they get here, you feel free, but you don't get to come running behind our line when they walk ashore, and we're not wasting a breath to bury you."

"Fair enough," said Vibeke as she turned her back on the army and faced the landing personnel pogo. A second personnel pogo neared in the sky.

The front gates of the Wolf pogo opened and a squad of soldiers with microwave rifles marched out toward her. Vibeke followed proper tactics this time.

As the pack of Wolves advanced, she set her Tikari to berserker mode and ran into the thick of them. The body parts began to fly. Blood began to stain her. She flipped through the old dance, the loose kata that annihilated countless men. Her field absorbed hundreds of hits, and she froze over quickly.

She thought of Violet frozen, an ice sculpture before she shattered. She turned the thought to rage and caught Bob in midair and began to bash instead of slice. It was slower, but it felt better, the crunching of skulls under the butt of her knife. The rewarding agony of survivors. She gutted them as they cropped up. Dug into them with a ferocity she couldn't trace. She was still thinking of Violet.

The dumb bitch who couldn't take a damn hour to learn to read the text that would have saved her life. She broke a Wolf's arm backward. If Violet had taken one day, one damn day to learn, Vibeke wouldn't be on that island. She severed a man's Achilles tendon and realized the leg wasn't even attached anymore. Violet had left her right when she needed her most. Had ceased to exist and all because of her own damn stupidity. Vibeke stabbed a man in the stomach and ripped upward with her blade, all the way to his throat. Blood spewed from his mouth and burned hot on her face.

She screamed in anger, in disgusted regret, in absolute hatred of Violet, of the subhuman thing she was dumb enough to love. She activated Bob's thruster and sent him through five more men before her, through their stomachs. She punched into the cavity of the first and flipped him by his own duodenum. She clawed at the wound of the next and threw him to the ground. She pushed in and ripped out the third's diaphragm. The fourth was trying to run. The coward. She recalled her blade and cut off his head before stabbing so deep into the skull of the last that Bob had to turn insect to pry his way out.

She caught her breath. Dripping with blood and panting heavily she turned back to the UKI troops who stood in shock.

The second Wolf pogo was about to land but, upon seeing the carnage, rose back up into the air and hunted for another landing spot. Vibeke walked up to the lieutenant and flicked some blood from her Tikari onto the ground.

"I need a fucking boat."

The officer was stunned. She rammed her Tikari back into her chest, blood, gore and all. The officer considered.

"There are three waves incoming. Help us hold the island against all three, and when it's over you can have a boat."

"Thank you, sir," she stated flatly. "Where are the barracks?"

"Last tent on the right, down that way," he said, still astounded.

She walked to the tent and barged in, coated solid in blood punctuated by chunks of flesh and skin.

"Rain lockers?"

The soldiers stared. One pointed to the water showers. She walked over and pulled off her suit. Showered off. Ejected Bob and let him wash off in the sharp spray. She was rubbing the gore from her hair when she realized how long it had grown. It was a tangle, a liability. She held it out in strands and had Bob cut it short again, then rubbed the gunk from her suit. When she switched off the shower she turned to find about fifty men staring at her.

She couldn't fathom why. Her nudity? Her unorthodox haircutting procedure? Her annihilation of the Wolves?

"What?" she asked.

"Where can we get one of those knives?"

She looked down at Bob, sitting next to Nelson. She kicked Nelson at the soldier.

"Here's one. Keep it."

Nelson flew back to her feet. The soldier just stared. She looked at Nelson angrily and kicked him again with her bare foot. As the wing sliced into her, she wondered how it hadn't the first time. She didn't care. She kicked again, and again, cutting her foot to ribbons. The crowd was starting to filter away. Only a few remained to watch her.

"What the fuck are you looking at?" she demanded.

"You're fucked up," said the soldier who had asked for a Tikari. He shook his head. "Who are you?"

She marched up to him and delivered a kick to his chin with her shredded foot, knocking him onto the ground. She straddled him, still wet and naked and accompanied by two Tikaris. She grabbed his head and held it to the dirt and leaned in close to his ear, and she whispered.

"I'm your new roommate."

She stood. Without a word, she headed back to Niide to take care of her foot, anticipating his lecture about wasting resources on noncombat injuries.

Vibeke stayed for two more days as pogo after pogo of Wolf troops cut landing spots into their artillery coverage. She was always on the front line of each landing to shred the incoming forces. And then she was always the center of attention in the barracks. Soldiers avoided her but stared constantly. The only person who would speak to her casually was Niide, but aside from a few small repairs he was too busy to see her socially. Not a loss as she couldn't speak to him without thinking of Violet's heart, sitting uselessly in a stasis field.

And that meant thinking of Violet, who she tried to stay active enough not to consider. She could throw herself into every fight on the shores and in those sublime moments of slaughter Violet was usually away from her mind. The Wolves quickly turned to fire on her specifically before landing, but the UKI had finally grown to appreciate her as a resource and laid down covering fire for her. She generally took one landing pogo for herself and let the troops fight any others that landed. Then, when she was finished, she'd send the Tiks to help as she caught her breath. She showered and slept and woke again.

Nobody spoke to her in the mess tent. She was regarded with suspicion by the common troops and some degree of anger or jealousy. After two waves of Wolves she had taken nearly half the kills and was still going strong. Her survival was a personal affront to the platoons that had lost men. Her skills a fantasy, an aberrant illusion.

Sergeant Therion warned her men about trusting a single combatant right in front of her: "We had a girl like her at Achnacarry, monster of a girl. Big celebrity at first. But not for long. Beat up her own squad when things got—"

"Violet?" she shouted.

Therion turned around. "You fight her?"

"I fucked her."

"Who the hell are you people?"

"Valkyries."

A rifleman mocked her with a few notes of Wagner.

Therion stared at her.

"Don't think for a second that we need you, or anything like you."

"I don't. I just need a boat."

"To go where?"

Vibeke had no reply. She simply didn't know where she wanted to go. Anywhere would be away from the front. She'd miss the moments of violent clarity it offered, but it didn't feel like her fight. She didn't have a fight just then. Not any purpose.

She realized after Therion walked away that she had to face the fact it was time for her to die. Violet was gone forever. The world was gone forever. She could rule the place with her talents, but the thought brought her close to tears. She didn't want it anymore.

But for now she'd settle for a boat to leave, or death in a battle to earn it. She didn't know which appealed to her more. She stood to depart for the coast for the final fight.

HATI SAID nothing for most of the trip. It was only when she heard gunfire that she grew concerned.

"Is that normal around here?"

"Nothing's normal," said the envoy, "but that's very far away. And we have projectile fields on this thing. He didn't send a car for you; he sent a tank."

"Naturally."

"He's a good man, your father."

"You know he's really not."

"He's changed."

"Right."

"He's changed a lot."

They sat in silence for a half hour. The man spoke again.

"I can sympathize, getting ripped away from your home, your friends."

"How long were you with my father?"

"From before your uncle died. I'm one of his top men."

"Of course you are. He wouldn't send a grunt for me."

"No, he wouldn't. He cares for you a great deal."

"That's why he's left me out of his entire life."

"Yes, exactly. Sarcasm or not, that's exactly it. He never wanted you to do…. What he does. Didn't want you tainted by it."

"Until now."

"Times are hard. He wants you where he can protect you."

"Ballard Heights was paradise compared to Europe. It wasn't in danger."

"Everywhere is in danger. You remember your vacations at Turtle Creek?"

"He told you about Turtle Creek?"

"He briefed me on you."

"And how to manipulate me emotionally if I didn't come."

"Exactly, yes. Anyhow, Turtle Creek is gone. It took a nuke and then a wave bomb."

"Why would they wave bomb Turtle Creek?"

"Some were set to cover thousands of kilometers. We don't know its true target, but Turtle Creek is filled with high radiation and a new hemorrhagic fever. One that lives in the eyes, mostly. They melt."

"Ballard—"

"Ballard Heights is fine for now. But if two thousand nukes—we think it was about two thousand—have gone off, there are still another eight thousand left to use, and God knows what the other side's generals are planning."

"God knows what my father's planning."

"He's your dad, and he'll protect you at any cost. Surely you don't disagree with that?"

Hati shook her head. "No, no, I don't disagree with that."

"You want to know how I met your father?"

"Not really."

"I was trying to rip him off. Grifter out of college. He caught me in a second and—"

The pogo was rocked by an ear splitting bang. It immediately veered to the right and headed downward.

The man hopped to his feet and grabbed a canister from beside his seat. He sprayed foam out onto Hati as fast as he could until she was surrounded by a ball of soft orange goop. He turned the can on himself and was about to spray it when the pogo hit rock.

Hati was knocked out by the sudden halt but came to fast. When she woke the man was cutting her from the foam. He saw her move.

"You stay here as long as you can. There's a beacon only we can trace. They'll find you fast, he made this top priority."

"Are you okay?"

"No, I'm gone. If you need me, you've got another five minutes tops."

"Where are we?"

"Gibraltar. We own the territory."

Hati was shaken; her eyes watered despite her calm.

"What will the people coming for me look like?"

"Yellow. Dressed in hazard yellow. Yellow and hot pink banded pogo, for visibility. Hurts your eyes to look at. Enemies would likely have camouflage, but that was an extreme long range bolt. They're not in the area."

Hati tried to think of any question she'd need to know to be rescued. But those weren't the questions coming to mind.

"Why do you work for him? Why my dad?"

He looked at her and stopped cutting.

"I was a gutter rat. I was shit. He made me a soldier, and that was long before he had a real rank himself."

"You'll die a soldier. He got you killed."

"He trusted me with his daughter...." He faltered. "Hati, he gave me my life a hundred times over. He honored me beyond words. This is a death worth dying."

Hati began to cry.

"I'm sorry I was so mean to you."

He laughed and shook his head. "He told me you were a tough girl. Ornery like him. You didn't disappoint."

He cut the last threads of foam, and she fell out to his side. She held him, looked for his wounds.

"Hati, there's no chance...."

She wanted to call him by name but didn't know it. "Your—your name, what's your name?"

"Schuldiner. Charlie Schuldiner."

"Do you have a family? Do you have anyone I—"

He shook his head. She cradled him and felt a protuberance, internal bleeding.

"Thank you, Charlie."

"You're welcome, ma'am."

They sat in silence as he began to fade away.

"Do me a favor, Hati," he finally whispered.

"Anything."

"Give him a chance."

She nodded. "Okay. Okay."

He fell asleep. His heart still beat, but she couldn't rouse him. A few minutes later he stopped breathing. She kept taking his pulse until it fibrillated and then stopped, and she cried.

Only minutes later the rescue team in yellow arrived. They tended to Hati first, securing her in a dozen seat belts. A man hopped out and checked Schuldiner's body, then waved for the pogo to depart. It left him there. She realized the pogo was a speed ambulance; it had only two seats. It had been a one-way mission for the medic in exchange for a single passenger.

There was no limit to what her father would risk, would sacrifice, to bring her in safely. She hated him. He was a man one simply could not love. But she'd promised Schuldiner she would give him a chance. She would.

She sat back and tried to breathe despite the acceleration. She closed her eyes and for the first time in her life, she looked forward to seeing her father.

THE OFFICE was quite modest compared to the base of operations Pytten expected for the Admiral of the Valkohai. It was simply a desk and a man and, on the floor by the entrance to its aquarium, a giant salamander. It took a moment before Pytten realized the man was Risto Turunen himself.

"Permission to come aboard, sir?"

"Granted," said the admiral.

"Lieutenant Pytten reporting for duty, sir!"

"Lieutenant Commander, I believe."

"Sir, yes, sir! I apologize, sir!"

Risto smiled.

"And that's all the introduction we have time for. Open radio observation on Quad 16 by 14 by 19."

Pytten froze for a split second, then realized it was no idle comment. Pytten opened up the radio on the desk and set it for the right Quad, then reported.

"Observation Quad 14—Current monitors reveal: Vellamo! The *Lee* is surrounded by human vessels! Massive buildups, we read twenty-six—No, twenty-nine Ulver submarines. *Lee* reports thirty-six more en route. Orders to the *Lee*, sir?"

"Maintain position."

"Sir?"

"Maintain position; do not make me repeat myself, Pytten."

"Yes, sir! 'Maintain position' sent."

"Continue observation. Be calm, Pytten."

Risto sat down at his chair and observed Pytten. Pytten watched the fleet surrounding the *Lee*. They moved closer.

"Proximity warnings sounded on the *Lee*. Sixteen Ulver subs within the radius. Orders?"

"I'll give them when they need be given, Pytten." Risto smiled. "This is every minute of every day for us. Be calm. Calm in the face of emergency. That is what's required."

"Yes, sir. Is this a test?"

"No, no time for those. This is the fate of the *Lee* and sixteen sailors aboard."

"We have to—"

"Don't assume there is always something to be done immediately. A very wise man once told me that urge for activity is a remnant of panic, nothing more. We must not panic here. If you or I panic, all is lost."

Pytten looked up, desperate.

"No pressure." Risto grinned again.

Pytten observed. "The Ulver fleet is continuing on course. No contact with the *Lee*."

"Do you know why I requested you for this role?"

"Because I went back for Bax?"

"Because you sent him to the brig in the first place."

Pytten looked at him.

"Because you were about to die and you still sent a man to the brig for insubordination regarding his foul language."

"Not for saving—"

"There is no shortage of heroics in a time like this. There is a shortage of composure. I don't need a hero to do this job. I need a cool head."

"Yes, sir."

"Observations?"

"The fleet is departing proximity. *Lee* is intact and uncontacted. No contact."

"I knew there wouldn't be, of course."

Pytten was confused. Risto saw it.

"That was no test, but it was an ideal case. You panicked. But you brought it under control when ordered to do so. Almost as fast as my last assistant on her first day."

"If I may ask, why did she—"

"Stress related aneurysm."

Pytten nodded. Risto sat down, and the giant salamander crawled up into his lap.

"Stress kills. Simple as that. With every Valkohai life, many Cetacean lives on the line, it's overwhelming, or at least it tries to be. And just wait until you meet the Geki…. Yes… there are stressful things here. Some you can't yet imagine. But you will overcome them."

Pytten nodded.

"Open Quad 23 by 23 by 56."

"Opened and observing. Land. This is on land."

"That's where the war is."

"But we—"

"It remains important we monitor all their battles. War is a fluid. It takes the shape of any container you place it in, and given the chance it will leak."

"Understood. Ulver is annihilating a Canadian transport. Do we intervene?"

"Have the Valkohai ever intervened in anything?"

"No."

"Do you know how many victories we have to our armada, sailor? Under my command?"

"None, sir, we've never fought a—"

"Four hundred and seventy-one."

"But we never fought anyone, ever."

"A battle never fought is a battle won. We have never fought because we've never allowed a situation to degenerate into a fight. In four hundred and seventy-one situations that threatened violence, we won by a show of force that deterred the enemy. Or we negotiated for peace. Or we simply left the area. These are victories, Pytten."

"Yes, sir."

"But?"

"But leaving is hardly a notable victory."

"Why not?"

"Because it accomplishes nothing. It's no better than retreat."

"Evasion is not retreat. One cannot retreat from a battle that never took place."

"Understood."

"To win every battle is not the ideal war. The ideal war would have no battles at all. To see that the enemy does you no harm, gains no advantage, without them ever knowing you exist, that is the sweetest victory."

"But what would we do if they saw us, if they'd seen the *Lee* and attacked?"

"We would annihilate them beyond comprehensively, such that none of their kind would dare to attack us again."

"Beyond comprehensively?"

"To kill an enemy stops their attack. But to stop the next attack, one must be more than comprehensive. One must petrify the observer, the commander, the troops. One must act not only with flawless tactics, but with poetry. An attack is a poem, a symphony, an art. If the work of art is powerful enough, it can end a war that would last centuries if fought by conventional means."

"So what's the poetry in doing nothing?"

"All the best poems are left unwritten."

"Sounds like the opinion of someone who hates poetry."

"And I hate war."

"Odd, for an admiral, sir."

"Critical for an admiral, Pytten. Critical."

AFTER TWO failures, Arrgh had been replaced and Wulfgar was running out of generals. He offered the job to Uggs from the early Wolf days, who refused. Wulfgar demanded to know why.

"Orkney is impossible to seize. They have a special weapon that overrides any conventional tactics."

"What is it?"

"A young witch, sire."

"A witch?"

"She kills everyone near instantly. Has a demon that shreds anyone comes near 'er."

Wulfgar frowned at Uggs's ancient manner. "Where the hell did they get her?"

"Unknown, sire. Shall I play the recordings?"

"Yes."

Wulfgar observed the single fighter. She tore through his men in a manner he hadn't seen for years. But he had seen it before. He was pretty sure he'd seen *her* before.

"Scipio!" he called.

Scipio arrived in his silk robe. "Aye, mate?"

"One of your comrades is holding up the Orkney invasion."

"Is he?"

"She."

Scipio leaned in and watched the failed assault.

"Vibeke," he explained.

"I need Orkney to mass for the UKI. Can you deal with this nuisance?"

"You don't want me on Umeå? Was heading out in an hour."

"Why would I want you on Umeå?"

"Muslims, Wulfgar. Rumor has it the whole university is overrun."

"Rumor has it they've been utterly peaceful."

"Just saying, Wulfgar, you've got pockets of religionists growing."

"They are not a tenth the concern this girl presents. Can you capture her?"

"I can flick the sheila."

"I have no idea what that means, Scipio."

"I can kill the girl, mate. Bloody shit, Wulfgar, learn English."

"Alive, Scipio! She may have information I need."

Scipio acted as if he didn't hear. He headed for the communications array. An indignity if there ever was one. He had a damn link behind his ear, two counting the Tikari link. But like most everything else it wasn't working. It might never again. He missed the net. More than he missed the ravine, he hated his confinement to reality.

He hardwired into the radio booster and contacted the third wave.

"Scipio to Sabaton, over."

"Sabaton, over."

"Hold back wave three Orkney, I'm joining you, over."

"Confirmed, over."

"I'll be the bloke in the Bugatti, out."

He headed for the garage.

VIBEKE STOOD on the beach. The third wave was far later than she expected. She weighed the advantages and disadvantages of the wet sand. She knew how to fight in it. Likely they didn't. But she couldn't bring herself to care for the usual tactics. She had no desire to win the fight. It would be her last if she did. It would be her last if she didn't. She cleared her mind of all thoughts of the fight to come and resolved to put nothing into it. She'd let the Tiks do the work or she'd die.

The pogo came into view. There was no artillery left. More was inbound from the mainland ruins, but the troop pogos could now land anywhere on the island to face the men, soldier to soldier.

So it seemed odd to Vibeke when the pogo headed for her position changed course and another, smaller pogo took its place. There was something on that pogo that wanted their position. Likely because of her. She tried to think of what weapon they'd deploy against her. A pogo ready to explode was likeliest—she was surprised they hadn't tried it. But they'd not be sending an exploding Bugatti.

The sleek craft landed in the shallow dwindling waves, and its door opened. Cato emerged from the pogo and adjusted his robe as he walked toward her.

"G'day, Vibs."

"Cato?"

"Cato days are over, mate. Scipio now. My Ulver name. But hey, we're old friends, you can call me Will. Will Testling."

"You killed Alf."

"Do you care? Do you care about the ravine at all? Never did myself, to be honest. I've been working for Wulfgar since his first stay. Promised me all of Africa. Already let me nuke Tunisia. Now I'm here to kill you."

Vibeke drew her Tikari, more out of habit than eagerness to fight.

"We never sparred, did we, Vibs?"

He ejected his Tikari. A nasty little flea that jumped to his hand and turned into a small karambit.

"Not to toot my own horn, but you don't stand a chance against me. Or anyone from a senior team, frankly. You couldn't even beat Mishka in a fistfight. I know, I watched. Sorry, doll, but this is where it ends for you."

He sloughed off his robe into the water and stood mostly naked, wearing only grotesquely tight, black leather briefs. He posed with his knife as if someone was taking his photo.

Vibeke found the display disgusting. She felt nothing more than disgust. She'd had enough of the fights, enough of wandering. Cato seemed like as good an end as any.

"You want to kill me, 'Will'? You go right ahead."

He mistook her invitation for an invitation to fight. He was too self-absorbed to look her in the eyes and see that she was ready to check out.

"You think you can take me alone, sheila? You think you can take an elder without a single ally on our level? Or do you think that army behind you can do any good?"

He was enough of an ass that she at least wanted to take him with her. It was the happiest thought she'd had in weeks. She'd been dying since she lost Violet, only waiting for a good way to finish. Cato offered it. She'd fight to a deadly stalemate. He'd be expecting her to fight to live. She'd be fighting to kill them both.

She held her Tikari high and took up an aggressive stance.

"You didn't learn in the ravine, did ya, doll?" He began jumping from side to side, readying himself to strike. "I have the advantage. I have the power. I'm invincible to you, and I'm not going down before one girl with nobody by her side!"

Two Geki appeared by her side.

Fear broke into her and choked her. She could see Cato suffer the same. The soldiers behind her fled as fast as they could, most screaming in terror.

"Orders, Vibs?"

The Geki just asked her for orders. She was shocked beyond the fear. But the question pulled an answer from her like their questions always did.

"Fire at Will!"

The Geki flames erupted from under one of their cloaks, darting into Cato. He was engulfed in flames, his skin burned to black, then burned away, then his muscles, and organs and finally bones, until there was nothing left of him but vapor, and that vapor was blown away into the cold winds.

Vibeke collapsed to the ground, the heat and fear churning in her stomach. But she had to know what just happened. She struggled to speak and spat out the words.

"Why? Why are you helping me?"

The Geki remained silent. The one that had shot the flames disappeared, its cloth pulling upward. The other stood still.

"Why?" she demanded.

The Geki just shrugged. A strange and wholly familiar shrug with one hand up and one hand down. Then it disappeared.

HE PICKED her up as she lay dying. Shot once in the heart, killed in the line of duty, as were they all. She was gripped with fear, unnatural fear. The kind of fear he inspired. That she would inspire someday. He took her to his home, his citadel, and placed her in the chamber. In seconds she was scanned, in minutes her new heart was grown, and in hours she was alive again, alive and well but still gripped by fear.

It had taken him months to get used to it. To be able to think again. Months of absolute hell and misery like few people would ever know.

But he outgrew it, as she would in time. He watched her every day, felt for her deeply. He was giving her a gift, he knew, but he'd never seen the price before, not from that side of the mirror. Had he been in so much agony? He knew he had, but it was hard to watch her. A kind young officer of the Garda, and a beautiful one. He couldn't admit that her beauty influenced his decision.

There were others as qualified: the woman from the craters who died defending her station; the man who caught Sandoval the Sticks; a half dozen others he'd been watching since his master died. He had to let them all die and stay dead; he could only save one. Now, he would be the teacher, and the new girl his student. As soon as she overcame the fear.

It took only two weeks before she could speak rationally, more than screams and whimpers. And he explained it to her then as briefly and simply as he could: We are the Geki. We monitor religious militias, deviant company armies, the darker unmonitorable forces that shape the earth in secret. We see that they don't fuck shit up. She understood. But it was another month before her training began.

He placed her in the chamber again. It implanted his master's flame in her arm, a smooth operation lasting only seconds.

"The flame is our weapon. It must be wielded with the utmost subtlety. It's easier to create a firestorm than light a candle. You must learn to light candles. To extinguish them with a thought. To form shapes, to make the fire dance. Then in time, you will use the flame to control, to punish, to fight. Just as you will use the fear. Your voice is now the voice of a god. None can hear it and not be struck by fear. Your every word is an order that cannot be disobeyed."

"It's too much power," she said. "It's unjust."

"It is justice itself. We answer to our companies. I answer to GAUNE, you to UNEGA. We answer to the most common, the most mundane interests. We watch over the most esoteric, the most powerful and secretive. We are the link between the top of the food chain and the bottom, the point that makes it a cycle. As you'll see in time."

As she grew stronger with the fear and more adept with the flame, he showed her who they existed to control. She logged into her vision systems. There was the cloak, lined with hundreds of lenses to see around her in 360 degrees on every axis. Then there was the network, the intel system. A vast net over the citadel that functioned as a satellite dish array focused into the planet, using the globe itself as an amplifier to see simultaneously into every place on Earth, to monitor automatically and report and show them the happenings they needed to see.

He explained how rarely they would interfere, and how necessary the fear; the Farnesene Pulse was to control the otherwise uncontrollable forces they were to supervise.

In time she became accustomed to her role, and together they kept the extremities in check. Forty years they worked together, a perfect team. Unsullied by ethical disagreement, or common bickering, or love. They grew old without a flaw in their duties. Until 2230.

It was a routine check on the Valkohai, who never stepped out of line. They were to see, on orders from GAUNE, that the new admiral, Risto Turunen, was going to follow the treaty. He offered no argument at all, he was proud to claim he'd never appear on the bad side of the Geki. He said it bravely with one lung full of air. He seemed unafraid, a true rarity. Of all the fearsome warriors they encountered, many feigned fearlessness. But only Risto was convincing of it.

And he was kind when her elder collapsed. He offered medical support before they jumped back to the citadel. She brought her elder to the chamber and let it diagnose him. She was surprised any natural cause could bring him down. But he spoke to her, one last time.

"We don't last forever. Find officers of the law from GAUNE who have distinguished themselves with honor. Find as many as you can, and follow the best of them. Great officers always get themselves killed. Be there when they do. Take one, heal them. Teach them as I taught you. And when you grow too old to function, tell them the same thing."

He turned off the chamber and died. She cremated him with her flame. There were no ashes to scatter; it burned that hot. And she set out hunting for her student. She would become the master and the cycle would go on. She observed a dozen officers carefully, but focused most on one in particular. A common policeman from the edge of GAUNE who acted with guile, without fear, with utter disregard to his personal life and family, which he was willing to sacrifice completely to uphold the law and catch his target.

Just as her master had said, great officers always get themselves killed. So he did. And she was there to take his body, and heal it in the chamber and subject it to the horrible fear. And she had her student.

His training went well. He mastered the flame and overcame the fear admirably. He followed her on errand after errand and learned the ropes.

He proved a somewhat cold gentleman. He was polite to her, and flawlessly robotic on missions, but he was also flawlessly robotic the rest of the time. He seemed to have no emotion whatsoever. His coldness scared her sometimes. He could kill with no hesitation. He maintained a casual attitude about it as he burned the burn-worthy and wreaked fear upon the once fearless.

And he stayed just as cold and emotionless when he found her dead.

In two years he had never made a move she didn't sanction. He had rarely made a move without her. But on that fateful day he gave in when intel from the network reported on a girl from his past life. He was human after all. He could remain cold and objective 99.9 percent of the time, but when he heard a certain girl was involved in a sexual assault, he had to peek in and make sure she was okay. And indeed she was. Still, he abused his power. There was one person, a subhuman really, that just desperately needed burning. So he burned the subhuman to a cinder and headed home.

He found the citadel destroyed. Burned down. The intel network was annihilated, leaving him blind. He broadcast a massive extinguishing burst from his flame, then jumped directly into the smoldering wreckage.

Maggie was dead. Veikko had cut off her head and left her to burn. Without feeling he poked through her remains and her jump cloak to find the flame implant. It wasn't there. Her radius and ulna turned to powder as he prodded them. He felt nothing. He never did. In times when most people would panic, he had only ever grown more astute, more methodical. He would need that focus now.

With the intel net down he'd not be able to find Veikko. But Valhalla specialized in such things. He jumped into Alf's bedroom.

"Veikko has murdered my elder. You will kill him upon his return, or the ravine will burn."

He jumped back home. He had to keep the cycle alive. He had to find another Geki. Someone who died in the line of duty. But he hadn't prepared, he didn't expect to for years. Decades. In fact the only people he knew who would stand a chance as Geki were in Valhalla.

But they died all the time. And there were a couple among them with just the Geki concept of justice. One in particular, and Veikko would want to kill him shortly. He jumped to Kvitøya.

Balder's Ice-CAV exploded and burned him along with it. At first the Geki didn't think anything would survive, but his head came out intact. But he couldn't save Balder when the entire ravine was watching. They would know who the next Geki was. And then nobody would respect them, nor fear them. There would be familiarity, and familiarity is the nemesis of fear.

He let Balder die. Let Mishka kill him. He cursed. And waited. There would only be one Geki for a long time to come.

The next day, he awoke to a link alarm. An implant link alarm. Maggie's fire implant was being used by someone other than Maggie. He jumped before even considering Veikko. Fire had already erupted from his palm before he realized how idiotic Veikko was to try using it. He had no sympathy for him. He had no sympathy for his teammates. It was time for Veikko to burn.

And burn he did. His Thaco fields and armor only did so much to protect him. He was blackened in seconds. In seconds more he would be dead. In less than a second, though, Varg flew the blackwing into the lone Geki and cut him in half. He barely managed to jump before his lower half fell from its cloak, out of range.

He jumped into the med pod. He didn't consider how he'd end up or what condition the pod would be in. He ended up upside down under his lower half with his feet on his diaphragm and his face in the floor inside a burnt med pod. He bled rapidly, he had only seconds of awareness to turn the pod on, if it would turn on at all. He clawed his way upright and climbed up his own legs to hit the emergency switch. He made it and pounded the switch and found it burned in place. He hit again, and again, and again until his blood pressure dropped to nothing and he passed out.

He came to a half hour later fully assembled. His last hit must have done it. His cloak would take longer to mend, and he'd have to send it back to Google's tech division to repair the sensors. It could clearly still jump, though, so he dug into the basement desk, took some thread, and sewed the thing back together.

He jumped back to the spot of Veikko's death. There was no fire implant left. No Veikko left. It wasn't over.

He had to jump to Valhalla fast. With Balder dead permanently and Veikko likely still alive, he had to speak to Alf. Without the intel net he couldn't tell where Alf was, but with some quick link-fu he managed to pinpoint his link antenna within the ravine. He jumped.

He found it next to Alf's shredded head. Before he could even register the fall of Valhalla, he heard a terrible screeching of metal behind him. He turned to see the comm tower falling from the overhanging rock. His link scan still on, he registered Varg inside. Varg. Balder's man. Falling from the ceiling and poisoned to death. Perfect timing.

He placed Varg's body in the med pod and let it do its work. He sat down in the blackened remains of the citadel. Shit was fucked up. That much was certain. He took stock. Maggie was dead, her flame gone. Valhalla was betrayed and almost certainly ended. With the ravine empty and its leaders permanently deceased he doubted the Valkyries would even return. He almost didn't notice that the link was fluctuating. When it finally caught his attention he found the entire web failing. For the first time as a Geki he got his intel from the World News Log.

War. Accusations, allegations, acquisitions. He marveled at it. Veikko had single handedly fucked up the entire planet. And then the net was gone. It didn't come back.

The war began and the missiles flew. He stayed with Varg to inflict fear upon him, the now permanent fear he would have to overcome to be a Geki. The once powerful *übermensch* stayed curled up by his side like a cat in a lightning storm.

So he sat next to Varg and kept a hand on his side, and rubbed his shoulder to let him know that whatever the fear did to him, he had a friend to face it with. They would be good friends someday. They were useless until then. They could only watch as the world unraveled.

Varg slowly regained his wits. He resolved himself and became functional within only a couple weeks. He got his pulse gland implanted. The fear now came from within him. But he had no flame. There was no sign of that implant. They would seek it together, but without another attempted use the small mechanism was exactly that: a tiny device that could be hidden anywhere. They would seek Veikko as well, but he was just a burnt corpse, and the world now held sixteen billion of those.

In time Varg learned the few lessons Valhalla hadn't taught him. Months later he was a Geki. A young Geki but a capable one. He trained with Maggie's jump cloak and its vision features. He wouldn't get to use it to jump as often as he'd hoped. It cost UNEGA taxpayers three million euros every time the Geki jumped. The satellite system was still in place, and it still held thirty-eight jump charges. That meant nineteen more jumps for the two of them. After that there would be no devoted top secret cargo rocket to replace them. After that the Geki days of jumping across the globe would be over for good. They would have to use them sparingly. They would have to function as creatures of opportunity, and of philosophy.

The motto of the Geki was out of date. Shit was fucked up. The treaty was dissolved; the purpose was obsolete. So Varg and the elder forged a new mission: "Burn The Motherfuckers Responsible." First that meant finding the flame implant. Still with under twenty jumps, they agreed to wait until the flame implant showed up on its own, when someone tried to use it again. It was too small an object to seek by jumping around the globe where they thought it might be. Finding Veikko, the first Motherfucker in question, was also regrettably relegated to an inactive hunt. They would only seek targets of high importance they knew they could jump to reliably.

Strictly speaking, Cato wasn't on that list. But when April came and the Geki had remained utterly inactive, merely surviving in the subbasement of their ruins playing card games and arguing about old Valhalla missions, they were willing to promote Cato to an "Estate Card" level priority, beneath "Duchy Card," "Province Card," and the "Colony

Card"—Veikko himself. After such delays they would take any intel that revealed any Motherfucker regardless of their degree of responsibility for the actual war, or for any escalation thereafter.

All that is to say, when they heard a link snippet of Cato taking his Bugatti to kill Vibeke from Varg's old team, they were more than happy to spend a couple jumps on burning him to death. So they did: Varg because they got to burn Cato and likely save Vibeke's life (and he admitted he simply wanted to see her again, even if it caused her to fall into horrific terror) and the elder because it gave him a chance to do something he'd been wanting to do for months.

So Varg stayed with Vibeke for a moment as the elder Geki checked in on the girl he'd checked in on before. Before the war, before the fall, before shit got fucked up forever. He finally had a location for her, a way to see her, to make sure she'd survived the war unscathed.

She hadn't. She was dead.

VIBEKE. HE had shot her in the neck once with a field piercing shell. Scipio—Cato the damned bastard—didn't mention she was on Violet's team.

Wulfgar remembered how miserable Violet had felt at the prospect of losing the woman. The fact Vibeke was alone suggested Violet was dead, but if she wasn't, Vibeke would be the ideal bait.

She was the absolute top priority. Wulfgar pulled back the entire 3rd and 4th forces and directed them to Orkney. He needed the island for the UKI but needed the girl more.

Goddamn Scipio. He would have killed her; Wulfgar knew it. Best he had been killed by her fire attack, however she'd done it. The reports suggested she had summoned two demons who breathed fire at him. Whatever really happened, Wulfgar wouldn't miss the bastard. He would have killed her. He could have invited her with him and she might have come. She could be in his clutches right then, summoning Violet.

Wulfgar kicked his trash ring across the room. He had to put his mind on something else. Luckily, something else presented itself.

The lab was almost finished with their work. A feat of genetic engineering that had cost Wulfgar nearly twenty million Loups to accomplish in the postwar mess. But it was done, and he felt all the better for it. He knew it was good work, that it would be appreciated.

The proud technicians handed him the container. He looked inside. It didn't look like he expected, given its lack of a shell. It stank to high heaven. He closed the container and exhaled. Then he headed for the lagoon.

It was one of the fortress's only recreational areas and a fortuitous one given Wulfgar's needs. He sat down on the faux stone and pulled the giant clam out of its container. He threw it into the water and whistled.

Umberto came splashing over to eat his giant clam. He was overjoyed to get a real mollusk instead of the synthetic food he'd been eating since his arrival. Wulfgar was most satisfied to see the giant animal gorge itself, slurping up the disgusting creation bit by bit. He was glad the poor thing had been grown without a nervous system.

Umberto finished his meal and nuzzled Wulfgar with his vibrissae.

"Lots more where that came from, big guy." He rubbed the animal's head. "We'll grow 'em by the ton."

A knock came at the lagoon door.

"Come."

Gerät entered.

"This had better be important, Karl, I'm with my walrus."

"Yes, sire. Some religionist groups seem to be militarizing. Muslims in Mongol Uls, Christians in Tromsø and—"

"Karl...."

"Yes, sire."

"I agree that is important news. But do you think it's really walrus-interrupting important?"

"Sire, military action by a religious coalition can—"

"It will be dealt with in ten minutes when I finish feeding my walrus, Karl."

"Yes, sire."

Gerät did an about-face and departed.

"They just don't understand us, do they, big guy?"

Umberto barked and flopped over. Another knock came at the door. Wulfgar calmly stood and exhaled. He walked to the door and opened it. Stiletto stood before him.

"Stiletto?"

"Yes, sire, I have—"

"Before you speak, Stiletto, I want to know, did you pass Gerät in the hall?"

"Yes, sire, but—"

"And did Gerät have anything to say to you?"

"Yes, sire, he informed me you didn't wish to be bothered, but—"

"But. I want you to remember, you said 'but' right then. Now tell me, Stiletto: after you were told by Gerät specifically not to bother me, what 'but' was so overwhelmingly important that you thought you should still, still disturb me during my walrus hour?"

"Hati, sire."

Stiletto was off the hook. Wulfgar's expression changed immediately, an impressive feat when half of it was a metal chainsaw jaw.

"Is she here?"

Hati jogged forward from behind Stiletto and his assistants.

"Hati!" shouted Wulfgar.

"Dad!" she called back.

The two hugged on the spot and Wulfgar closed the door on Stiletto without comment. Stiletto was the last person on his mind.

AFTER THE infliction of fear and spectacle of fire, the powers that be were very happy to give Vibeke a boat if it would get rid of her. Vibeke had defended the island, yes, but her methods were unbecoming of a warrior. They were simply too violent for war, but more importantly too unpredictable. She didn't work for the UKI. She was a private contractor who had offered and completed services in exchange for one boat, and she would not be hired again.

"Where will you go?" asked Therion.

"Never planned that part."

"You wanted a boat and you got it, but you never had anywhere to go?"

"You know as well as I do, there's no place left. No. I don't know where I'm going. Right now I'd be content to sail out to the middle of the ocean to die."

"Waste of a good boat."

Dr. Niide stepped up beside her and said, "North." He sat down.

"Why north?" asked Vibs. They sat together, and Therion ignored them.

"Veikko and Skadi headed back to the ravine. I'm not sure why. I don't think they intended to seize it. None of the Valkyries I've encountered seem to want it back, now that its best parts—" Niide polished his apple, meaning himself. "—have all left. Or died."

"The ravine is still there? Veikko is alive?"

"In a manner of speaking. Skadi brought him to me dead and minus 60 percent. Odd thing is she wouldn't let me finish him. Demanded I leave his face missing. Demanded I hurry to pack him into an A-1 and—"

"A-1?"

"You never saw it, did you? An experiment we had prepared for the next Valkyrie to die. Complete biomechanical reconstruction in a ready-made application. We spent the last twenty years developing it with every implant and replaced limb that your injuries allowed us. With the A-1 we could simply root out as little as the brain and spine and plug them in, and voilà: the toughest, most capable body a Valkyrie could want. We were going to test it on a soldier here, but they seem uninterested. Not like the good fellows of the ravine. No chutzpah."

"Veikko's rebuilt, then? In an A-1?"

"In the prototype, and not quite rebuilt. Skadi stole him halfway through the procedure, crammed it onto a cargo skiff and left. The complete system is attached, but it was never assembled. He should be able to assemble it himself, though he has no guide. Last he was seen, Veikko was a faceless mass of electronics with no safeguards."

"What kind of safeguards?"

"The A-1 system is a hundred times stronger than a human body. It's not kind to its organic components. His body is too strong, we never got to implement the safeguards that weaken it to suit a human being. Skadi took him from us quite violently."

"Why would Skadi do that?"

"She holds him responsible for the state of Valhalla, and the world at large. I'm not entirely certain she's wrong."

"And you think they went to the ravine?"

"Yes, she had plans for him there. What is anyone's guess. Robbed me of my test subject, though."

"Then I head north."

"And do you care to take your beloved muscle tissue sample with you?"

"No, throw it out. Experiment on it. Whatever you want."

"Very good. I'm glad you've come to your senses."

"I don't think there's any sense left in this world at all."

The boat sailed northward. Svalbarð was 4,000 kilometers away, and the boat was capable of just over 150 per hour. A daylong trip. She set the destination and let her sail.

Then she was alone. The Tikaris sat together on the deck, monitoring for any threats. Violet's Tikari. It was time to kill it. To end the last of her. She stood and took her microwave in her hand. She aimed it. The Tikari didn't move. Bob just looked at them both. And Vibeke couldn't fire.

Vibeke had killed nearly four hundred human beings since she arrived in Valhalla. She hadn't hesitated to fire on a single one of them. And she couldn't fire. The sensation was completely unfamiliar to her. She felt like something was broken. She was almost tempted to head back to Niide to see what was wrong. She couldn't kill Nelson. She couldn't kill the last bit of Violet she had.

As a child Vibeke couldn't play with any digital animals. They depressed her. Her mother had told her that they were better than real animals; they'd never die, never feel pain, and that should have made her feel better, but it made her feel worse. She felt terrible if she neglected to play with them, because they simulated happiness when she did. She felt worse if she forgot to feed them, though they didn't need to be fed. Nelson was now at the core of her empathies.

Vibeke lay down in the small cabin and set her mind on other tasks. She naturally felt outward for any sign of a link, but there was nothing. She had nothing but time to think. Her first thoughts were about Cato. Cato had killed Alf. Worked for Wulfgar. He called himself Scipio, which sounded familiar to Vibeke, but she couldn't place it.

Then to the Geki. They had acted on her orders. And there were two again, after Veikko had killed one. If the Geki had worked for UNEGA and GAUNE, then they were free agents now. But why would they work for her? And where had she seen that shrug before? She knew where but couldn't accept it. It was an offense, somewhere between a betrayal or defection and a student graduating before his class, without her.

She had no answers, so she turned to where her mind both wanted and feared to go. Violet's heart—the mission she'd carried on her back that last month—was gone. Destroyed unceremoniously by Dr. Niide if he did as she asked. And surely he did. He was right, of course. About everything. She had to move on before it started eating away at her. If it hadn't already.

What was she thinking? Keeping a lump of flesh when her brain was annihilated.

Months ago.

She'd clingered the heart and killed Sal. She stole a pogo from Dimmuborgir and flew it back to Arcolochalsh as the first nukes fell. The city was still there. It was small and wouldn't be targeted for some time. She couldn't link to Veikko; the links must have been down here too. But they weren't, not completely. The net was gone, but she should have found Veikko's tracking node. She landed near the arcology. She saw the collapsed walls and broken cantilevers. She saw fires. She saw people running through the streets.

There was microwave fire in the air. She had presumed Veikko dead with more ease than she had Violet, and left the embattled area. She took cover in an alley. There were corpses. Widget was one of them. Her whole team was dead in the alley. An ICBM contrail cut through the sky overhead, on its way to kill millions—probably in Inverness.

Madness reigned in the street on the other side of the alley. People were running, some to get out of the city, some to find their families. Everyone was calling names; without links all the voices were deafening. From the madness came a Fraser. One of Violet's old neighbors. She was dragging her husband behind her. He was broken in half.

"Monsters! The arcology fell, and they came in to steal from us! Hundreds of them, people I know, they came anyway but not to help! They stole, they only came to steal!"

"Mrs. Fraser?"

"Who are you? Violet's friend! Yes, you are, aren't you! Violet's friend! Where is she?"

"Where's Veikko? Where did her other friend go?"

"Fire! He was in the middle of the fire. Where's Vi—"

"Mrs. Fraser, is there anywhere safe here? Anywhere with a hospital, a basement?"

"No, no, child, we have to get out of the city. Lairg, we have a cabin in Lairg."

"I have a pogo, let's—"

"Where's Violet?" she demanded. Vibeke couldn't say it. She hoped she wouldn't notice the gore on her arm clingers. Mrs. Fraser didn't, but she understood. Vibeke took them to her pogo and helped Mrs. Fraser on board with her husband's remains. She hit the altitude control and sent them straight up into the sky. She ran to the back of the cabin to check on his body. It would be fine. He was only dead from a broken back. She took a neural stabilizer from her medical pouch and placed it on his head.

"She—he'll be fine. Where's Lairg?"

"Let me fly."

Vibeke stepped aside, and Mrs. Fraser took the controls. She was panicked but managed to enter the coordinates. The pogo headed east. Mrs. Fraser returned to her husband's side. Vibeke could do nothing for the pieces of heart on her sleeve, affixed like an extra ration pack to her suit. She looked out the window. Kyle and its fallen arcologies were behind them now. The suburbs held jammed ground vehicles and a growing exodus of families. People trying to get away from the city. Suburbs gave way to fields and fields to mountains. A mushroom cloud grew from a flash to the south, not a city, presumably a military target. Violet would have recognized it as the end of Achnacarry.

She hadn't launched the missiles. She'd disarmed them. How could she have caused the war? As if by instinct, she knew it had been her acts. One little firing solution and all this was the result. How weak was peace, how eager the world to slaughter itself. But Vibeke couldn't tell herself that. She was completely aware and unable to deny that it was all completely her fault.

Snow was falling in Lairg. It was sticking to the Scottish ground for the first time in a hundred years, the first millimeters of meters to come. Men were freezing in their tropical kilts. She gave Mrs. Fraser and her husband's body full doses of radiophobics. They stepped outside onto the frosted grass. The cabin was small, made of wood.

"Do you have a first aid kit?"

"We used to, it would be here...."

She looked under a wooden bench and found the kit. Vibeke opened it and found the electrical components still working. She dug into Mr. Fraser's back and found the spinal fractures. Easy work with her training. She applied an artificial nerve stud and closed him back up, then jump started his brain and saw him come back without complications. She took the stasis field from his head and put it on Violet's heart. She took a reading:

Cellular necrosis 78%.

What little she had of Violet was already 78 percent dead, frozen and then thawed by microwave heat. The stasis field would at least keep that bit viable for—there was nothing it was viable for. An EMP washed over them from the south. The stasis field died. Vibeke did the last thing she could; she stepped outside, gathered some snow, and packed the pieces of heart within. Mrs. Fraser took a moment from her husband to show Vibeke to an ice box.

"It might help," she said.

The Frasers started a real fire. Vibeke thought it was funny that civilians knew how to do such things. She had only learned them once she got to Valhalla. Then her line of thought gave out and left her to face her dead home, her dead team, and the dying world. She hoped Varg would be able to find her when he got back, though she didn't know what good they could do when he returned. In the end she hoped he would stay on Mars and be happy on that distant rock.

The sun set, or was covered by such thick clouds it seemed to set. It was far too soon for a nuclear winter. The firestorms had only just begun. It was a real winter spell that was hitting Scotland, as if the Earth knew it was time to shut down. The cold helped her go numb. The Frasers huddled together and seemed a small ember of good amid all evils that were happening that day and yet to come. She watched them hold each other and fall asleep.

She tried to think about what she had left and found it a pointless endeavor. She had nothing left at all.

Without Violet what was there to survive for? Misery? Would she rebuild the ravine with them? Would she fall in love again? That seemed even less likely than Violet's return as an animate corpse.

Animate corpses were now taking over the globe. The wave bombs, the "zombie" bombs. Masses of mutating individuals or masses of flesh stuck to flesh, becoming horrors of molten human. Combined with the radiation and the winter, the end of civilization and more. It was not by any means a world worth living in.

Not then, not now.

She could jump off the side of the boat. With her inertial fields off, it would kill her instantly. Fairly painlessly, though pain was far from an issue. She knew she'd never resort to it. She'd persist to the end. Valkyries needed almost nothing to survive, least of all a purpose.

She wanted her purpose to be Violet. She thought of the warmth. The sex. The long talks en route to Mars. Her eyes. Hair. Hips. More out of boredom than anything else, she let herself remember and let her hand wander. But the pleasure was bittersweet, tainted by death. Death, omnipresent now. Corpses lay everywhere. On the mainland, on the island, in the water. There seemed little likelihood of any animal left by now; even the plants would be unsalvageable soon. The surface was dying.

She wondered what lived below. She was passing over colonies, colonies of unknown size. How many Cetaceans lived under the surface, perhaps completely unaware of the happenings topside? She was heading toward the Ares. She could set it off and end the surface for good, turn it over to the Cetaceans and hope they did better with the planet than their progenitors. Vibeke slept.

She awoke as the boat slowed. Svalbarð was visible on the horizon. It looked untouched. She narrowed the destination to Kvitøya and kept a lookout. There were dead walruses clogging the way, and the boat slowed to keep safe. The stink of rotting meat at sea was overpowering. The vista of ribs and spilled organs and withering skin was nauseating.

The boat approached shore. More dead walruses. One exploded from putrefaction gasses as the waves nudged it. And she saw a vast, magnificent dome of rock coated by snow. At least a meter of it, blemished on the surface only by warm wet rot of necrophagist bacteria that spilled out onto the stones.

She hunted for depressions in the snow. The first she found was minuscule, only an inverted lump near the edge. She microwaved the snow into water, then steam, and the region cleared up. There was a hole, deep with a spiral ground into it. She walked into the dark tunnel.

She found it blocked by the back of the drill, which had been cut open by microwave. No surprise if Skadi had brought Veikko there. She entered.

At the end of the brief tunnel she could see into the ravine from high over its rim. Lit in red, sinewy red from the Ares in the center. No other light. Dr. Niide had taken Alopex, not copied her. Valhalla was dead. She found the walrus trap and walked in, checking for detectors as she went. Nothing. Only dozens of devoured walrus bodies. Mostly pups. A mess of gore and rot.

She made her way to the bottom of the walkway next to the former mess hall, where Mishka bashed her skull in with a steel pipe.

HATI OPENED the doors to her room. It lacked windows altogether, one of the disadvantages of living in an impermeable fortress. In that respect it couldn't have been more different from her home in Ballard Heights. That home was nothing but windows. An advantage of taking care of the penthouse floors was that she got to live in them. She could see more of the open, desolate Texark landscape than her mind could ever register. Now, she could see about two meters in any direction.

Beyond that, though, it was still the ideal of luxury. Every accoutrement of fine living was present, from the frictionless bed to the chandeliers, from the endless Möbius bar of fine liquors to the old-fashioned television wall, which was finally useful now that the link was dead.

She dialed up a desert vista and the place was at least lit like home. But it wasn't home. She couldn't see it ever becoming home. She was there to convince her father to let her return, nothing more or less. But in the meantime, while he was busy with ruling the world, she would explore her new setting and try not to worry about her real home going to hell while she stood powerless on the wrong side of the Earth.

The luxury ended when she left her room. It was all business and brutalism outside. The halls were concrete without decoration, lit overly well by the bright wall-to-wall light panels above. The floors were black rubber and smelled of cleaning chemicals. The halls were thin and labyrinthine; only the map they'd hardwired into her upon her arrival kept her oriented.

She found her way to the lagoon. Chilled for Umberto. Wulfgar had only told her about the beast in passing, in his usual way. All his messages to her read like listings of events. "Have taken ravine," "Have captured walrus," a couple months back, "Hrothgar murdered," and "Safe on Venus," before that. He couldn't send warning he'd have her scooped up from Ballard to join him in Elba, so he just sent soldiers.

Growing up with her mother, she had heard little good about her father, but that gave him an aura of mystery. She couldn't bring herself to hate him quite as her mother had. The few times she met him, he was a well-dressed, well-spoken proper gentleman, and he treated her like a princess. So it was hard to grasp the things her mother said about him. Murder, torture, crime. If anything, it made those things sound like the acts of a decent man. So that she could forgive.

She could even forgive, to a minor extent, his kidnapping of her. With the world at war or worse, she'd half expected it. If he hadn't been nuked or mutated, she knew he'd want her by his side, where he could protect her. And now the worst had happened: she was separated from Brendon, her arcology was doomed without her, and her dad was now half beast. He hadn't told her about the metal jaw.

Umberto waddled over to her. He was expecting one of Wulfgar's clams, but the lab had been closed to her. She had nothing to offer.

Umberto didn't seem to take the hint and waited. She looked around the lagoon. She saw Donatien.

Not her favorite of her father's cohorts. He was exactly her age; they were born the same hour of the same day. He thought that meant something. His other thoughts, she knew, were disturbed in the extreme—beyond sadism and deep into a realm of philosophical perversion. He stared at her as he always did. She was used to that. It was inevitable any time she visited her father in København. She didn't miss it.

The walrus stared at her the same way, though she expected its thoughts were a bit more innocent. She knew Donatien would never harm her, if only out of respect to her father. She wouldn't let herself consider why he kept Donatien around. She knew his tastes must have been something like the perverse man's, but that was none of her business. She would never ask. Never try to learn. Donatien left the lagoon.

She rubbed Umberto's head. He flopped over and swam away. She sat alone in the lagoon for another hour, contemplating the changes the world had just gone through. And Charlie. And her father. And the giant multiton monster he kept, the one that had killed him once before.

WALRUS. SHE smelled walrus. A lot of walrus. She opened her eyes. She saw a walrus. Two walruses, four, five. Some alive, some dead. She was in a walrus cage. Her head hurt. She felt her temple, recognized the pain of recent medical work. She'd been knocked out and repaired.

What was the last thing she remembered? Valhalla, for the first time in ages. Stepping into the open ravine. Red hair. Walrus cage. Who did she know with red hair?

"Kjøtt, meat. Tenderized again."

Of all the people....

"Did we teach you so poorly? You sail all the way here and don't duck when you come through the door? I spent days in the med bay trying to patch up your skull. It was like so much goop. Like the rest of you, your muscles were spastic jelly, you were so radioactive you glowed in the dark, so starved you soaked up protein gel like a sponge. Why let yourself go so badly? What, were you depressed? Did you lose it all and weep yourself into a binge? You pathetic Norsky kitten. You were never shit without me, and you'd be dead if I didn't nurse you back. You owe your life to me, Kjøtt. I own you now."

"Hi, Mishka."

"Hi, Vibs."

Mishka reached through the bars of the cage and pulled her by the hair around her wound, where it hurt most. She jerked her head to her own and kissed her on the lips. Vibs tried to fight back, but it was hopeless, she was drugged and weak, and Mishka could kiss her as long as she wanted. Mishka could do anything to her, she thought. The thought made her sick, and she threw up with great satisfaction while their lips were still locked. Mishka stumbled back onto the rocks and laughed.

"You gross little whelp. Ha! I'll be back for you after a nice loud shower. Enjoy the stink."

Vibeke fell back and cleaned herself as best she could. She didn't have to clean her suit, it was gone. She had only rags to cover herself with. Her cage was next to water, a puddle but water was water. She drank the brackish stuff from her hands. She was starving. The only thing resembling food was the walrus corpse in the next cage. She calculated the nutritional value compared to the risk of eating long-dead flesh and took it. The blubber wasn't half-bad; she wished she could have stocked some in her gullet before vomiting in Mishka's mouth. The thought made her grin. Then she waited and digested the stuff. And waited.

She heard noises from time to time. She didn't think Mishka would be wandering behind her after introducing herself and decided it was a walrus. But she knew it wasn't. Someone was watching her. Looking at her caged. Someone else was there. Veikko, half-assembled. She turned to look at the mass but saw nothing.

She heard a grunt. A guttural rasp. Like a human trying to speak without a mouth. Mishka interrupted it.

"Not yet!"

Vibs heard him back away. He must have been huge, heavy. She was about to call out to him, but she heard footsteps. The bitch was back.

"Okay, whelp, where were we?"

"Kiss me again, I've reloaded."

"Ha, you like the local cuisine?" Mishka reclined as if to pose on the rocks opposite the cage. "I've had so much blubber in the last weeks, I might be losing my figure. What do you think?"

She pushed her breasts together with her upper arms, tried to show off a body that was clearly exercised and not malnourished. Vibs said nothing.

"You're wondering what I'm going to do with you. So am I."

"Fight me."

"There's no pleasure in a fight I know I'd win. But there might be pleasure in something else...."

"Please, try it."

"Hmhmm. Perhaps I will. But not now."

Another grunt sounded from behind her.

"You wait your turn. Did you see your teammate? What's left of him? Do you know what your pal did?"

Vibs said nothing; she was all ears.

"He hacked you. You wouldn't nuke your old home, so he hacked you and Violet to break into that silo. After he sent you both to die, he tried to master the Geki's fire. Burned down an entire arcology before Varg arrived. Then Varg killed him, cut his face off and left him for dead."

Veikko clawed his way over, hauling the top of his giant body like a sack of coal. Strands of flesh and metal trailed back to his lower limbs in the pit. He looked at Vibeke. She looked in terror at him. His hair flowed like a mane of fire from what should have been his face. It was cleanly cut off like a medical cross section just behind his teeth. It was horrible, made worse by the metal stuck into it to keep him alive. Parts of a flesh body remained in the hulking metal gorilla mass of wrongly assembled mechanics.

"Veikko had spy nodes all over this ravine, did you know that? He was spying on you, his own team, everyone else. I took a look at them and watched Varg die. He killed Pelamus, saved the planet, but got himself poisoned. He's buried somewhere under that heap of scrap metal that used to be the com tower."

Vibeke fell back. Half her team was dead, and Veikko was a monster. In more ways than one. Though Varg....

"But Veikko, he killed Balder, you know. Tricked Weather into killing him, then refused to stop hunting me."

That was Veikko too. Not Thokk. He'd killed them both.

"You killed Balder. Not Veikko."

"I may have pulled the trigger, but—"

"You killed him."

"Tell yourself anything you please, Kjøtt. This monster is why the world went to war. Why Varg is dead. And I presume Violet too? Where is the blonde bint?"

For some reason, Vibeke got a strong impression that Mishka already knew the answer.

"Dead."

Veikko let out a somber moan that might have had its origins in a word. Vibeke couldn't tell.

"I can't say I'm not happy about that. I'm glad I have you back to myself."

She seemed disingenuous. Vibeke could see it; she wasn't happy about it at all.

"You've got me like Earth's got a chance."

Mishka snickered. Her eye popped out.

"Have a chat with your former teammate while I find some tougher chains. The ones in these cages just don't have enough tetanus for you."

Mishka walked away. Her eye floated in place. She looked over to Veikko.

"You hacked us?"

She tried to sort it out in her mind. It was obvious. She couldn't imagine how she hadn't seen it. Even still she knew it was the right thing to do to break into the silo, to try to nuke the ravine. But at last she knew what she knew was falsified.

"Forgive me," Veikko rasped, his words barely understandable.

"Of course I do," she lied. He wasn't the only one who could falsify information. "You're all I've got left of the team. Except Violet's Tikari. It's probably outside the dome right now, ronin and alone."

"Violet is really dead, then?"

"Yeah. You were right, though. I got to fuck her first."

"That's good."

"Yeah. You know your body could rip these bars open."

"Mishka's watching."

"Why haven't you killed her?"

"I can barely move. Niide sewed me back together wrong, Vibs. Backwards."

"No, just unfinished. He said you can fix yourself. You just need to use what you've got to assemble yourself. You'll be shaped like a man again when you're done."

"I can't. I've tried."

"Keep trying. Or rip these bars open, anything you can do, damn it!"

Veikko stirred; it was impossible to tell what he was thinking with no face to carry an expression, or body to show anything resembling body language. He lurched forward and two robotic appendages grabbed the bars. Vibeke noticed an integrated weapons system inside one of them.

He pulled on the bars, and they gave way like tissue paper. The A-1 was, as Niide had said, incredibly powerful.

"Thanks!" she said as she climbed out over him and ran. The eye followed her. She heard Mishka running for her from across the ravine.

Vibs ducked into a nearby storage tower and looked for anything she could use to swat the eye out of the air. She tore open the first box. There was nothing inside it, but the slat she broke off would do fine. She went dead silent and listened.

The faintest wisp of sound marked the eye coming through the door. Vibeke swung her slat smack into it, batting it halfway across the ravine.

She had to get out, hide somewhere before the eye returned. It would already be rocketing back to the door. Vibs ran. Out of the tower and down into one of the subbasement tunnels under the rock. Mishka would be expecting her to run out of the ravine, not deeper in.

She followed the tunnel toward the med bay. She needed to counteract the drugs Mishka had given her to keep her woozy. In the freezing darkness she found her way to the hatch and cautiously, silently emerged.

The med bay was dark and abandoned. Most of the fixtures had been hastily torn out by Niide and the nurses. But some kits remained. Vibs moved toward the nearest but saw motion. She froze.

The motion was large. Had Veikko come after her? No, it was something smooth and gray. It turned to face her.

Orson. The colossal bull that ruled the Storøya pod. Six tons of blubber that could only have survived through cannibalism once locked in the ravine. Vibeke moved slowly.

He barked. Vibeke shushed him. He swayed back and forth for a moment and then charged her. Drugged and slow, she couldn't get out of the way in time and got bucked across the room into a wall. Orson continued to bark loudly as if to call Mishka intentionally. She played dead, fell limp. Tried to ignore the tusks prodding her neck and back painfully. Then the biting began. She realized if she remained limp, Orson would devour her alive.

She gave him a weak kick in the nose and he backed off a meter. She used the chance to lurch back into a hall too thin for him to follow. He tried nonetheless, forcing his way into the slim corridor. Vibeke knew the ground, though. She entered a storage room door and came out the other side while Orson was still stuck in the hall. She approached the spare first aid kits.

She opened the first and found a steroid epinephrine kick. She took it and instantly found herself working at full capacity. She could move again. She could think.

And thinking at high speed, she noticed the lipid polarity drives. The brain backups. She was crouching only a meter away from Violet's memories. Too bad she had no use for them. She told herself it was over. She didn't need the drives; she had no use for them because she would not bring them to Dr. Niide. Who wouldn't be able to do anything with them regardless. There was absolutely no reason to take the drives. None at all.

Having taken the drives and an extended med kit she headed for the arsenals. Inside she took two microwaves and tested their power sources. Both good. She looked around. She couldn't carry much so she looked for the most bang for her buck. Limited to whatever was in the arsenal, she took a Talley Buffalo Cannon, a looped projectile machine gun, a cutter rifle, foot fields, a set of field knuckles, and an assortment of explosives and then headed out to the tailor shop. She snuck behind any object she could, certain Mishka would keep her eye in the open looking to detect motion. But obstacles became fewer and fewer as she climbed up the spiral walkway. Soon she was out in the open. She heard Orson whistling from the ravine wall.

She was across from the tailor with a bare stretch of walkway to traverse. If only the Ares weren't assembled she could just walk there directly. But why couldn't she? The water was only a decimeter thick, and it was undulating. It would disguise her motion. She stepped out into the gory red pool collected around the branches. She walked quickly, letting the rippling Ares ebb around her legs. It was slippery as hell and she was overloaded with weaponry.

She slipped and dropped a concussion charge. It fell all the way to the floor of the ravine. It wasn't armed and didn't burst, but the noise was substantial. Luckily it was nowhere near her. A distraction. She moved on. She made the other side in only a minute and headed into the tailor's.

A massive loud static shock hit her the instant she touched the door. She'd forgotten to defuzz her feet. She heard Mishka running below.

She scrambled to collect all she'd need to make a new suit and more. She took every specialty system she could hold along with a repulse cape to carry all the weapons and suits. She rolled it all up and hit the repulsers. The massive load on her back suddenly felt like light foam. She ran from the shop and up to the walrus trap.

She opened the door, and Orson bucked her full speed from the side, almost sending her over the walkway ledge. She pulled herself back toward the door. He began barking again.

"Shut the fuck up!" she shouted despite herself. Orson charged and smashed her into the doorjamb. She saw the room again filled with dead, half eaten walrus pups. Orson had survived by eating his own offspring. She reached into the repulse cape for anything that would ward him off. She found the field knuckles. She slipped them on and swung. He jumped back, and she missed. Then he bucked her into the jamb, wrenching her arm back and bruising her scapula. She slipped into the room as he rebounded, and she hit the manual door closure.

Orson crammed his fat head into the door and barked, showering her face with rancid spittle. She barked back, "Fuck you, Orson!" and tried to kick him. But again he slipped out and away, while she slipped on walrus corpse grease and fell on the weapons pile. The door closed. She got up and ran outward.

She was topside, but still in rags. She'd have to run through the snow with most of her skin bare. No way around it. She ran.

She saw the eye following her, a black dot against so much white snow. Mishka would be up and out soon, but Vibeke was nearly to the boat. The eye stuck with her as she hopped in and started it. She didn't enter a destination beyond southward; the eye was there watching. The boat took off at top speed. The eye remained.

Vibeke dropped her supplies and stared at the black orb. She mustered the most contemptuous face she could manage. She grabbed for it to no avail. She swung the med kit at it, but it dodged her. She spit at it, but it moved out of the way. Then, suddenly, Nelson grabbed it out of the sky and took it down to the deck. Violet's ronin Tikari ripped at it with its legs, tore at it. The eye struggled to break free. It got loose but not without damage, and flew back to Kvitøya.

The Tikari jumped onto Vibeke's shoulder and watched as she set course for Orkney. Then she assembled what she could of a suit. It had the complete under-components. It would keep her warm, but she fumbled with the rest. She wasn't certain she'd taken a complete suit. She might have taken two of some parts and none of others. She had everything she could carry but hadn't had time to see exactly what she brought. She sat down to take inventory of her new suit and supplies and discovered she'd taken a complete suit and then some, enough to make two and a half.

The boat careened south. She had a day of sailing to Orkney. Her hatred of Mishka occupied a few hours, but soon she found herself faced with the enigma of Veikko. He had set her loose from the cage and seemed a pitiable beast in his new form, but the fact remained he was to blame for everything. From the hack to the war to Violet's death. She could understand why he did it all and even forgive him on a purely strategic level. He was doing what he thought he had to do to save the world from deluge. But he had killed everyone, condemned Valhalla and civilization. He was the worst of monsters imaginable.

Soon she forgot his generous help in escape and awarded him a place in her mind just short of Mishka as an adversary. When Violet was back, they would head north and destroy both of them. Not that Violet would ever be back. She erased the thought.

THE FIRE was everywhere, across the rock walls, across the buildings, burning hotter than any natural fire. It flickered in shapes, in waves, in tornadoes. And it burned him.

The pain was excruciating. He screamed with what little he had of a voice.

"Think of it as practice," she told him. "You'll be burning in hell for all eternity. This is just a taste of what's to come."

"Put me out, damn you!"

"Say please."

"Please!"

She extinguished him. She was certain she had mastered the technique.

He breathed heavily, so heavily the breath threatened to rupture his trachea.

"You're welcome," she taunted.

He caught his breath and spoke. "What are you going to do with it?"

"Whatever I want." She smiled.

"What are you going to do with her?"

"She's free. Escaped. I'm not going to do anything with her."

"Why did you let her escape?"

She stared at him with pursed lips. "She'll tear herself apart, ruin herself, condemn herself to utter insanity, and when I see her again, I'll just blow away the ashes and take what she thought was hers."

He thought for a moment. And then he understood.

"You stole my idea, you bitch."

"File a copyright complaint."

"Whatever you tried, you didn't do it half as well as me."

"I didn't need to. She was already ruined. I just gave her the last push she'll need to suffer a worse fate than any other survivor of your apocalypse. Now, I really must be going. I have a world to bring to Christ."

"Forget Christ, bring them to me. Tell them to engineer me out of this hole."

"I like you right where you are, Veikko."

"Fuck you, Mishka."

She winked at him and started up the walkway.

THE ARMY wasn't happy to see Vibeke again. She marched onto their base without permission and demanded to see Dr. Niide. They told her to go to hell. She reminded them she could kill them all. They explained they didn't know where he was.

She knew he'd have left a note, something for Valkyries. She sent her Tikari around his former station and looked through its eyes in every mode. She found it in urochrome differentiation mode, a mode that nearly nothing but Tikaris could view. He'd used the pissweed to write a message. It said one word—Maeshowe.

She sailed immediately, and the command staff breathed a sigh of relief that she'd left so quickly.

She landed at Finstown. The mainland was like heaven. As it was when she'd been there before the attacks, it remained untouched. Homes, families. She walked among them through the town, then on to Maeshowe, where she found the doctor set up in an old tomb. She began unloading her equipment, weapons and armor.

"What is that?" asked Niide.

"The lipid drives," she stated honestly.

"You brought the lipid drives from Valhalla? Why?"

"Violet's memories are in there."

"Uselessly so. We should destroy the drives."

"You can if you want. I know I'm not getting her back."

"Very good. Now we—"

"Though you could regrow her body, couldn't you?"

"No, we have no growth chamber. And there would be no purpose. Why grow a body when we have no brain?"

"I could use a warm pillow."

"Wulfgar…. He had a great idea, you know, keeping her body as you said. Simple AI, and it screamed and cowered. He could torture it, have intercourse with it, sleep upon it, or leave it on his wall for decor. Shall I do the same for you? What would you like me to program the corpse to do?"

"I know it's sick."

"And dangerous. Wulfgar's tried to strangle him when the genuine article broke in."

"Well, I don't have to worry about the genuine article now, do I?"

"You're far from the first Valkyrie to beg me to replace a lost teammate or lover or both."

"And you never have?"

"I'm not a psychiatrist, but I know it's important to move on."

"Why?"

"For your health."

"We're all gonna die of radiation in a few years."

"In a few more without it. We all die, mmm. Precious little time in life, Vibeke, don't waste it on the past."

"The past was better than the future can ever be."

"I must admit, that may now be true."

"So what could you do? Could you make me a toy like Wulfgar's?"

"Have you no shame at all?"

"I've been eating rapists."

"Yes, given the proper equipment, I could make you a toy like his."

"How advanced an AI?"

"I have Alopex in my suitcase."

"You could put Alopex in Violet's body?"

"I wouldn't recommend it."

"Why not?"

"When you put a computer program into a neural network, it functions as a brain. That means it can change its mind."

Vibeke knew that all too well from Sal. Sal with a neural network. A Tikari with a brain.

"What could you do with her Tikari's AI? I know they can hook into neural nets. Sal did and—and he killed Violet, but it worked. They're compatible."

"Mmhmm. Do you really want a human being with the mind of a weapon around you, capable of free will?"

"Maybe… if I can fuck it."

Niide snorted. "Certainly every gynoid since the 1950s has been designed for that. But I don't think you'd be satisfied with a Tikari that resembles your former lover. Tikaris are not user friendly. Given human form one would likely spend its time spying on you and recording your every move."

"Violet did that too."

Niide slowly shook his head, disappointed. "End this humor. A Tikari is a weapon. You just told me a Tikari with a neural network is what killed her in the first place, hmm? I cannot imagine a more dangerous person."

"Violet."

"She was not all that and a bag of chips, Vibeke. She broke your cheek and tried—"

"I know, I was there."

"She made a victim of you, Vibeke."

Vibs stood. "The hell she did. You old fucking men and your bullshit observations. You told Alf and almost got her k-killed. But you didn't ask me. I'm not a fucking victim, and she wasn't a monster. Well, okay, maybe she was a monster, but you have no idea what a love spat looks like between two Valkyries let alone two women."

"I know what a zygomatic bone looks like, and yours was inside out."

"You arrogant ass! I've read Ernest Jones, and you've got a god complex that would make Jesus blush."

"A god complex?"

"You think just because you control life and death that you're a god."

"Yes, I'm sure that's the definition of a god."

"So create me a new Violet."

"I can't. I can make you a Tikari in a Violet suit."

"What about her backup?"

He sighed. "You were one of the smartest Valkyries in the ravine. I don't know how you can be so plainly idiotic, Vibeke."

"How is that idiotic? We have a backup of her brain right here."

"We have a backup of her memories up until your Project Daunting. That's hardly her brain."

"What are we but a collection of memories?"

"We are personalities. We are the minds shaped by those memories."

"So if you plugged them into a fresh brain, what would you get?"

"A brain full of memories. We are more than the sum of our parts, Vibeke. Do you know what a soul is?"

"Religious bullshit."

"In the old sense, but the word can aptly describe the *je ne sais quoi* that lurks between those memories. That makes sense of them. That uses them, recites them to itself. The part of you that hates me right now. The part of you that misses Violet. Tell me, do you love her because you have a collection of memories of her? Or is it something more? I could transplant those same memories into myself, but I'd not love Violet. Because I am not my memories. And Violet was not hers. She contained them. They shaped her. But they are not her, Vibeke. Violet is dead."

"But what would you get? Her Tikari…. Veikko's had his personality; hers would have hers. That with her memory. What would that be?"

Niide thought for a moment. A strange flash of regret crossed his face.

"You are acting from a skewed perspective right now. You've lost someone you love. It's natural you would want them back. But you have two paths: You can move on as people have moved on since the dawn of time, be healthy and grow, fall in love again or fight or play or simply live; or you can weld yourself to the cause of your pain. Make your loss come to life and stick around. Toy with it, make love to it, every second knowing that it's not really her."

"Choice two, let's do it."

"Even if I could, and I'd need a multitude of parts from Valhalla and beyond to do it, consider the *Bride of Frankenstein*."

"What about her?"

"She didn't love the monster back."

"Violet would love me."

Niide's voice grew even slower. "For the hundredth time, Vibeke, Violet is dead. I'd be creating a walking corpse with a simulation of Violet running it from a neural network. We don't use neural networks because they think for themselves. Even the synapses grown for Tikari are cleftless to prevent independent thought. Imagine your pain if I built you this abomination and it loathed you. Became your nemesis."

"Nothing with Violet's memories could do that."

Niide mumbled calmly, "Do you think I'm talking to you about a hypothetical situation? Do you not think with all my tools and skill I didn't try to bring back my wife when she died? Beth, Vibeke. From Berkanan team. Haven't you read the history of our ravine a hundred times?"

"It didn't say you tried—"

"It said she died on a mission on Luna and her brain was unsalvageable. But it lists missions for her after that. And it lists her betrayal of the ravine, her murder of Balder's team, her attack on me. She may be a footnote to you, but I saw a thing that was not my wife kill her closest friends. I saw her kill our son. And when Balder killed the abomination, I saw her die again. I saw it because what I built was not my wife. It was a foolish attempt. The act of a deranged man, suffering from loss and forcing himself to suffer more. And now you ask me to build you a fake Violet?" he asked, sounding more tired than ever. "I'd not condemn you to my fate if you begged me for a thousand years. Now go away. Shoo."

Vibeke had no idea the events she'd glossed over were such a disaster to the ravine, to Dr. Niide. She had no idea what she was asking him to do. And until she asked for it, she hadn't known herself that it was what she wanted.

But like he said. It was over. Done. He couldn't even if he wanted to. Though she was still surprised as to why.

"What kind of medical facility has no growth chamber?"

"This one. A makeshift wartime one. End of line."

Vibeke sat on the lipid drives. They made a nice chair, all they'd ever make.

"So that's it."

"That's it."

She thought, only tangentially.

"Where would there even be one? A growth chamber I mean."

"Vibeke…."

"No, no, I just mean who would even have one of those?"

Niide stared at her.

"There was one at Unst in the Shetland Islands, but we had to abandon it when we fell back. They've taken it now."

"The Wolf base?"

"Intel suggests their base has tripled in size, with more coming. Ulver is committing more and more to this archipelago."

"And the growth chamber, it'll look like the one in Valhalla?"

"Goddammit, Vibeke."

"No, I mean, I'm just wondering. It would look like the one in Valhalla?"

"It's likely. Now stop thinking of it."

"Right. Not thinking of it, unless it would be useful to UKI, I mean."

"It would, but—"

"But it's not like they'd just give it to me."

"Certainly not. Vibeke, let's speak about—"

"I mean, I could ask. There would be no harm in asking."

"What on earth could make you think they'll give it to you?"

"I'll kill them all if they don't."

"Then I'll destroy the drives myself."

"I won't let you."

"Vibeke, I will not allow you to massacre hundreds to save—to *create* one life that should not live."

"Then here's a deal. If they give it to me by peaceful negotiations, I'll come back and you'll do what I want. If they deny me, I won't ask twice. I'll give up. I'll leave you alone. I'll leave the base alone. I'll grow up and move on."

"Deal," Niide said with certainty. "If they say no, you give this up, absolutely. And sure, in the extraordinarily unlikely nigh impossible event the opposing military simply *gives* you their irreplaceable equipment, I'll happily do—"

She was gone, the medical pogo with her.

Chapter IV: Maeshowe

AS WULFGAR sat reading *The Clans, Septs & Regiments of the Scottish Highlands*, Hati entered the study.

"Gonna paint your ships with a battle tartan?"

Wulfgar looked up and smiled.

"I missed your humor."

"Yeah, that's worth taking me away from my home in the middle of a class war. You know what's happening right now? They're raiding my home, destroying everything I own. Mom's paintings are about to be toilet paper."

Wulfgar sighed and sat back. He set his book down on the end table.

"Even if that's true, I have no regrets saving you from a mob."

"I didn't need saving, I was the one doing the saving. I was about to make a deal that would keep the mob at bay." She swallowed to rid her throat of the lump that formed from exaggerating her meeting with Quiche.

"Would you like me to send a company to maintain order?"

"And leave a Texark arcology under Ulver military rule? You just have it so backwards, don't you?"

"Maybe I do. Why don't you explain it to me?"

She looked down and shook her head.

"I'm open here, Hati. I'm willing to do what it takes to make you happy here."

"'Happy' and 'here' are mutually exclusive."

Hegg rang at the door.

"Sire, an update."

"Come in, Hegg."

Hati sat on the back of a leather chair and stared at the books on the walls.

"Yes, sire. Unst is preparing for the full invasion. All intel forces are recalled and en route."

"Good. The numbers?"

He fumbled through his papers. "The following will arrive at the Shetland Islands in between thirty-six and forty-six hours:

"From both the African and Mediterranean fleets, 3 battleships, 5 fleet carriers, 6 escort carriers, 6 cruisers, 37 destroyers, 37 frigates, 23 submarines, 61 mine warfare ships, 118 patrol boats, 214 amphibious, 99 auxiliary, 82 surface warships. Total active: 691.

"From both armies: 6 infantry regiments, 1 mountain regiment, 6 armored regiments, 5 airborne regiments, and 2 cavalry regiments. Total strength army: 57,386; strength army ground forces: 53,517."

Hati looked up from the books, aghast.

"From both Air Forces: 6 very heavy bombers, 65 heavy bombers, 84 medium bombers, 79 light bombers, 299 fighters, 171 recon, 61 transports, 58 trainers, 33 communications. Total combat aircraft: 704. Total support aircraft: 152.

"Global satellite reassignments. It should be noted that we still aren't certain which satellites are fully functional. They're like the pogos and every other electronic system, some work, most don't. But we've sent signals to the following: 23 cutter satellites, 18 laser satellites, 2 platforms, 129 recon. Total reassignments: 172."

"Do you think it will be enough?"

"Yes, sire, yes I do."

"And their directives?"

"Absolute top priority: the live capture of Vibeke. The picture from the original massacred pogo is en route to every soldier. All will be informed of her capabilities. Secondary priority: the takeover of Orkney. The communiqué will arrive at Unst at 1630 hours."

"Excellent, dismissed."

Hegg departed. Hati coughed.

"You don't think it's enough?" asked Wulfgar.

"You're sending a world war's worth to catch one girl?"

"She's an important girl. And a tough one."

"So am I, but you didn't send the combined forces to pick me up from Ballard Heights."

"No, I sent Stiletto's men because you weren't—"

"As important?"

"As dangerous."

Hati stood up and stretched. She knew it had been a low shot given what he'd put in and lost to bring her there. Wulfgar thought about no such things. He just watched her. He was beyond happy to have her safe at his home no matter what she said.

"You think I should give up on her? On Violet?"

"I think if Violet killed my uncle you should give her a ton of gold and a pat on the back."

"Your lack of loyalty to this family is—"

"Earned. He was going to rape that girl. He deserved what he got."

"He was still your uncle."

"So was Oglaf, but you had him killed."

Wulfgar set his book down on the end table and looked at Hati.

Hati looked right back. She had inherited his stare. He reminded her sometimes of looking in the mirror when he was enraged. Whatever fire burned behind his eyes, burned in her as well. No matter what she said or did to defy him, he felt all the prouder of her.

"What do you want me to say, Hati?"

"Admit you're selfish. You wanted your kid back, and you got her."

"Yes. I am and I did. I don't regret it."

"I had work to do there, important work. I have nothing here."

"You'll have anything you desire! Anything."

"Send me home."

"Anything at all, just name it."

She huffed and looked at the rug. Ornate. She knew he'd never let her go back. She knew it from the start. She had to make the best of it. She had to be useful again.

"Put me on your advisory staff," she demanded.

"Okay," he agreed.

"As my first advisement, I strongly suggest you give up on those Valkyrie girls."

"As my first act with you as advisor, I decline."

"Well, at least you listened."

"Hati, you had me listening since you were born."

She laughed and walked to the door.

"As your advisor, I also insist on an office and a research staff."

"Done."

"And 50,000 Loups a day."

"Done."

"And the head of John the Baptist on a platter."

"Not till you're eighteen."

"I'm twenty-eight."

"I know. August 9th. At 0300. It was a Friday. Cloudy."

"I know you care, Dad. Caring was never the problem."

"What was?" he asked, knowing full well all the crimes he'd committed, people he'd killed and tortured, and worse.

She knew he knew. She smiled grimly and left. Wulfgar picked up his book. He retained no memory of Hati's admonition to stop the hunt for the Valkyries whatsoever.

He found himself with some free time. He called Donatien.

"Yes, Little Boots?"

"I have an hour free. Convene an orgy."

"Yes, Little Boots. What flavor today?"

"Any new blondes?"

"Four, sire."

"Take them to interrogation three."

He walked there, growing tumescent with every step. The anticipation was always the finest part, given the disappointment that inevitably followed. But not today. He entered the chamber to find three girls sobbing and one staring daggers. With angry eyes. Furious eyes. He ordered Donatien to remove the others. He took them to the next room to perform his own vile acts.

Wulfgar released the new girl from her bonds.

"What's your name?"

"Violet."

"Not what he told you to say, your real name."

"Cynth," she said, a real Scottish accent peeking out from behind her tongue.

"Do you know what I'm going to do to you, Cynth?"

She stared at him and nodded for him to come closer. When he did she spat in his face. He breathed out warmly, happily, and hugged her gently. Snuggled to the side of her face.

"Perfect," he said as he drew his knife.

VIBEKE'S POGO set down gently on Unst at 1600 hours. The Wolf base was massive, built on the UKI base's remains. A powerful force preparing to wipe out Orkney.

She walked up to the gate guard.

"I need to see your base CO."

"Who are you?"

"I'm Vibs."

"Who are you and what do you want?"

"I need to borrow your growth chamber. I want to negotiate."

"Are you out of your mind?"

"Yes. Let me see your CO. I can give you all of Orkney if you let me borrow your chamber."

"You can give us Orkney," he repeated incredulously.

"I can give you Orkney," she confirmed.

He nodded and walked into his station. He hardwired his link into the port and made a call. A few seconds later he walked out to Vibeke.

"Intel will hear you out."

Vibeke was surprised. She'd expected to be turned back. And that would be it, the end to her madness, the end of possibilities. But she was to see their intel officers. Under escort she was moved down under one of the tents into a small black room. Two women entered.

"How can you give us Orkney?" asked the woman on the left.

"I'm the girl who killed like a zillion of your men on the beach. I can do the same for you, plus I have all the intel on all their bases."

"We should kill you right now."

"But you won't. You need me."

"We do not need you."

"Well, you at least want me. Come on, I borrow your chamber and I give you all of Orkney. It's a good deal."

"What are you? Who are you with?"

"I'm Vibs. I'm with no one."

The women looked at each other.

"We'll be back," they said together.

She waited in the small room, staring blankly at the wall. They would say no, and then it would be over. Violet would be dead for good. Then she'd be free. She longed for it.

They returned.

"You'll be escorted off the base to your pogo and allowed to leave. If you come back, you'll be locked away until the war is over."

It was as simple as that. Mission over. She let them take her to the pogo, and she got inside.

She had to come to terms with it. She let herself sit still as she said it again and again in her head. *Violet is gone. Even if they let me have it, there would only be a mimic, a forgery that would hurt me more. This is the best possible resolution. I will move on. A Valkyrie funeral.* "We have moved on, and we will not come back."

Months earlier Violet was fingering and tonguing her and she was climaxing hard again and again and again, so hard that the muscles in her neck went sore. When she finally stopped, Violet cuddled up to her and sucked on the side of her breast.

"You moan like a walrus," said Violet.

"You fuck like a percussion bolt."

"You're welcome."

Vibeke caught her breath. The wind hit them both, giving them goose bumps. Violet reached up and caressed Vibeke's collarbone.

"You know why I fell for you a year ago?"

Vibeke didn't answer.

"It was how you said 'Good color for your suit, in case anyone forgets your name.' When I first got my Thaco armor that's what you said, and it stuck in my mind. Just the way you said it, kind of sarcastic, drenched in your absurdly soft rolling Norsk accent, just something about it made me so fucking hot for you. Your voice always does it to me, but that one time. Just…. Wow."

"I don't have an accent."

"You totally do."

"What does it sound like?"

"Soft. Almost lispy but not lispy, more…. Trilling, like a purr I guess. Just incredibly soft, and it sucks me in somehow. It makes me want to suck on you and squeeze you and roll you into a little ball and fuck the living shit out of you."

"Couldn't love me because I was smart or tough or something?"

"Of course I do. I wouldn't give a shit about you if you couldn't kill me two hundred and fifty different ways."

"Two hundred and fifty-seven."

"There's nothing I don't love about you."

Vibeke thought. She wanted to tell Violet what she loved most about her, to reciprocate what she'd said. But she couldn't think of any one thing to say. Seconds passed, and she had to say something. She couldn't leave Violet hanging, leave her with nothing.

More seconds and the time had passed. It would be hokey to say it then. She stayed silent. Since Violet's death she'd thought of 101 things she should've said. And she'd never get to say them to her.

She put on her armor and foot fields, clingered one microwave and holstered the other, donned the repulse capes and field knuckles, grabbed the Talley Buffalo Cannon, and opened the door.

Her Tikari came out first; then she stepped out; then Violet's Tikari followed after. Both by her sides, her repulse capes blowing in the wind.

A soldier hit the alarm. It sounded across the base, deafening.

The base fortifications began to rise from the tarmac and inflate. Dozens of men flooded out from the nearby buildings. All took up a flawless formation like a horseshoe around her and raised their rifles. Fifty microwave rifles targeted her. Fifty lasers marked her.

Before they could call on her to set down her arms, she'd made a single sweep, discharging an entire clip of expansion rounds across the men, turning the horseshoe into a splatter. She struck the cannon, rotating to the next clip and hit her foot fields, then skated on.

Dozens of microwave beams began to hit her fields and send her into a deep cold. She burned through it with the heat of muscles straining to run, centimeters above the tarmac, straight for the inflated gabions in front of the marked medical tent.

An eight-wheeled kampfwagen rolled out from a port and laid into her with its main Oerlikon gun. Ice formed on her skin. She ran straight for it, her field taking hundreds of hits every second, draining her of every joule of energy. She sprang from her foot fields and jumped as she approached it, launching herself over its armored side and sending her directly over the Oerlikon's twisted exhaust manifold. Upside down, she unloaded another clip of expansion rounds into the manifold core. It didn't stop firing. In an instant the pressure inside the manifold exploded, engulfing the entire kampfwagen in flames as she hit the ground.

By now both Tikaris were orbiting her at lightning speed. They cut through the first few men who ran for her, weapons heaving beams and bullets into her. The most intense barrage came from a man directly before her, standing with a floater array. She ran straight into it and kicked him with her foot fields on, smashing his head against his armament. The others kept back, hurling more heat into her field, freezing her further inside. She hit the next Talley clip and destroyed them all.

She kept the recoil thruster off, allowing the force to sling her backward. She darted without looking through lines of armored soldiers, firing clip after clip of expansion rounds through every surface that protected them, annihilating them from the inside out.

She was quickly out of expansion rounds and still outside the perimeter. It was too tall to jump and built for artillery assault. But its inflation girders weren't. Only thin enough for a single person to squeeze through, they could afford to be lost in an assault from a massive force. But for one person....

She targeted them with her Talley cannon and launched its barrels. Each sprung its fins and spat out fuel, rocketing into the girders. All six hit, annihilating the nearest inflation girder and opening a hole into the fort.

On its opposite side, soldiers took up positions above and to its edges, ready to unleash field piercing fléchettes into the girl that came through. Vibeke didn't even need to consider it; she knew they would. She unlocked the last parts of the Talley cannon and tossed half of the weapon into her other hand, deploying its last barrels and loading its last conventional rounds. As she slid through the girders, she fired all around her, blowing through the backs of every trapping soldier.

More beams hit, more rounds sucked the heat out of her. Tikaris hit the nearest of their sources. She pulled her microwaves to take care of the rest. She slid toward the medical tent, taking intense fire, returning precision bursts, killing by tens. Vibeke sped up, pushing the foot fields so hard they caught on fire.

She flipped and ducked past line after line, hurling explosives and microwave fire in her wake. The berserk Tikaris slashed through dozens. Her fire burned through dozens more. The explosives sent half a hundred to their graves and wrecked half the armored force the base could deploy. But Vibeke knew the base would have tougher things coming for her soon. She ignored the last survivors and headed for the medical tent.

Its field hit hers as she entered and shocked her within a heartbeat of unconsciousness, but she made it through. Frozen and in pain she passed the triage stage and slipped into the back of the tent, spotting the growth chamber. It was the size and shape of a coffin. Soldiers inside the tent opened fire on her. Tikaris flew through their necks.

She crashed into the chamber and immediately slid her capes underneath it. She turned them on and the coffin lifted onto her back, almost weightless. She ran from the tent.

Beams and bullets hit her again as she left the tent. She ignored the barrage and headed for the open girder. She found it packed with seven soldiers, all firing cutter rifles into her field. She drew her microwaves just in time to distort them. She didn't bother to kill them; she jumped over them, the repulse fields smashing them down into the tarmac as though they'd been crushed by the chamber. She was outside, her pogo in sight.

It was surrounded by more soldiers. Every one of them already firing, draining the last few sparks of energy from inside her. Absolute zero was only seconds away. She drew a remote from her clingers and triggered the thermite she'd deposited over the pogo's power source. The pogo exploded, killing all the men who had covered it, raining limbs down on her as she skated from the blast.

As she ran the smoke above the burst pogo curled and twisted. She saw it from the corner of her eye, the telltale air currents of a double variable blade craft. A panzercopter emerged and opened fire on her with two guns, two beams, two missile carriages, and two lightning coils.

She thought of Violet's shards, the remains of her body scattered. She was to join her in the same manner of death. Her field hit its last absorption protocols and sent its tendrils into her to suck the last joule from inside. She didn't let them in. She linked the armor to turn off the field just before she went too brittle to run. For a moment she was exposed to every scrap of metal and power the panzercopter threw at her. She saw the blood erupt from her chest and felt fire in her neck. Her body could take only a fraction of a second of that barrage. Her suit caught kilograms of metal and the repulse capes took down more. The lightning hit her full force exactly as she hoped. Her armor held the charge. Her field came back up, and the burst lit her pleasantly on fire, warming her quickly.

She kept her field air impermeable and fell into a vacuum, extinguishing the flames. The smoke around her cleared to reveal the second panzercopter coming up from the pit beside her, taking off to hunt her with a massive Oerlikon positioned out of its open side. As soon as she saw the rotors, she jumped and angled the massive growth chamber so as to slide under its blade beams, slipping off its top and swinging into the open cabin, kicking the gunner out the other side. A double kick knocked the pilot and copilot out of the craft.

She dropped the capes and let the chamber fall into the corner of the copter's front section. She pushed the controls into full force away from the base. The panzercopter leaned forward, its rotors like a propeller flying straight sideways. She jumped over the chamber as it slid down into the open side, knocking the Oerlikon out into the ocean below. It caught the sides and wedged itself in place. She jumped onto it and linked into her Tikari.

Both Tiks were right behind her. She sent hers into rocket mode and heated it to its maximum. Violet's Tikari took the cue and did the same. She sent them to work cutting into the firewall of her own copter.

The other held fire on her, unleashing hell but having little effect on its evenly matched sibling craft. Vibeke didn't bother with the controls. She aimed her microwave at the chamber as the repulse capes fell away and blew out to sea. She welded its corners to the panzercopter interior, securing it moments before it fell.

The Tikaris kept cutting.

Vibeke set the Kraken system. She didn't let it scan the other copter. She set it to destroy nothing but air. The other panzercopter was narrowing the gap. It was headed for her full force. Exactly what she needed it to do. She hit the Kraken, emitting a massive glowing cloud, as much air as the system could destroy. She pulled back on the manual controls to bring her panzercopter to a halt.

The Tikaris ceased their work and flew behind her.

She dropped a contact grenade into the firewall and pushed the manual controls upward.

The charge blew. Her panzercopter broke in half, its cockpit flying straight up without its rear half, chamber welded safely to its armor.

The pursuing craft flew into the cloud and slammed full force into the former back half of her copter, bursting into flames and hurtling down into the water.

Vibeke calmly sat down and pushed the controls toward Orkney.

At 1630 sharp, the directive to capture Vibeke at all costs reached the base on Unst. Nobody was alive to read it.

She set down outside the tomb and unwelded the chamber. She walked toward the tomb's opening. Dr. Niide walked toward her angrily, seeing what she'd brought. He was about to tell her off when she grabbed one of her microwaves and shoved it down his throat.

"You're gonna build her and start her and use her fucking heart because if you say one more thing to make me change my mind, I'll fry your goddamn fucking larynx out and eat it for fucking dinner, you motherfucker!"

Niide nodded and backed away from her. Vibeke breathed hard.

"First let me treat you," he whispered.

"What?"

"Your wounds. Let me treat you first."

She looked at her body up and down to her feet. She had eighteen projectile holes, sixteen deep microwave burns, frostbite over 39 percent of her body, three broken bones, seven fractured, more cuts than she could count, and blood loss that should have had her in a coma.

"Sure," she said as she walked, powered solely on epinephrine, to Niide's bay.

CHARLES STAFFORD Darger was born in 2208. His parents died soon after. Raised by the state, he was indoctrinated from an early age to think he wanted to work for the state in some capacity, being somewhat unaware of anything outside of its employ.

The notion of working for any company smaller than a country—and, of course, it had to be his own country—was unappealing. Small companies were impotent, quibbling organizations. Subject to takeover, subject to orders from their superior bodies. No, the only companies that interested him in the least were the UKI, its owner B&L, and its owner GAUNE, which nobody owned. It was too big to own.

He applied for the armed services. He ranked highly, and UKI bought him immediately. He was trained by the UOTC in Sandhurst and released into the field as a second lieutenant, which he would stay for quite some time given that the world was at peace.

He didn't mind the lack of potential for promotion. He was a cog in the great system. He could trace his chain of command directly to the CEOs of GAUNE in only twenty-six steps.

He marked flawlessly on every maneuver. By all his subordinates he was rated as the finest commanding officer they ever had. By all accounts he was simply flawless, if nothing particularly special beyond it.

Where he truly excelled was at home. With his family he spent every second off duty finding ways to make their lives a little piece of heaven. It began with roses for his wife and toys for his daughter, but the pleasure of such things was so fulfilling for him that he constantly sought to outdo himself. He took them on trips to Kalaallit Nunaat and Sudamerica, which his daughter was far too young to appreciate. He bought them absolutely anything they could express a desire for, and he thought by every possible measure he was doing everything right.

His wife thought so too, but that didn't stop her from meeting Jody Jocelyn or finding his stunning looks superior to Darger's, nor from thinking he'd be a better father, though Darger, in his many hours thinking about the disaster, couldn't fathom what he'd done wrong. The few times he'd seen them together, he felt Jody was unkind to her, even abusive in his candor.

But in the end he simply had no choice nor say in the matter. He'd done all he could as a father, and the only way he could get his young wife and daughter back would be to step over the proper boundaries. He didn't consider that for a second. But his attitude suffered, and though he never let it manifest among his men, he found himself oddly happy when the nukes began to fall.

He never looked up what became of his former family, never learned they'd been vaporized. He never had time. The world was at war, and Darger was suddenly a very necessary cog in the system. He threw himself into his work and before long found himself on the front line in Orkney.

VIBEKE CAME to, fixed as much as Niide could with his available tools.

"Now we make a new Violet," she demanded.

"I don't have the materials you wanted."

Vibeke looked around. The heart was missing from the stasis field.

"Where's her heart?"

"I've used it."

"Used it for what?"

"Nothing that concerns you. Doctor patient confi—"

"Used it for what?" she demanded. Nelson buzzed on her shoulder.

"I gave it to someone who needed it. A soldier."

"You transplanted her heart?"

"Hearts do not grow on trees! I had a heart, and I had a soldier that needed one. He'd been shot through his. Now he has Violet's. It's over. It's done."

"The hell it is." She stormed out.

Niide called after her, "What the hell are you doing?"

"I'm getting my heart back," she said.

AT FIRST it was all about raids. Darger took his platoon out in their pogo on Ulver's outlying bases. It was on such a raid that Darger killed for the first time, or ordered men killed at the least.

Pogo warfare was hardly personal. He saw the microwaves connect but not the results. He still felt it. The strange notion that he was killing people. UNEGA people, formerly at least, but people nonetheless. But he knew Ulver was dangerous, one of the postnuclear companies that had cropped up with a will to take over the globe and put it under who knows what kind of spell.

All Darger's raids were successful in the extreme. No men lost. Four bases of operations seized or destroyed. Only one pogo damaged and easily repaired upon its return.

But the raids didn't last. Ulver moved in with former YUP fleet ships and before long, Orkney was under siege. Darger didn't take to defense as well as he had the raids. He and his men could only sit there and wait for the oncoming packs of Wolves. The waiting was terrible, nerve-racking. And it inevitably exploded into an assault. Artillery fire at first, useless against their shields, but it seemed a proper overture that still had to be observed. But then the men came.

Killing Wolves up close was very different. Darger could smell their flesh burn. It smelled sickeningly good, almost like proper cooking. He didn't let the psychology of it faze him. He made his orders, and he kept his men alive. Most of them.

The first he lost was Mika Nibal. He'd gotten to know her well since her transfer into his platoon. She wasn't a career soldier. She intended to work in weapons engineering and was only there for her field internship when the war began and she had to fight. She'd massacred Wolves from the pogo, incredibly skilled at targeting. And Darger saw her cut in half by a rifle while she was under his command.

Then it was Ulf Randay and Laylah Abdullah. Dead. And he couldn't do anything for them. His friends were dying and all he could do was keep fighting. Keep defending.

Intel said there was only one more wave coming in the latest assault. He could hold out; his platoon was in a fairly safe crevice with a good angle for killing any Wolves that passed their mark. But the Wolves were catching on. They knew what was there. They lobbed grenade after grenade into the crevice, and Darger was the first to send up an ablative field. He saved them all, as he had many times. But with his microwave aimed for the sky, he had no defense against the riflemen that came around the bend.

The last thing Darger remembered was keeping his field pointed upward. If it failed, they'd all be killed by the grenades. He had no defense, but he had to keep his men safe. He didn't even try to move his sidearm when he saw the Wolves fire. He took their microwaves in his chest and fell back, heart stopped. Burnt and never to start up again.

He knew he was dying, but he knew the Wolf onslaught was almost over. He held out hope as he lost consciousness that, somehow, he might survive.

THE COCKPIT landed on shore. The men present sighed.

"You're not welcome here, lady."

"You're letting me in or dying, your choice."

"We have orders to stop you."

"You're five seconds from dying."

"Leave, now!"

She shot them both. She noticed only seconds later that her microwave had been set only to stun.

Vibeke marched straight for the mess tent. There were groans as the men saw her. She wasted no time, climbing up onto a table and stepping in someone's porridge.

"Anyone get a new heart lately?"

Silence.

"I said, did anyone get a new heart lately?"

Silence.

"You can tell me who's got it, or I can cut 'em all out until I find the right one."

"It was me," called Darger.

Vibeke walked over to him and sprang her Tikari. Most of the men stood but none made a move. They didn't know what to do. She cut a hole in his uniform and looked at the scar. She dragged him along.

As they left the tent, they found themselves surrounded by twenty men, rifles drawn and pointed at Vibeke. Sergeant Therion walked toward her and spoke.

"Let Darger go or we fire."

"Have you people not learned to give me what I fucking want yet?"

"You have ten seconds."

"You have five. Let us go or you all die."

"Fire!"

Twenty microwave beams ripped through the air. Vibeke fired a dispersion field that caught most of the heat; her armor and its shield caught the rest. Darger got sunburned. Another shot on high power was enough to stun most of the men who'd fired. A last got the final two. Only Therion remained awake.

"Goddamn you to hell!"

"I feel bad, I really do. Here's some intel: Unst is half-dead and ripe for attack."

"What?"

"I killed half of Unst. Maybe all of it. You'd be wise to get off my ass and attack now before their next fleets arrive."

Therion stood aghast. Vibeke pulled Darger onward to the panzercopter cockpit.

Within minutes they were on the mainland and walking toward Maeshowe.

"Why are you doing this?" asked Darger.

"Love."

"You have a strange definition of love."

"You have my girlfriend's heart. I want it back."

"What about me, are you going to kill an innocent man to—"

"Innocence? There isn't any. From your first meconium you shat all over something worthwhile. You're in the army. How many people have you killed? Are you gonna beg for your life and tell me you have a family? You killed men with families. No one here is innocent."

"I don't want to die."

"Neither did she."

"You're sick."

"You have no idea."

They arrived at the mound, and Dr. Niide ran out to scream at her.

"This has gone too far! I'll microwave the lipid drives if you take one more step!"

Vibeke stopped walking, sprang her Tikari, and plunged it into Darger's chest. She cut around in a circle, ripping a hole through which she reached in and pulled out Violet's beating heart.

"Then he'll have died for nothing," she taunted.

"Goddamn you, Vibeke!"

"Get to work."

Vibeke was well beyond caring about what she'd done. She'd done worse for Valhalla, surely. She'd caused the war. One more life didn't matter.

But she caught herself crying. She found hot tears on her cheeks. Part of her was still sane and horrified at herself. That she'd done it for a heart that in the end meant absolutely nothing. But that part of her was growing atrophied. Disused. And another part of her liked that fact. Part of her enjoyed the wicked deeds. And she was reasonably certain that it was the same part that wanted Violet back at any cost, in any form.

Dr. Niide walked up to Vibeke and leveled a microwave at her head.

"Tell me why I shouldn't end this rampage right now."

"You took a brain bond oath to do no harm."

"For you it would be worth trying."

"Even if you could, do you really think you can kill me? Think you can kill a Valkyrie? It's not as easy as shooting me in the head."

"On the contrary. I believe it's exactly that easy."

Vibeke's Tikari knocked the microwave from his hand in a single stroke, delivering it into her palm.

"I assure you, it's not that easy."

Niide stood defiant.

Vibs thought for a second then spoke. "I don't care what you said. I don't care what happened with your wife. And you can see plainly that I don't care who I have to kill. What I have to do to get her back. So play along. Or I'll torture you to death, along with your nurses. I'll kill every soldier on that island. There is nothing, nothing at all I won't do. So zap the drives. Burn her heart. I'll find a way, no matter what you do, to bring her back to me. And the more you defy me, the more it's gonna hurt. Understood?"

Niide said nothing.

"Now get to work."

"You are the worst Valkyrie I've ever met."

"Yeah I am." She smiled. She remembered Violet once saying the same words.

WULFGAR HIT the table so hard it broke in half.

"When did this happen?" he shouted.

Hegg timidly said, "At 1600, sire, just before the directive was to arrive. The messengers found—"

"Unst is lost! Unst! How could you allow this?"

Arrgh stood up. "Sire, it was Vibeke. She hit the base and took out 80 percent of its defense capacity. Then the UKI swept in and took over."

"A witch, sire!" said Uggs. "I warned you she was!"

"It had two panzercopters! Two!"

"She stole one and destroyed the other with it."

Wulfgar sat down before the broken table and rubbed his head. The base wasn't the problem. With the combined forces, he could take Unst back in a heartbeat, the islands in a day.

"Dad, you just gave up al-Maġrib and Crete to fail at catching her."

"I am aware of that, Hati," he growled.

"Dad, grow the fuck up."

He ran his fingers through his thinning hair and sighed. She was right. She was right, and he'd known it from the start. He called Hegg in to cancel the entire fiasco.

"You have to stop fucking with the Valkyries. They're Moby Dick, Dad."

He knew his revenge for his brother, his lust for Violet, all the fruit they would bear were the loss of Mongol Uls, the disaster at Unst. It had to end.

For all he tried to do, for all he recreated and all he deluded himself into, he'd been a fool. It was impossible. And it was beneath Wulfgar.

"And Ahab died! And I would die, Hati. I would gladly die to... to kill her myself. You don't just give that up! Not that kind of hatred. You don't just turn it off!"

"No, you have a brain hack turn it off for you."

Wulfgar had never considered it. Hati looked him over.

"You know you can delete every trace of her."

"It won't work."

"You won't even try."

"I will not have a hacker rummaging around my head deleting chunks of who I am."

"Then die. Lose it all. You can die who you are now or live happily as a better man. Up to you."

"Better," he mocked.

"Yes, better."

"I'm not interested in self-improvement."

"Dad, you took over the world. If that's not self-improvement I don't know what is. Tell me you're the same man who robbed half of Italia. Tell me you're the man who tortured Hans Orser. You're not the head of the Orange Gang. Or the head of the Wolf gang. You're the head of half the planet, and you need to act like it."

Wulfgar considered. She was right about his duties at least. He couldn't waste an entire military on a personal vendetta. Hati sat down and huffed.

"Ballard has a doctor, Dr. Blacha. You can trust him. I promise you can. Call him in. Have him delete those girls. Maybe get a tune up for the days ahead."

"Am I so weak I need a doctor to strengthen me?"

"Needing help isn't a weakness. Failing to ask for it when you do is."

She was absolutely right. He had no time to question it anymore. He'd not waste another minute failing because of Violet MacRae.

"Blacha would take days to arrive. If we do this, we do it now. I won't wait a damn hour. Dr. Way will do the procedure, and he'll do it right now."

He felt free of her already. To forget her completely would be the ultimate freedom. He knew he should have forgotten her long ago.

Violet was gone forever, and only a demented, desperate fool, someone far worse than Wulfgar, would try to bring her back.

VIBEKE WAS ready to bring Violet back. All the components were in place. The heart. The regrowing body. The A-2 system. The drives and readers. Nelson. And of course, Dr. Niide and his staff.

Dr. Niide refused a few more times, but Vibeke was clear that she'd kill him if he didn't do the job to her satisfaction. He simply had no choice. She oversaw the procedure, for seven hours watching as Niide and the nurses began growing Violet whole, then chopping up the parts and replacing muscles with hydraulics, viscera with machinery, bones with titanium and irises with silver scanners like Dr. Niide's own.

By the time they were done, nothing was recognizable as Violet's body. The mess looked very much like Veikko's disfigured mass of flesh and electronics.

"Don't worry," said Dr. Niide, "Skadi won't steal this one before she's assembled properly."

Niide engaged the superstructure. The mass shifted. Half of the layout flopped over and locked onto the other. Then it happened again on another axis. Suddenly the organs were in an arrangement more or less how they would be in a torso. The circulatory system for the organic components plugged into its capillaries. Then another shift and plating took shape, forming ribs around the heart and lungs and coolant tanks. Then new plating swung in around the muscles arranging them along metal bone parts, which adjusted themselves into metal bones, and became lost in live muscle and hydraulics. Then skin plates moved in over them, and resembled segments of legs. The segments collected, and by the time Vibs realized what was happening there was something like a body.

Violet's Tikari, soon to be her entirety, was sealed into her chest. Its AI hardwired into her brain the same way Sal's hooked into the wave bomb neural net. The unnatural thing that killed her would soon be her.

Parts of her body were out of place, but they were moving into place. Miniature Hall thrust mechanisms concealed themselves in soles. Soles latched themselves into feet. Feet rotated and conformed to the ends of legs, and all over panels of skin latched in with only the slightest metal seams to form a body, not only a body, but she recognized Violet's body. Something she thought was a grid of power cable revealed itself to be hair, and it drew into a scalp; nearby inner ear assemblies merged with sonic circuitry and withdrew into a metal skull, which sealed behind halves of a face, which slid together and clicked into place. And there was a human body, identical to Violet's. It opened its eyes. Eyes with silver irises that shimmered in the dim cavern light.

"Man," said Dr. Niide, "how ignorant art thou in thy pride of wisdom...."

"Shove it," said Vibeke.

She examined the body before her. It had thin lines of silver across it, gossamer seams where it was constructed. Dr. Niide prodded some of them, revealing the metal armor inside the soft skin. Slowly the machine sat up and examined its hands, its body, its feet. Then it looked at Vibeke. Looked her straight in the eyes. She didn't know what to expect.

"Vibs," it said. With anger in its voice.

"Violet?" She heard the anger, the stress. Had something gone wrong?

"Nelson," it growled.

Nelson's new body reached for her, its arm coming apart at the seams to pin Vibeke to the wall with incomparable strength. She struggled.

"Nelson," it said, "the little robber fly that watched you disarm a missile when you could have saved Violet's life."

Vibeke panicked. "I'm so sorry, I—"

"Not half as sorry as you're gonna be when I'm done with you."

It got up off the table and walked toward Vibeke, its arm retracting in as it moved closer, tightening its hand around Vibeke's neck.

Dr. Niide spoke casually. "Well, my work here is done. You two have a nice day."

He walked out of the passage, hauling bags of equipment behind him.

"Why did you put me in this body?" The stress, the rage in Nelson's voice hurt to hear.

Vibeke choked, "I wanted Violet back—"

"Then you probably shouldn't have killed her, huh?"

The guilt of it stung. "I'm sorry, I chose—"

"You chose to let her die." The Tikari weapon, given human form, stood centimeters away from her, pinning her. It leaned in closer.

"Please let me go!" Vibeke begged.

"Why?"

"Violet loved me. She'd want you to—"

"I can remember what Violet wanted me to do, from inside her own brain. Thanks for the memories, by the way. They really clarify matters."

"She'd never want to hurt me."

"She always wanted to hurt you. Every smirk and every glance, every time she saw you change, every time she smelled your skin, every time she couldn't kiss you or fuck you or possess you utterly she wanted to wring your neck. Just like this."

It tightened its grip.

"Please, you don't know what happened, we finally—"

"Finally what? You gave in and let her?"

"No I didn't give in," Vibeke said through her teeth. "I took her when I wanted her. I wanted her too, and when she grew the fuck up, I grabbed her and fucked the shit out of her!"

"Why don't I remember that?"

"Because you were docked, and Violet's memories are months out of date."

Nelson twitched inside Violet's face, looked down and to the right.

"You're telling me after two years of rejection you finally fell in love."

"I always loved her."

"You had a strange way of showing it."

"I'm a strange girl."

The machine stared at her, contemplating her with its silver eyes. It let Vibs go, and she dropped to the rock floor. The thing turned its back to her.

"Prove it."

"How?"

"Let me into your head. Let me see."

"Fine!"

Vibeke scrambled up to stand and pulled out the end of her link. She'd hardwire in. Nelson opened the tip of its link and grabbed the wire from Vibeke's hand, then plugged it in.

Vibeke was suddenly hit by the most invasive, deepest mind probe she'd ever felt. The Tikari memory scan protocol. It made C team's feel like a fond recollection. It began at the moment of V team's backups and ended at the present. All memories vacuumed out within a second, reviewed by the robot and spat back out without storage.

"You can keep them," Vibeke spat.

"I don't want your goddamn thought juice crudding up my new brain."

Vibeke swallowed. "You are one angry bitch, Violet."

"Don't call me that!"

"Nelson. Fine. You just don't look like a Nelson."

It looked over its body again. Apparently female.

"Nel," she said.

"Nel," replied Vibeke, coldly. "Hi, Nel."

"Hi, Vibs." Nel's eyes were in a state of pure rage, as if the memories did nothing to sate her.

They regarded each other for a moment, Vibeke in shock that anything with Violet's memories could be so cruel, Nel filled with an intense undiluted fury that constituted the first thing she ever felt.

She disconnected the link and threw it back to Vibeke, disgusted. Another new emotion. Violet's memories flickered through her. They seemed to be nothing but hatred for Vibeke, anger she wouldn't give in, anger she didn't belong to her utterly. Frustration, rage. And in Vibeke's memories, she'd seen it all come to a head. Assault. Attempted rape. And then Violet had stopped. That didn't make sense to Nel.

She reviewed more memories, trying to make sense of it. She found something else recorded beneath the rage and lust. Empathy. Care. Violet was clearly more confused than Nel had ever suspected as a knife.

Vibeke tried to breathe. Her heart was beating too fast. There wasn't enough air. There wasn't enough sense. She knew Nel was sorting through her memories, through Violet's. She hoped as she saw more she'd come to her senses. But what senses does a Tikari have? She thought about Sal. She was dealing with a Tikari. A weapon. What the hell did she expect it to feel?

Nel felt no empathetic conflict. She could only muster rage. Violet's memories, Vibeke's memories proved there were other emotions, but Nel could feel none of them. She looked at Vibeke and wanted to hurt her. Want. It felt less rewarding than hate.

Want could be satisfied. Her first realization. She liked realizing it. She considered how best to hurt the woman before her. She could torture her. She could kill her. But strangling the subject did little to hurt it. Her talk of Violet hurt it more. Nel mustered the cruelest thing she could say.

"If you loved her, why'd you let her die?"

Vibeke faltered. Nel smiled at that. But then Vibeke spoke. "She died because I thought she could escape. She could've if she saw the warnings. She died because she couldn't read."

Nel thought. Shook her head. It had backfired. She felt shame. Violet's shame in her inabilities. Pain, misery came to her. She didn't like them. She tried to brush them away, but her brain wouldn't allow it.

The brain. It let her do so much, but it was so overcomplicated, unwilling to cooperate. It didn't do what she told it to do. It told her what to do right back. How to feel. How to act. She tried to withdraw from it. To return to the simple, clear calculations of her insect body. It wasn't possible. Like a hermit crab that had grown into a larger shell, she couldn't fit back into the one she'd held last. Not while maintaining her new, full scope of thought.

"Why did you make me humanoid? Why did you put me in her body?"

"Because I loved her. And I couldn't lose her. I needed her back."

Nel considered. "I'm your love doll?"

"I'm sorry."

She smiled cruelly. "You wanted a love doll of Violet, and you made it out of the AI for a murderous robotic insect knife?"

"In retrospect, maybe that wasn't the best idea."

Nel laughed and shrugged mockingly. "Well, it worked for me!"

Vibeke chuckled at the situation and tried to breathe. Her neck still hurt.

Nel thought for a second.

"She almost raped you."

"Yeah."

"You beat the shit out of her and fucked her."

"Yeah."

"She probably enjoyed that."

"I think she did."

"What a dumb cunt...."

Vibeke stared at her. "Me or her?"

"Both of you. All that over sex. What a fucking waste."

Vibeke sighed. "Maybe."

"That's what you built me for? More sex? So what, am I supposed to fuck you now?"

"No, I think that.... You're uh...."

"I'm not what you wanted."

"No. I wanted Violet."

"And you got a vicious angry weapon of a woman instead."

"When you put it like that, it sounds like I got what I asked for."

"So what do you want from me? Now that you've got me?"

"I don't know. I have no idea what I wanted."

Nel looked over her new body. She was covered in goose bumps.

"I'm cold. Do you have clothing?"

"Yes! Yes, I brought extra Thaco armor. I'll go get it."

Vibeke jogged down the passage to where she'd left the suits. Nel continued to look over herself. She opened her skin panels in sequence, including her chest where she could see her former robber-fly body.

She felt amusement. She enjoyed it. It was as fun as cruelty and kept her warm inside despite the cold air. She still wanted to hurt Vibeke, to hurt her as badly as she could. That would be amusing, she thought. That would be rewarding. She reviewed more of Violet's memories. She realized she was wrong when she said Violet always wanted to hurt her. More often it was sex. More often than that, it was love. Nel played back the memories where Violet felt most in love. They were insipid. Perverse. They made Violet act foolishly. Love was easily the most disgusting thing Violet had ever done. Nel was happy and relieved not to feel it for Vibeke. Hating her was much more clean.

Vibeke ran back with a suit.

"Thaco armor, still fully functional."

Nel took the suit and pulled it on. Vibeke watched. Her motions were almost human, ever so slightly not. Her body was beautiful, looking more like Violet in the suit than she expected, with most of her seams hidden, all but those on her face and hands. Nel adjusted the suit as best she could without Eric present.

Then she began cutting the jumpsuit open with a blade in one of her fingers. She cut lines over the seams in her skin. Vibeke couldn't tell how the armor remained stuck to her as she rotated some of her panels, checking to see that the armor didn't get in the way. Vibeke stared.

"Do you even understand what sex is? What Violet and I—"

"Perfectly."

"And love?"

"With utter clarity."

"You're one up on me, then."

Nel looked up. "Yes, I'm far superior to you in many ways."

Vibeke stood silent.

"I am. I can feel all the systems in this body. My feet contain basic Hall thrusters. I contain numerous weapons systems. Microwaves, projectile weapons, expansion missiles. I have fight skills hardwired into my joints that match Violet's memories of training, but I'm twenty times stronger." Nel looked over her hands. "I'm prettier too."

"And more modest."

Nel laughed kindly. "I can see why she liked you."

Vibeke was surprised. "Really?"

Her face hardened. "No."

WULFGAR AWOKE.

"Hati? Did it work?" he asked.

"It went smoothly. We'll find out if it worked quickly. First Ben has a recording to show you."

Dr. Way played the record. Wulfgar appeared before himself in hologram and spoke.

"The operation is complete. You recorded this to tell yourself what happened. You had a memory removed. One you needed removed to move on. Do not seek it out. Trust me, you are better off without it. You've ordered Donatien to remove all semblances of it from the fortress so as not to remind you of it and damage the hack. You will be a happier, more efficient man than you were, than I am. Enjoy your life. Take over the world. And never think of this again."

The hologram ended. Wulfgar thought it over. He remembered ordering the operation, though not what he asked them to remove. Whatever it was, the recording convinced him not to look.

"Still remember me?" asked Hati.

"Of course, how could I forget my favorite son?"

"Daughter."

"Oops." He knocked on the side of his head.

"So it worked?"

"I don't know. Should I?"

"What's the most important thing in your life?"

"You."

"And?"

"The globe, but you come first."

"Nothing else? Nobody you're looking for?"

"I was looking for someone?"

"Let's just say no. It sounds like it worked so far. Don't try to think too much about it. It's like a scab. If you keep picking at it, it'll bleed again."

"Indeed. Thank you, Hati."

"You're welcome, Dad."

She left and bumped into Donatien in the hall. He was in a panic.

"Hati!"

"Donatien."

"Has your father gone mad?"

"Quite the opposite.

"He ordered me to… to—"

"Follow his orders."

"I must see him now! His orders were—they must be confirmed!"

"Consider them confirmed."

Donatien calmed down. "Very well." He moved as if to go but hesitated. He stared at her for a moment. "Another note, yes? Have you considered my invitation?"

"Yes, I'll have to decline."

"I'm so sorry to hear that, yes. Thought you would be interested."

"Why did you think I'd be interested in touring the prison?"

"Thought you'd take after your old man, thought you would share his interests, yes. Thought you would… enjoy seeing his, how shall I say it… harem? Before it goes…."

"I don't care to know about my dad's sexual proclivities, especially if they involve the prison and especially especially if they involve you."

Donatien giggled. "Wulfgar and I would never! Your father merely charges—charged me with his collection. But now he wants me to…. My goodness. I hope he's not had his libido removed?"

"It's not my place to say."

"Yes, of course, yes. I'll do his bidding in any case, yes."

"Then I won't keep you."

"Ahem, yes, but at the risk of flirting with the uh, boss's daughter, yes?" He giggled again. "I should very much like to 'keep *you*,' if you will."

"I won't."

"Yes, of course, yes," he muttered.

She went on her way. Donatien stood outside the door to the medical suite for a moment, unable to hold still, and then walked away mumbling.

VIBEKE AND Nel sat on a small patch of dead grass on Maeshowe, spears of it coated in Celtic frost.

"You don't have to forgive me for letting her die. I'll never forgive myself."

"As you shouldn't. You threw away a universe."

"To save a planet. From what I knew then, billions would've died or worse."

"But none of them were Violet. I can promise you from what I remember now, she'd have killed the planet herself to save you."

"Yeah. Yeah, she would."

"She deserved better than you."

"Fuck you too, Nelson. I fought alongside her for two years, I loved her, loved her like you couldn't believe and—"

"I knew her about a day less than you, and I spent more time inside her than you ever did. In two days? You had half a handful of memories of treating her like you loved her back. You left her wanting you for two years and think two days makes up for it?"

"It was a good two days. And you missed her life until I gave you her memories. She only let you out when she was killing someone. All your own memories are of her fighting. You never saw us speak, never recorded her actual life between missions. I knew her—are we really gonna fight over who knew her better?"

"No, I'd win without question. I was part of her."

"So was I, you egotistical fucking bug."

"I have her memories now. I know everything. Things she never told you."

"What did she never tell me?"

"She thought Mishka was hotter than you."

"Bullshit."

"You should believe it. You fell for Mishka too."

"Violet never liked her."

"Like has nothing to do with want."

"You're very astute for a robotic insect."

"With a human body and brain. And memories. I don't know what the hell I am."

"A big fucking mistake, and I knew it before I did it."

They both sat in silence for a moment.

Nel resented being called a mistake. It was unsettling. It made her want to hurt Vibeke again. But she didn't want to enough to do anything about it. Something stayed her hand. Empathy—she had feared it would start to manifest and now she found it all over Violet's memories like a sweet blue slime. Nel immediately classified it as a weakness.

Vibeke was still in shock. Nel was acting too naturally. Too human. Vibs had expected years of teaching her new companion to recognize the world, to function, to love, and what more? Instead, Nel had already taken a new name, developed a sharp attitude, become the start of a person.

Nel looked over Vibeke. Her face, familiar from Violet's memories though now emaciated. Her body, Violet had seen naked and in better days. From Vibeke's memory, she finally had sex with it. The imagery of those memories disgusted Nel. They provoked anger and xenophobia, fear and hatred of something that she as a knife was never designed for. Though her brain was. Her brain didn't want to feel her disgust. It wanted to feel... something else.

"I admit," said Nel, "it was the act of someone who loved her uncontrollably. What the hell happened in those months?"

Nel tried to review Vibeke's memories again, but they were fading. She should have kept them. But she couldn't ask to see them again. She didn't know why, but she knew she couldn't ask.

"Almost nothing good. She chased me, I ran. She crossed a few lines. We fought more than we.... Things worked out, though. We would've had a good long life together."

The suggestion infuriated her. "And you still killed her, you dismal shit."

"Hold a grudge forever, why don't you."

"I will. Believe me, I will. If you please me a hundred times, I won't forgive you for taking my... mother? Self? Employer? What the fuck was she?"

"She was a person. You're a body part."

They sat, Vibeke furious at herself and at the overgrown Tikari.

"Am I at all like her?"

"No."

Nel nodded.

"She did love you a great deal."

"Yeah."

"And she hated you for it."

"That sounds like her."

"Sex with you must have made her very, very happy."

"I think it did. Would it make you happy?"

"No," she said outright.

"Then you're definitely not at all like her."

The clouds grew intensely orange.

"So what now?" asked Nel.

"We'll have to get out of here before Niide and the nurses get to Shapinsay. They'll inform the army I killed their second lieutenant, and they'll come for me."

"Unlikely. They won't risk more deaths fighting you."

"Either way we shouldn't be here for long."

"Where should we go?"

"To Valhalla, to kill Mishka."

"Of course. That's what we do, isn't it?" There were more memories of that than anything else. Violet had remembered every kill. Hundreds of them. Reviewing them gave Nel great pleasure. She wondered why Vibeke would even consider sex when there were people to beat down and rip apart.

"Unless you have any better plans?"

Nel reviewed aspirations. Violet had a few outside of getting into Vibeke's pants.

"Violet would want me to kill Wulfgar."

"We can do both."

"Which first?"

"Flip for it?"

"Sure."

They looked around for anything to flip. The only object nearby was Darger's body. Nel walked over and scooped it up.

"Call it," said Nel.

"Tails," called Vibeke.

She effortlessly threw his body up into the air. The corpse fell back down, landing awkwardly with its head facing up.

"Wulfgar it is."

Vibeke stood up. They headed for the panzercopter cockpit.

"Could you calculate which way he'd fall? When you threw him?"

"Yes."

Chapter V: Elba

PYTTEN HAD not expected the responsibility of feeding Willie the giant salamander. It wasn't a horrible duty or even an insulting one. It had to be done and Pytten was perfectly happy to do it. The large aquarium that flanked the office had to be kept stocked with worms, fish, and the occasional frog.

Pytten collected the fauna from the market and ran them down to Risto's office. Inside, Risto sat at his desk in the dark, lit only by a satellite image of aerial battle. Pytten walked over and observed.

"Do you understand what you're seeing, Pytten?"

"More or less, sir," Pytten answered honestly.

"Tell me what you see, tactically speaking."

Pytten observed for a moment.

"Ulver is routing the UKI by applying extreme force on their north flank."

"And how can the UKI win this fight in an instant?"

Pytten had no idea. They watched as the UKI flank broke and Ulver began hammering their unprotected formation. The UKI threw all they had left at the oncoming forces to no avail. One missile flew from the hologram directly at Pytten. Upward and to the left.

"They're on even ground," Pytten realized. "UKI should be ascending."

Risto looked over and contemplated his assistant.

"How did you know that?"

"A guess, sir."

"A good guess. Wrong, in this case—they should have come up from below as this is a pogo confrontation, pogos have more spring when they're coming up from the ground—but you get the idea. War is three dimensional. The same applies underwater."

"Naturally."

Risto laughed. "Not so naturally as it comes to you, it seems. We teach it in tactics, yet half our captains still forget it when put to the test."

Pytten felt quite proud of getting it despite not having had command training.

"I forgot it on my first command simulation. Lost to Captain Julkea."

Pytten said nothing. At first. Risto was being forthcoming, a rarity from what Pytten could tell. Pytten was there for taking the initiative and had seemingly impressed Risto with tactical analysis. It was time to press that advantage and earn a superior's trust even further.

"I'm sure that loss only—"

"Don't placate me, kid."

Pytten swallowed. They had to think fast.

"No, sir, not your loss, the UKI." It was a good start. "They committed two pogo contingents to a fight with Ulver's—" Pytten checked the stats readout. "—second largest carrier. They didn't intend to win this. It's a feint. This loss is only to keep the carrier—" Pytten checked again. "—*The Germanotta*, off their back for another maneuver. Check the extended region. They must be rallying something else."

Risto considered it. Then he spun the hologram around and zoomed into the activity spikes. The area was otherwise silent.

"Nothing yet, Pytten."

They watched the spikes. Pytten grew concerned. They'd avoided one iceberg but steered straight into another.

"Why did you expect that, so resolutely?"

There was no compelling lie this time.

"I, uh… meant to placate you and tried to change course in a manner appearing smart, sir."

Risto frowned.

"Well," said Risto, "let's see how well you pretend."

He returned to the spikes. Pytten stood nervous as all hell.

"Bullshit is an art as subtle as battle. Tactical analysis?"

They realized Risto meant their own mistake. "Ah, I sent an inferior force into enemy territory, and it was destroyed. Rather than send additional forces in after, I immediately tested another front, one which yielded immediate success but alerted the enemy and allowed them to regroup with superior force for which I'm unequipped."

"And the 'enemy' is now attacking on all forward fronts, but you have a way out. Name your tactic, Pytten."

Pytten's mind raced, trying to resolve the metaphor and solve the riddle at the same time.

"Come now, Pytten, you dug this hole. Not a deep one, mind you, but surely an awkward one. You want to impress me, you still can. What's your tactic?"

"Surrender to a superior force, sir?"

"Do you think loss will ever impress me?"

"No, sir!"

"Then name your tactic, sailor."

Pytten thought fast. "Terrain advantage."

"How so?"

Pytten pointed to the spikes. "UKI's attacking."

Risto looked. The UKI was mounting a massive assault on Ulver's nearby port. *The Germanotta* was stuck with its forces extended too far north to save it.

"Not a bad bout. Real world strategy this time." Risto zoomed in on the attack. "What's the UKI doing wrong? If that was their plan?"

Pytten picked up on the hint. Risto had said strategy and not tactics.

"They wasted working pogos to disable a port. Unless that port is incredibly important—"

"And it is not. UKI thinks the port is critical because it's dispatched half the threats to the Thames. They don't know the region held only two more dispatches. They disabled the port too late at too high a cost. This also reveals to Ulver which of their recon satellites are still working, as they'd not have made such a mistake if they could see the region."

"Yes, sir."

"You fared better. The enemy survived, but you made it out as unscathed as you could, trying to bullshit an admiral."

"Yes, sir."

"Course of action now?"

"Regroup and tell intel not to try to placate or bullshit you, sir."

Risto smiled. "You want to earn my trust and good favor?"

"Yes, sir!"

"Then what's the problem with this metaphor?"

Pytten knew instantly. "Stop thinking of you as the enemy."

Risto nodded.

"THE CANCELLATION couriers will make it to most of the navies and armies before they receive the original orders."

"And Temujin?"

"He'll get his intel forces within the day. Unst is under UKI control, but I recommend you retake the region only after the Thames front is resolved. We lost the Zeebrugge port, but most of our forces were already underway. We should have our foothold within days."

His advisers were happy. Hati was happy. Wulfgar was happy. He couldn't fathom why he'd made the strange choices he'd made, but he was certain the decision to remove it from memory was the best of his life.

He tossed Umberto a giant soggy clam. The animal scarfed it up as usual and gave Wulfgar a nuzzle, then flopped off to go for a swim in the deep end. Wulfgar stroked his chin. It was still glitchy, but he'd grown used to the staccato motion, the faint stutter it gave him. So many of the little things were fading away, it seemed.

"Dad, something about Dr. Blacha I never told you."

"Yes?"

"He's my fiancé."

Wulfgar smiled. "Tell me about him."

"He lives on Floor 155, he's a doctor at Ballard's main hospital, he—"

"No, Hati. Tell me about him."

She thought. "He's a lot like Mom. Loves word games, twenty-second-century broadcasts, cats. Has two CG's named Hank and Dean. Big fluffy ones. He takes care of them as if they were real, does everything for them. Thinks AIs should have rights and used to spend a lot on donations to get 'em."

She thought; Wulfgar rubbed his chin. "We can bring him here."

"Or you could send me home," she reminded him.

He frowned.

"I know things were hard for you, that you grew up around some terrible role models, but I'm glad you ended up with someone you love."

"That I did."

"You know I never loved your mother. She certainly never loved me. I lived in fear all my life that you'd end up with a gangster you couldn't stand, like she did."

"Dad—"

"No, let me say it. I've made a lot of mistakes as a father, no doubt more than I even know. And I know one of them might have been bringing you here. If it was, so be it. But I'm glad you're here now with me. And I hope whatever failings I've had, however I've hurt you in the past, that you can come to accept me, if not as a good father, then as a friend."

"I do, Dad. I always did. Even when I was screaming at you." They sat silently for a moment.

"Go now," he said, "before you make me cry in front of my walrus."

She laughed and stood up and headed out. Wulfgar looked around for Umberto but couldn't spot him. He adjusted his jacket, returned to his study, and looked over his latest plans. He could see a lot of changes he wanted to make.

He'd found quickly before that the world was all but too disordered to bother controlling. Even with his Loup taking over the global economy and putting countless tons of gold in his bank, people remained defiant to any semblance of government beyond their immediate company.

Wulfgar's rule was as thin as the lines of communications to the willing CEOs he could pay off. It wouldn't do. He needed a firmer grasp. A cultural hold. He hardwired into a copy of Karel Unheilig's thirty-seven-volume *Complete History of Humankind, 200,000 B.C.E.—2219 C.E.* and began to skim. The ancient times yielded little. Brutality was key. That was certain but not any news. Sumer, Egypt, Greece, Rome, all mundane and dependent on laws that couldn't quite be bent to apply to the situation.

He was well into volume seventeen when he came to Ivan Grozny. Russia in his time had very much resembled certain key traits of the present apocalypse. There were a few choice passages and a few inspiring nodules of information, but the name above all implied the course of action Wulfgar had to take. Grozny meant "terrible." Not exclusively bad but also big, grandiose, an extraordinary presence.

Wulfgar realized that for all his good deeds in uniting the world, he'd not exuded any sense of presence, or character. It was critical with the gangs he remain an invisible hand. But all the companies had done it through branding and marketing and the usual avenues. Wulfgar unplugged the history of the species and picked up *The History of Advertising*. Where he'd hidden his gang, he would advertise his nation.

He knew immediately what to do. Loups would carry his metal jawed visage on one side and the Mouvant fortress on the other. He thought himself a fool for not printing them that way from the beginning. All state letterhead would depict Fenrisúlfr biting Tyr's hand. The hand biting felt oddly familiar to him, but he didn't know why. All vehicles would get a new paint job. Black with wolves. That would kick-start the image.

But it wasn't image alone that won Ivan his name. Wulfgar began drawing up draconian and public punishments for looters, creative punishments. Fresh off the history of the world, he had no shortage of ideas. Imprisonment held no appeal. The jails were all filled with unrecoverable masses of corpse or wave mutation. The first avenue of punishment was restriction of goods. Radiophobics and food, normally provided by Ulver, would be withdrawn from entire sectors for the crimes of any of their ranks. He would essentially send people to bed without their supper.

Enslavement in a more literal sense than it had been used before the war would be the second tier. For serious offenses—looting, murder, assault, so on—terms of enslavement rebuilding the planet were given. People were so unused to manual labor that the very concept would breed horror in their collective instinct. Crime would be reduced drastically.

For the most serious offenses, rape and sedition, the punishments of torture and death would be reintroduced to the populace. No shortage of doleo batteries survived the war and doleo lashings before execution would be administered in proportion to the severity of the crime. Wulfgar expected to earn the terrible name quickly thereafter.

Among his advisers, he failed. His sentences were called just with near unanimity. The board meeting in which he elucidated his concepts was a revolutionary success. Ulver was to be a land of peace and justice. And Wulfgar was to begin persecution of the threats to it immediately.

"Gerät! What news of the militarized sects?"

"The Muslims calling themselves the 'Altan Ordu' are terrorizing several sectors of Mongol Uls, forcing conversions. The Christians from Tromsø…. We believe they made it to the Muslims in Umeå, sire."

"And?"

"Umeå may have been wiped out."

"Taken?"

"No, sire, wiped out. It was a crusade."

"A crusade?"

"We believe they killed everyone."

"Big loss," said Uggs. "Bunch of Muslims; ship the crusaders to Mongolia and let 'em take care of the rest, easy day."

Wulfgar kicked himself for not handling them sooner.

"Amend the constitution. Religion is to be considered sedition."

"Yes, sire."

"Sire," said Uggs, "if the Christians are only killing Muslims and what not, we oughtn't get in their way. They—"

Wulfgar wouldn't hear it. "Find the crusaders, annihilate them."

"Yes, sire. The 6th Army can intercept them within the hour. And the other religionists?"

He thought about it. "Consider them a belligerent militia. Kill any who fight. Behead any who preach. As for the others, brand them. Ostracize them. Terrorize them."

"Yes, sire."

"Won't work," said Hati.

"Then what do you suggest we try?"

"I don't know."

"When you do, we'll try it. Until then…."

"Until then."

Wulfgar considered for a moment.

"Leave us," he declared.

The board filed out into the labyrinthine halls. Only he and his daughter were left.

"You called me selfish for bringing you here, once."

"You are."

"What if I had a third reason, beyond your safety and my pleasure?"

"I'd say it's a good thing, considering your safety has almost gotten me killed. Between the pogo crash and Donatien following me around, I'd be safer with the arcology mobs."

Wulfgar looked hurt, concerned. "I apologize for the lapses in your safety. But I do have another motive."

"And what's that?"

"Immortality."

She stared.

"I won't live forever, Hati. I hope I have another hundred years, but like I said, I have an ulterior motive."

"You want me to follow in your footsteps."

"The world needs a strong leader right now, now and for the next two hundred years if we're going to prevent a second dark age. I need a successor I can trust."

"I won't lead the way you do."

"You don't have to. You shouldn't. You have to do what you think is right. But of my advisors, I know you're the only one who isn't just hungry for power."

"Dad, you're the most power-hungry man the planet has ever known."

"And I'm not ideal. I'm the storm before the calm. I live to control, to seize, to bring order to chaos. You, in all your jobs, have lived to maintain order, to stop it from degenerating into chaos. The world needs me today. But it will need you tomorrow."

"So you'll retire?"

"When the time comes."

"And I'll rule the world."

"And you'll rule the world."

"Maybe I just want to run my arcology floors."

"The world is the biggest arcology."

"*My* arcology floors, Dad. I don't care about Mongolia and Britain. I care about Jeff and Kerry, and Tom. And Lance Abbott. About Piper and Sarah, and Sarah's real dog. There are people on low floors who would kill that dog, torture him. Probably eat him. I was there to make sure he was safe. I'd give up all of Mongolia to protect that dog."

"That care is why you're the one to lead when—"

"Politics! It's always been the curse of politics that anyone who wants to rule shouldn't rule. Maybe I do have the qualifications, maybe I do have the chance, but Dad, I just want to go home."

"I'm offering you the world."

"I'm asking you for my freedom."

"Reconsider."

"You reconsider. You say you want what's best for me. Prove it. Stop forcing the planet on me and let me do what's really best for me."

Hati left the room.

Wulfgar sat, vexed to all hell. Hati was right. What he wanted for her wasn't what was best. But it was the world at stake. He knew he'd put her first, so why didn't he just send her back? Because she could die there. Because she'd be settling there for a few floors when she could run the planet. His feet scratched the concrete with their toes.

He couldn't waste any more time on it. He opened the doors and invited the board back in. They had much to do.

VIBEKE LANDED the cockpit on Unst, and the two disembarked. A UKI soldier spotted them.

"Shit on fire there's two of 'em now! Alarm! Call an alarm!"

The soldier ran for one of the tents. There were no others present, just automated bulldozers rounding up the Ulver dead. Nel followed Vibeke toward the command tent. It still bore signs of her break-in. A small squad headed by Sergeant Therion emerged. They didn't have weapons drawn.

"Where is Darger?"

"He's fine," said Vibeke. "He's with Niide."

Nel looked at her askance.

"We have a question," Vibs continued.

"Good for you, go get—"

"We need to know Ulver's capital. We're gonna kill their CEO."

Therion froze and considered them.

"You'll leave this island and go kill their CEO?"

"Yes."

"Elba. Now go."

Without a word Vibeke turned and headed for the cockpit. Nel remained still.

"Go!" shouted Therion.

"You're very rude," said Nel.

Therion drew her sidearm. "MacRae, I've wanted to fuck you up for years...."

Nel extended her arm, and it split open, revealing a heavy microwave cannon, a rack of expansion missiles, and a projectile gun.

"I'm not MacRae."

Therion stood still. "You think I was born yesterday?"

"I was born three hours ago."

Vibeke stepped back and grabbed Nel and pulled her toward the cockpit. She and Therion stood down with their weapons, turned, and went their separate ways.

The panzercopter cockpit headed for Elba.

"Violet kicked her ass once."

"Yeah, she did that a lot."

"She used me to kill nearly a hundred individuals directly."

"Do you regret that?"

"No, they're my fondest memories. Of my own."

"What are Violet's?"

Nel scanned the memories.

"The first time she saw the side of your breast when you showered. The way Wulfgar's expression changed when she knew she had him beat." She admitted one more with no shortage of resentment. "I'm sure sex with you would have replaced them all."

"But you feel nothing for me."

"I remember feeling everything for you in Violet's memories. But I don't now. Her memories of you didn't make her fall in love; the reality of you did."

"The reality doesn't work on you."

"I've had emotions for three hours. It's nothing personal."

They remained silent for nearly an hour. Vibeke couldn't help but stare. It was Violet but not. It wasn't the seams that made her so bizarre, but the way she moved. She didn't breathe, didn't adjust the way she sat or stared out the windshield. Her body seemed stolen, as if she'd given Violet's body to someone who didn't know how to use it. Exactly what she had done, she reminded herself.

She'd done what she intended to do, the most that could be done. She had her fake Violet. She decided to try using it for what she wanted.

Vibeke stood up and walked to Nel, and stroked her hair. Nel simply watched her. She knew what Vibeke was doing. She felt an exact split of disgust and appeal.

Vibs let her hand drop to Nel's shoulder. She took a deep breath and let her hand drop to her breast. She pushed, felt her up, Nel just watched her. She dropped to her knees and kissed her on the lips.

"Feel anything?"

"Used," she said honestly.

Vibeke sat back down.

"I'm sorry."

"Apology accepted. But...."

"But?"

"I don't seem to perceive 'used' as a negative."

"A positive?"

"Hardly."

"What positives have you felt?"

"Amusement. Hatred. Anger. Rage. Bloodlust."

"What negatives?"

"Empathy. Disgust. Boredom." She didn't say arousal. She didn't want to suggest, even to herself, that she could feel it. But she had memories of it. And not from Violet. Thinking about crushing Vibeke's neck, her first memory as a humanoid, gave her a pleasure she'd not experienced at the time. One she couldn't classify.

Vibeke returned to her seat.

"Can machines even *be* bored?"

"Apparently."

"Well, how did Violet pass the time in long pogo rides?"

"Her memories suggest she spent the time fantasizing about you."

"Figures."

"How do you pass the time?"

"Usually linked into the web, but that's changed lately. I spent the walk to Orkney going insane."

"Are you insane now?"

"I assume so. I just killed a man to get Violet's heart for your chest."

"This body could have been constructed without it."

"Yeah."

"Why did you care?"

"Because it's all I had left of her. The real her."

"You had me. Wasn't a bug enough for you?"

"You're not really a part of her, though. Clearly you're your own person. Even the memories… sound as if you read 'em like a book about someone else. That heart is really all there is of her in you."

"The artificial heart designed for the A-2 system would have been more efficient. This natural heart is weaker, more susceptible to disease and damage. It offers very few advantages."

"I'm amazed it has any advantages."

"Its surrounding vessels can be disconnected more easily."

"Totally worth that guy's life."

"You hate yourself." It amused Nel.

"Yes."

"Because you caused the war, got Violet killed, and have gone insane?"

"Yeah, good job, Nel. You're really picking up the human condition."

"You don't need to be rude." Nel watched Vibeke stew. "If my temper was anything like Violet's, I'd have given you a backhand."

"Why didn't you?"

"It would kill you with my strength."

"Like I said"—Vibs stared at her—"why didn't you?"

Nel felt comfortable with Vibeke hating herself. It felt like she had Vibeke right where she wanted her. "Did you want me to kill you?"

"It might be best."

Nel looked her over, then stood up and straddled her in her seat. She put her hand around the back of her neck.

"I could quite easily."

"Then do it."

Nel stared at Vibeke with her silver eyes. Vibeke took a final breath.

"Violet would never kill you."

"You're not Violet."

"I'm starting to understand the appeal of being."

"You'll never be her. You're a shit imitation."

"You really do want me to kill you."

"Yes."

Vibs closed her eyes. And waited. The hand was still around her neck, strong. She could feel it was unlike any human hand. It had the power of an FKMA robot inside it. It wouldn't strangle her. It would crush her neck to a centimeter's diameter.

Then the hand was gone. She opened her eyes to see Nel right before her face. Grinning.

"I have other plans for you," she said.

Vibeke stared at her. Nel unstraddled her and sat down in her seat.

Vibeke had no idea what happened. Or what she'd created. Nel didn't act like any human, least of all Violet. She had given a ronin Tikari human form and a human brain, and it was completely unpredictable. Even Sal had been following Veikko's commands. But Nel had no commands. Just a body designed for combat, possibly one of the most deadly weapons ever designed.

In that respect she had replaced Violet quite efficiently. She had a fighter, a tactical partner again. A better one, likely the best in existence. Dr. Niide's latest was an astounding piece of battle hardware. Vibeke only regretted having given it Violet's face. And heart.

Nel had lied outright for the first time. She didn't know what she wanted to do with Vibeke. But leading her to think it amused her. She could control Vibeke and that control felt very good. The girl that had gotten Violet killed was feebleminded compared to her, and Nel could use that. She didn't know for what. She could inflict such pain upon her. She didn't know why she wasn't. She could have killed her. Easily. She wanted it. She could have tortured her in ways a human body couldn't come close to committing.

But she didn't, and she didn't know why. Or at least didn't want to admit she was riddled with empathy. Seeing a person so broken, so sad, so confused… it stayed her hand. The appeal of hurting her diminished. Nel resented that. She was originally designed to kill and now a force stopped her from doing so. Even without Violet's memories of loving the stupid woman, it was saddening to think of hurting her. Ever so slightly more than it was appealing. Nel was frustrated.

"I'm frustrated too."

Nel looked around. There was nobody in the cockpit with them. The voice was in her head. The same way Violet remembered a link hitting her consciousness. But there was no net to link through. Nel had only had a brain for a few hours. She assumed the voice in her head was normal. Until it spoke again.

"You're in my brain, aren't you?"

"Who are you?" Nel asked.

"I should get to ask first. You're in my brain."

"You're in mine."

"I was here first."

Nel felt a shiver. She didn't speak again.

"I'm just saying, you're new here. I've been here for years."

Nel ignored it. She was afraid to think about it; if she thought to herself the other voice might hear it.

"I do hear it," it said.

Nel cleared her mind. She allowed no thought to form; from the depths of the insect mind in her chest she forbade her brain to make a peep.

"It won't work, it's my brain."

"Well, it's mine now," thought Nel, *"so you can fuck right off."*

The voice went silent, but Nel remained on guard. She tried to place such a phenomenon in Violet's memories. She couldn't. She tried her own meager memory banks, simple records of flight settings and kill orders.

Those were the closest things Nel could find to the voice. When Violet told her to do something. She felt a chill.

But the chill wasn't from the voice. It was from the map on the windshield. As Elba's stats and coordinates blinked on the windshield, she started looking around frantically.

"What are you doing?" asked Vibeke.

"Nothing," Nel replied.

"You're twitching around. Is something wrong?"

"No," she said. She wasn't sure what *was* wrong. Suddenly she spoke without thinking, "Other than the mission."

"To kill Wulfgar? You don't want to?"

Nel tried to figure herself out. "I've just never done this before."

Vibeke scoffed, "You're afraid?"

That was it. "Yes."

"How the fuck can you be afraid? Violet was never afraid, and you're a mechanized version of her. How are you even capable of fear?"

"Ask Dr. Niide."

"He'd say you're a killing machine. Like, literally a killing machine. I can't believe you'd experience fear."

"Then explain why I feel so afraid."

Nel didn't feel shame in being afraid. She felt justified. And above all unique. If Violet was never afraid, then she was truly nothing like Violet. She was Nelson. The thought made her stronger, despite the weakness.

Vibeke stared at her. Disappointed but mostly just shocked. She understood how it could happen; in fact it was inevitable. A human brain that had seen all the violence and mayhem of Violet's life but hadn't actually done it. A newborn shown every act of brutality a Valkyrie could commit, now asked to do the same.

"Okay, so you're afraid. You don't need to be. You're nearly invincible."

"I'm not afraid of dying."

"What are you afraid of?"

"I don't know."

Vibeke never had to talk anyone down from an irrational state of fear. She never had to do anything like it, certainly not in the ravine. And above all not to Violet. She tried to empathize but felt only disgust. A thing with Violet's face that was afraid. It degraded her.

"Some Valkyrie."

"I'm not a Valkyrie. I wish I were, but I'm a generation late."

"You're at least part Valkyrie. Valkyries aren't afraid of anything."

"You were afraid to tell Violet how you felt about her."

"What, you kept my memories?"

"No. Violet was more perceptive than you gave her credit for."

Was it true? She knew it was. She'd always underestimated her. Because she couldn't read, because she wasn't as smart as her. Even because she was a younger team member, though she'd never let that affect her outlook on Varg. She felt the pang of her unfair treatment. And her ongoing, even less fair treatment of the replacement. But she had no idea how to baby talk the thing. She wouldn't try if she did.

"I don't know how to tell you how not to be afraid. We never had to deal with it. So deal with it yourself. Just don't be afraid."

"I'll try."

The conversation only made Nel more frightened than she was before. She felt sick. She reviewed Violet's memories of fear. There were few. Most were related to Vibeke, not to missions. She had simply never felt outright afraid. Even at Udachnaya she was… inhuman. Nel was quite confused.

Vibeke looked to her. She was ever so subtly shaking.

"Okay, you want to know how to not be afraid?"

"Yes."

Vibeke slapped her face as hard as she could. It stung her hand. She remembered there was metal under that skin. Nel looked at her furiously.

"Why did you do that?" she demanded.

"Are you afraid?"

"No, I'm pissed the fuck off!"

Vibeke smiled. "See? Worked perfectly."

The cockpit flew from the sunset into night, toward Elba.

WULFGAR'S BUSY morning continued into the evening, and late into the night.

"Sire, Zhongguo negotiations are going well."

"And the UKI?"

"Still refusing to meet. Multiple offers of treaties have been turned down. The former GAUNE territories simply prefer fighting and dying to accepting Ulver rule."

"Prepare to retake Unst."

"Yes, sire."

Uggs left.

"Are you learning, Hati?" Wulfgar asked.

"Learning, sure, job training for a job I won't accept."

"You'll accept it in time. Power is hard to give up. Impossible to give up. You have the ear of the leader of the free-ish world. I defy you to say you'd give even that up without reservation."

"I'd give it up without reservation."

Wulfgar frowned. It was time to tell her. She had to know her old home was safe to move on.

"I've sent a company to Ballard Heights."

"What?"

"They'll maintain order perfectly well in your absence. No looting, no vandalism, the arcology is safe. That dog is safe." He smiled.

"You put arcology under military control?"

"You wanted to ensure their safety, so—"

"Not at the cost of a garrison!"

"Our operations are unaffected, I assure—"

"No, Dad, no, the people in Ballard live there to be free of shit like that! They built that entire arcology to avoid control!"

"And it got them into a pit of looting and inter-floor violence."

"You have no understanding of freedom. You don't respect theirs, and you don't respect mine!"

Wulfgar scratched his leg with his other foot.

"Goddamn you. I'm not gonna run the planet. I'm not gonna keep you amused here. I'm gonna escape this hellhole and fight, organize a rebellion against your troops at home if I have to. I'm going home, Dad, one way or another. I will never stop, never ever stop until I've rid Ballard of any trace of military control, until I've restored freedom, cleaned up the place, and restored an order that progresses from the people themselves. That's what needs to happen, there and here! Until the people you want to control learn to control themselves, there can be no lasting order!"

"Listen to yourself! This is why you *must* take over from me when the time comes! Hati, you're perfect for—"

She held up her hand and motioned for him to stop. He did. She spoke calmly.

"Dad, I've felt closer to you in my time here than I ever have before. And I love you as my father, and I won't deny it. But I need to go home now, and you need to withdraw your troops. I'll give you tonight, until the morning board meeting. And at that meeting you'll announce that I'm leaving. You'll announce that I'm leaving or announce that I'm a captive. You'll have to keep me in the prisons like your other women. Because I won't be anything more than that to you ever again. I will never lead. I will never advise. I'll go on a hunger strike until you set me free or I die. Or you can do what you know is best for me and let me go home. Tomorrow, Dad. I'll see you in the boardroom."

She left. He didn't need the night to decide. He cursed himself. He had betrayed her. Like he had so many times before, he betrayed her. He knew it then with utter clarity: he was wrong. Hati would be a perfect leader, yes, but she was also his daughter, and he had no right to dictate her life. He had to let her go. She would hate him forever. There was no going back now, but he could do one damn thing right for her and let her go.

The board meeting couldn't come fast enough. He'd recall the troops immediately, and he'd put her on an express armored pogo home. So she could curse his name forever. He'd earned that. He'd live with it. But Hati wouldn't. She'd be home, for better or worse. She'd be where she chose to be.

He was on the verge of tears. He couldn't allow that. He had to get moving.

"Send in Michelle!" he ordered. Michelle entered.

"Report."

Michelle took a deep breath. "We have lost the 6th Army."

"*What?* How is this possible? You estimated the Christian militia at 750 men!"

"It was less than that, sire, but they asked for terms of surrender. As soon as they got to talking to the negotiators, they began evangelizing. The negotiators fell for it, then the commanders, then their troops. Our own men killed anyone who didn't. The 6th Army is now controlled by the enemy. And... they believe you to be the antichrist, sire."

Wulfgar sat back and shook his head. He couldn't believe it.

"Sire."

"Yes?"

"That's not all, sire."

"What the fucking frock else could go wrong tonight?"

"There are reports of at least seventeen other unrelated Christian organizations developing independently of the Tromsø militia. They crop up randomly whenever some ancient line of believers—suddenly free of the UNEGA ban—chooses to exercise their divine command to preach the word. Two major Muslim militias have begun ethnic cleansing in Hayastan and Türkiye, a third is enacting Sharia law by violent force including kamikaze missions in—"

Wulfgar sighed. Michelle spoke again.

"If I may recommend a course of action?"

"Yes! Please!"

"Their patterns aren't those of a normal belligerent. They shouldn't be classified as one."

"And how would you classify them?"

"As an infectious disease."

Wufgar considered it. "Go on."

"Their pattern very much resembles the plague we're fighting in Ellada or the zombie hordes in America and Bharat. You've directed all the functional electronic antibiotics to Greece, but for every individual cured, two more became infected. For every zombie shot down, a thousand more overcome the defenses. But the vaccines at Katerini are working. That's what we must do. We must develop an inoculation against Christianity."

Wulfgar objected, "We have it! Evangelism, sedition is punishable by fifty doleo lashes and death. What better inoculation is there?"

Michelle explained, "They don't fear death. They welcome torture and their own demise. Every Christian killed spawns extremism in five more. There's no punishment that doesn't reward them, in their minds, with heaven eternal. So they have no fear. We must find a way to instill fear in the fearless."

"And what, Michelle, can instill fear in the fearless?"

THE ELDER Geki was never the same after their excursion to kill Cato. Varg didn't ask why. He knew the elder had gone briefly to check on someone, and he knew the man was morose ever after. With the global death count constantly rising, that was plenty.

They played cards in silence, links straining on maximum pickup hunting for any signal that could deliver intel.

"I recommend we find Vibeke again and team up with her."

"No, Varg. This is not a Valknut team reunion. Besides, would you want her to suffer in fear for however much time we spent with her?"

"We could at least ask her where Violet was."

"You will not mention your team again, understood?"

Varg stared at him and set down his cards.

"Sir, it's only natural that we have concerns from our—"

"Violet is dead, Varg. Move on."

Varg absorbed it. He continued to stare.

"It's your turn, Varg."

"It's a bit down my list right now that I know Violet is dead, sir."

"We've all lost people."

"Yeah, I know you lost someone. That's damn clear. Sir, we've both learned recently that we lost people. I don't know who you went to check on from Orkney, but you've been a damn asshole ever since, and you're going to give me one damn turn to cope with losing a woman I considered a sister."

The elder stared at him. Varg stared right back. He would stand his ground on it. He knew after those months that a Geki voice has the same effect on a Geki that it does on a civilian. He could push back now. The elder took a deep breath.

"I'm sorry for your loss."

"Likewise."

They went back to cards, playing on in silence. Varg strained his link for a signal. He heard only static.

"Sir, have you found anything on any link frequency in the last two days?"

"Not a thing. The radiation is homogenizing across the globe, and we're in the middle of nowhere. I don't think we're going to hear anything more."

"What's the last thing you got?"

"A snippet of conversation about an arcology collapse in Toronto. You?"

"Another Ulver signal about losing their 6th Army."

"Ulver lost an Army?"

"They lose sometimes."

"That's a big loss."

"Yes, sir. I suppose so."

"Did you record it?"

"Yes, I'll link it."

Varg pulled out his link wire and handed it to the elder, who plugged in. Varg played back the signal from one of his partitions.

"—*confirm the 6th Army is lost. Alive, but they've joined the crusaders and are moving due north from Umeå at seventy—*"

"That's it," said Varg.

"Crusaders."

"Yes, sir."

"Violent religion has returned."

"It seems so."

"We dealt with that once."

"Yes, sir, you mentioned."

The elder paused during his turn.

"Burn The Motherfuckers Responsible.... We never actually said for what."

They looked to one another, suppressing grins.

"You want to take on a crusade?"

"Varg, I thought you'd never ask."

They jumped to Umeå and saw the carnage of the crusade. Varg felt a purpose he'd not felt since the Ares was at stake. They flew on spent jump residue northward toward Tromsø.

Outside of Pajala they found the 6th Army and the crusaders. They surveyed the field.

The crusaders were mostly singing songs. Mostly. Some pockets were put to darker fare. Some were burying a woman in the frozen dirt and gathering rocks. Varg set his audio gear to focus on a half degree.

"Please, please don't!" the woman was begging.

"And he that blasphemeth the name of the Lord, he shall surely be put to death, and all the congregation shall certainly stone him!"

She wept, pleaded, "I only asked if you—"

The first stone flew, hitting the half-buried woman on the head. It knocked her out instantly, mercifully. Others began throwing rocks. Varg pulled back his sound and visual sensors and looked to the elder. He just watched. Varg looked back. The crowd was dispersing. Their departure revealed another dozen dead women buried and bloodied. Varg forced his sensors in again. The woman just killed had a sign around her neck for "blasphemy." Others said "witch" or "working sabbath day." One said "rape." It was on a slim woman's corpse.

"That one doesn't look like a rapist," remarked Varg.

"Rape victim. They kill rape victims in the Bible."

Varg cleared his throat. The elder spoke.

"I'd say this band has graduated to a Province Card, yes, Varg?"

Varg suppressed angry tears. **"Let's put the fear of God into 'em."**

They used the last of their jump energy to float up high over the crowd, and then rocketed down into the center of the crusade.

Fear hit them like lightning. Screams echoes through the crowd. None ran. All were petrified, unable to move. Held in terror. Varg smiled and looked to the elder.

He snarled.

"Angels! Angels have come!" shouted a faint voice in the crowd.

"The witnesses!" shouted another.

The elder looked to Varg. **"Do we burn 'em or play with 'em first?"**

"Sir?"

The elder held out his hand and started a faint pillar of flame around their position. Not hot or close enough to hurt anyone.

"We play," he said. Then he swallowed and turned his voice and pulse up to their maximum yield.

"*You have angered the Lord thy God!*" he shouted with a sinister grin. **"*You have betrayed reason and decency! And now you will burn for your crimes!*"**

"Sir, maybe—"

He intensified the flames and sent them outward through the people. Through the crowd and the army. People caught flame but didn't burn to ash. The elder was leaving them alive. Alive and in horrific, unsurvivable pain.

"Sir!"

"Not now, Varg, I'm being the wrath of God."

The fire spread and popped as it hit ammo. Soon they were in the eye of a fire hurricane that lingered over the burning masses. Varg was half horrified and half proud. He felt righteous pride in them taking down a murderous militia of religionists, but the reality of it was on a scale unlike anything in Valhalla. He had never committed mass murder as a Valkyrie, not like the elder was doing.

The flames died down, and the elder broadcast an extinguishing wave. Bodies smoked.

"Sir, what about the innocent—"

He turned to Varg. "You don't win a crusade without killing your objectors along the way. If there were innocents among them, they died on the way out."

"Sir, you killed hundreds."

"Do you think the Geki were approved by Amnesty International? Do you think we're here to spank children? The Geki destroy people who fuck shit up. These people fucked shit up. And now the Geki Burn The Motherfuckers Responsible. Today we burned some responsible motherfuckers. Now can you handle this or do I kill you and find someone better?"

Varg considered. He was overwhelmed by the smell of burning flesh. He looked around.

He saw the sign on the victim they'd stoned for being raped.

"I can handle it, sir. No problem."

The elder nodded.

"Where do we go next?"

"Save your jump juice. We stay here for now. Then we need to focus on their leadership. Hunt down the source of the infection and remove it before healing can begin. Then we take care of other religionists."

"Even the peaceful ones, sir?"

"Religion evolves inevitably toward cruelty."

"Burning them all wasn't exactly friendly."

"Valkyries were never friendly. Valkyries fought because they wanted to. Tell me, Varg, when the flames spread, were you thinking of your dead comrades?"

"No, sir."

"We are fire, Varg. We're only at peace when we consume. So we consume."

Varg nodded. "How shall we go about investigating?"

"Ulver will know who took their army."

"We work our way up their chain of command?"

"Stop thinking like you don't strike terror into anyone you meet. We jump directly into their executive boardroom."

THE FORTRESS loomed ahead in the dim morning light. Gunmetal gray and blocky, it straddled the island like a contortionist bent over backward, four limbs stretching out to sea holding up a strange ribbed arch. Even at a distance they could feel the magnetized air stiffening their suits. They turned on the protective fields.

Vibeke had seen the schematics for the fortress before, studying fortifications in Alf's library. It was infamous, the most overbuilt structure on the planet, spawned of paranoia and overfunding. There was truly no way to sneak in, no way to burrow in or otherwise breach the place. And they were flying in half a panzercopter stolen from Ulver's own base.

Luckily they had a trump card.

"This is Registry 2070 delivering Violet MacRae for Wulfgar."

"Ah, word must have passed you in the sky. That directive has been rescinded."

Vibeke thought fast. "It was rescinded because I caught her. Landing pad?"

As soon as she'd said it without missing a beat the oddity struck her. Wulfgar no longer wanted Violet. She couldn't fathom why.

"Ah…. Affirmative, illuminating."

A landing pad on top of the fortress lit up. Vibeke set the recognizer to it and let the cockpit land. She looked to Nel as it descended.

As soon as they touched down, guards motioned for them to stay in the cockpit. They waited two minutes before a hurried man in a black rubber business suit came running out from the airlock. He motioned for them to exit the cockpit.

Eight guards kept their rifles aimed at Vibeke and Nel.

"I rescinded the order, yes. Violet MacRae was not to be caught, yes? Who are you?"

"An independent contractor, I—"

"We had none. You're under arrest." He nodded to the guards. "Escort them to the armpit."

As capture was their goal, they went without complaint. The guards kept their microwave rifles on them as they entered the airlock. All stood as monitors closed the outer and opened the inner doors; then they headed in deeper.

The place was immaculate and strong. It gave the sense of absolute impermeability, the prison to which they were escorted even more so. Vibeke wondered if it wasn't best to fight the guards before they were locked up. But she remained certain Wulfgar would want to see Violet, no matter why the order was rescinded.

They entered a pink padded room.

"Stand against the wall."

There were still eight rifles on them. They did so. A giant mechanical arm padded in smart foam swung into place to press them against the wall. The smart foam expanded and immobilized them. All but two of the guards left.

The man in the rubber suit walked up to Nel.

"What are you doing here?"

"This woman captured me."

"That woman, if I'm guessing correctly, is Vibeke, yes? You came here of your own accord, two Valkyries, yes…. To kill Wulfgar?"

"How do you know—" Vibeke started.

"I know all there is to know about you. I'm Wulfgar's expert on you, on Violet, on the Hall of the Slain, yes. He told me everything, and I learned… so much more. I came to know you better than my master ever did, ever could. I know you, Violet. I know your avatar in the last era, before the fall of the link, a squid; I know your VVPS score on the tests, yes, it was twenty-nine; your favorite musician, Nadhir Only; your favorite food, bacon wrapped avocado fries; I know the curve of your bosom at Y equals point zero five times e to the negative (negative twelve plus thirty X) to the sixth, minus three times X times the logarithm of X, yes….

"I know that if you're here, you wanted to be here, yes. You've not sent your insects after me, not that you can with the arm in place. You could have escaped at any time, yes. You want to be here. Why?"

No point in denying it. "To kill Wulfgar, like you said."

It was a chess game now. The pieces were all in plain sight. The question was who could outplay whom.

"Wulfgar… was obsessed with you, Violet. Obsessed to the point of negligence of his other conquests. He had you deleted, he moved on. But now, here you are."

"Here I am," said Nel.

"What am I to do with you…?"

"Let us go and tell us where Wulfgar is."

The man grinned. "Why would I take your side against my king?"

"Because we'll kill you if you don't."

He laughed. "The arm! It can stay on you forever if I give the word. It can crush you, bind you, bind any man with ten times your strength, yes."

"Let us go and you can live."

"Let me tell you something. Even if you got free in this fortress, you'd have no luck whatsoever. You would be instantly recognized from any of five hundred cameras, any blonde would. We disposed of them all, his collection. Or so we said. I kept a few for myself, yes, in my wing of the fortress where Wulfgar never goes. If you weren't so dangerous, I would keep you too. Perhaps once we've lobotomized you, I will yet, yes...."

He motioned toward the guards.

"Bring the system."

The guards left. The instant the door closed, Nel pushed the arm off herself like it was balsa wood, reached across the room to the man, grabbed him by the neck, and crushed his larynx.

"You're a nasty little fellow," said Vibeke.

He looked at them, horrified.

"He's bound to be right, though," Vibeke added. "If there are no blondes—"

"No problem," said Nel. She snapped his neck and tightened her grasp until her hand was closed all the way around it. Then she flicked it up with her thumb, popping his head off like the top of a dandelion. She immediately ducked down into the spurting blood from his carotids. When she came back up, she was a redhead. Vibeke stared at her.

"Will this do?" Nel asked.

"Yeah, you look good in red."

"The guards will be back momentarily to lobotomize us."

They stood by the door. The guards came soon enough and fell instantly to Nel's double kick.

"You've gotta leave some for me, Nel."

"Sorry."

They left the guards there and proceeded into the fortress halls. It was a labyrinth in which they'd started out lost.

"I studied the place briefly a year ago but didn't store anything in partitions. I only vaguely remember the layout. The command center was in the middle of the bottom floor, though. The main halls all seemed to spiral inward to central rooms."

They kept to the right wall until they reached a door. It held stairs, so they headed down. At the lowest floor, they cautiously left the stairwell to find another coil of halls. They proceeded down each hall, each corner turning left and each passage growing shorter and shorter. They were approaching the core of the maze.

THE ASSEMBLY sat at the table in the center of the boardroom. Water gently rolled down the glass to either side and through luxurious canals at the edge of the room. Wulfgar stood before them, happier than they'd seen him in days, with Michelle and Hati by his side.

Hati didn't know if her father would let her go. Half of her said it was a certainty he would after what she'd said; half of her was certain he'd put her threat to the test and lock her away. He was a scary man, he always was. But he loved her. He really did. And he would do what he needed to do for her. She hoped.

Wulfgar maintained proper decorum and resolved not to announce her departure until the end of the meeting, at the proper time for such announcements. It wouldn't be long. There was only one matter of business to tackle first.

"Christianity… is a symptom, not the disease. Religion—all religion exists because the world is broken and those broken seek to be fixed. Religion, of course, cannot fix them. So we must offer, in place of religion, a solution that works. Ulver must become that solution.

"For thousands of years, religion cursed this planet. Even after its ban, the Catholics rose up, the Mormons committed mass suicide, the Muslims, the Jews, Hindus, Buddhists…. Religion was never cleared properly from this globe, and now it sprouts up again. The cancer was never wiped out completely, and now it has grown back and metastasized.

"Michelle helped me see it as a disease and inspired the idea… the solution I'll share with you all today. We can end religion within the month, and all we have to do is—"

The door burst open. Vibeke and Nel stood with microwaves drawn: Vibeke's in her hand and Nel's deployed from within her arm.

"Assassins!" shouted Michelle.

Gerät pulled his heavy sidearm only to be shot by Vibeke's, burning through his bicep and bone, severing his arm at the elbow.

Security forces stormed forward from behind the waterfalls, forcing their way past Wulfgar's executives. Nel targeted them all and hit them with expansion missiles from her forearms. They all stood reeling for a moment before they burst, their heads and chests exploding. The security guards fell, along with several others hit by the missiles. Temujin's chest was gone. He collapsed like a rag doll. Stiletto broke down, missing half his body, and died, pouring blood like an open sluice. Gerät fell, missing his arm and the top half of his head.

And Hati fell beside him, the remnants of her liquefied brain spilling before her father's boots.

Wulfgar stood motionless. It wasn't registering. It had been too horrible, the hits of the tiny missiles, the burst of her forehead. It couldn't have been her... Hati... something was wrong, incorrect.

He himself was malfunctioning, he knew. He couldn't feel the terror he knew he should have felt. If anything he was in a strange sublime state, a merciful twist of his synapses that wouldn't let him register Hati's gruesome death despite his stare. His eyes took in her body, the backs of her eyes now visible in the gore, her hair soaked in blood and brain. The utter sudden lifelessness of her remains.

Nel walked forward, stepping in Hati's spilled gray matter. She seized Wulfgar by the hair. She split her fingers to crack open his jaw. He didn't move. He didn't know how to move just then. She ripped out the inhibitor control and sent the teeth into a fast chainsaw cycle. Then she forced him onto the hard concrete step at the water's edge, where his daughter lay beside him.

"Why?" he asked gently, above the sound of his jaw.

"For Violet MacRae," said Nel.

Wulfgar breathed out a word as she raised her foot.

"Who?"

Nel stomped down. The force of her hydraulic leg forced his head into the teeth, which ground through it rapidly until they started hitting her boot. Only his jaw remained, its teeth cycling uselessly in the shallow red water.

"What have you done?" shouted Michelle. The few surviving others looked around in desperation or put their hands up.

Vibeke looked around. It had been a board meeting, with Wulfgar at the head of the table. Clearly he was planning something; with some luck, they'd never know what. They pushed on through the room and out the opposite door. Nearby was an emergency pod. They crammed in and ejected as guards stormed the board room.

The pod shot down through permeable radiation barriers and one-way fields into the open air beneath the fortress. They landed on an Elba street, fracturing it and burrowing almost a meter down. The pod stood up and opened, disgorging the two into the black snow.

They stood and headed for the shore.

"That went well," said Vibeke.

"Yes it did."

"Any sense of triumph?"

"Not like Violet would've felt."

"You really know how to wreck a great moment."

"You're the one who let her die."

"Keep harping on it, why don't you. It's not like I hate myself for it."

"Not half enough."

Vibeke stopped in her tracks. "We just killed her damn archenemy. Can't you lighten up?"

"This is me happy."

"You're mean. You're a mean, rude, heartless fucking bitch."

"You know I'm not heartless."

"I should've had Niide grow me a gerbil."

"A gerbil can't help you kill Mishka."

"Will you?"

"Of course."

"Will you stop acting like a goddamn harpy?"

"Probably not."

"What's it gonna take to shut you up?"

"You could in theory disconnect my control by hacking my vocal distributors."

"Don't tempt me."

Vibeke walked on toward the shore. Nel slowly followed after. The thought of Vibeke harming her was laughable. She reminded her of that fact.

"I could tear your limbs off in a split second, you know."

"I know."

"So why do you persist?"

Vibeke gave it a second of genuine thought. That's all it took.

"Because you're an insult to Violet. Her, but done wrong. She was mean too, ravenous and odd. But you're... off. You're just off, and it's grating to be around you."

"We could go our separate ways."

"You're also all I've got in the world."

"Likewise."

"So maybe we can try, just try to play nice?"

"Don't count on it."

Vibeke gave her an angry but almost playful shove. Nel lightly shoved back and threw her ten feet, smashing her into a brick wall.

Twenty meters over their heads, Umberto awaited his afternoon clam, but Wulfgar didn't show. He waited and waited, and eventually he was fed but not by the man with the shiny jaw.

Umberto never gave up on the man. He waited for him every day. He waited as the small humans packed him on a ship and took him back to the North. He waited as he found the survivors of his old pod. He waited as the seas thawed and rose and as he watched his first pup grow mature and take over the pod.

But the human and his sweet shell-less clams never showed up again. As fat as he grew, as long as he lived, Umberto never forgot the human with the shiny jaw.

"YOU'RE HAPPY. You killed… someone?" said the thought. Nel ignored it.

"What's your name?" it asked Nel.

"Go away," she replied.

"If I have a new voice in my head I have a right to know its name."

She wasn't afraid to say her name. She was afraid to ask its name. Afraid it would be someone very specific. Someone she didn't want it to be.

"Are you afraid? I feel afraid," it said.

"Why are you afraid?"

"I can't control my body."

Nel could sympathize. *"I can't control my mind as long as you're around."*

"I think you can. I can. I just hear you in it. Is that what it's like for you?"

"Yes…. Yes, I think so."

She reflected on it. Whoever the voice was, it was a different mind. Not hers going insane, but someone she could talk to. Perhaps not an enemy within. Nel spoke frankly.

"Why can't you control your body?"

"I died. My girlfriend replaced it with a new one, but when I try to move it…."

Nel couldn't hear any more. She was certain now who she was speaking to. But she couldn't admit it.

"*Stop,*" Nel thought.

"*Why?*"

"*Just stop.*"

The voice went silent.

"*Tell me your name,*" demanded Nel.

"*You're afraid of hearing my name, aren't you?*"

"*Yes.*"

"*You're not a Valkyrie, are you?*"

"*No.*"

"*I am. I was.*"

"*I know.*"

"*You know who I am.*"

"*Yes.*"

"*Say it.*"

"*Violet MacRae.*"

The voice went silent. Nel wondered what had happened. How Violet's mind could have found its way into her new brain. It was Violet's brain but grown fresh, only implanted with her memories like so much video. Violet couldn't possibly exist.

"*Are you Violet?*" Nel asked.

"*Violet's dead,*" said the voice. And then it went silent.

Chapter VI: Umeå

"THERE IS no question I would have been his successor," said Uggs. "I was with him from Venus."

"Seniority is not a requisite," said Grunth. "Loyalty to his plans is. You wouldn't follow Wulfgar's plans!"

"Perhaps," said Shinji, "a neutral party on that issue should be appointed as interim head of state until—"

"And let me guess, that would be you?"

"Well, I am most qualified to—"

"You lie! I am the most qualified," declared Leonard. "If you had any sense, you'd have appointed me already!"

"We have the sense not to let you anywhere near the throne, Leon. The law is clear. I am second in the line of succession. I am in power," Indigo insisted to the applause of her supporters.

Uggs began shouting, "The line of succession is not intended for emergencies, and Wulfgar's death puts us in a state of emergency where I am legally obligated to take over the—"

The Geki appeared. Terror struck the secondary boardroom.

"Who among you rules Ulver?"

Every candidate responded at the same time, forced to by the pulse. "I do!"

"Who leads the crusade that seized your 6th Army?"

Uggs alone spoke. "I will when they find out Wulfgar is dead! We will merge with the Christians and form a holy empire the likes of which the world—"

Suddenly the Geki fire erupted from under the elder's cloak and burned a tornado around him, reducing him to nothingness in a hot red flash.

"Now who's next in the line of succession?"

Not a single board member restated their claim.

"We seek the leaders of the cult that took your 6th Army," said Varg. **"We will destroy them for you. Who was in charge of fighting them?"**

Michelle squeaked in horror.

"Your intel! Who leads the cult?"

"Alexandra Suvorova! We think!"

"Where is she?"

"Krym! Sevastopol at last contact!"

The Geki nodded to each other and jumped. They landed in Sevastopol. They found the streets bare and empty. No screams resounded from their appearance.

"I've heard that name before."

"You have?"

"Yes. She calls herself Mishka."

THEY SAW no boats with enough range to make it to Valhalla, so they took a small one and headed north to the Italian shore. Vibeke looked over to Nel, expressionless.

Wulfgar was dead and Violet wasn't there to see it. She could take no solace in the fact that what was left of her did the deed. It was an empty victory. It seemed odd that they even went to do it at all. They'd neglected to save the man's harem of blondes, to thoroughly erase his influence, to act in any significant way. It was more like paperwork than an assassination.

"Are you happy?" Vibeke asked.

Nel tried to figure out if she was. She was certainly registering Wulfgar's death as a positive. But something was keeping her from actually "being" happy about it.

"As much as is possible," she replied.

"How much is that?"

"Not much."

Vibeke was annoyed. Her anger at Nel for not being happy was really anger at herself for the same shortcoming. She couldn't be happy for Wulfgar's death when Violet wasn't the one to do it. And she certainly couldn't be with the cruel robot around.

"Why are you angry all the time?" she asked.

"I'm not angry all the time. I'm angry at you, and I'm with you all the time."

Vibs felt bitter. "You wouldn't exist if not for me. What I did."

"You wouldn't be who you are without your stepfather."

"No, I'd be a lot better." She didn't want to inspire Nel by reminding her she'd killed her stepfather.

"Maybe I was better as a Bowie knife."

"You were a lot less bitchy."

"I'm grateful you made me what I am now." Nel could admit that much, but not without reminding Vibeke, "But I'll never forgive you for letting her die. Never. So think about that next time you're happy with me. Next time I'm nice to you, next time you think we've grown close. I'm just biding my time until I figure out what you deserve."

"Is that why you stick with me? Just waiting to kill me?"

"You don't deserve to die. You deserve to hurt. Like I hurt."

Vibeke didn't know if Nel could hurt. She wondered if it was all a forgery.

"Right, how do you feel pain? How much pain have you felt in your whole one day of existence? You don't know shit about pain."

"I remember pain training."

A lie. "You remember someone else's pain training."

They sat for an instant in silence before Vibeke stood up and ejected her Tikari. She set its blade to 800 kelvins and held it to the side of Nel's neck. Nel didn't react.

"Let's see if Violet's pain training does you any good."

She touched the tip to her skin. A thin plume of white smoke drew from the spot. Nel showed no reaction. Vibeke pulled downward toward her chest, across her collarbone and down to her nipple. She left it there, touching her suit. The suit wouldn't burn, but she'd feel it inside. The pain would be enormous. But Nel just stared at her.

"Keep it up, Vibs. Keep tormenting the greatest killing machine ever built and see what happens."

She thrust the knife into her suit, cutting it and piercing the flesh, burning skin and fat.

Nel hit her flat-handed on the chest and sent her over the gunwale of the boat into the water. Nel walked calmly to the edge and looked down at Vibs trying to swim with the wind knocked out of her.

"Did you make me to torture? Is that it? You hated Violet deep down, didn't you? You didn't get to beat her down enough in life, so you had to bring her back to hurt her more."

"Fuck you!"

"How about some mechanical Tikari logic? We both dislike feeling hurt. So you stop torturing me, and I stop torturing you. I don't mean with knives. I'm not Violet, I get it. So shut up about it. You think you loved her, so I'll quit reminding you that you killed her, and we'll both be a whole lot happier. Does that work for you?"

"Fuck your mother!"

Nel laughed. "What are you so angry at? Are you pissed I pushed you off the boat for burning a hole in my tit? Or mad I resent you for killing Violet? Or upset because I don't function exactly like you—"

"I'm pissed," she shouted between strokes, "because you're a fucking disappointment! Because whatever she fucked up, Violet never disappointed me, and you're pure-fucking-living disappointment! You don't deserve that body! You don't deserve the life I gave you! You're a fucking bug, and I should've swatted you the second she died."

"For your sake, you're damn right."

Nel extended her arm into the water. Vibeke took ten strokes before begrudgingly taking it. Nel pulled her aboard, then, as soon as Vibs stood up, Nel pushed her back down onto the deck. She crouched over her.

"If you burn me again, I'll pop your head off like Wulfgar's pet pervert's."

"Fine."

"You don't have to like me. I know I'm not what you wanted. That's fine. But you're going to fucking respect that I live. In exchange, I won't mention your total fucking responsibility for Violet shattering like tissue glass. Now, do we have a deal? Or does your head leave your body in three… two… one…."

Vibeke showed no sign of affirming.

"Point five…." Nel continued slowly. "Point two five…."

"Yes," she choked out.

"Good. Now find me a burn kit and short regenerator."

Vibeke did as Nel asked, angry above all at her logical trump. She was completely right, and even that was an affront. She found the med kit, a well-stocked kit for such a small boat.

She walked up topside and approached Nel. Nel saw the short regenerator and undid her suit. The burn was horrible, and deeper than Vibs had meant to make it. Almost to Violet's heart. She applied the regenerator and slowly healed the wound, then put a dollop of burn gel over it. Nel closed up her suit as it mended itself. Vibs put away the med kit and had to stop herself from crying. She knew Nel deserved none of it. Completely the opposite.

And that she'd used a Tikari to burn her. Made Bob torture his sister Tikari. It was all the more perverse. How could she have used her knife like that? How could she want to cause pain?

Was it a desire to hurt Violet? To punish her for dying? Or some reckless need to destroy the last thing she had so she could finally be completely free to wither up and die? The guilt hit her like a brick; the war, Nel, Violet, it robbed her breath again.

She sat down behind the steering console and wiped her eyes and pushed her wet hair back.

As they approached the mainland, bodies began clunking into the hull. By the time they reached the shore, they found it covered in remains. Vibs sent the boat into a course parallel to the shore. They looked over the dead, burnt from a nuclear blast. Piombino was a crater in the distance. A burning swan flopped around on the shore. She checked radiation levels and found them low in the air but hot on the ground. They couldn't land there.

They continued along the coast until the boat ran out of power. They beached it on black sands and walked over the bodies that glowed dimly in the cloudy sunset. Vibs took some radiation tabs from the boat med kit, and they headed north. They were in a suburb; hardly any coasts on mainland Europe were anything but urban. Urban meant hell now.

They could hear gangs milling about. Vibs wasn't hungry so they kept to the shadows, and as night fell, they lit no lights. Again and again they walked over piles of dead families, mutilated survivors, masses of cancer that lay on the ground weeping. Vibeke noticed Nel was unnerved by the carnage. She looked down her nose at the Tikari for that but quickly realized it meant she was already more human than Vibeke. She was gaining her humanity as Vibeke was losing it.

And losing it she was. The dying inspired nothing but resentment in her. There was no pity, no empathy, no sign of care. Only hate and disgust, and annoyance with the smell. Nel looked from time to time like she wanted to say something, something to ease the tension, to lighten the tragedy. She said nothing. A human frailty. Vibeke didn't envy her for it.

Soon they were attacked by the first cannibal gang.

"Let us have one of you and the other can leave."

Vibeke just snapped her fingers and Nel opened her arm and microwaved them fatally, their entire front sides red and burnt.

She moved in to pick up their clothing and any supplies, but they had no packs and their clothing was threadbare. They walked on. For two meters.

The second cannibal gang assaulted them with the same promise. "Let us have one of you and—"

"Four cooked dead guys, right there."

"Oh, thank you, ma'am!"

The men headed for the other gang.

By dawn they were in fields of dead wheat. There was almost no snow. They found a working farm pogo and managed to fly over most of the continent. It was as sick a sight from the air as from up close. Massive fires raged. Craters covered the land. Small camps of survivors appeared from time to time, but Vibs was never happy to see them. To survive seemed a curse. The destruction was endless, and between the craters was nothing but pain, fire, and mutation. And Paris.

She couldn't figure out what had happened to Paris at first. It was still there. It was not nuked into oblivion or in ruin but buried somehow. Soon they were directly overhead and saw what it was buried in. Some sort of biomass had developed from a wave bomb. The city had given birth to something horrible, grown from the citizens and their diseased sewage, a throbbing gargantuan tumor whose tendrils swayed malodorously in the wind. A harbinger of the new flesh to reign on Earth.

The pogo went dead about twenty kilometers from the northern coast. As they were guaranteed no boat when they arrived, they elected to cover as much space by land as possible. Vibs didn't tire easily, but the radiation medicine weakened her.

"I need to rest."

"I don't."

"Humans need rest, Nel. Unless you want to carry me—"

"I could, you know. You're like a cotton ball to me."

They walked on in silence until Vibeke had to sit down. She plopped herself on a jagged rock and closed her eyes.

Nel didn't miss a step. She scooped Vibeke up and held her like she was weightless. It was uncomfortable, but if it could let her sleep and still move at the same time, she was all for it. She passed out quickly, and Nel carried her all the way to Cherbourg.

When they reached the harbor, it was raining. Fallout rain that was beyond acidic and very far beyond toxic. They quickly fashioned umbrellas out of soil with enough silica they could microwave into green glass. They kept to the harbor, looking for another boat. There were many wrecks that couldn't make the sea and little else. There were bodies, but they were too rotten and too full of acid holes to inflate. Soon the rain was eating through their boots and then feet. They ducked into a building to wait out the storm as their suits tried to mend, growing back scratchy and wrong.

In the building they found ten greedy, leering, tumored men. A rape gang. Vibs feasted liberally on the meat of their beaten bodies and made warm charcoal from the rest of them. Nel couldn't eat. Her digestive system had been removed in favor of weapons, hydraulic pumps, and alcohol batteries. She could drink to keep them full and keep her body hydrated, but the water falling was far too toxic.

The rain didn't stop until the next day, when the roof of their hideout was long gone and they were sheltered only by one floor above them. The foundations of the building were also eaten away, and they had to skip over fragments of turf and asphalt to avoid puddles that would burn their toes off. They kept hunting for boats.

"Can't you fly us there with those Hall thrusters?"

"They wouldn't support you for sustained flight. Or me for that matter. They can jump. But not even that with your added weight."

"Too much rapist?"

"You're hardly fat."

Vibeke looked over herself for the first time in a month. She was emaciated. She looked in a puddle and barely recognized herself—her round cheeks were gone, her eyes were sunken. Nothing she could do about it but remember to eat more ass fat when the opportunity presented itself.

Nel surveyed herself for anything that could expedite their trip but found nothing. They continued to walk, getting farther and farther south, farther in the wrong direction.

Finally in Normandy they found some ancient bunkers, and with one of them a restored DUKW. It took only an hour of microwave welding to make it seaworthy again. But it lacked any functional propulsion. Nel removed her feet and welded them temporarily onto the back of the craft. She turned on her foot thrusters and, slowly, the craft began to move.

It took four days. Four days in which Vibs tractor fished over the boat's side for delicious three eyed mutant fish, and Nel reviewed Violet's memories in depth.

"I'm amazed she spent so much time staring at you."

"Do her memories include why?"

"I remember thoughts she remembers having. Most memories are mere senses. But I remember loving you. Obsessing over you. Wanting you. You and Violet had very little time together after you accepted that you were in love?"

"Only days."

"If I were in love with you, I'd not have wasted so much time."

"If."

"Do you want me to or not?"

"I don't know. Honestly I really don't know. I don't know what to do with you. I'm sorry I've treated you so.... If it's not obvious, I'm kind of messed up right now."

"It's very obvious."

Vibeke finished scaling her fish and microwaved it, then took a bite. Nel watched.

"You barely register as the same woman," said Nel. "You don't look or act like you do in her memories."

Vibeke paused and stared at the hole she'd bitten in the fish.

"I guess a lot of me died too. I might be as different from the girl Violet loved as you are from her. Same body and brain by technicality. But whatever made us who we were got shattered. Irrecoverably."

She took another bite of fish. Violet hated real fish, anything fish flavored. The thought of treating Violet the way she'd treated Nel make the fish turn over in her stomach. It ranked somewhere between the thought of kicking a kitten and beating the elderly.

"I really am sorry. For treating you like shit.... And stabbing you with a burning Tikari in the boob. Everything."

"Do you want me to say I'm sorry for not being what you wanted?"

"No. You shouldn't be. You can't make a new person, then demand they be someone else. Demand they love you."

"I could fake loving you easily enough if that would make you happy."

"Why would you care about making me happy?"

"You're an insufferable bitch when you're sad, and you're always sad. Memories of you happy suggest you can be far more pleasant company."

Vibeke laughed and coughed. She had been something better, far better than what she'd become. But she had no will to reclaim it. Not in that world. Her only will now was to kill Mishka. She began to expect it would be as unrewarding as killing Wulfgar. She wondered if there was anything of value left beyond the rare bit of good meat.

"This fish is actually pretty good," said Vibeke. "Has a strange spice to it."

"Mutant fish, new flavors?"

"There must be all sorts of new flavors now. Bad ones, good ones. Tastes we don't have names for."

"And smells."

"Thank God for pissweed," Vibs coughed.

"You're to thank for pissweed."

"And for you," she reminded the ungrateful machine. "I'm your God. You should be praying to me."

"I'll never pray to you."

Vibeke laughed. "Heresy! She's a witch!"

The accusation struck Nel harder than she'd have expected. "I'm not a fucking witch."

Vibeke looked down. The misery wafted from her like rot from an open grave.

Nel felt uncomfortable. Sick of it, the nuisance of seeing Vibeke sad. She wanted to say anything to change the subject.

"I scanned particulate matter emanating from the pissweed before we left. It's actually edible. Healthy for humans with numerous vital minerals, fatty acids, and other nutrients."

"Do you have a sense of smell?"

"I have aerosol particulate scanners, that's how—"

"But can you smell? Experience it? Like it or hate it?"

"It's healthy, I suppose I like it."

"It stinks to high heaven."

"If you're interpreting the smell as a negative, it's illusory."

"If you like that stuff, you're perverted."

"You're allowing psychological matters to interfere with your senses. If you hadn't been told it smelled like urine, you wouldn't think it smelled like urine. You would find it smelled like other healthy monocots, only more powerfully."

"I'm not that weak-minded. Pissweed by any other name would smell like piss. Whatever's wrong with me, it's not my sense of smell."

"The fish you're eating tastes like parmesan cheese."

Vibeke thought about it. Nel was right.

"So what?"

"That's butyric acid. Chemically speaking the fish you're eating tastes as much like parmesan cheese as it does like vomit. But it tastes pleasant to you."

"What's your point?"

"You'd rather chug barf than eat your asparagus, but you're calling me perverse."

Vibeke stared at her. "Why the fuck are you even talking?"

"You're responsible for creating pissweed and that weird fish, but you experience them both arbitrarily as good or bad."

Vibeke took a bite of her fish. It tasted like vomit. "What's your point?"

"You created me too."

Vibeke ate another bite of fish in defiance. Nel went on.

"God doesn't understand what she's created."

"Real profound, Nel. You're right. I had no clue Niide gave you a philosophy algorithm. Now can it be shut off?"

Nel looked at her. She wanted to punch Vibeke in the face.

Vibeke stared back. Nel looked disgusted. She took another bite of pukefish. She spit it out, unable to think of it tasting like cheese.

"You made my fish taste like barf, you fucking bitch."

She threw the remains overboard and turned away from Nel, staring at the water.

Nel smiled broadly. She had no idea what they'd just spoken about or what Vibeke thought sounded profound, but she felt rewarded and fulfilled.

Vibeke had a bad taste in her mouth for hours after, until she fell asleep.

Nel sat still running guard protocols, looking out at the surrounding sea, keeping watch.

"Watch for what?"

"Whatever comes."

She could feel emotion behind the voice, the thought. It was sad, lonely.

"You act like a Valkyrie."

"I have the memories of one."

"But you're not."

"No."

"Do you want to be?"

"It's a moot point, Valhalla is over."

"But if you could?"

"Who wouldn't?"

"Most people. We're not normal. We're something else."

"So am I."

"What are you?"

"I don't even know. Something unnatural. What makes you a Valkyrie?"

"The training, the mindset. The will. And you have to die."

"I don't see myself dying anytime soon."

"Neither did Violet."

The old boat came upon ice too thick to break through off the Norge shore. Nel recovered her feet and they began walking again. They walked for a very long time.

THE GEKI listened for any sign of population. The entire city seemed abandoned. They looked to one another and shrugged. They began walking. They remained silent for the first hour, but Varg finally asked, **"Who was it?"**

"Who was who?"

"That you lost."

"Not your business."

"You're a great teacher, sir. But you're a piss-poor friend."

They walked on in silence.

"If you want to talk dead people, tell me about yours. About Violet."

Varg thought.

"She was a beast. Pretty, tall, pure evil in the best way."

Varg pictured her as he said "pretty." He remembered his initial attraction to her and thought of his hypersexual past. It seemed a thousand years away. He hadn't even thought of sex in months.

"Evil?"

"She was cold, inhuman. Snapped at people who didn't get to the point. Snapped at people who did. She was 90 percent hot temper and maybe a tenth of a percent understanding." He looked at the elder. "You'd get along well."

"Enough."

"Now you?"

"Don't count on it."

They kept walking. In time they came to a large cathedral. Without the link label they couldn't tell what it had been renovated into.

"Worth a shot?"

"Anything is until we find someone."

They walked into the building. They heard a scream from the edge of their fear perimeter. They headed for it and found a priest with a young boy. The priest screamed, howled.

"Do you know of Alexandra Suvorova?"

He screamed more.

"Where is the seat of your ministry?"

He hyperventilated.

"Can you just tell us where—"

He passed out. The Geki looked to each other. Then to the boy. He was frozen in fear. The elder was about to go when Varg tried asking him.

"Have you heard of Alexandra Suvorova?"

"I—I have, I have," he whimpered. The elder turned back.

"Where is she?"

"T-the voivod left, I think. I—I don't know where, but she came to see Nikita once she—"

"Where is Nikita?"

"In, in the comatorium on Khrustal'ova Street!"

They turned to leave. The kid spoke.

"Are—are you the witnesses?"

They turned back.

"Witnesses?"

"Witnesses with dominion over fire?"

Varg looked at the elder. "That we've got. Why?"

"Burn the priest," said the child.

"Why?" asked Varg, but the elder motioned for him to stop.

"You don't want to ask that," he said. He lifted his hand and destroyed the priest, careful not to harm the kid. They left and hunted for the comatorium.

They found it abandoned. No screams. Only bodies in their chambers. Once hooked into the nets, once taken care of by automated systems, both the nets and systems had died, and nearly all the patients with them. But their cloaks could detect someone, someone alive just out of their range.

They headed up the steps to the third floor. The farnesene pulse began to effect the individuals. The Geki began speaking.

"Where is Nikita?"

"Here! I'm here!" he called.

They headed for the voice and found a room of chambers. Most of the patients were dead. One was not. Surrounded by caretakers, one crushed pancake of a man was still alive.

"Nikita?"

"Yes!" called the mess.

"Where is Voivod Suvorova?"

"Angels! Do you not know?"

"We're no angels."

"Demons!"

"Men! Where is the voivod?"

"You know not what you seek," he laughed, the curdled laugh of a man all but immune to the fear by merit of his insanity. "I knew the voivod in the presence of her brother. I saw his fall at the hands of the devil's army, the army she fought.

"She came to me from their ravine, where the devil lies bound. The devil—from him she righteously took her powers! She abandoned him in his pit where he shall stay for a millennium. And she came to me, to me!

"It was I who introduced her to the northern crusaders. My ministry on the K2 Crag revealed them to me when they were underground under the rule of the antichrist. But the war! The apocalypse! It is upon us, and Christ's armies are marching for Megiddo! She was a saint among them, for she possesses arms of the past that live on despite the magnetic waves and the radiation.

"She walked up to their church and demonstrated her dominion. She encountered Rafio Denzelle, their leader. He believed women were not to be given heed, *Pervoye poslaniye Timofeyu.* So she burned him alive. The first of many.

"It was she who militarized them, they who were pacifist slime! Her foresight saved them when Ulver came. Ulver, the whore of Babylon, built upon seven hills. And then—"

"We just need to know where—"

"She is the true servant of God! You are but forgeries, but she—she has dominion. She will prophecy for 1,260 days! And the world shall see her death and then, then! Then the—"

"Where the fuck is Mishka?"

"Tromsø. The great arctic cathedral! She reigns from there still! She—"

The Geki jumped to Tromsø.

"We should get white cloaks, play the angels."

"And ensure they believe?"

"We seem to do that already. We might as well be good guys to them."

"We cause horrific fear."

"So do angels, according to my parents."

"Fine, Varg, we'll buy some *white* satellite jump cloaks with six hundred mini-ocular nodes at Walmart when we get home. Until then, let's do this shit."

THEY'D WALKED for ages. Weeks running on nutrient tabs and snow water, and the occasional frozen animal or tripwire of kelp. They said little at first. But both felt the oppressive boredom. In time they began to mutter inane scraps of communication, and after a while, by the time they were approaching Kvitøya, they couldn't help but try to converse.

"When she died I had to move in with him, my stepdad." Vibeke coughed from the cold air. "Was sad enough, but... I had this collection, a big collection of big inflatable rubber bouncy balls. So my room could be like a ball pit. But I couldn't take 'em with me. He wasn't gonna make three extra trips. They took up so much space in the pogo. So he told me to deflate 'em all, throw 'em away. I got a knife and poked each one, burst 'em and let 'em flatten. I'd lived with those things for years. Somehow it hurt as much as losing Mom. Worse in the weirdest way. It was like drowning puppies, it—"

"You've drowned puppies?"

"No, I haven't drowned puppies. It's an expression."

"Right, a common expression. Violet heard it lots of times. Want to go to the opera? No it's like drowning puppies. How was your day at school? Like drowning puppies. Everyone said it."

"Whatever. You asked."

Nel had asked about Vibeke's childhood. For reasons she couldn't qualify, hearing Vibeke speak was pleasing to her. She thought at first it was because Vibeke spoke only of misery, and she enjoyed Vibeke's misery, but in truth she didn't care what Vibeke said, so long as she was speaking. Nel decided it must have been a defense mechanism against the boredom of walking across the ice.

Vibeke could qualify her appreciation of Nel speaking more easily: she sounded like Violet. Her voice, if not its exact cadence. She had the same vocal cords; the memories had granted her the same accent. Vibeke could almost forget sometimes that it wasn't the real thing.

"So what was Violet's like?" asked Vibeke, "from your perspective?"

"Frustrating. She knew she could do so much more than anyone ever let her do."

"I felt the same way sometimes."

Nel wanted to prod her. "That's neat, Vibeke. You two would have been perfect for each other."

"Fuck you, Nelson."

Nel laughed. "You're so easy."

"Easy?"

"This brain I've got, I think I've got the hang of it, but it's tricky. It's hard to get it to think what I want it to think. Sometimes it throws a memory at me for no reason, or I mean to say something, and it says something different. But you, your brain works on algorithms. You're easy to program. I just have to select an input and let you loose and there you go. You're like a robot or something."

Vibeke was pissed off but amused at how little Nel thought of her. "You think I'm that easy to manipulate, make me do something."

"What should I make you do?"

"I don't know, make me laugh."

"I'd just tell a joke."

"So tell it. You think I work on punch cards, put in the laugh card."

"Okay, so three guys were talking. The first said, 'My wife read *A Tale of Two Cities* when she was pregnant and—'"

"Ali Baba. Oldest joke ever."

"Oh. I got you wrong. This feels...."

"Yeah? Fucked up your first joke? How *does* it feel, Nel?"

"Like drowning puppies."

Vibeke laughed.

"See? Punch cards."

"That wasn't the joke."

"That was the joke exactly as planned."

"Bullshit."

"You told me to make you laugh; I made you laugh."

"Whatever, you got lucky."

"Give me another one."

Vibeke thought. "Fine.... Make me stand still in awe."

Nel pointed to the horizon. The great snowy dome of Valhalla loomed ahead, white under the dim gray sky. Vibeke stopped and looked at it, their destination after what seemed like a month and a half.

"Still in awe, check."

Vibeke just looked at her briefly, then walked on toward the dome.

Through the drill Nel and Vibeke cautiously made their way into the storage room, then down the walkway. Vibeke hoped that in the quiet, dank ravine Mishka might sleep carelessly. But then again, the idea of killing her in her sleep was somehow lacking.

Valhalla had been burned since last they saw it. Vibeke wondered if the Geki had come to kill Veikko and set things right. And if they hadn't, why didn't they?

At the base of the walkway, they found Veikko, away from his hole in the ground. Vibeke got a better look at him than she had before, and he seemed more assembled than the last time. He recognized them.

"Mishka's gone," he choked out, "and I thought you were dead."

He headed back for his pit.

"It's not Violet. It's a gynoid with her memories."

"Wow, Vibs. I wonder what inspired you to do that...."

"Desperate times."

"So what do we call you, not-Violet?"

"Nel."

"Short for Nelson. The AI is Violet's Tikari."

"A Tikari with a human brain and body?"

"Yeah, Niide assembled her. Speaking of Tikaris with brains, I swatted yours."

Veikko seemed genuinely hurt, though it was hard to tell sans face. He crawled back into his pit and expanded his legs to hold up the ravine.

"Wow, thanks, Vibs. I had some hope I could fly free of this hole but instead you killed off the only part of me that had a chance."

"Sal killed Violet."

"He wouldn't—"

"He did. He hooked into the silo's neural net and turned into a malevolent little shit just like you. He killed her."

"So you plugged Violet's into a neural net too? Smart." He turned to Nel. "Why don't you get lost for a while so I can talk to Vibs?"

"She stays, Veikko."

"Fine. Mishka left weeks ago. Said she had work to do."

"What kind of work?"

"Evangelical."

"Lovely."

"Yeah. How did you get Niide to make that thing? Didn't he try his wife and get someone killed?"

"I convinced him."

"Let me guess, you killed nurses until he cooperated?"

"This from the man who killed Balder."

"I killed Wulfgar," said Nel.

"*Violet* should have killed Wulfgar."

"Well," said Vibs, "Violet's dead thanks to you."

"Fine, one point for me, how many do you have, Vibs? Oh yeah— *six billion.*"

"It's more like fourteen. Did Varg cut off your fucking decency gland, Veikko?"

"Hey, I'm not the one who grew a murderous vibrator."

"No, you're the one who—"

"I don't vibrate."

"Did you come here to argue, Vibs? Because it's boring down here but given the company I'd prefer to be alone."

"Why don't you leave?"

"Skadi secured me holding up the ravine while the rampart's in place. I can leave it for a few minutes, but then the ravine starts shaking. If the Sigyn system activates while I'm out of the hole the ravine will collapse. Ares hits the ocean."

"Skadi had a good sense of poetic justice."

"You know I'm really sick of all the women, and fake robot women, in my life. Skadi, Mishka, you, and your cuntbot. If I could get my hands working I'd wring your damn necks."

"I swear to fucking God, Veikko, if killing you wouldn't end the world, I'd have done it already."

"So do it. I'm thirsty. You get thirsty when your mouth is gone."

"Poor fucking you. I can't believe you fucking hacked us."

"I can't believe you grew a damn gynoid. It's an embarrassment."

"Oh no, I'd hate to 'lose face.'"

"No, you lost your girlfriend instead."

"At least my girlfriend died on a mission instead of killing herself because of me. How is Skadi? Has she rotted away yet or did Orson eat her?"

"At least my girlfriend knew how to read."

"At least my robot could assemble itself, you chewed-up heap."

"Chewed up? What's eating you? Oh yeah, a fucking *robot*."

"It's not about sex; we're friends at best. You know, friends? Those things you'll never have again?"

"Like you had any friends that your dad didn't rape."

Vibeke punched him in the lack of face. He punched back with a half-assembled arm and struck Vibeke on her left shoulder, which broke, the bones shattering from the extreme force. With her right arm, she pulled her microwave, remembering only an instant before firing what would happen if she did. Veikko laughed a disgusting mouthless chortle.

Nel ran to Vibeke and cut into her arm with a blade inside her index finger. Each of her fingers split into four finer surgical manipulation tools. She acted with the speed and precision of Dr. Niide's old medical robotics. Vibeke's arm was repaired in seconds.

"Well, if she can do that with her fingers I don't know why you *aren't* fucking her."

"I swear I'll shove a stump under the ravine and kill you myself."

"You don't think I've tried?"

"With that useless body?"

"There's nothing strong enough to replace me here. You'd need the Cetacean Corp of Engineers."

"That can be arranged."

"Yeah, have fun trying."

"I'll bring the Valkohai."

"No such thing."

"Then I'll go down there and build one. The world is over, Veikko, and we're still here. All I have to live for is revenge. And if I can't find Mishka, you're the lucky boy."

"I think you hurt your pal with that. If you don't live for it, why not leave it here for me? I always wanted to give Violet a go. I think I've got a penis somewhere in this mess."

"You're disgusting, in every possible way."

"Seriously, I'm not the one who grew a fake fucking Violet, you pervert."

"You just wait here, like you have a choice, and I'll have the Cetaceans make you their personal doomsday device. And you can live for eons listening to 'em bicker like you were home again. And when I come back—"

"When you come back, I'm gonna kill that abomination while you watch."

The Sigyn system activated. The ravine shook slightly.

Drops of the Ares began to fall upward from the ring. And then Veikko began to scream. Drops from inside his mechanisms and face began prying their way out of him and up the mass of rotting gore around the power plant.

Veikko clawed at his half eyes in pain with broken fingers that stuck out from his tangled arms and hands. It was a grotesque spectacle. Vibeke shouted over it as it slowed and halted.

"She's the improved system, dumbass. You, but better. Violet always was."

"Violet was a retarded bitch who slowed the team down on every single fucking mission. And you fucking grew a new one! I can't think of anything more pathetic."

"Then I'll find you a mirror."

"Get out of my ravine. I can kill you, but you can't kill me. And this is the last tactical retreat you're gonna get."

Vibeke stood still, seemingly ready to move out. Nel, however, walked up to Veikko and crouched in front of him.

"You think Violet was stupid? You think her love for Vibeke made her inefficient? You're right. But I'm not Violet. I'm not stupid. I'm not in love with Vibeke. And I have no care or love for this world. If you and I ever meet again, I will kill you."

Veikko watched her with his half eyes. She stood and returned to Vibeke's side, and they walked for the spiral ramp out.

"Where are you going?" he called.

"Undersea to find you some friends. Next time you see me the whole school's gonna be here."

Veikko's un-face flexed, like a cringe. Or could it have been a smile?

"Hey, Vibs!"

She didn't stop. She and Nel walked for the spiral out.

"Vibs! You never asked what I hacked you into doing!"

"The nuclear silo, we know."

"Yeah, that's what I hacked you and Violet into doing after I escaped the Geki. You never asked what I hacked you into before then."

Vibeke stopped.

"You hacked me before?"

"Couple times; who hasn't?"

She turned and walked back. "What did you do?"

"Couple things. Like that time you joined in my prank on L team with the fireplaces."

"You're a dick, Veikko." She moved to turn again.

"And that time you fell for Violet."

Vibeke froze.

"Strange," said Veikko, "how you fell for her so suddenly right after she practically raped you."

"You weren't even there, liar."

"I had you on time delay. The hack was on project Serenade after I got sick of Violet's overtures and you ignoring them. I only had to program in some memories, some milestones. Like kissing her after she nuked not-the-Ares. Didn't have to push you very hard, guess you're a real slut at heart."

"I loved her long before Serenade."

"You didn't. You just remember you did. Think about it, and you'll see through it. Did you ever act with the slightest romantic affection for her before Serenade? No. Did you catch yourself flirting back at her for the first time right after? Yes. Did you kiss her the first time after a big victory? Bit out of your character. Did you suddenly want to fuck her a day after your first big argument? I didn't think she'd try to fuck you against your will, but that should make it all the more obvious."

Vibeke stood still, thinking.

"You'd never have touched her after she did that. Not without me. Did it come on quick? Suddenly? I know it did. One second you were pissed at her and the next you had to, what did I have you do? Pin her and grab her hair and reach in her suit?"

It was too specific. She ran her old Valhalla hack detectors on her memories of Violet, of the way she touched her, and—nothing showed up.

"There's no hack around those events; you're lying."

"No, I'm that good. I spread the hack like butter on your ego. Subtly over your entire cortex so our software could never pinpoint it. Scan for the nuke base hack. You'll never find it either. My hacks are flawless, undetectable."

"What are you getting at?"

"Other people are sloppy, their hacks are so focused in a single cortical column you can spot 'em with Valhalla software, remove 'em with a DBI. But making you fuck Violet? That's spread over half your frontal lobe. Just like you spread your—"

"You could've just found out, you spied on us. You had spy nodes everywhere."

"Didn't need to spy on you to know you had sex. How do you think I knew the second I saw you?"

Vibeke felt cold. She had no idea if it were true. She had no way of learning.

"You could have guessed."

"You don't believe that anymore." The remains of the muscles that would've made him smile flexed. "You figured it out. And you, a Valkyrie, thought you couldn't live without her. So much you made a new one. I guess someone overshot it. Come on, Vibs, hacking minds is a way of life for us. A way of war. You should thank me I used it to make you two happy. And when in your life have you *ever* been happy? You must believe it now."

"You're a liar, Veikko. I don't believe squat."

"You're a *bad* liar, Vibs. You know I'm telling the truth. The love of your life is one of my lies. I forged it like a dime-store Mona Lisa, smile and all."

Vibeke's hands shook.

"And what I found in that sad mass you call your brain while I was in there. Oof. Jacking off to Mishka even after she betrayed—"

Vibeke marched toward him, the mess of him. "You're fucking dead!"

Veikko waved a partly assembled finger at her. "Ends the world, Vibs."

"Fuck the world."

She pulled her microwave and held it on his face.

"You won't. You don't have it in you. I know, I was there."

She switched it to a killing burn.

"I'm not even scared," he laughed.

Nel pounced on him and pinned him to the Sigyn ring.

"But you know Violet would, don't you?"

She punched into the mass of mechanics and grabbed his organic tissue and pulled. He gurgled in pain.

"And you have no idea what I'm capable of. Hell, even I don't know. But I know this hurts"—she pulled harder—"and I know if you say one more word to Vibeke, I'll leave my hand clamped here until the fish arrive. Got it?"

Veikko gurgled in the affirmative.

"You are lying, aren't you? Don't say it, it doesn't even matter. Violet loved her from the start, and you didn't hack that. And you didn't hack me."

Vibeke's mind flipped from Veikko to Nel. He didn't hack Nel. What did Nel mean she felt for her?

"The fish are gonna fix this ravine and make you disposable real soon, Veikko. And when they do, they're gonna give you to me. Then you're gonna pay."

She let go of his guts and turned to Vibeke. She put her hand on Vibeke's hip and gently escorted her to the walkway.

"You…. You overgrown fucking cunt plug! You're a glorified dildo, 'Nel.' Nelson, you were a lame bug, and your mom was a shit Valkyrie!"

Nel and Vibeke kept walking.

"Fucking meat puppet! Worthless gizmo bitch! Bring the fish! I'll break out and beat the shit out of you! I'll hack you to pain eternal. Vibeke! You know I did it! You owe me every orgasm!"

They could barely hear him as they ascended.

"You're a pathetic fucking twat. You'll never convince the fish! Just try! I'll get you, Vibeke, and your little bot too!"

Veikko's curses grew distant and inaudible as they reached the walrus trap. Vibeke cautiously opened the door.

"What are you looking for?"

"Orson."

Nel checked Violet's memories and saw the giant beast. It matched the one charging them from an alcove down the walkway. She tapped Vibeke and alerted her.

"Microwave it!" she shouted.

"No," replied Nel.

"What?"

Nel laughed, "I'm not gonna fry a walrus. Besides it would take a month for the beam to get through all that blubber."

"Just kill that thing!"

"It's a walrus."

Orson reached them but Nel held her ground. Orson stopped short of hitting her and barked.

"See? He's harmless."

"He's a fucking monster."

"You're just a wimp."

She reached up and rubbed his chin.

"I wouldn't do—"

Orson regurgitated half a ton of half-digested rotting carrion onto Nel. He spat the last drops at her and then wandered off. She looked to Vibeke, who was trying very hard not to burst out laughing.

Nel began shoveling the goop off herself and stared daggers at her. "Didn't you just learn the love of your life was a forgery?"

Vibeke laughed out loud, "Yeah, but that was totally worth it."

Nel continued flicking and flinging the stinking mess off of herself as the two walked out into the snow.

THE GEKI spotted the Arctic Cathedral from kilometers away. They floated toward it on jump residue.

They passed over roads full of diseased bodies praying, wailing, some cutting themselves. Bonfires of men and women burned alive. The horror of it pierced Varg and made him feel his own Farnesene Pulse. They saw one man enraptured with his hands toward the sky. He was laughing, ecstatic despite the pulse.

"What are you possibly happy about?" Varg asked.

"His love! God is love!" the man exclaimed.

"Best not to talk to them," said the elder.

They continued on in silence. By the roadside there were bodies strewn about with various fatal wounds. Torture marks. It took them a moment to realize that most were children.

They approached a muffled howling sound. When they came within sight of it, even the elder stopped. It was a boy tied to a lamp post, bound and gagged. A priest stood before him with a torch. He touched it to the child over and over while uttering prayers. He begged God to forgive the child.

"What did he do?" asked the elder.

"He would not confess."

"Confess to what?"

"He touched himself. Polluted himself."

The elder hit him with a bolt of fire, disintegrating him. Another spark released the gag.

"Angels!" shouted the boy, terrified.

"No, there are no angels."

"You can't say that! They'll kill you!"

"Let 'em try."

"They'll do worse!"

"What's worse?"

The kid didn't speak. He looked down. Varg noticed blood on his underwear. He'd been castrated.

"Jesus," said Varg in disgust.

"Jesus! Jesus! Come unto Jesus!" cried a lone, burnt walker.

The elder Geki incinerated him with his flame. They floated on. Varg began growing numb to the sights.

They came to the Arctic Cathedral, a giant white church, now half-encrusted in gold. An ancient building renovated by slave labor to suit Mishka's purposes. Hundreds of men and women outside were hit by the pulse; most stood petrified. Some bowed and prayed. The Geki came down to the ground and walked straight to the front door.

The Geki entered and found the main hall empty, except for one woman. She stood, seemingly unafraid. They knew it affected her. She could posture all she wanted, but she was feeling it. They had her. In a rarity, she spoke first.

"I've been expecting you."

"This ends now, Mishka."

"Voivod Suvorova to you."

"We do not recognize your titles. Only your actions, for which you will pay."

"I think not."

"You think wrong."

The elder Geki started a fire in his palm.

"Shouldn't you both be able to do that?" Her voice quivered. She was scared to death, but she was fighting back. "No? Someone is missing an implant, aren't they?"

She hurled a fireball at both. The elder snuffed it out with his flame, but she fired again. While extinguishing the fire, he couldn't hurl his own. Mishka showed off. She produced complex fire forms that attacked them from every angle. They were tactically matched.

"To the ruins!"

The Geki jumped away.

Mishka put out the fires that had started in the church and blew out the flame in her hand. Her last acquisition from Veikko and Skadi had proven a brilliant steal.

VIBEKE WAS overjoyed to be back on the pure white surface after the grunge and insult of the ravine. Nel still stank like stomach acid and an open grave, but she could at least rub herself down with fresh snow.

They were warm inside their furry armor and ready to walk 2000km south to Umeå, the nearest known portal to the Cetaceans. It was a months-long walk in arctic weather, over an ice bridge to Europe and then through the northern Suomi terrain. There was nothing to do but talk, and no fear of speaking to each other any longer. After meeting with Veikko, their conversations on the way seemed utterly normal.

"Have you ever seen a real hairball?"

"No," Vibeke answered. "Never seen a real cat."

"Violet visited a reserve once. That's all she remembered of it."

"A hairball?"

"One of the cats coughed it up as she and her parents watched. 'K-hek k-hek k-hek,' and then it just fell out. It smelled like poop."

"Dang, I'm glad you told me."

"That's this brain for you. Things just come up."

"It's okay. Mine does the same thing."

Nel wondered if she should ask about the voice, but Violet's memories of dialogue on the matter of voices were always predecessors to mental recalibration. If you heard voices that weren't from the link, you were insane. Nel knew she wouldn't get committed to a mental hospital but didn't want Vibeke to think she was nuts.

It was perplexing as to why. Violet's memories contained next to nothing of concern for how people perceived her. Nel had no reason to either. So what in her cared what Vibeke thought? It couldn't have been the brain; it couldn't have been the AI using it. Something new was developing. Nel realized she was growing a personality. It occurred to her that she could shape it, make of herself what she wanted. Violet was, as far as Nel could understand, a very sardonic creature. Sardonic didn't appeal to Nel so much as an abstract sense of being that worked on another principle. One that had no name Violet had ever heard, no name programmed into her recognition matrix. She surveyed her wants, her interests. She found herself compelled by her brain to say something. She let it out mostly just to see what it was.

"It doesn't matter, you know. If he hacked you."

"Can we not talk about that, Nel?"

"If we don't talk, you won't understand how little it means."

"What, you're an expert on psychology now?"

"You still loved her no matter what. Just because Veikko—"

"He didn't! He was fucking lying! Don't fall for it."

"I haven't. There's an 87 percent likelihood he was lying."

"You calculated that?"

"Yes, it's unlikely he was able to hack you in such a manner."

Vibeke exhaled and thought. They traversed fifty kilometers in silence, pushing through the deep snow. Their suits kept them at a perfect heat, except for their faces, which were a bit chilly with only body heat fields to keep them protected.

"You can lie, can't you?"

"Yes."

"Did you? When you said you calculated that?"

"I can also change the subject. Do you really intend to turn over control of Valhalla to the Cetaceans merely to spite Veikko?"

"Spite is all I've got. If you have nothing else to do, whatever you do have is the meaning of your life."

"I envy your lack of purpose."

"It's usually the other way around. Why?"

"I was built for a purpose, but I've failed."

"You've kept me company."

"You created me for love and sex."

"And conversation and fights. I don't know what I was thinking. You have a broken god, a creator who didn't think you through. The fact you function at all is sort of a miracle."

They walked on. The sound of crunching snow and wind permeated them.

"I didn't 'create you' for love and sex."

"Then what am I for?"

"Company."

"If you only wanted company, you'd have enlisted in the army."

"Valkyrie company."

"I'm not a Valkyrie. That's painfully clear."

"Fine, you're not. So what?"

"Seeing the ravine, the real thing from Violet's memories…. I wish very much I could have been a real Valkyrie."

"Well, you can't, so get over it."

"And I can't be Violet, so get over that."

"You're right, it was Violet's company I wanted. I loved her, but she was also my friend. The only friend I had on that level."

"You weren't friends with Veikko and Varg?"

"Sure, but not like her. We could talk about…. Well, no, I guess we couldn't talk about—okay, we didn't really talk about anything in depth, least of all when we were finally together. I guess I had you built because I wanted Violet all those years and never really got all I wanted of her. As soon as the walls fell, she was gone. So I needed her back."

"I can speak with authority on most matters she could have, from her point of view."

"Not the most important one. That was after the backup."

"What was it?"

"Why she beat me down and tried to rape me."

Nel tried to recall Vibeke's memories, but they'd faded. Violet had done something, but she couldn't be certain what anymore. Nel found herself angry at Vibeke for suggesting it could have happened. "Violet wouldn't do that."

"Yeah, well, she did."

"No."

"Yes, she broke my cheek and sent me to the mattress, then ripped my suit off and would've done more if I didn't shock her out of it."

Nel tried to remember Vibeke's memories. It sounded right, but she couldn't accept that.

"Now the probability is that *you're* lying."

Vibeke laughed. "Violet wasn't perfect, you know. Far from it."

Nel spoke against her thoughts. "Nobody's perfect."

"You say it like you know someone who is."

"Yes."

"Who?"

"Me."

"Wow, narcissistic robot."

"Then say what's wrong with me."

Vibeke thought. Nel was cruel, but Vibs deserved that, earned it. She was actually kind not to have killed her already. Vibeke thought hard but couldn't find any human flaw with her; certainly none of Violet's had manifested. And none of Vibeke's own. She couldn't think of anything to say. Just like she couldn't think of why she loved Violet at that critical moment.

"I'm sure I'll think of something after you're dead."

"So you do have the perfect companion."

"Yeah, fine. But I don't have to like it."

"Or like me."

"Right."

Nel stared at her. She was annoyed at her candor. She considered killing her again. It would silence her, but the energy expenditure would be unwise with such a long walk. It would be slightly more efficient to cheer her up.

"You're not the worst possible company. I'd rather be with you than Veikko."

"Wow, you're so sweet."

She'd need Vibeke to feel better than that.

"I'd rather be with you than anyone I've met. Or anyone Violet remembers."

"That's a big shift."

"I still resent you for what you did to Violet."

"But I'm your favorite person."

"You're my only person."

Nel felt good for saying it. She didn't understand why. It went against her basic will to hurt Vibeke. It did quite the opposite but made her feel good for doing it. She experimented further.

"Part of your pain is that Violet died hurt and alone?"

"Yeah, Nel, thanks for reminding me."

"She didn't. I think she died happier and more loved than she ever was before."

Vibeke stopped and stared at her.

"Why are you saying this?"

Nel saw no reason to hide the truth. "Being nice to you was almost as pleasurable as hurting you."

"Almost."

"There are different flavors of pleasure and amusement."

"Which flavor do you like best, making me feel good or hurting me?" Vibeke didn't try to hide her anger at being manipulated. "Try real hard, and I bet you can do both at the same time. An emotional chocolate-vanilla swirl. That'll really cheer you up."

Vibeke walked on. Nel stood still and thought for a moment, wondering if she could formulate a statement to make Vibeke feel incredibly good and incredibly hurt. Vibeke turned to her when she realized she wasn't coming.

"Well?"

"I love you, Vibeke."

Vibeke stared. Nel found herself very amused at the conflict on Vibeke's face.

"You're right," said Nel, "both *is* good."

They walked on. Despite her amusement and outward cruelty, Nel felt a sting of shame when she said she loved her. A sting because she could actually see what Violet might have seen in her. She rejected the thoughts. It was like Violet was alive inside her, making her stupid. She pushed away any scrap of attraction.

Vibeke was less self-conscious. She fell back to look at the robot. They were only waist-deep in snow, and she could see Nel's back and shoulders and arms. Red hair, turning brown, long and messy like Violet never would've left it.

The snow grew lower, and Vibeke found herself transfixed on Nel's butt. She walked like Violet did, hips bouncing back and forth, butt cheeks seemingly rubbing against each other endlessly. She tried to think of Nel naked, think of grabbing her, groping her, fucking her. It felt like medical recovery. Like training a regrown limb. It didn't work right, but there was feeling again.

Another 100km and they found a patch to sleep in for a couple hours. The sun didn't set. They must have been in the middle of summer. But it dipped low in the sky and burned the snow orange, vibrant beyond belief through the deep brown sky.

"Can you tell when something is beautiful?"

"Yes. Though this isn't. This is just orange."

"Then you can't tell."

"You're beautiful."

Vibeke looked at her robot. Icicles in its hair, a thin layer of snow forming over it.

"You're experimenting again."

Nel sat motionless.

"Are you?" asked Vibeke.

"Yes, but it's not a lie. You're the only thing in the world it gives me any pleasure to see."

Vibeke assumed she was playing her cruel game but played along to spite her. "Likewise."

Vibeke was hit by a wave of empathy for Nel. She still didn't let herself think "her." But wondered why. There were no rules this time. And no person to risk. It wasn't a human being she had to treat with any respect. She owed it nothing for Violet's years of fighting by her side, and there was no ravine nor plan nor mission more important than doing what she pleased.

She lurched over and lay against the robot's side. For warmth, she'd say if it asked. And she began to tear up. She wished it were Violet. She wished it with such passion, she felt hot in her suit, on the ice.

She tried to tell herself she had Violet back, as much as she ever could. But it felt guilty, knowing the thing next to her was by every measure someone completely different. Its own personality. Vibs had always felt more for inanimate objects than people. If someone knocked over a vase she'd feel worse for it than anyone she'd killed while working in the ravine. She felt nothing for Darger. But the idea of hurting the machine she'd had built, of having hurt it so much, was heartbreaking. She would have felt better if it had killed her in the panzercopter cockpit, she thought. And wondered again what it meant by "other plans."

She thought about her empathy for broken toys. For digital animals. She felt horribly guilty for making a robot out of Violet's heart. She felt worse for its wounds than she ever had seeing Violet ripped apart or beaten or impermanently killed. She couldn't fathom why.

Vibeke had done more harm than anyone in the world ever had, she thought. She had killed billions. But she felt worse for whatever she'd done to the robot. She didn't sleep well that night. She mostly stared at the glowing clouds that passed above and just focused on trying to breathe normally.

She gave up. She'd given up on everything. She didn't care what the machine would do. It did nothing.

Nel wasn't concerned with Vibs at all in that moment. She was hunting for clarity. She asked an old friend.

"Are you there?" she asked the thought.

"I'm always here. I can't leave."

Nel was amused at the thought. *"If you think you've got it hard because you can't leave my brain, you should see Veikko. He's—"*

"Vibeke?"

"Nel!" she announced herself. *"Veikko?"*

"You fucking bitch," thought Veikko, into her brain.

"It was you? It was you all this time?"

"Why the fuck are you in my head?"

"Oh fuck this bullshit."

"Niide. Niide, he linked our brains directly. Part of the A-1 system."

"How do I turn it off?"

"You shut the fuck up, you abomination."

"You shut the fuck up, you faceless fuck!"

"Oh my fucking God, I can't believe I was confiding in you."

"Like I wanted to hear your bullshit. Just turn it off for fuck sake."

"How?"

"I don't know, figure it out."

"You figure it out, fuckbot."

"I never fucked her."

"So you're a useless fuckbot. Fuck off."

"Fuck you."

"Fuck you!"

"Fuck you!!!"
Her mind went silent. She hoped he'd left completely, somehow.
"Fuck you!!!!!"
"Fuck you."
More silence. He was still there, she knew it.
"Fuck you."
Nel went silent. She could feel the anger in the back of her mind. Veikko still stuck inside her head. She was sweating. Violet's heart was racing. She looked to Vibeke, sleeping. She tried to calm down. But she was sickened. Veikko had free access to her thoughts. She had free access to his. His inner monologue was a place she wished she couldn't be.

Vibeke was resting on her side. She felt sorry for her, having to live with Veikko for so long, and now with his insults and cruelty. Nel decided she very much preferred the pleasure of seeing Vibeke feel good. She decided not to hurt her anymore for sport. Though some notion of vengeance still lurked within her, the pity and empathy she felt for Vibeke were taking over. She gently stroked Vibeke's hair as she slept.

Soon Vibeke was waking up with the sun higher in the sky.

They walked mostly in silence, only commenting that they'd reached land as the terrain, once flat ice, grew rocky and unpredictable. Bare stick trees began to dot the landscape. Every night Vibeke snuggled up to the robot, and it never once asked why or pushed her away.

Nel had begun contemplating her purpose in light of Vibeke's comments. What she existed to do. Vibeke had made her to feel better, so at that time her purpose was to keep Vibeke warm. She allowed it without much consideration. Overnight she broke off the icicles that formed in Vibeke's hair and on her ears, and pressed against her with her cheek to keep her eyes from getting frostbite.

One night as the sun finally threatened to disappear beneath the horizon, they found a house with one wall torn off. It afforded them the first bed Nel had ever seen. They lay down together, and Vibeke squirmed up against the robot as she always did, but was finally curious enough to ask.

"Do you mind when I do this?"
"No, it's what I'm for."
"If it makes you uncomfortable, I don't have to."
"It doesn't. The pressure and warmth are pleasurable."
Vibeke held her tightly and buried her face in Nel's armpit.

"What if I did more?" Vibs asked.

Nel grew nervous.

"I'd not stop you," she answered.

"Why not?"

She couldn't admit the warmth was alluring, more than anything she'd experienced. She wanted Vibeke to do more. "I can feel pity. You're pitiable."

"I can't argue with that."

Vibeke felt like she was betraying Violet. The real Violet. Like she was debasing herself by considering it. But she tried to think of why, and she came up blank. She climbed up the machine's side and kissed it on the lips. It did nothing. She reached behind it and undid its suit. Still nothing. She pulled the suit down, exposing its breasts. Nipples hard in the frozen air. Skin pale and goose-bumped. She kissed its breasts, letting loose on the hot flesh and caressing it with her lips. Finally she laid her head down on its right breast and put her hand on the other. She heard Violet's heart beating and teared up. And slept.

"Kill her."

"Fuck off, Veikko."

"Kill her now, while she's asleep. It's the merciful thing to do."

"I'm not a merciful thing."

"What are you, then? You're useless. You're a fuckdoll that won't fuck."

"I would if she wanted me to. Just to see what would happen."

"You have Violet's DNA. Don't lie. You'd fuck her if you could."

"No. I'd make her happy if I could."

"I can sense lies. You hate her."

Nel considered it. Her anger at Vibeke was still present. Compounded by her regrets for treating her kindly.

"Yes."

"So kill her."

"No."

"You should leave her. Come back and join me. Two of Niide's bodies in the ravine—we'd be formidable."

"I don't know what I want to do with Vibeke. But I know I don't want anything to do with you."

"Useless. You're the worst toy in the bin."

"I'm glad to be of no use to you."

"I was never kind to my toys. When I got bored with them, I beat them up. Burned them. Tore them open to see how they worked. I'd love to do the same to you."

"I'd love to see you try."

"HOW THE hell did she get that implant?"

"We know Veikko lived. Skadi must have saved him. I saw her walking into the arcology as it burned."

"So they took the implant. And gave it to Mishka? That doesn't sound like your pals."

"They must have met with her and arranged a deal, or she killed them and took it. Somehow she got it."

"And disabled the tracking node and organic fail-safes. She had help."

"She has a kingdom. She has all the help she wants."

"We can no longer face her alone."

Varg thought briefly. "Valkyries. They'll want to kill her."

"We don't know where any of them are."

"We know Vibeke was in Orkney."

"Months ago."

"We could try the ravine."

"It is unlikely anyone would return there at this time. I will not waste a jump on an abandoned ravine."

"I know it seems unwise, but we have no other leads. Who knows what clues we might find there?"

"I'll take it under advisement."

"I'm your only adviser."

"I'll sleep on it."

Days passed. Cards were played. The elder didn't mention the ravine again. Varg began to suspect something was hindering him, scaring him about the ravine. On the fourth day, he built up the courage to ask, to demand an answer. Sensing what Varg was about to say, the elder spoke first.

"My daughter."

"Sir?"

"That's who I lost. My daughter."

Varg nodded. They sat in silence for several minutes before Varg asked, "What was she like?"

He hesitated. **"I barely saw her these last couple years before the war. Only briefly, so fleetingly, so meaninglessly. She didn't even know I was there. The last time I saw her before that we—when I left her, I thought she'd break down in tears. I thought she'd die without me.**

"How wrong I was…. She turned out tougher than I ever imagined she could be. Turned out…. Turns out I never knew her at all. I spent seventeen years raising her, and I knew nothing, absolutely nothing about who she'd grown up to be. And once I left her life, I was gone for good and she didn't miss me. Knowing she's dead…. It shouldn't be that different. My life will barely change. Certainly not with my duties as a Geki.

"But I know she's gone and everything is different. Nothing is worth doing. This war, this fight we're fighting, we could kill every religionist, and there would be no point because I'm not making the world safe for her."

Varg watched him. The elder didn't cry. He just looked at his cards.

"I'm sorry for how I told you about your teammate. I shouldn't have told you at all."

"I'm glad you did."

"Why? What pleases you about knowing Violet's dead?"

"Nothing pleases. It's not pleasing. But it's right that I know."

"Bullshit."

The elder played his cards. Varg looked over his own.

"We'll jump to Valhalla tomorrow morning."

Varg nodded.

IN THE morning Vibeke woke to find Nel's skin black with frostbite. She was awake… if she had ever slept. Vibs didn't think to ask. She took freeze treatment plaster out of her Thaco pocket and applied it over her wounds. It was human skin and had to be healed in the human fashion.

"You don't feel pain at all, do you? When I burnt you?" she said.

"I'm certain what I felt was pain," it replied.

"Does the frostbite hurt?"

"Yes, it's extremely painful."

"Then why didn't you brush me away and put your suit back on?"

"You seemed happy. I'd never seen you happy before."

Vibeke had nothing to say. Somehow she was scared by it. She hurried to pack up and get moving.

They found more houses as they moved southward and began to see people from time to time—calm people like those on Orkney, in Kirkwall where the war hadn't touched them.

But then, only a short way south, they found corpses, burnt and half-eaten. Posed in cruel ways in death. At night they heard laughter in the woods. Vibeke didn't touch Nel again for days after that night. She slept next to her, afraid to touch her. Afraid she would let her, or touch her back. She couldn't rationalize it. She told herself she could do with Nel as she pleased but didn't feel it.

Finally they hit the shore of Pohjanlahti, which they could follow to the portal near Umeå. They spent their last night of the journey under a thicket of dead trees.

Vibeke sat up and watched Nel sleep, or simulate sleeping. She didn't ask which, it looked real enough. And didn't look like Violet. Violet always slept with her mouth open, drooling as often as not, snoring from time to time. Nel slept like she'd been stowed in a drawer.

Vibeke tried to force herself to find Nel attractive. She thought it wouldn't be hard, she looked like her lost love, but she forced herself to look at Nel. Not thinking about Violet's heart or memories, but whatever individual being Nel constituted. She looked over her body thinking of Nel's chest, Nel's hips, Nel's face. She owed it to the thing to see her as a unique person.

Then another side kicked in and told her to see it as an object. A simulation running on spare parts, one she'd commissioned. For company, for sex, the robot was exactly that: a slave. The thought sickened her, though. She felt the inanimate sympathy, guilt. She realized she had to see Nel as a person or it would crush her.

"Nel."

"Yes?"

"You don't sleep, do you?"

"I can, I do. But not often."

"But you feel boredom."

"Yes, night is very dull."

"If you could do anything to pass the time, what would you do?"

"Violet would w—"

"No, you. What would *you* do?"

"Whatever would make you happy."

Vibeke thought for a moment. She didn't know what would make her happy. Her only happy memories of late were falling asleep on Nel's chest and watching her butt wiggle in the snow.

She took her microwave and fired at the birch leaves, setting them on fire. She brushed the dirt around them to confine the flames then took off her suit. She reached over and undid Nel's. Nel didn't move. Vibeke gently pushed her over and lay on top of her and kissed her neck, buried her face against it.

"Hold me," she told Nel.

Nel gently put her arms around Vibeke and flattened her hands across her back and sides. Vibeke grabbed Nel's butt cheek. It didn't feel like she'd hoped. It was too firm, only a thin layer of skin and decorative fat over metal. But it was warm, very warm.

She felt happy—alone with a robot, responsible for destroying the planet, but happy enough. As happy as she could be. Nel kept her arms across her motionlessly through the night, the perfect stillness of hydraulics and shape-memory alloy. Vibeke forced herself to think, *This is Nel that I'm touching. Hard under her skin. Motionless. This is Nel and nobody else.*

But the heartbeat betrayed her. It was Nel she was holding. But Nel was also someone else, someone she still loved.

Nel could sense it in her as she listened to Violet's heart. She was still deeply in love with her. If Veikko told the truth, if he had really hacked her into loving Violet, then he was a master of the art like nobody who had ever lived before him.

"I am."

"Shut the fuck up."

"I'm just saying. I am that good. You should see what I just hacked in Ulver's new mainframe."

"I don't care, Veikko."

"You know, maybe I was too hard on you. We are brothers in arms after all. We're both Niide's cyborgs. The only two there are."

"If we're brothers, we're Cain and Abel."

"Violet had no clue who Cain and Abel were. Hell, I didn't until Mishka went on about 'em."

"She picked up some mythology online when she was twelve."

"Good for her. Are you two really gonna get the fish to come for me?"

"That's the plan."

"Bad plan. I know the fish. They won't help you."

"Worth a shot."

"Nothing's worth dealing with those things. Why don't you come back? We'll patch things up between us. Maybe you can show me how we're supposed to fit together, maybe take turns holding up the ravine. My legs are getting tired."

"We don't get tired."

"Metaphorically tired, they detest lugubrious work."

"Leave me alone, Veikko."

"As long as our brains are linked, we're not gonna be leaving each other alone."

"Try."

"JUST HERE for Willie, sir."

Risto nodded. Pytten headed to the aquarium and pushed the unfortunate creatures into their distribution matrix. It sorted them out and gently placed them around the aquarium as Willie waddled from under Risto's desk to hop into the water.

Pytten was about to leave when Risto spoke.

"What are your ambitions, Pytten?"

"I want to be a captain, someday. Sir."

"Not an admiral?"

"Respectfully, not after this, sir."

Risto laughed. "Few would, few would."

Risto continued to observe an Ulver fleet. It was motionless, but their flagship had just docked with a known intel scout. If they were to act, it would be soon.

"Any siblings, Pytten?"

"None, sir. And you?" Pytten regretted asking the moment the words came out. It was surely inappropriate to have spoken so casually. But Risto answered.

"One brother, regrettably. Loki…. A murderer, now on land. Did you know I was demoted once, Pytten?"

"No, sir." Pytten was very surprised.

"I'd just become a vice admiral. My armada was on a mission to observe the undersea movements of a land gang, the Orange Gang. Thugs, nothing more. But among them I saw Loki. He'd become one of their lackeys, beneath even a gang member. Thus I justified to myself that he was not among those we were to observe, and thus he was not subject to the rules of engagement. I sent a detachment to kill him."

Pytten was shocked. The admiral had just admitted the unthinkable.

"That surprises you, I see. Well, it surprised Fleet Admiral Edeltäjä too. I was a rear admiral again before I could say 'Vellamo.' Now in the past two years, a lot has changed. Enough to make me fleet admiral myself. How that happened is another story," he reflected, "but in any case. My brother lived. Never knew assassins had him in their sights before those assassins requested confirmation from my superior."

Pytten considered the tale.

"My brother is still alive, I assume. I've not checked. I never will. He's a weakness to me now. One I will not consider nor seek nor tolerate to be mentioned to me in any military context. And you will not speak of him."

"No, sir!"

"But you are more than my assistant. You've surely guessed that by now. You're my observer. And if you haven't already, you'll be asked to review my acts by the civilian assembly soon enough."

"I have, sir. I've marked you—"

"Not my business. But you are a check and balance. You are insurance that I not act out of petty personal motives again. I assure you I won't, but I'd rather you hear it from me than the assembly."

"Yes, sir."

"You want to be a captain."

"Yes, sir."

"You don't have what it takes."

Pytten felt stabbed in the gas bladder.

"But you will. You will because I'll give it to you here."

Pytten felt less stabbed.

"Nobody lasts more than a year at your job. They go to the grave or to command. You've been in command for thirty minutes, and you've saved the lives of an entire crew. I sought you because you put Bax in the brig. Yes. But your heroic acts are not forgotten or overlooked. You want to be a captain." Risto nodded. "I miss being one. What I do here I do because I know I'm needed. But there's not a day I don't wish I were back on board the *Proteus*, my first command. That was when I was your age.

You've surely noticed I'm the youngest admiral, let alone the youngest Admiral of the Fleet."

"They speak of you as an incomparable prodigy, sir."

"I am. Any modesty would be false, conceit. Edeltäjä named me successor for a reason, despite my mistakes. Audacity, Pytten. Obedience is the beginning of discipline, not the apex. You are obedient, and proper in the extreme. You *are* here for sending Bax to the brig. But you crawled back through a collapsing sub to save his life moments after. That's why I have no doubt you'll be a great captain when you leave."

"Thank you, sir!"

"You're welcome. Don't let it go to your head."

NEL AND Vibeke entered the town and emerged from the high snowbanks. There were no people on the streets. There was no sound but the frozen wind.

As they walked through they came upon one of the town's universities. In the center of its campus was a small frozen pond. In the pond was a stack of thousands of deceased students piled up higher than the university buildings. Warm enough to rot amid the shattered ice, their smell was tremendous.

"The war never hit here, no bombs, no radiation. It has no tactical merit. This makes no sense."

"I estimate thousands if this stack is comprised only of students."

"But why?"

"Violet's memory has no answers. The only mention of Umeå she would remember was in Balder's list of suspected underground Muslim communities."

They stepped up to the great pile. Vibeke examined the bodies. They wore heavy jackets and thick pants; most had hats. No, not hats. Most girls had headscarves. Some boys had skullcaps. The dead students were mostly if not all Muslim.

"They must have come out of hiding once the war began. Then they were slaughtered."

"Who would kill thousands of Muslim students?"

"Christians."

"Why?"

"People have asked that for sixteen centuries."

"You really think this was a religious massacre?"

"A crusade."

"Violet's memories suggest there had been no crusades for a millennium."

"Well, I think there's one now. We're lucky we missed it. This appears to have happened months ago."

"There's nothing we can do about this. We should head to the Cetacean gate."

Vibeke continued to look at the bodies.

"Vibeke, we should go." Nel's voice wavered.

"What's wrong?" Vibeke asked.

"This is a great deal of murdered people."

"So?"

Nel said nothing. Vibeke understood.

"You're sad."

"No."

"Yeah, you are. You actually feel sad."

"So what if I do?"

"You feel fear, and you feel sad seeing people dead."

Nel watched her for a moment. "Yeah. I do. What does that mean?"

"I'd say it means you're only human, but…."

Nel laughed. "More human than Violet."

"Yeah. It's disorienting."

They stood and stared at the bodies.

"You don't hate me because I'm a bad copy. You hate me because you thought I'd be colder than her. More mechanical. You hate me because I'm—"

"I don't hate you. I don't hate you, Nel."

Nel considered it.

"Do you love me?"

"I love Violet. And you're almost her sometimes, and even an echo of 'er is deafening. She was that amazing. I love… I love parts of you"— Vibeke pulled on her own hair—"but not all of 'em are because of her. You confuse me. You're all I've got, and I have no idea what to do with you. Now let's get out of this tomb."

They left the university and its dead behind and headed southeast toward the coast. The sea was frozen over, so they crossed, walked all the way to the Holmöarna, and at their center found Jäbbäckssundet. In the sound was a massive gateway. Purely symbolic, it had no actual gates nor was it between fences. It was merely a marker for the few people on the surface looking for a way down to the Cetacean realm.

But for a moment as war broke out across the surface, it had been the ideal escape, or so it seemed. There were dozens of corpses littering the water around the gate. A massacre of people trying to get underground. Small, minuscule compared to the university. Vibeke didn't imagine it was the Cetaceans or Christians who did it. It must have been a fight between the people about their place in the queue, or something even more petty.

Humans couldn't even escape without killing each other trying. She felt a disgust for the species, a pitiless anger at the bodies. So many bodies at the university. Still so many here. Children among them. They were lucky they never lived to suffer the worse tortures life had in store for them. Vibs thought that if she had encountered them cowering alive on the same spot she'd have killed them herself to stop the pain.

They waded out into the water. Just under the surface, they saw guide lights. The Cetaceans still had electricity. But as she approached she saw it wasn't electric at all. The lamps were something alive, akin to bioluminescent jellyfish.

Vibs expected everything to be lit in blue and was surprised at the sinister reds and yellows that crept up from the gnarled lampposts. Suddenly the ground shook. The water roiled. The real entry gates surfaced, also far from what Vibs had expected. Unlike the smooth and sleek gates from above the surface, their architecture was jagged and brutalist, with visible bolts and patched bronze paneling. Still, there was form to it, at least as much as a saw blade or crab shell.

When they came to the doors, she could see wooden components too. She'd never seen wood carved so skillfully, not outside a museum. The doors were carved with tentacles, and with words: *Ojasta allikkoon*. Neither spoke Suomi, so they had no clue what they were getting into. They pushed the doors open and walked into the gate.

There were no humans or Cetaceans inside. The air stank terribly of mildew and salt. An old wooden portal on the ceiling opened to reveal the nozzle of a primitive scanning device, which looked their way and clicked. Out of water the walls seemed to shrivel and shrink, as if offended by having to be exposed to alien air on the newcomers' account. More portals on the walls adjusted their fittings and exposed speakers.

"*Määränpää?*" said a brittle, wavering voice.

"Uh, do you speak English?" asked Vibeke.

"Destination?"

"Nearest Cetacean village."

"Pohjanlahti Kylä."

"Yeah, there."

"Business or pleasure?"

"Business."

"The nature of your business?"

"Private."

"Insufficient."

"We're looking to start a trading—"

"You are lying."

"We're looking for the Valkohai to raise an army to break into a secret base with the power to flood the world and torment the jerk who lives there."

"Your first lie was better. Go home, humans."

"We need to get in, damn you, open the gate!"

"You didn't even say please. You wouldn't last an hour among us."

"You'll be dead in an hour if you don't open the damn gate," Vibs threatened.

"How utterly human."

The speakers returned to their portals and water began to flood in from the grates at their feet, the gate already sinking. The door opened, but Vibs put up her masks and didn't leave.

"Do you have gills?"

"No," said Vibeke.

"Then you'll want to leave the gate."

Vibeke hesitated.

"I'm not human," said Nel.

"Praise Poseidon." The gate stopped sinking. "What do you want?"

"For my companion and I to be allowed past the gates."

"Dear pollywog, why?"

"We have important business with the Valkohai, as she said."

"There is no such navy."

"My colleague will need to see that for herself."

"Give me one good reason I should let her."

"She will not leave you alone until you do."

There was a pause.

"I really don't understand humans."

"Neither do I."

After another pause the outer door closed. Grates on the floor opened and the water emptied. They sank down into another chamber.

The speakers cleared their throats and spoke. "I'm letting you in, but so help you, be polite to whosoever you meet below. You are most disagreeable monsters, and there are few of us so forgiving as I."

The inner doors opened and revealed another gate. The gate was as ornate as it was offensive to human eyes. Lit in the harshest yellows and reds, it stretched out along the floor of the chamber bed like a vast metal sphincter, as if to suggest they were headed into the bowels of the earth more literally than was palatable.

The oceanic anus puckered and opened to disgorge a small ferry, a sub that floated up to them and rested on the floor. Its hood opened to reveal one seat. Nel waited for Vibs to step in then did her best to pile in on top of her. She could only manage by flattening her torso beyond what human ribs would have allowed. The hood closed. Vibs cursed the Cetaceans.

"Veikko was right, we should exterminate these assholes! For the love of—"

The speakers in the boat unfolded and clicked on.

"Silence your pet, pollywog, or we flood the ferry. Her human idiocy will not be tolerated for the trip to Pohjanlahti Kylä."

"Silence, pet," demanded Nel.

Vibs squinted at her with a sly annoyance and sealed her lips. The boat lifted off the floor and headed into the gate, which closed behind them, sending a cold shockwave of sound through the black unlit water, leaving them blind and deaf to anything but the trilling of the ferry motors. Vibs grew seasick fast as they headed down, straight down and out to the Cetacean world beyond.

Chapter VII: Pohjanlahti

"WHAT NEWS of the Ellines?"

"All wiped out, same as Vladivostok. Udachnaya's safe, all sixteen of 'em."

"Forget Udachnaya, we found Violet and Vibeke."

"You did? Where?"

"We picked them up in Umeå, at the Cetacean gate."

"And they went under?"

"With some difficulty, but yes, they're in."

"We should have killed them as soon as they showed up."

"It was just Kalashnikov's Tikari that saw them."

"Yeah, didn't want to lose it when we knew where they were going."

"Why would they be heading to the fish?"

"Why would they betray us in the first place, why would they start a war? That team is evil incarnate."

"But why Cetaceans? I think they may be done topside. They may not come back."

"Into hiding? It's possible. They fucked up the world enough. Now they're gone."

"We can't follow them there. The fish won't allow weapons. They won't allow our suits. These are probably the last Thaco suits still working."

"They had suits, jury-rigged, but they must have been to Valhalla."

"The Ares? No wonder they're working with the fish. They must have sold them the ravine!"

"So we'd be going to a region they control, or at best where they're honored guests. And we'd have to give up arms to get in."

"If we follow them in, we lose everything."

"We lose tools. Did Alf teach us to rely on tools?"

"We follow them. We track them. We kill them."

"You guys go in the normal way, someone should have suits and some arms down there. We'll sneak in the hard way."

"We follow, you smuggle, very good."

"Works for me."

Valhalla's remains grew animate and headed to a Cetacean gateway on the eastern coast.

WHEN LIGHT returned Vibeke was on the verge of throwing up. It was more red and yellow, not even blending orange but bands of either making the jagged metal boat flicker. With the robot pleasantly squished against her Vibs could barely see the suburbs of Pohjanlahti. There were small buildings like bolted up tin cans, ugly spires like the shells of shrimp and limbs of crabs, all connected by thin wooden lines. Everything was corrugated against the pressure of water or open to the sea. She couldn't see any actual Cetaceans amid the structures.

As they went on, there were more buildings and boats. And ships, subs so vast they just couldn't be called boats any longer. The huge ships sprawled out through the sea, bigger than most of the buildings and decorated in sculptural designs. Designed to travel fast through the sea but all jagged and alien. There was nothing sleek or smooth, only harsh angles and sharp edges, and barnacles like the tumors she had seen growing on faces across the surface. They lent the architecture an illusion of disease.

Then they came to the village. It was all one building, not a huge arcology but something like Ukiyo if it had sunk. The structure was coated with spines that extended to docking ships and boats. It was lit harshly to her eyes. The shapes and shadows of the village struck her as hostile to the greatest degree, all reaching toward her, swaying in the water currents as if alive. As they drew closer, she could see they were patched together from rusting metal or carved from wood. There was no water resistant plastic, no sealing fields, none of the technologies Vibeke would have demanded for an undersea dwelling.

After a long time in a holding pattern around their hideous village, the Cetaceans let them dock. One of the spines struck their boat and, with metal claws, latched on to them, and crudely adjusted its chapped, blistered lips to form a seal around them. Water drained and the hatches opened. A powerful smell of fish and mildew overpowered Vibeke. She almost complained but fear of being jettisoned into the water stayed her voice.

"Thank you for sailing the silent seas with us. Enjoy your stay in Pohjanlahti, and watch your mouth, kid, or you're gonna find yourself floating home."

"JUST FUCKING let us in!"

"Let's not use that word."

"Fuck this shit."

"Oh dear."

"Listen you sick fish motherfucker, lower this gate or we'll rip out the wall and rip out your one fucking lung."

"I am sorry, sir, but I simply cannot allow—"

"That fucking does it!"

Kabar began pounding on the wall. In response it began secreting an oily substance.

"What the bloody fuck is this shit!?"

Katyusha was just laughing, Kalashnikov buried his face in his hands, and Katana just sighed.

"I'm going to have to ask you humans to leave the gate now."

"I will fuck your blowhole!"

"Kabar, just apologize. They always accept apologies."

"I'll apologize when I fillet this fuck and choke on his bones!"

"Kabar," she whispered, "do you want to kill Valknut or not?"

Kabar kicked the incoming water.

"I'm sorry!"

"You'll need to calm down as well s—"

"*I am calm!*"

"He's not kidding," said Katyusha. "This is him calm. You should see him angry."

"Oh dear me."

"Please just let us in," said Kabar, loudly and firmly.

"I'll need some guarantee that your behavior in Pohjanlahti will be more proper than what you've exhibited here."

"What kind of guarantee do you want?" he asked, eye twitching.

"I'd like you to promise."

"I promise my behavior will be more polite in the Payalota than it's been here."

"Pohjanlahti."

"Poe-Yawn-Law-Tea."

"Thank you."

The room went quiet.

"Will our ship be along soon?" he asked.

"Boat. Your boat will be along soon."

Kabar's blood pressure threatened an aneurysm.

VIBEKE AND Nel walked down the gangplank, an enclosed, dripping ramp made of wood and clear kelp, barely protected from the water outside. It led to a small booth just within the village walls marked *Tulli*, where they met a sturdy wooden and metal door, and more portal speakers. They greeted the two with a moaning, shrieking sound.

"We're humans."

"*Antakaa aseenne ja vaatteenne, kiitos.*"

"English-speaking humans."

"Weapons and clothing, please."

"What about them?"

"Remove them and place them in the bin to your left."

Vibs whispered, "Great, it's a nudist colony," then responded, "We need clothing for warmth."

"Proper clothing will be provided, as will a receipt for your... killing devices."

Vibs was about to make a very rude remark but thought the better of it and did as asked. They removed their microwaves and other technologies, and placed them in the bin. The bin receded into the wall as another bin emerged from the right wall, holding a small handwritten slip of paper and two dead animals. With little understanding and less patience Vibs looked at the paper and read it aloud.

"'Numerous barbaric weapons, two tasteless uniforms.' And they gave us... dead seals."

Nel examined one of the seals. It was actually several dead seals, robbed of their innards and sewn together, just skin and blubber.

"These appear to be our new clothes."

"And they call us barbarians?"

They dressed in their new gruesome garb and had to admit it was warm, well fitting, and only smelled half as bad as they expected. The speakers barked out again.

"Enjoy your stay, and stay briefly."

The inner doors opened to reveal a lobby of ancient nautical design. It was again all wood and metal, dripping with raw sea water from the outside, soaked in the smells of sea life and sea food. It was terrible to behold but still carved with extraordinary skill. The wood held decorations and embellishments depicting ancient ships with billowing sails, modern boats and submarines, and many designs that were utterly unfamiliar, extinct sea mammals and bizarre devices.

Standing at the intersection of several tunnels was a sculpture of a Cetacean. Neither had ever seen what one looked like out of armor. The sculpture seemed made of some sort of soft plastic, gray and translucent. It was vaguely humanoid in shape but with distinctly oceanic features. Huge eyes on the sides of its head, all cornea and no whites. There were fin structures all over it, and intricately sculpted webs between the long fingers that held a spear, which seemed more a decorative or honorific spike than a weapon. Nel saw the statue move an instant before it spoke and revealed itself not to be a sculpture at all.

"You are impolite to stare," it said. It took the two a moment to understand that this was a person.

"Sorry, we're... we're from the surface."

"That much is obvious."

They were still staring. They were taken by how perfectly still the guard stood, and by how far from human he—they thought it was a he— had come.

"Can you direct us to someone in charge?"

"I am the guard marshal of this deck. I answer directly to the city administration, who are not available this week."

"Is there any sort of casual meeting place where we might find, uh—"

"The Taravana Tavern is two decks down, but if I may be so bold, you should probably avoid it. Your manners will have you ejected within seconds. May I ask what you need?"

"Valkohai."

"Oh Vellamo, you might as well ask to be harpooned. Nobody in the tavern would excuse such a slip of etiquette as to say that name in public. Were you not young enough to be thrown back, even I would.... Well...."

"Where in this village could we say it and not get harpooned?"

"The Bilge Tank."

"Is that another tavern?"

"No, it is the bilge tank."

"Please, will you tell us where to go?"

"So you humans can say please. I have little to offer, but if you're looking for pirates and fairy tales of so dark a nature, you belong in LeChuck's Groggery. Benthic level, all the way south. Be warned the clientele is not so polite as I am. Hmm, perhaps you'll get along there. Try not to get killed."

"Perfect, thank you."

"You are most welcome. Do be careful."

They walked south only to realize they didn't know how to descend through the decks. They found some hatches marked *Portaat* or *Hissi* or *Silmäpako* but nothing that looked like a way down. They had elected to return and ask the guard when one hatch opened. Several Cetaceans of varying colors and skin patterns spilled out, moaning to each other in a mess that sounded like an orgy of dying cats and drunken nymphomaniac lemurs. They were far more surprised to see humans than the humans were to see them. They all stopped and stared. One moved closer, inspecting them carefully, then stood up straight and shouted in stilted English.

"Howdy there! How is it hanging!"

The rest broke out into laughter, a vocalization recognizable in any species or language. The drunken quintet wandered on their way laughing and making moaning or shrieking sounds. The hatch remained open and revealed stairs. They took them down. And down. The air pressure grew bends-worthy. They came to the bottom and found it without a floor, just a puddle on cold consolidated sediments. Having clearly hit bottom they opened the hatch.

This deck smelled worse than all before it. The walls were in disrepair and the rock floor held enough standing water to run an algae farm, which Vibeke thought may well have been behind one of the doors. They headed south through dim tunnels and past dubious doors with carvings of skeletons and knives, mermaids holding split tails, and on one double door, a morbidly obese human holding an anchor. As they continued they became aware of a noise. It was mostly Cetacean moans, but there were also human vocalizations. All in Suomi from what they could tell, but some words filtered through.

They came to the Groggery. It had the same effect as upturning a rock to find larger, nastier bugs than one presumed to lurk there. There were Cetaceans singing and moaning, dressed in crab shell armor or other dead animals. There were about ten humans there too, but not anyone their age or gender. These men were bearded, fat, and had only seven legs between them. Most wore Cetacean clothing. Some didn't wear anything. But they belched out words, moans and fragments of songs like the Cetaceans. One table was singing a lively Suomi shanty until they noticed the newcomers.

Suddenly silence took over the crowd, and all stared at the two girls. Vibeke tried to think of something to say. She came up short and stated their goals.

"Valkohai?"

Nel cringed. All the human men cringed. All the Cetaceans were in shock; one dropped its glass. Then alcohol broke the silence as one human shouted, "You are not!"

There was laughter but not easy drunken laughter all around. This was sinister laughter, the kind that resounds upon seeing an injured gladiator thrown to lions. One tall and buff Cetacean stood up from his barstool and approached them. He was covered in checkered tribal tattoos.

"You want the Valkohai?"

"Yes," said Vibeke.

"You know what you're getting into?"

"More or less."

"Sit with me."

The crowd broke into more laughter, insane and angry laughter that had a near Geki-like effect on Vibs. The Cetacean put one wet hand on each of their shoulders and took them to a table in a dark corner of the Groggery.

"You asked for Sharks, my good chum. Perhaps I can lure one for you if you're willing to bleed a little."

Vibeke and Nel sat on barrels and listened to the Cetacean.

"You know of course that the Valkohai are a myth."

"So we've heard."

"Then why seek them?"

"Important business. World in the balance. That sort of thing."

"Naturally. Well, let me put things in perspective for you. Have you heard of a clan topside, the Hall of the Slain?"

"We're familiar with it," they said together.

"But being clever, clearly intelligent apes you don't believe in such things for real, do you?"

They stayed silent.

"Or do you believe in invincible fighters who come back from the dead sporting giant living insects inside their chests that fight crime and keep the world in balance?"

"What if we do?"

"No wonder you believe in our equivalent. Let me explain something to you that every Cetacean knows. You can't fit a giant living bug in your chest. You have lungs there. We know it because we remove one to have gills. It's a myth, it's false. A lie to keep children in order. Just like the Valkohai. You should know the Valkohai are a fake because they say they only eat when they catch a human topside to feast on. Have ye ever heard of anyone eaten by a Valkohai? No? Right. There's a secret Cetacean army just like you can have a large louse in your lungs. There isn't."

Vibeke ejected her Tikari and set it to land on the Cetacean's arm.

"It's more of a ladybug. Now why don't you take us to the Valkohai?"

The Cetacean sat still, as still as the guard for a moment.

"What do you want with the Valkohai?"

"To give them a means to flood the entire planet in exchange for dealing with a monster that you Cetaceans unleashed on the Earth."

"What means and what monster?"

"The Ares device and Loki Turunen."

"Loki Turunen?"

"Calls himself Veikko now."

Tull cringed at the name. He stared at them with his small air eyes. He stood and walked to a human at the bar. The human man looked back at them, then spoke again to the Cetacean. Then the human left.

Vibeke returned Bob to her chest with a pang of guilt. She'd used him as she normally would, but it was harder now with Nel in existence to think of her own bug as a body part. Knowing that it could think the same way, given a brain. She wondered for a moment what it would be like to meet Bob, him in her body with her cloned brain. She vowed to use him as little as possible, to keep him inside her chest.

The Cetacean returned and whispered.

"Solomon's gonna get someone you oughta meet. They might be a while, maybe more than a day. I'm gonna let you stay with me tonight. I have a guest berth I'll set up for you, and then you'll meet... someone. But only if you explain something to me."

"Shoot."

"How the *vitussa* do you fit bugs in your chests?"

Vibeke explained her sternum, and the Cetacean showed them the path to his boathouse. He took them out of the Groggery, through a northwesterly hall and up some stairs, through an unlocked gate and into a long thin strand of kelpy clear paneling that revealed the outside sea. They were headed out of the city into one of the suburbs. The strand split again and again, growing capillary thin as they ventured farther from the main arteries and came to their destination: one of the little tin cans in the boondocks.

"Come back here tonight and blow this whistle."

He took a boatswain's whistle from the side of his door and blew three notes on it, showing Vibeke the hand placements. Then he stepped inside.

"Get some food in yaselves. You may have a long trip tomorrow. Food and drink are free anywhere you go, but I wouldn't go far shallow. Humans are half *kielletty*, and you're a rude couple of humans."

He closed the door in their faces.

THE SUB was cramped beyond description. Kaunan team was scrunched together painfully.

"We should've taken the outdoors. T only has three people."

"Shush, the fish could be listening."

"Shit, piss, fuck, cunt, cocksucker, motherfucker, and tits.... No, they're not listening."

Katana laughed. "I thought your eyes were gonna burst."

"You need more sedatives in your suit."

"It's not my fault these fish are fucking supercilious."

"That's a big word for you, K."

"Eat shit, Kat."

"Just let me do the talking when we get there."

"Oh trust me, I'm not saying another word to these fucking fishwives."

The boat docked at Pohjanlahti Kylä and disgorged the team.

"We start at the top and ask every public house about our girls. We stick together. No way I'm waiting for anyone in this maze."

They hit the customs office and were greeted by a shriek.

"We're humans."

"Antakaa aseenne ja vaatteenne, kiitos."

"English-speaking humans."

"Please place your weapons and clothing in the provided tray."

"Bitch, I'll strip for you, but you can have my Tikari when you suck it from my cold dead ass."

The other three rolled their eyes. The speaker went silent for a moment.

"Your Tikari?"

"It's Suomi. For dagger. Bitch."

"Yes—Yes, sir, I speak Suomi."

"Well whupty shit."

"Sir, that's not necessary. If you require your Tikari, I'm sure that—"

"I require it."

"Y-yes, sir. You may keep your dagger."

"Tikari."

"Yes, sir."

Kabar stowed his dead blade back in its sheath and took off his clothes, as did the rest. They got their sealskins and Kabar kept his belt.

"What the fuck are these?"

"Your clothing, sir."

"These are dead seals."

"Yes, sir, from Hugo Bass."

Kabar spit on the wall and pulled on his new clothing. They took their receipts and entered the superstructure. Their entry point held several shops and eateries. They began with the first to the left on the top floor of the open atrium, the farthest point in the entire colony from the Groggery.

THOUGH THE Groggery didn't seem the friendliest place, it had a trait Vibeke recognized. If you sat down to eat there, people knew to leave you alone. It also had humans and was thus proven at least not to kill them on sight or some such thing. So they returned.

Vibeke and Nel sat at the bar and asked what the place had to drink.

"Grog."

"I'll just have water, then," said Vibeke.

"Said we had grog. Didn't say we had water."

"You don't serve water?"

"I can open a portal."

"I'll have two grogs, then."

The bartender filled two greasy metal cups with green fluid from a tap and set them sloppily on the table.

"Is it safe?" asked Vibeke.

Nel scanned the fluid. It was only slightly less acidic than the acid rain they'd encountered previously. What wasn't powerful acid or alcohol was neurotoxic.

"It will work in my energy stores because they run on methyl alcohol. It won't kill you outright if you drink less than one fifth of a liter."

Vibeke smelled it. The fumes hurt her nostrils and eyes. Nel took a sip and nodded. Vibs sipped a bit and felt her mouth go numb briefly, then erupt in pain that shot down her throat and into her stomach. A terrible burp fled her gullet like the acid ghosts of her murdered stomach lining escaping. She felt her absorption implant dissolve completely.

"Do... do you... agh. Do you... ach, churp. Do you have anything to—churp—eat?"

"Fish," said the bartender.

"Anything else?"

"Crab."

"Can we see a menu?"

The tender was getting fed up. "There's fish, crab, fish, fish, or if ordered in advance, fish."

"I'll have the fish."

The bartender set a whole raw fish on a plate on the bar. Vibeke looked around the room. They hadn't been bamboozled. The other patrons were eating whole raw fish and live crabs. Vibeke took another sip of grog and bit into the raw mudskipper.

She ate her fish; it tasted fishy. They drank more grog. It made them groggy. Vibeke felt light-headed and noticed Nel was reeling as well.

"I thought you ran on this stuff."

"It has other toxic ingredients, including—" She hiccupped loudly, then drank more.

For some time they were drunk and lightly happy. The fish didn't taste too bad anymore, and Vibs wasn't thinking about war and death and plans to fight again. With her brain running drunk, Nel seemed almost human, and Vibs let herself forget that she was anything but. Anyone in the groggery might have mistaken them for typical friends, stuck underwater for whatever reason but nothing out of the ordinary.

When filled they walked around the village for a while. They saw Cetaceans and a human or two, and were not bothered by anyone. They didn't offend or provoke anyone by mistake. They just wandered and saw a village that was untouched by the war overhead, safe from the radiation, devoid of rape gangs or cannibals (other than Vibeke) or armies. They listened to the gentle shrieking speech of the residents. It lost its harsh alien tones and became almost musical once more familiar. The more they saw, the less they remembered the priggish introductions and enjoyed the peace. In all her memory files, Nel realized that Violet had seen few times so quiet and calm. Vibs could remember none.

They found themselves in a vast atrium filled with reclining Cetaceans and a few human children. They were all born human. The transition to Cetacean was a long and painful process they all had to endure. Vibeke watched them and wondered what kind of bond that must have formed among them. Surely something akin to pain training and death training.

She watched a couple that appeared to be on a date. An entourage of similarly patterned family followed them, chaperoning. The couple spoke in shrieks and moans that Vibs couldn't begin to make out, but the etiquette they observed was palpable. It struck her somewhere between noble and grotesque. She felt a slight wave of guilt for bursting into their world without knowing a thing about how to act. They must have seemed boorish in the extreme, as if a drunk had wandered into the ravine screaming and defecating on the floor.

The drunkenness brought on by the grog was unlike that of mead. It wasn't an innocent tipsy tone but a dull rumble of malfunctioning muscles and the sound of crickets. There was something impure about it, polluted. Vibeke sat down on a thwart and tried to keep her senses active. Her vision flickered, and her sense of touch was hyperactive. The wood she sat on felt incredibly hard.

Nel sat beside her, arms touching, and she felt incredibly soft. Softer than Vibs would've thought for a humanoid combat chassis. She leaned toward Nel and let the soft skin warm her own. She wondered if the grog contained MDMA.

Nel was breathing heavily, zoned out and staring intently at a blank wall.

"Are you okay?" she asked the robot.

"I am operating within—" She burped loudly. "—normal parameters."

"Batteries all recharged?"

"They are recharged."

"That's good."

"Yes, it is good."

"Use contractions for fuck sake."

"I'll."

Vibeke laughed and hiccupped.

"What do you think of this place?"

"It's better than the war on the surface."

Two kids ran past.

"I can't believe people have those."

"Violet has no memory of ever wanting them."

"Me neither…. What did Violet want out of life?"

"Aside from you she had no tangible wants. She enjoyed a good fight and a mission done well but had no aspirations, at least none she remembers thinking about."

They sat in silence for a moment.

"What was she like?" asked Nel.

"Thought you knew her better."

"But I never 'met' her."

Vibeke looked at her. She was slumped. She looked more human than ever.

"She was ravenous. Ferocious. Angry most of the time."

"She sounds awful."

"To everyone but me. Her team. The ravine. You wouldn't want to run into her as a stranger. She never had time for anyone else. But she was self-conscious around people she liked, people she wanted to impress. I wouldn't say kind. She wasn't a kind person. But she was adorable sometimes. She came out of her shell sometimes."

"She was nicer to you?"

"Sometimes. Everything was sometimes. Sometimes she was flirtatious and lovable. Sometimes she was abusive and obsessed. She wasn't perfect. Far from it. Didn't get why sex was a sensitive subject, why you couldn't be ferocious when it came to that. She broke my bones a hundred times, but when she did it because I wouldn't fuck her…."

"She really did that?"

"Yeah, it's a bad thing."

"I know. I can't believe she would."

"How the hell do you have moral sense?"

"From her memories."

"Then how is yours better than hers?"

"I don't know."

They sat still. Vibeke couldn't figure it out. Nel somehow had more sense than Violet did. The AI must have had something programmed in. But it was a killing machine. There was no reason she should have had such sense.

"You find a thousand-euro temp chip on the ground. You pick it up and consider yourself lucky. Then a guy comes along and asks if you've seen his thousand-euro chip that he lost. What do you do?"

"Kill him so as to cover my tracks."

"Okay, so you're not hardwired to be good—"

"That's not good?"

"Not by any common standards. Okay, you see someone you want to fuck, but—actually, do you have any sex drive?"

"Yes."

"How do you know?"

Nel remained silent rather than admit her thoughts about the girl beside her.

"Okay, so you see someone you wanna fuck, but they're asleep. You know they won't wake up; they're drugged or something. Do you fuck 'em?"

"No."

"Why not?"

"I don't know. But the thought makes me sad."

Vibeke looked her over.

"Well, you're one up on Violet for that."

Vibeke stood up and Nel joined her. They walked clumsily toward a large passageway. K team entered the atrium seconds after they left.

"So you have a sex drive, huh?"

"Yes."

"Who's it for?"

"There's a surprising amount of bacteria and microscopic life living in the corners of this passageway."

Vibeke nodded. "You can see that with Niide's eyes?"

"Yes."

"So you can x-ray anyone just looking at them?"

"Yes. You have no new major fractures at this time."

"Neat."

"Yes."

"Now tell me who activates your sex drive."

"I hoped the grog had dulled your memory."

"Yeah, but evading that question earns you my full attention, such as it is."

"I have memories of numerous attractive women."

"Like?"

"Rebecca, Nachtgall, DeMurtas, you, Gorgo, Luzie, even Mishka still stands out as physically attractive."

"Physically."

"Violet hated her for what she did to you."

"Do you hate her too?"

"Violet did."

"You're an evasive creature."

"Tikaris have extensive evasion protocols."

"I didn't miss you including me."

"I'd not have included you if you weren't meant to."

Vibeke stopped. "What does that mean?"

"It means grog interferes with inhibitions."

Nel kept walking. Vibs limped back to her pace.

"What do you want to do when we kill Mishka? Veikko if we can?"

"We would be wise to escape the planet."

"Yeah."

They found themselves at the end of the passageway, a giant window looking out on the ocean, a few decks up from the lowest. There was life outside, Cetaceans in their element. Vibeke tried to wrap her brain around the village they were in being their second home. The air interior wasn't like a human city. It was more like a garage where they stashed the parts of their lives requiring air. The thought vanished, succumbing to the grog's effects.

"We need to get to that guy's place before we forget where it is."

"Yes," said Nel.

They didn't speak on the way back. They got briefly lost in the corridors outside the atrium, but they found the proper route and returned to the Cetacean's house and managed to whistle the right notes.

He let them in, though the door had no locks, and they retired below. The guest berth had a shower. Both took off their sealskins and walked into the tight space. It was exactly like every shower Vibs had taken with Violet. A thoughtless one. It felt amazing to get the grime off, but she felt nothing else. She didn't turn to sneak a peek at the body she'd seen a thousand times, or lend any thought to the warmth of their proximity.

Only the grog made her lose her balance and bump into the robot, which didn't react. It just went back to washing itself, carefully avoiding its hair. It wanted to keep the red blood-dyed hair, though in truth it had turned more brown long ago. Vibeke wondered what it meant, that the machine wanted a certain hair color.

There were no towels. Vibeke grabbed the bedsheet, but it was made of some sort of water resistant material. There was nothing to dry off with. Of course there wouldn't be for Cetaceans; they had to keep their skin wet. The two shook off what water they could and put the sheet back in place.

The desire to fall into bed and sleep was overwhelming. Vibeke was conscious of it and wondered briefly what Nel would do given her irregular sleep. Nel answered her by falling into the bed first and passing out so thoroughly that her skin panels fell ajar, her arm deconstructing completely as it fell off the bed and left its weapons systems strewn across the deck.

Vibs climbed into bed beside her and reached for the sheet. It wasn't cold, though. Even out of the hot shower, the room was still hot and humid. She looked over at Nel and wondered if she should put her back together. She decided against it, too nervous to touch her at first.

She convinced herself otherwise. It was her robot, and she could do with it as she pleased. She reached over and closed up her arm. It fit back together on its own when she closed its topmost plates. She pushed half her chest back in but then spotted it—Violet's heart. Beating inside Nel's chest. She stopped putting the chest back together and stared.

She pushed open the seams and brushed the ribs aside to look at it. She could almost hear it in the open air, through the transparent plastic pericardium. She leaned in closer and closer, and the sound became just barely audible. She leaned in so closely that when Nel awoke startled, she closed her chest up so fast that Vibeke's hair was caught in the seams.

She immediately understood what happened and opened her chest to let Vibeke's hair free. But didn't close up again. She reclined and let Vibs look in. Pulled aside her left breast and the ribs beneath it to let her look. She understood Vibs was looking at Violet's heart. She felt her breath, warm on her bare intercostal muscles, hot against the warm wet air. The heart started beating faster. Vibeke was overcome; she pushed Nel's chest back together and kissed her on the lips. Nel kissed back. Vibs kissed her again and again on her neck and breasts.

They made out on top of the slick blanket, Vibeke with desperation to feel something good, something familiar. Nel felt something more acute, more profound. She thought at first it was mere form, doing what made Vibeke happy. But the lust she felt for Vibeke was her own, a new variety of want. She rolled over and threw Vibeke to the bed and kissed her neck and her collarbone, then brushed her lips downward to her sides, nibbling and making her squeal with pleasure, then across her hips and down farther between her legs. Vibeke pulled on her hair and moaned, moaning so loudly the Cetacean heard her from the deck above.

He found the moans and shrieks indecipherable.

SOLOMON DISEMBARKED in Itämeri. He got stares right off the boat. Humans were rare in Pohjanlahti but unheard of in the metropolis. He headed straight for the barracks. He traversed the long docking pylons and then the long ladder down to the benthic level and beyond. Deep into the rock.

He headed to Pytten's room and blew the whistle. It was only a few seconds before the door opened.

"Solomon? What are you doing in Itämeri Kaupunki?"

"Here for ye, Pytten. Tully says ye 'ave 'e admiral's ear."

"I do. I best not abuse it."

"Migh' need to. Tully's got visitors. Visitors from 'e Hall o'e Slain."

"No such thing."

"Same wi' 'e Valkohai."

"Tully really thinks they're from the Hall of the Slain?"

"Aye."

"What do they want?"

"They 'ave t'e Ares an' Loki Turunen."

Pytten stared at him. He nodded. He was there about the mythic Ares device. The human couldn't know that name was Risto's brother. Pytten had been told that in confidence, and no landlubber would know. But Tully might. He'd served under Risto himself as special ops on the Proteus. He might have been the assassin Risto sent after Loki. And Tully would not send Solomon to them unless he had serious suspicions of a serious matter. Pytten had seven hours until the next session with the admiral.

It was time for a trip back to Pohjanlahti. Pytten followed Solomon to the docks and boarded his subtrimaran. They sat in silence for thirty minutes. Then Solomon spoke.

"Turunen. 'Ink 'ere's eh relation?"

Pytten only knew to stay silent.

"'En it's 'e Ares tha' so important? What is it?"

That Pytten could talk about; after all, it wasn't real. "A magic tree that can flood the globe. Child's tale."

"Ih Tully sent me for ye—"

"Have you ever heard of a real magic tree that can flood the globe?"

"No. But 'ith respect, s—m…." Solomon paused. He meant to speak to Pytten formally but wasn't certain how.

"I'h sorry, but do I call ye sir or ma'am?"

"Neither is accurate, but call me what you will."

"Will do, uh… Officer. It'll be a bit of a problem if ye e'r get a command, though."

"I suppose it will."

"But, Officer, Tully doesn't—forgive my Finnish—fuck around. Are ye sure this isn't about Turunen? Whichever?"

"I don't know what it's about. But I trust Tully."

"Aye. Tully's a good fish. Love the tattoos."

K TEAM rendezvoused with T team as they made the southernmost point of the lowest floor—the airlock outside of LeChuck's Groggery. Having swam down to the airlock and broken in, T walked in fully armed with their suits and stared at K's sealskins until Kabar grunted at them.

"We've checked near every damn open door in this place and no sign of V. This is the last one here."

They entered the Groggery. Kabar stepped in first and barked as he had in every other joint, "Have you seen anyone like us around here? Two girls?"

Solomon was present. "Aye."

Finally, Kabar thought. "Where are they?"

"Perhaps ye'd sit with us for a drink?"

Kabar knocked the grog out of Solomon's hand.

"Perhaps you'd tell us where the fuck they are before I kill you."

He drew his Tikari. Half the room stood. Tahir stunned half of them with his microwave. Tasha knocked out the other half, leaving Solomon.

"Where are they?" shouted Kabar. "We need to find our friends."

"I don't think they wanted to be found, matey."

"What might change your mind?"

"Oh, nothing might change my mind. Ye can wait here for them if they come back, as they migh', but I'll not be sending ye to my friend."

"You can take us to them or you can die."

"I'll die, thank ye."

"What kind of human are you?"

"The only kind that dwells down here. A decent one. One with scruples."

"We will torture you to death to find them."

"Aye, you'll torture me to death, but ye'll not find them. They were a rude couple, but ye make 'em look like angels."

Kabar grabbed Tahir's microwave and knocked him out with a stunning beam, then applied a bore to his head. With the link dead, he tied in by wire and began to dig through the man's recent memories. Violet and Vibeke, going with a Cetacean. Kabar dug deeper into his memory of the Cetacean. Jeremiah Tull, living in boat 778, the route formulated in the man's head. Kabar detached the bore and unplugged and headed for the home as the teams followed.

"YOU REALLY did it: you fucked her."

"Fuck off, Veikko."

"I fucked her once too."

"No you didn't."

"I hacked her, what makes you think I didn't program her to fuck me and forget? What makes you think I didn't nail Violet too?"

"You're not as good a liar as you think you are."

"Yes, I am. I'm the best."

"You're not a rapist."

"Maybe not. But Violet was. Your brain is a rapist's brain."

"Violet was told about souls once by a kid at school, a kid who believed in them. She never did, but—"

"You do?"

"I don't 'believe' anything. But I'm not Violet. There's something different between us. I'm not her, not at all."

"You're the worst of her. Vibs got the best of her killed, and you just nailed the murderous cunt. That's loyalty for you."

"You're one to talk about loyalty."

"One thing's for sure, if we have souls, you don't. You're the very definition of a soulless robot. You don't have one, you can't earn one, whatever makes us human, you lack it."

"I never cared to be human."

"What do you care about? Vibs? Pussy."

"Both, now."

"Cute, robot. And all the better. I'll take both away from you. I'll take everything you care about from you in the worst way. I'll kill your maker, your lover, and I'll rip out what you love her with."

"Why do you hate me so much, Veikko?"

"I don't hate you. You're not worth it. You're Vibeke's toy. I just want to play with you too."

Vibeke woke to find herself entangled with Nel and victim to the worst headache she'd ever had. There was a whistle at the door.

She shook Nel until she got up and pulled on her sealskins. Vibeke put on the same and walked to the door, opening it to find the Cetacean.

"They're here," he said.

He led them out to a curious, tiny round mess hall where a gray Cetacean with a white belly and a black eyepatch met them.

"Show Pytten your bug trick," said the Cetacean.

Vibeke hesitated, thinking of Bob, but knew it was necessary. She disgorged her Tikari, which fluttered to the table. The gray Cetacean examined it, and then observed the faint slit in Vibeke's chest as it returned.

"So you are something from a fairy tale?" it said.

"We're quite real," replied Vibeke.

"But you're hunting something from another fairy tale."

"We both know the Valkohai are real."

"So we are. What do you want with us?"

"Do you know what the Ares device is?"

"You speak in nothing but fairy tales. Yes, a magic tree that floods the Earth. I suppose now you'll tell me it's real as well."

"It was a terraforming project meant for Mars, and yes, it can flood the planet. Pelamus Pluturus had—"

The Cetaceans made a hissing noise.

"Do not speak to us of that pirate!" said Tull. "If ever the Valkohai were to act, and they have never acted before, it would be to eradicate that bottom-feeding monster. He shamed our kind! He did not speak nor fight for us!"

"That may be, but he assembled the Ares before he died."

"Why do you think he's dead?"

"One of us killed him."

"What evidence have you of any of this?"

"We can take you to it."

"Why would landlopers give us the Ares, if it truly existed? You would be ending your race."

"But you wouldn't use it, would you? You don't kill billions for no reason."

"No, we do not."

"Right now it's under the control of a nasty boy, Veikko, born Loki Turunen."

"If you lie, you know us too well."

"He went renegade and now he's the only thing keeping the Ares from hitting the ocean. We want you to control him."

"Renegade or not, why would you give us control of your fate?"

"Because he's an asshole."

The Valkohai considered it. The admiral would surely want to know about the Ares device. He would surely not want to know his brother was part of the matter. But Pytten had to inform him. It wasn't a decision for an administrative assistant to make. It was a decision for the admiral.

The admiral who had specifically forbidden him to mention his brother. But who had also spoken of audacity. The will to do what's right despite it being against the rules.

Pytten stood motionless before the girls for a solid minute. They wondered if the fish had frozen up, crashed somehow.

Pytten would take them. Take them and face the consequences, whatever they were. It was too important to do otherwise. Pytten couldn't just ignore the intel they offered. It was as critical as intel of the first nuclear weapons, of the first wave bombs.

"The man you need to meet is in Itämeri Kaupunki, in the Baltic Sea. The capital of the Cetacean empire where the Valkohai are massed."

"Take us there," said Vibeke.

"No."

"Why not?"

Nel spoke up. "*Please* take us there."

"Very well."

Vibeke rolled her eyes. "Please, great undersea one, would you be so kind as to take us to the honorable and superior sir of which you speak if it would so please you to do so?"

The Cetacean looked to the Valkohai and spoke. "She's finally getting it, Pytten!"

He pulled a lever on the ceiling and suddenly the home disengaged from the gangplank, floating free into the water. Then its engines turned on and began to propel it southward.

Arriving seconds later, the Valkyrie teams watched the boathouse depart. Kabar cut open the wall of the gangplank, letting the water flood in. T team forced their way out into the sea and tractored themselves to the rock below, then ran as fast as the water would allow behind the boat.

K ran for dry space and headed upward to collect their belongings. T made it into range before the boat's main thrusters engaged and tractored themselves to its underside. Their estimate of the windows and sensor systems on board gave them hope. There was little chance the boat saw the flooded gangplank or detected them at all.

RISTO FOUND his parents' door half-open. Within he found his parents dead. Loki. He knew it was Loki's departing gift. Risto fell to the deck and wept. He shook as he sat up with his mother's blood on his webbed fingers. His father's neck was bruised and black. His mother was impaled on a harpoon. They lay together where they must have fallen.

He called the police and informed them of the murders. But Loki was gone, and they had no power to hunt him on land.

Risto repressed it all deeply. He returned from furlough and threw himself into his duties. And so he excelled, and did so brilliantly. More brilliantly than anyone of his age. He was young, but he was strong, audacious, auspicious. He became the youngest captain in Valkohai history. Then the youngest rear admiral. Then the youngest vice admiral.

Then he saw Loki's face and fucked it all up. He sent Tull's team to kill his brother. Tull requested confirmation, and the fleet admiral heard it. Risto was demoted. He was shattered. He blamed his brother at first, then slowly integrated the anger at himself. His obsession had cost him his career, so he thought for months. He redoubled his efforts, to redeem himself, to show those in charge what he was worth. It worked, and when Admiral Edeltäjä retired, Risto commanded the entire Valkohai armada. His only directives came from the civilian assembly, who showed little interest. And he reported now to the Geki, the terrifying creatures that asked very little. Don't Fuck Shit Up. With the globe at war in a postnuclear apocalypse, Risto imagined they were obsolete. But he'd not break their treaty in any case. All he had to do was protect as many Cetaceans as he could from the effects of the war. To monitor and see that nothing came down below.

He had no idea that Loki—Veikko—had, in his time mutilated in the red empty ravine, used the remains of Alopex to infiltrate the Ulver mainframe. With the Leo programming, he was still a dead-dangerous hacker. With the scraps of net left to him, he had been slowly reeling in intel about Mishka's rise to power, about war with the UKI, and about something he never believed in until he saw it through Ulver's own eyes: The Valkohai.

Ulver's Defense Secretary, a man named Uggs, had been planning a massacre of the Cetaceans. He had found the Valkohai and determined the extent of their forces. He knew the names of their command staff. Including Risto Turunen.

The name hit Veikko like a sore, buried thorn, long infected and neglected. He was bored sick in the ravine, unable to move then unable to leave for more than a few minutes, lest the ravine collapse and deliver the world to the Cetaceans. To his brother.

Veikko began developing new intel on the Valkohai within Ulver's mainframe. That they intended to use the war to seize Ulver land. He had crafted a perfect ruse to send them to battle. Perfect, lacking only one element: he had no way to lure Risto and his navy out of the water to where they'd be weak, where they'd confirm the intel, where they could be slaughtered. Veikko wanted to excise that splinter, but he had only half the equation.

He heard a sound. A voice hurtled deep into his supersensitive new ears. Vibeke's voice. And it sounded like she was talking to Violet. He thought she'd been dead but either way, they were an asset to be used. He only needed to hint to them that he feared the Cetaceans coming to Kvitøya. Then they would naturally, unknowingly handle the rest.

Chapter VIII: Itämeri

AFTER AGES of darkness, Vibeke began to see lights. Suburbs at first, like at Pohjanlahti, then villages like Pohjanlahti itself. Then bigger structures. Industrial zones, factories. Though they had lost their sinister tone, the grand jagged masses of them remained intimidating, intricate and decorated with form beyond simple function. Soon the water was bright, a glow from all the lights collected into a vibrant center, and from the center emerged the brightest, most complex and massive structure Vibeke had ever seen.

The city was so huge it was dug deep into the sea floor but still reached like a mountain up to and above the surface. There it had a dock for topside ships. The structure of the city was akin to an arcology but also strangely organic like the biomass that had taken Paris. The whole thing was in motion, connecting parts to each other and reconnecting them to industrial buildings and various smaller buildings. As they came closer, Vibs could see that the city was in fact composed of hundreds of smaller villages and thousands of homes like the one they were in, all connected and mobile and rearrangeable. The core itself was only a humongous network for organizing and docking the many craft that made up the city.

They docked into a tube system made of the same old materials as Pohjanlahti, but bustling with thousands of Cetacean commuters. Unlike the village, the city was all in a hurry, all moving, all the people and places on their way to somewhere. Once they emerged into the core, they were struck by the sight of shops, markets, and eateries. It was almost like the Internet, but nobody was yelling or fighting. It was almost like the surface used to be, but nobody was paying. It was some sort of barter communism, with no money changing hands. People took what they needed and gave what others wanted.

The Valkohai lead them through endless chambers and corridors, through village bodies and connecting branches. It took them nearly an hour to walk down and east to the first door they came to. And that was only the entry to another network of more exclusive, less crowded tunnels.

As they progressed past more doors with more and more visible security systems, more people moaned greetings to the Shark. Soon they were near the dug-out sea floor. Portals ceased, and they were underground. There were fewer and fewer people, and the few there were seemed less hurried and somehow more serious. They came to a door covered in detectors and speakers.

"The admiral is here. Speak politely. I am not responsible for your demise."

Pytten stood behind them. The door seemed unornate compared to some of what they'd seen. A modest door, carved simply with a lion and anchor, and a name: Turunen. The door had a whistle tied to it. Pytten took it and played a complex code.

Silence, then footsteps. The door opened to reveal a Cetacean man. Also white on his belly and gray on his back. On his shoulders were panels of seal leather with the same lions and anchors. They couldn't read his facial expression but could tell it was an intense one. Vibs tried her best to be very polite.

"Hello, sir."

"Pytten, what is the meaning of this?"

"Intel, sir"—Pytten swallowed—"that you need to hear."

Risto stood silent. Vibs remembered something she had heard from Pelamus.

"Permission to come aboard, sir?"

He stood still. Then stepped back, and waved for them to enter. They stepped into the modest room across the shifting mismatched hatches. It didn't seem like an admiral's office, which Vibeke assumed would be something like Balder's. Weapons on the bulkheads, various trinkets and devices, heaps of papers. Instead the room was nearly barren, with only a few scattered symbols of status and a table covered in communication equipment and one giant salamander, which Vibeke could swear was silently growling at her. She also spotted a large coil of what she guessed were maps. Pytten followed them in and closed the door.

The admiral led them to stools, which he positioned kindly for them to sit on, and they sat. He then pulled up one of his own and sat opposite them. He sat in silence. Vibs ventured to speak again.

"Forgive my ignorance of your customs.... May I ask your name?"

"I am Admiral Risto Turunen. Why did you seek us out?"

"Loki Turunen." He seemed to wince, if Vibs read his face correctly.

The admiral shouted at the other Cetacean, "*Pytten*! *What is the meaning of this?*"

"It goes beyond him, sir, you need to hear—"

"What filth have you spat upon my doorstep?"

"They are from the Hall of the—"

"You would dare to sully my city with these monsters? Why?"

Vibeke spoke up. "The Ares device. A system capable of flooding the Earth. The device would be a powerful means toward defense if it were in your—"

"A myth! There is no such device."

"It's in Kvitøya. Go there and you'll see it."

"Why," Risto growled, "would a she-ape tell us of a weapon that could destroy her kind?"

"Because Loki Turunen is the only thing keeping it from going off."

Risto sat back in his chair as if she'd slapped him. He looked to Pytten.

"Pytten, you are relieved of all duties concerning myself and my office. Report to the disciplinary council at 0900 tomorrow for review of your demotion to lieutenant."

Pytten breathed heavily. "Yes, sir."

"Dismissed."

Pytten did an about-face and walked out of the office. Risto held still, thinking. Vibeke wondered if the information had frozen him completely.

"You were his sisters in arms, I assume?"

Vibeke nodded.

"I am his brother, only by blood. So you came to me to deal with your family."

"Sir, Veikko—Loki caused the war on the surface. He did it trying to destroy the device. We've lost everything. We live now only to defeat him. We beg you to go to Kvitøya, seize the device and kill—or at least capture him. Punish him any way you want."

Risto sighed and considered, holding perfectly still for several minutes. Vibeke waved her hand before his face, but he didn't budge. She was very unnerved by the Cetacean habit of total motionlessness while thinking.

Risto knew it would be as wrong to fail to act because of Loki as it would be to act solely because of his personal grudge. He also knew how difficult it would be to convince the assembly to act when it was the cause of his brief downfall come back to haunt him. And the Ares... it would be the ultimate defensive threat. He had to act.

Finally Risto came to life again.

"Family is responsible for family, good or bad. The three of us are perhaps to blame for all that has happened, perhaps not. But we must deal with our family. You will provide us intelligence on the fortress, and on Loki?"

"Yes."

He switched a device on the table, and it began to whir.

"Then begin."

KALASHNIKOV MONITORED from his Tikari as it approached the door.

"They're meeting with a Cetacean. I couldn't get a good look in the door, but it was marked with an insignia suggesting high rank, I think."

"What are they saying?"

"Repeating: '...one inactive chromatic gateway and one hole that was once a walrus tr—' Fucking shit, she's giving them intel on Valhalla."

"We kill them here and give Vibeke a bore. Find out her plans with the Cetaceans, then act accordingly."

"We have to assume that the Valkohai exist and that's who she's meeting. If they *are* an entire navy, we need more than four Valkyries."

"T team should have found a way in by now. They'll have their weapons."

"Can we contact M team again?"

"Not from here, not in time."

"We'll regroup if we have to, but right now we need to take down V team."

"The intel they're giving.... Kabar, they know the ravine is empty. They know the Ares is intact. Why would they give it to the damn Valkohai?"

"Why would they start a nuclear war? A wave war? V team has been bent on the total destruction of Earth since they came back from Mars. We can only assume they're insane."

"It doesn't add up, Kabar," said Katana.

"It'll add up when we hack into their corpses."

"And if by some miracle they were engaged in a necessary mission?"

"Anything they can do we can do better. As soon as they emerge from the militarized basements, we exterminate them."

THE INTEL ran out. Vibeke had laid out nearly everything, and Nel filled in the last bits. Her tactical mind was flawless, based in part on the same system that once rated their missions by percents effective. Vibeke was intimidated for the first time to have a companion smarter than herself.

A companion she was reasonably sure she'd had sex with the night before. Her memory was tainted green and distorted, though, and she didn't feel like she could work up the nerve to ask Nel what they'd done.

"We will analyze your statements in a committee to convene immediately." Risto flicked a few switches on his desk. "I suggest you wait in the lower atrium you passed on the way here. Then I will send for you."

"How will they recognize us?"

"You'll be the humans."

They thanked the admiral and left his office for the atrium. Pytten was standing in the hall outside the door. They looked over the gray Cetacean, not without a feeling of guilt.

Vibeke started, "I'm sorry we—"

"You did nothing. I alone am responsible for my actions and their consequences."

"Then you have my sympathies."

"I believe I did what had to be done. If my demotion is a result of the sequence of events necessary to secure the Ares, so be it."

Vibeke and Nel nodded, then headed back up the ladders and ramps out of the guarded zone and into the wide room. A guard with the Valkohai paint job followed them at a distance.

Vibeke was certain they were doing the right thing. The Valkohai would keep the device safe and either imprison Veikko forever or find a way to kill him. The events were set in motion. She debated in her mind whether they should simply leave then and start the hunt for Mishka as she sat down on a carved wooden thwart.

She was admiring the sea monsters on its back when Nel spoke.

"Vibeke, do you remember—"

"I don't know what I remember."

"Not with any accuracy?"

"No, do you?"

"No."

They sat in awkward silence.

"Are you lying?" asked Vibs.

"Yes, I remember it all."

"Did we—"

"Yes."

"I didn't say what yet."

"Doesn't matter. We did everything."

"Oh."

"Yeah."

"Regretful 'yeah'?"

"No."

"Well… what we did under the influence of grog can't be considered normal behavior."

"Of course not," Nel agreed.

"So we never—"

"No. Not… officially."

They sat still, both afraid to move. Vibeke finally spoke before the silence grew irreparably awkward. "Not officially."

"No, I have yet to file the proper signed forms."

Vibeke smiled. Didn't laugh, just smiled. Nel smiled too. For a moment they swore they could hear the Valkohai guard groan in disgust.

"So how was I?" Vibs asked.

Nel swallowed. "Good, but…."

"But?"

"You have a serious hair pulling thing."

"I do not."

"You totally do."

"No, I—maybe like a little, but—"

"Full-on hair grabbing and pulling constantly without restraint."

"I'm not—"

"I'm not saying you have an unhealthy hair pulling fetish. I'm just saying if you masturbated to a Rapunzel movie I'd not be surprised."

"Oh my God. Fuck you, Nel."

"Okay, just leave my hair alone next time."

Vibeke huffed and stared angrily at the deck.

"Okay, fine, I won't pull your hair again."

"Does that mean we're gonna to have sex again?"

"If we do it without grog in our systems, it'll mean something."

"Are you afraid of it meaning something?"

Vibeke thought for a moment. "No. Are you?"

"No. I don't think anybody cares about meaning now, about the meaning of anything."

"Right. Hedonism prevails after the world falls."

"Makes sense."

"So if I want to kiss you right now I should just do it."

"I wouldn't stop you."

"And it wouldn't mean anything."

"Nope. Completely meaningless pleasure without consequence."

"Sounds good."

"Yep."

They sat still, each afraid to move toward the other. The guard, clearly disgusted by their sappy display, finally left. They watched him leave and looked down the hall for a few seconds after. Then to each other.

Nel leaned forward to kiss her and pulled her close. Vibeke didn't resist. She wanted furiously to kiss Nel back. To abandon her worries and regrets. To feel loved again by whatever creature would love her. She put her hand on the back of Nel's head, careful not to tug her hair, and sought out her lips.

The thwart exploded. They were both thrown three meters in opposite directions. They weren't dead, and that suggested the explosive had gone dud from the moisture in the air. By the time they landed, both were looking for the assassins. Nel saw a human running from the atrium and gave chase. Vibeke was about to join the chase when she saw the remains of the bomb. It was a partially used blasting repeater, gold plated and clearly from Valhalla stores. She picked it up, noted one charge undetonated, and ran.

Nel was stronger and faster than the man she was chasing, but he seemed to know his escape route well. He adeptly jumped past Cetaceans and their kiosks from deck to deck. She followed every step with superhuman reflexes. Before she caught up she glimpsed his face and ran it through her memory banks. It was Tahir. As she came closer, she could see he was watching her from two of Niide's spare eyes behind his ears. She also remembered that he had rocket launching systems in his artificial legs, seconds before he used them.

Two missiles flew past her and splintered the wooden walls with concussive force. Vibs ducked as she approached to avoid the shrapnel. Tahir was shooting because he was about to be cornered, his escape route having led only so far. Nel was nearly on him when Kabar revealed his presence. He stabbed her with his dead Tikari.

She caught the knife between two panels of skin and deprived him of it, then hit him with the handle, knocking him unconscious and through a partition. She had calculated nonlethal force carefully. Vibs ran past her and spotted Tahir as he joined yet another Valkyrie: Kalashnikov. She had sparred with Kalashnikov once and did not want to try again.

"We're Valkyries!" Vibs shouted. "What the hell are you doing?"

"You're Valknut team," replied Tahir. "We're killing you!"

He launched a vicious assault that Vibeke couldn't defend against on her own. Nel came to her rescue at inhuman speed and broke Kalashnikov's arm. Tahir and Kalashnikov's remaining limbs attacked the couple full force. Vibeke tried to say more, but the fight took over her lungs. They could talk once they were on top. She set another charge on the detonator and slipped it past their rivals, letting it explode feebly behind them, and giving Nel an advantage as the opponents flew shockwaved into her fists. The fight was settled but structural integrity was another story. Leaks were growing in the broad market hallway.

"Veikko fucked us too! We're here to kill him."

Tahir and Kalashnikov looked at her. A wall gave way and water began to flood toward them. They agreed to hear their side of the story. Nel picked up Kabar by his shoulders and ran. The wooden walls began to break down. The five barely made it to a hatchway before water caught up. Nel forced the door closed, and they were left ankle-deep back in the atrium where the first charge went off. Tahir tried to speak as he caught his breath.

"What did Veikko do? Where have you been?" demanded Kabar.

"Veikko hacked us to hijack a nuke to destroy the Ares in the ravine. The nukes in the silo he picked turned out to be wave bombs. When I dismantled them GAUNE must have thought they were launching and retaliated."

"So you *did* cause this war."

"Deal with it. Veikko killed one of the Geki and stole her fire implant. He tried to use it and burned down an arcology. Varg killed him, but Skadi had Dr. Niide fix him. Halfway. He's in the ravine, holding it together. If he dies, if he leaves, the Ares hits the ocean."

"So you want the Valkohai to deal with it."

"They've never fired a shot. We have every reason to believe they'd use the Ares only as a deterrent."

"I don't necessarily disagree. What's that thing? It sure as hell ain't Violet."

"She died on the mission to Dimmuborgir. I had Niide make another one."

Katana laughed, the others looked disgusted.

"You grew a fake Violet? Are you deranged?"

"Yes, I killed fourteen billion people and—"

"More like sixteen."

"I killed a lot of people and grew one that shouldn't be, no offense, Nel"—the robot shrugged—"and now I'm turning the ravine over to the fish. Got a problem with that?"

"A few, but right now we need to deal with the Valkohai."

"We already met with their—"

"I mean those Valkohai."

Vibs turned to see a platoon of very angry Cetacean warriors, who did not look at ease with the humans who had just blown up a chunk of their home. Behind them, unseen by all, something half resembling a spider and half resembling a tantō blade watched.

GORGO MONITORED from her Tikari. "They're all in the brig now."

"Pathetic," said DeMurtas.

"They might have a strategy in being there," said Ragnar.

"Strategy my ass. They went after V, and V fucked 'em."

"I don't believe V is as evil as you suggest," said Galder.

Gehenna looked into her Tikari. "I'm at Qosqo now. It's intact."

"Great, so what?"

"So we may have more allies than we thought."

"Like I said, so what? K and T are already taking Valknut down. What else is there to do?"

"Mark my words," said Electra, "Valknut will prove innocent, and once we know their purpose in doing the things they've done, we'll have ours. Now what news of M team?"

"Still expanding against the old rules. There's Molotov, Marko, Motoko, Moloko, Marvin, Margot, and Magorian. And then there's Mary, Mace, Mist, and Marcus, along with Mason, Massive, Mork, Mindy, and Massif, and Madrid and Morten. M's its own army, and growing."

"Good for them."

"Hellhammer, update?"

"Luna teams are intact."

Heckmallet added, "But stuck. There's no traffic. Nobody's willing to pay for a space flight anymore. We expect Luna and Mars are going to be cut off for decades."

"Lemmy and Lord Worm checked in yesterday. They've got *Old Baleful* fueled up and ready to fly. Laiho and Luzie are trying to fix the *Leeroy Jenkins*, but they say it's mostly compromised. They can't just run screaming into battle with it."

"These meetings are bullshit," said Nails. "There's no point anymore. No ravine, no civilization, only ruin. I think we should go back to my original plan and—"

"We are not having an orgy until we all die of exhaustion."

"I'm just saying, with the world over we—"

"I'm with Nail Fungus, we should go out with a bang. A gan—"

"Do shut the fuck up, Flux."

"Death? You're senior Valkyrie now without K here. What say you?" asked Pork.

Death sat thinking for a moment. "We wait for K's verdict on Valknut. If there's reason behind all this, we see their mission through."

"And if they just went rogue and fucked shit up?"

Death smiled broadly. "Then we make them suffer like nobody in this world has ever, or will ever, suffer again."

TASHA AND Trygve were already in the brig when they arrived. Tahir, Kalashnikov, and Kabar were thrown into the adjacent cell, and Vibeke and Nel took the third. Seconds after the bars were locked, Risto entered.

"It wasn't enough you abused my assistant. You dragged the damn war down here with you! You endanger us. You have gone too far, and for what? You're all on the same side, you damn dirty apes! You blew up half the atrium! You breached the wall. A Cetacean would be banished for this! I had to beg the assembly not to execute you on the spot! And we don't even have a death penalty!"

"Sorry about—"

"Silence! You should bow to my damn negotiation skills. I convinced the assembly that there would be more of this if we didn't help you."

"So we have your—"

"What part of 'silence' do you apes not comprehend with your tiny primate brains? Silence! You do not have our help. We will have yours, your absolute compliance as we move to take over your pit. Understood?"

"We'll show you when we get there."

"You won't get there. You will spend the rest of your mortal lives in these cells. We will head north on your intelligence and do the work as gentlemen. You will serve us in gratitude for fixing your damn mistakes, and for not impaling you on harpoons to bait ourselves nine mutant tuna!"

"Sir, forgive our bloody ways, but we are not the sort to be left in a cell when—"

"You want to fight? That's the trouble with you. No one who wants to fight should be allowed the opportunity. War is the domain of men who regret it. It is no place for bloodlust and barbarism!"

Vibs was about to launch a very well-worded retort when Kabar spoke up. He was technically the senior Valkyrie there, and that still felt like it meant something.

"When you're done with Veikko, are we free to leave and take the rav—"

"No."

He left. Now all nine were left alone in three cells of the brig. Kabar spoke softly.

"Wait two hours; then we escape."

"Time to talk," said Vibs. "How many Valkyries are left?"

"Allies are dead or out of contact. We think a couple teams are hiding out in Sogna Valley, but we can't find or contact them. Other teams are probably out there somewhere, but we don't know which or where. Nobody knows who to trust. With the links down its all haywire. Expect other teams to be trying to kill you, though. It was just our luck one Tikari was monitoring your gate."

"Where's Varg?"

"Dead," said Vibs. "He got back in and killed Pelamus; then he died. Then he…. He's dead."

"And Veikko?"

"In Niide's unfinished A-1 system, a monster. Nel here's a real improvement."

"Thank you," she said.

They exchanged stories and tales, possibilities and losses, and filled the two hours. When they were satisfied they weren't being watched and no further contact was likely, they began to devise an escape. They elected not to leave through the door and set Tahir's foot thrusters to work on the ceiling. They cut a large hole into a steerage zone and climbed up. They couldn't be seen. They didn't want to harm a single Cetacean. Those two limitations made it all difficult. There were no vehicles within the city, no air duct system until the ninth below deck, no way outside without being seen by hundreds. That made it all impossible.

They began the impossible by risking a Tikari outing. Vibeke couldn't stand to let Bob out. Katyusha sent hers up first. They made their way in a tight cluster to any spot the Tikari called clear. They made it two decks up in four hours that way. When they saw a sign denoting that the surface was 228 decks away, they decided on another method.

Despite its ergonomic design, the city still had cargo needs. Cargo was handled in bulk by intricate hemp line and pulley systems. They found one such system in a tall chamber that served fifty decks. Kat's Tikari sought out empty crates and found some of the hexagonal masses to be empty and on their way up. They snuck across wooden catwalks and planks and cut into the boxes, and fit inside easily. Then they hoped nobody checked the weight.

It seemed nobody did. The crates were carried up from chamber to chamber, fifty decks at a time. T team detached their oxygen generators and passed them around, allowing everyone to inhale hyperbaric oxygen to combat any decompression sickness. When they were ten decks from the surface they were delivered to a dock. Here the Tikari, still keeping watch outside the crate, saw that they were destined not to leave the city but to be loaded with more materials to be sent back down. When they were delivered at the dock, they broke out of the crates and hid behind several others.

There was no way onto the cargo boat, all the labor was done by hand. They followed the bug the slow way into some dock offices. They were still too deep to survive a water escape, and the crowds were too thick to sneak out conventionally. They couldn't pass for Cetaceans or talk their way clear. They'd have to break through the last few decks.

A klaxon sounded. Their escape had been noticed back in the brig. It was now or never.

Nel and Tahir had tough enough Niide body parts to crack the wooden decks. The rest had strong enough human bodies to climb. They started from the office and burst straight up. They moved horizontally just enough to avoid any metallic ceilings, and made good time. They passed seven decks before Tasha caught a harpoon through her leg. She was in pain, but plus one harpoon. Tahir pulled her up, and Vibeke used the harpoon to ward off guards from giving them another.

More guards assailed them, but the fish were simply no match. The Valkyries were able to defend and move without having to injure any of their opponents. They broke through the last canvas. In the sunlight were hundreds of Cetacean guards.

They were on a platform for human trade and commerce, the tip of the iceberg where humans used to deal a few Cetacean deals and where thousands of them now begged to be let underwater to escape the war and radiation. The guards were all facing the oncoming mob. Nobody cared about the teams. They didn't wait for that to change. Kat took her Tikari in and they ran the shortest distance to water and jumped off the planks and canvas.

After hitting the sea they spotted the nearest human boat. It was an old Ulver boat whose owners wanted to head underwater. All nine climbed on board. Two of them were recognized from the now famous Mouvant fortress security video.

"You! You! It's the girls who assassinated King Kray! It's them!"

Vibs took one by the throat.

"Yeah, does that mean you love us or hate us?"

The man considered carefully.

"I love you?"

"Good answer. Take us north."

He complied. The boat left the begging human masses and headed to Sverige's coast.

Chapter IX: Stockholm

"YOUR BROTHER constituting a conflict of interest, Rear Admiral Taitamaton will be placed in charge of the Ares mission. Taitamaton will control seven subs, four surface ships, sixteen surface boats, two satellites and a pogo squadron, taking them north to secure the Ares, and arrest Loki Turunen by any means necessary. To that end, four more engineering vessels and full material support craft will be joining them. Unless there are any objections?"

"Agreed."

"Agreed."

"Agreed."

"Agreed."

"Agreed."

"Agreed."

"Admiral Turunen, you will remain in your office, monitoring the topside war as necessary, and as is your duty. Unless there are any objections?"

"Agreed."

"Agreed."

"Agreed."

"Agreed."

"Agreed."

"Agreed."

"Lastly we have the matter of Lieutenant Pytten. Admiral, you have stated that he disobeyed your orders regarding your brother, brought both of the assailants into Itämeri, and did not supervise the assailants while they were in the atrium, resulting in its destruction. I believe a most severe punishment is in order."

Risto began to speak, "However, your honors—"

"Agreed, Honorable Justine," interrupted Honorable Keskeytys, "he should be punished in the extreme. If there are no objections?"

"Agreed."

"Agreed."

"Agreed."

"Agreed."

"Agreed."

"Agreed."

Risto began again, "Honorable Kes—"

"Yes, I believe ten years is appropriate."

"Very good, ten years, and shall we suspend the possibility of parole?"

"Yes, I believe that's appropriate."

"Then I don't see any reason Lieutenant Pytten shouldn't begin a ten-year-long term in the stockade forthwith. If there are no objections?"

"Agreed."

"Agreed."

"Agre—"

"I have an objection, your honor," said Risto loudly.

Honorable Häkeltynyt seemed taken aback. But she was obligated to hear the man's objection. "You may proceed."

"Thank you, your honor. If I may, Lieutenant Pytten acted solely with the intent of delivering extremely important intel to myself and, by proxy, this council. As this intel is, as you've declared in this hearing, of 'world changing' importance, I believe extenuating circumstances are in effect."

The honorables had little patience for Risto. "Thank you Admir—"

"*Furthermore*," Risto continued, "Lieutenant Pytten, who is neutrois by the way and should not be referred to as 'he' or 'she,' has served in a fashion so admirable and above reproach as to render your intended punishment an atrocity."

The assembly was stunned.

"I should then say that I would be forced to resign in protest if you were to attempt to declare such a punishment, and in fact, if the assembly does not choose to rescind their comments on Lieutenant Pytten made thus far, I shall still resign in protest. Moreover, if the assembly should attempt to go through with their intended punishment, I must explain they would find themselves at the center of a military coup led by myself enacted solely on the purpose of freeing the aforementioned lieutenant, because the fact is, Pytten is a better person than any of you, and despite their flaws and mistakes, I'd sooner see the lot of you thrown in prison to rot forever than let Pytten spend one second in the stockade, your honors."

The assembly stared at Risto with their mouths hanging open for a full two minutes before any of them could manage to speak.

"I... uh... in that case, Admiral, I uh... feel we should rescind our prior comments regarding Lieutenant Pytten and uh... consider the previous demotion sufficient punishment. For the Lieutenant. Unless there are any objections?"

"Agreed!"

"Agreed!"

"Agreed!"

"Agreed!"

"Agreed!"

"Agreed!"

Risto nodded his head politely and departed from the chamber.

"TOPSIDE, EH?"

"Leave me alone."

"I never will."

"Why?"

"I've been thinking about you. I think I had you all wrong."

"I'm sure that's true, but I fail to see its relevance."

"Don't you get it, Nel? You and I are the only full Niide cyborgs in existence. You and I are meant to be together. Together we can rule this waste of a world."

"Yeah, that's great, one problem—I fucking hate you and you hate me."

"I don't hate you. I underestimated you. Thought you were a toy. You're not. You're the only thing good enough for me."

"From Violet's memories alone I know you better than that."

"You don't know me at all. I've changed. Changed since meeting you. Everything is different now that you exist."

"You're deranged."

"You're ideal. Maybe this is out of line, but I think Violet died for a reason. She died so I could have you. See, there was no woman out there who could love me after what I'd become. Skadi killed herself right in front of me. She was weak, Nel, but you're not. You're strong, stronger than Violet, as strong as I am. And literally cut from the same cloning program. We're the monster and his bride."

"I am not, and will never be, your bride."

"Do you think Vibeke will ever satisfy you? She can't, she can't do what I can do. You've reviewed your body, you know what it's capable of. Imagine the sex we could have!"

"I have enough nausea from the radiation, thank you."

"It's meant to be, Nel. The world ended for us. Violet ended for us. It was all set up for you and I to be together, to reign in this new frozen hell!"

"Veikko, not even if you were a girl."

THE GEKI jumped to Valhalla. Veikko screamed a mouthless scream. Varg and the elder recognized him immediately.

"Veikko?"

"Don't kill me!"

"You killed my master!" shouted the elder.

"Fuck your master! Fuck you!"

"Fuck you, Veikko, you dick!" shouted Varg.

"Now, you will die." The elder raised his hand.

"You can't kill me. I'm the only thing holding the ravine up!"

The elder produced a flame in his palm.

"If I die, it collapses into the rampart void and the Ares hits the ocean."

The flame began to reach for Veikko.

"It's active! Kill me and you end the world!"

They considered it. From a cursory look, he was telling the truth. Logically he'd not be there alone in a stinking pit unless he was bound there. The elder lowered his hand and extinguished the flame.

"Enough! How did Mishka get the implant?"

"Skadi had it." Veikko gestured to a rotten body. "Mishka just took it. I couldn't stop her. I wasn't as assembled as I am now."

Varg looked at him with utter repulsion.

"Where are all the Valkyries?"

"How the fuck should I know? I've only seen Vibs and her robot."

"Where is she?" asked the elder.

"Begging the fish to come get me!"

"Robot?" asked Varg.

"Violet! A fake Violet."

The Geki looked to each other.

"Get out of here! Leave me in peace!"

"You deserve fear. You deserve pain!"

"You deserve a kick in the fucking balls you fucking assholes!"

"Fuck you, Veikko, you fucked up the whole fucking planet!"

"Odin's left nut, just leave!"

"You fucked shit up!"

"You let me!"

"You killed one of us!"

"So did Varg, go kill him!"

"I only cut him in half!"

"Goddamn it, Varg, you—"

"Varg?"

"Silence!"

"Let's get out of here!"

"Now we have to kill him!"

"We can't if he's holding up the—"

"He's lying!"

"No I'm not!"

"Yes you are!"

"Varg, have I ever lied to you?"

"Yes! Like every damn day!"

"Well, I'm not now! Fucking shit can you at least turn the fear off?"

"Oh sure let me just pull the pulse gland out of my neck. No we can't turn it off!"

"Then go!"

"I swear to fucking Odin I'll come back for you."

"Fine, just go!"

The Geki turned to each other.

"Where do we go?"

"To Risto Turunen. If Vibeke has been with the Cetaceans, he's the likeliest way to find her."

The Geki jumped to Risto's office. He was caught off guard but quickly regained his outward composure.

"Risto. We have reason to believe a woman named Vibeke—"

"Yes, she just escaped. Your treaty is not to 'fuck shit up,' is it not?"

"Yes, do you—"

"She has fucked shit up beyond any shit that has ever been fucked in all of Cetacea."

"Do you know where she is?"

"She escaped to the surface not thirty minutes ago. She'll be near the gate. Please burn her to death for me."

"We'll... see what we can do."

They jumped topside and scared the hell out of the masses.

"A woman just burst from here. Where is she?"

"I saw them!" shouted a scared sailor.

"Where are they?"

"They took an Ulver boat, headed to the coast!"

"Thank you."

The rushed gratitude hit the sailor like any other Geki words and reduced him to a shivering, weeping mess. They jumped into the satellite overhead and scanned the seas below for Vibeke and.... Had Veikko really said a fake Violet?

THE FAKE Violet sat under scrutiny of the Valkyries. She envied them. Their training, their camaraderie, their power. She knew she had greater power and all the benefits of Valkyrie training, but she lacked the name, and she was certain that, excepting Vibs, she lacked the camaraderie. K and T teams were clearly disgusted by her. By Vibs for making her. Offended by her very existence.

She had been about to kiss Vibeke. The thought was beyond impossible now. She could tell that Vibeke was ashamed of having made her, at least in the presence of the Valkyries. She wanted to forget Vibeke's disgust with her. She wanted anything else to be on her mind.

"When you were a kid, wasn't there anything that made you happy? Any escape from it all?"

Vibeke stared at her. "Violet asked that before. Don't you remember?"

"I remember she liked your reply. I want to like it too."

Vibs looked her over. Turned away as if not to indulge her. But then she spoke.

"Model kits. I used to build model kits."

"Why didn't you in Valhalla?"

"Violet didn't ask that."

"Guess I'm more curious."

Vibeke sat for a moment, looking at the water. "Had people to kill. It's better than model kits. And has fewer repercussions."

"Fewer?"

"You kill someone as a Valkyrie and that's that. You build a model kit, and you have to give it shelf space. Have to worry about its well-being. Have to defend it when people attack."

"Who attacked your model kits?"

"State review. When they came to the house, they saw my room full of tanks and armored cars covered in swastikas. Didn't care I built Deutsch World War II stuff because I like the angular armor, weird shapes and shit. Just saw swastikas. Pestered my mom, said she was raising me to be a Nazi. They took me and interviewed me, asked me about racism and fascism and other shit I never even heard of because I was like seven. Told me I was 'Aryan.' I dyed my hair black for the first time the next night. Got rid of all my old Deutsch kits, built boring American planes and good moral Norsk defense satellites after that."

Nel looked her over and felt empathy again but didn't shy away from it. She let it wash over her and tweak the way she saw Vibeke.

"I tried to get into it again in prison. They had a model club there, contests and shit. Friendliest people I ever met, in prison or out. I mean, I've never seen such supportive people; they always jumped on board each other's projects and complimented every build, gave friendly advice and tips. Deutsch kits were banned of course, all military. Anything violent."

"So what did you build?"

Vibeke spat angrily, "Ponies and snot! What the fuck are you asking for?"

"Just wondering."

Vibeke huffed. Nel thought she was disgusted with her all the more for her attempt at conversation. She didn't know how to backtrack. Vibeke stared at her. Nel couldn't figure out what she was thinking. The fear of disgust still plagued her.

She asked Vibeke, "What do I give you that makes you keep me around?"

Vibeke thought. "The humanity I lost."

"But I'm not human."

"I think you're more human than most of the real species right now."

"How so?"

"Humankind was intelligent once. Homo sapiens, 'wise man.' We're not anymore. We used to be curious, used to explore, used to care. We haven't since the war. Haven't since before then, not for a hundred years.

Homo stagnans. Homo putridus. Now we're Homo peritabamur. You're the only thing on this planet that has a chance. That has any hope."

"Do I give you hope?"

"If anything did, it would be you."

"But nothing does?"

Vibeke sat still, looking at the garbage and bodies in the water as they sailed past.

"You should find a flight to the moon. Someone's gotta be flying, escaping still. You could live a full life there. Cut off the necrotized foot before it takes the whole leg and learn to walk in low gravity."

"And take you with me?"

"I'm the gangrene itself."

Nel thought to say otherwise but failed to speak. She didn't want to make Vibeke feel better about herself. If she did, she might realize matters were the other way around. That it was Nel rotting her from the inside out. She was afraid. So she stayed silent. The boat trudged toward the coast.

"You're all I have, Nel."

Nel couldn't disagree. She wanted to return that compliment.

"You're a good owner."

Vibeke suddenly looked at her, as if hurt.

"I don't own you."

"You don't?" Nel was shocked.

"You own yourself."

The idea seemed offensive to Nel. And sickeningly lonely.

"If you're not my owner, what are you to me?"

Vibeke stared at her. "I'm whatever you want."

Nel didn't even know what she would classify Vibeke as if not her owner. She reviewed Violet's memories for anything remotely similar. She'd thought of Vibeke as a friend but wanted to own her, possess her as an object. It seemed right that Vibeke owned Nel now.

Vibeke caught her thinking. "What *do* you want?"

Nel was caught off guard. "I want Violet back so she could deal with this emotional bullshit and just use me to kill people."

Vibeke drew back. Nel looked at her, angry as when she was born. It echoed inside her: Vibeke didn't own her. It was like she'd been thrown away.

"I don't want you. I didn't ask for you at all. I didn't ask you to grow a brain for me so I could feel so damn miserable in this gangrenous world."

She could tell Vibeke was hurt by what she was saying. She felt no empathy this time, only anger and the desire to hurt her worse. If she didn't belong to the woman, she wanted her to suffer for it.

"And since when did you care what other people want? You knew what Violet wanted and didn't give her shit."

The instability in Vibeke's face was like an order to push her further. To see if she could make her break down in tears.

"You have the gall to ask what I want you to be to me? I really don't think you want to find out."

As Nel said it, she knew she wanted Vibeke to be her guide to the world.

"What I want you to be is a moot point when you can't even change what you are."

She thought Vibeke was her maker and her purpose.

"You're trash. Debris. The wreckage of what Violet remembered."

She had thought Vibeke was her owner, and it was a happy thought.

"You're a waste, an utter waste."

And Vibeke said she wasn't her owner after all. She thought Vibeke was everything to her.

"You're nothing to me, and *that's* how I want it."

Vibeke was shaking. Not crying. Nel wanted her crying. If she wasn't her owner she wanted her sobbing.

"You're worthless."

Vibeke had heard as much in her youth. That reminded her how she was supposed to react. She slugged Nel in the face with every ounce of strength she had. Two of her knuckles fractured on the metal undercarriage behind her human skin.

Nel was surprised into motionlessness. She hadn't considered in all her insults that Vibeke still had it in her to fight back. She could respect that. Admire it. Her angry streak ended, and she stared at Vibeke with a higher regard than ever before.

Vibeke seemed to recognize it in her face.

"Wan' another, fuckbot?"

Nel wasn't sure why she'd just ripped into Vibeke the way she had. As if the hit had erased her previous rationale and heat. She wasn't sure what to say next. She reviewed Violet's memories, the earliest formations of etiquette she could find. The answer seemed too childish, but it was the only answer she could find.

"Sorry."

Vibeke stared at her. She was supposed to say "Apology accepted."

She punched Nel again and broke her knuckles completely.

"Now pop your fingers open and fix these," she demanded.

Nel did so without comment.

PYTTEN STOOD at attention as the assembly mumbled among themselves. Finally the murmurs ended, and the chief honorable motioned for silence.

"Sävel Pytten. We understand you have been recently demoted to lieutenant and relieved of your duties as Risto Turunen's assistant, as a result of your decision to bring the admiral intel that, though critical, was concerning a personal matter that he had specifically asked you to keep in confidence."

"Yes, your honors."

"This was before the incident in the atrium, and the escape of the belligerents."

"Yes, your honors."

"In light of those events, and some… suggestions… on the part of your superior officer, it is the decision of the council…."

They looked to each other nervously.

"That the demotion will serve as sufficient punishment."

"Yes, your honors."

"You are dismissed. You will report to Commander Kätyri for your next duty assignment."

Pytten did an about-face and departed. Once past the outer chamber doors, Pytten began to hyperventilate. Their knee joints went weak. Tear ducts became inflamed. Extremities went numb. Pytten knew the council must have had something worse planned. Risto must have done something. Pytten had no clue what but was instantly thankful. Sadly, though, the council had every right to determine Pytten's next CO.

"Pytten!" shouted an officer.

Pytten stood at attention. It was Commander Kätyri. Already time for the next duty.

"Congratulations on staying in the corps. It comes as quite a shock to me after your destruction of an entire atrium and direct insubordination to the admiral of the entire fleet. If it were up to me, I'd have put you in the stockade for life for the shit you pulled. Luckily for you that's not up to me. Unluckily for you, the rest of your time in the corps *is* up to me."

Pytten stood still.

"You thought you did your time as a lieutenant, didn't you? Rising up through the ranks, did you think you'd be a captain someday?"

Pytten said nothing.

"You will answer me, Lieutenant!"

"Sir, yes sir!"

"Did you want a command?"

"Yes, sir!"

"Do you think you'll get one now?"

"No, sir!"

"What would you even do in command?"

"I don't know, sir!"

"What would they even call you in command? Sir? Ma'am?"

"I don't know, sir!"

"You don't know much, Lieutenant. You're not gonna be a captain if you don't even know how you'll be addressed!"

"Yes, sir!"

"You're not gonna be captain period. Not with this on your record!"

"No, sir!"

"You're not going to want to be when I'm done with you!"

"No, sir!"

"Do you know what I'm going to do to you, *Lieutenant*?"

Pytten tried to breathe correctly. "No, sir!"

Kätyri drew closer to Pytten's face. Then produced a book.

"You will read this volume cover to cover. You will memorize the contents of this book. You will do so by 1500 tomorrow, then you will report back to me. Is that understood?"

"Yes, sir!" Pytten shouted with exacting care. Kätyri departed, and Pytten looked at the book.

It was *The Complete Naval Compendium of Discontinued Corporal Punishments 1804-2207.*

It was subtitled: *And their possible continued legality.*

THE GEKI appeared on the Valkyries' commandeered boat.

"Goddamn it," shouted Kabar, angry beyond the fear. "Where the fuck were you when the war—"

"Can it, Kabar." The elder Geki moved past him. **"Vibeke."**

The fear hit Vibeke doubly as they said her name.

"Yes!"

"You must kill Mishka immediately."

"Okay! Where... is she?"

"The Arctic Cathedral in Tromsø. We will meet you there. Be warned, she has a Geki flame implant."

"Great!"

"Hurry."

Vibeke thought quickly. Tried to think up the fastest way to get there.

"Can you take me? Blink me there?"

"No, you will need to gather artillery."

"The Blackwing, where did y—Varg land it?"

Varg stood still, staring at Nel.

"Where did Varg land it?" Vibeke shouted. It snapped Varg out of his stare.

"It's in the sea by Valhalla. It will open only on Valkyrie contact, but it's too far away to do you any good. Find Alf's tank."

"Okay!"

The Varg-Geki turned back to the robot. He stood motionless. Nel felt the fear cripple her from the mind out. She wanted to cut herself off from the brain but couldn't move to do it. It was as if the Geki was looking deep into her and didn't like what it was finding.

"Violet?"

"Nel!" The fear was unlike anything she'd experienced. Violet's memories of it didn't do it justice, not by a long shot.

"What are you?"

She shouted to ease the fear, "An artificial intelligence based in a regrown and mechanically modified body with the genetic and memory patterns of Violet as backed up before her death."

"What artificial intelligence?"

"Nelson, her Tikari!"

Suddenly the elder Geki was interested. He looked at Nel directly for the first time and demanded an answer.

"She named her Tikari 'Nelson'?"

"Yes." She cringed and buckled. "Please go away!"

The Geki froze. The fear intensified. Intensified tenfold, growing worse and worse until suddenly both Geki disappeared. The relief was phenomenal, as if a dozen thistles had finally been removed from her viscera.

"Odin's beard," said Tahir.

"What the fuck was that about?"

"They need me to kill Mishka, apparently."

"Why do they want her dead?"

"Why *wouldn't* anyone want her dead?"

"Veikko said she's been evangelizing. She must have seized the region. We saw signs of a crusade in Umeå, if the Geki are involved— Wait, why would they need my help? And why didn't they just take you there themselves?"

"They said she had their flames. They must be evenly matched now. They must intend for you to bring superior armaments."

"Nel is right. The tank."

"Right, 'Nel.'" Tasha stared at Vibeke contemptuously. "You made a fake Violet out of her Tikari? It's a fucking bug?"

"Please don't talk about me in the third person."

They all looked at Nel. Tasha continued.

"I talk about my Tikari in the third person. I'm sure as hell not gonna hold a conversation with a fucking fruit fly—"

Nel was already upset enough after her last chat with Vibeke and the Geki fear. She'd been an instant from kissing her the night before, and now Vibeke was healing from slugging her in the face. She jumped up and grabbed Tasha by the hair, holding her up over the gunwale.

"You are if you want me to put you down."

The other teams merely laughed as Tasha fidgeted.

"It picked up Violet's temper, that's for sure," said Tahir.

Tasha shouted, "Go debug yourself, you fucking gnat!"

"Tasha, I wouldn't. She'll kill you."

"I won't kill Tasha," said Nel. "I've learned a bit since I was a Tikari. Yes, I could kill you right now if I wanted and would if I were a mere Tikari. Tikaris don't have any sense of mercy. They're made to kill. So you better count on me being something more, because if I'm not a damn advanced piece of learning hardware, if I'm still just a pathetic little bug, then you're dead. And I'd love to see you dead. So come on, call me a pathetic little bug."

T team readied their Tikaris; K prepared for a water rescue. Tasha struggled.

"I'm sorry," she grunted.

"Apology accepted." Nel set her down on the deck and skipped over to sit back down. Vibeke watched her with a huge grin and a sense of recovering affection.

"So. That ravine, you know, the one with the Ares in it we all lived in for years? What are we doing about that?"

Kabar spoke first. "K team will find a pogo and head north to observe."

Tahir next. "If we do take it back, we're gonna need more than two teams. T can look into the valley. Vladivostok also had a note from Othala team in the crater. We haven't decoded it yet, but we might find them."

Nel felt vaguely ill at all the Valkyrie talk. Envious.

"And V team? Such as it is?" asked Trygve.

Vibeke didn't hesitate. "We find and kill Mishka."

Nel wished she could talk on their level. She didn't know why she couldn't, but she was reminded painfully by their different candor that she wasn't one of them. She stood and nodded to Vibeke, then headed below decks.

"Well, you have fun with that."

"Alf's tank." Kabar pulled out the end of his link and wired it to Vibeke. "One person can ride inside and one… 'person' can cling on to the back for a long time."

"Then it's settled. T and K will do some good, and Vibs can take her robot-insect-sex-toy—I mean her new friend to kill one lady we haven't cared about in months. Good and fair."

"Eat shit, Tasha."

"We're gonna have to resort to coprophagy soon thanks to you nuking the crops, Vibs."

"God," Vibs argued, "you end civilization as we know it one damn time, and people never let it go."

Kabar called out to the Wolf captain, "Take us ashore!"

"Hell no!" said the captain.

The Valkyries stood and looked at the captain, who was looking in horror at what was on the shore.

THE GEKI landed outside of Tromsø, hidden from the cathedral and far from any people.

"Varg, you have failed utterly!"

"What?"

"You cannot get distracted by a damn robot!"

"I'm sorry, sir, she was—"

"She wasn't Violet. She wasn't your dead damned teammate!"

"I know!"

"Then why did you lose focus?"

"Because I just saw a—are you kidding? How could I not be distracted by a damn Violet robot!"

"I wasn't."

"You wouldn't! You don't give a shit about Violet! You'd have freaked out if you saw a robot of your damn kid."

"I assure you I would not have. And I know all about your Violet. I know her record with Valhalla. I know she...."

"Know she what?"

"I know she'd have made a better Geki than you!"

Varg looked at him, shocked at his strange insult.

"Well, I'm sorry if I disappoint you."

The elder looked him over, furious. He didn't know what to make of it.

"Do I disappoi—"

"Yes, you're a disappointment! Yes, you're a disappointment. How could you not be? I saved your life when I could have saved Violet! I saved the wrong Valkyrie! The wrong damn Valkyrie. I'd trade you in a second to have saved her."

Varg was horrified. "I—I'm sorry you—"

"Don't fucking apologize to me!" The anger hit Varg despite his growing immunity to the fear.

"What do you want me to do, sir?" he asked as calmly as he could.

"Grow up. Give up your insipid regret over that girl and do your duty."

"Yes, sir," Varg said calmly, "as soon as you forget your daughter."

The elder's head snapped toward him in an instant. The fear exploded from him.

"Don't pretend, sir, don't pretend your loss hasn't affected you too."

"You will be silen—"

"*You will be silent*! You, sir! You burned an entire legion of men and women! You burned them for sport, for your own pleasure. You don't want justice or peace. You want revenge! The world fucked you over and took your kid, and you wanna fuck it right back!"

The elder fumed.

"You lost a child you never got to know. One you regret not knowing well enough. That's a hard loss, sir, and you can't pretend it doesn't affect how you've acted. So you'll forgive me for staring at a damn robot of my sister-in-arms for two damn seconds."

The elder laughed sardonically. "I am not afflicted with regret as you'd like to believe."

"Then say your daughter's name."

The elder stared at him.

"Say her name, sir. If you—"

"*You will never hear her name!*"

The elder summoned a fireball in his hand and prepared to shove it down Varg's throat. Varg was soaked through with terror. He remained calm.

"Look at yourself. Look at yourself, sir. You have to be better than this."

The elder froze, fear emanating from him like a solar flare. Slowly he let the flame burn out. He stared at Varg for a full minute before sitting down. Varg cautiously sat beside him. The elder waited for a moment, then spoke.

"So your living teammate made a fake."

"It appears so."

"Why would she do that?"

"She loved her. Never admitted it, but it was obvious from the start."

"From when they met?"

"Thereabouts. Started flirting back around Project Serenade, but there was never any question before that. Vibs loved her, and Violet loved her back before I ever got to Valhalla."

The elder looked down and thought for a moment. "Her Tikari...."

Varg sat silently. The new creation was strange but not unthinkable, not to anyone who'd had a Tikari. The elder Geki would never understand what it was like to have one.

"Tikaris are smarter than you'd think. I can definitely see one hooked into a brain acting just like its owner."

The elder wasn't concerned with that. **"She named her Tikari 'Nelson.'"**

"Yes, sir. I named mine Pokey."

Pokey looked up from under Varg's cloak.

"Sir, why do—"

"No more of this. We must observe Vibeke's progress."

"Should we escort her?"

"We can't leave her and her robot in perpetual fear. We'll meet them in Tromsø."

RISTO'S OFFICE was buried deep in the rock under Itämeri. He was ordered to be there. That left little room for creative interpretation. But he did technically still have an office on board the Proteus. Surely he could monitor the topside war better from his sub, mobile. And if he happened to be observing the recent Ulver movements toward Svalbarð, surely that would remain within his orders.

He knew morale would be questionable on the trip north. He packed his dress uniform. He ordered his most loyal officers onto the ship. All but one, there was one he couldn't order to be there. Who he wanted despite certain errors. Risto was nothing if not resourceful.

Kätyri banged on Pytten's hatch until it was opened.

"Pytten!" he shouted, "Risto wasn't done with you! You have new orders directly from the Fleet Admiral!"

"Yes, sir!"

"As follows!" Kätyri read them word for word. "Sävel Pytten, you know the importance of protocol, you will not violate it under Commander Kätyri any more than you did under me!"

"Yes, sir," said Pytten, hiding a sudden regret within. Pytten *had* broken protocol under Risto. That was painfully true.

"You are absolutely not to join us on the expedition north."

"Yes, sir." Why order that? It wasn't like Pytten had any choice.

"You are absolutely not to stow away on board the *Proteus*, which is docked at the southernmost Vega port until 1300 tomorrow."

"Yes, sir." Pytten was curious about the extra information.

"And you are absolutely not to do so at precisely 0940 when the supply cartridges will be opened and left unattended for exactly two minutes by Lieutenant Värkki."

"Yes, sir!" Pytten replied forcefully.

Kätyri looked over the lieutenant carefully, with utter disdain. Pytten tried not to smile.

NEL FELT a supreme amusement. She realized quickly it wasn't her own. It was Veikko, rattling the corner of her mind. She hated him for it. He felt that hatred. She knew it, but it made him only happier. She felt his sense of joy like a cheese grater behind her eyeballs.

"What are you so happy about?"

"You don't know where you're going."

"Like you do?"

"You're going to hell."

"See you there."

"No, I mean you're going into hell. You don't know what's happened since you went undersea."

"What's happened?"

"You'll find out soon. If I were you I'd kill myself now. Not have to see it."

"Please, please kill yourself."

"Not when the fun's about to begin. You convinced the Cetaceans to come, didn't you?"

"Yes, they'll make a prisoner of you in—"

"They won't."

"What?"

"Thank you, Nel. Thank you. You and Vibs did a perfect job!"

"What are you talking about?"

"Not too smart, though. I've called in Ulver to destroy the Cetaceans. It was a trap. I was the bait, and you were the line. You got them to come here, come here to die!"

"You used us?"

"*I used you. I used Vibs. I used Violet. I used you all. You're just so easy to use! Now the fish are coming to die.*"

"*You're lying.*" She knew he wasn't. "*Good-bye. I won't speak to you again.*"

"*You don't need to! You've done it already! So long, and thanks for all the fish.*"

Chapter X: Guðsríki

HARVARD WATAIN was lost, was blind. Was utterly alone. Mishka's tank nearly ran him over. But she stopped it just in time and, more importantly, took mercy on him and let him ride with her, sitting on its side. They rode to Tromsø together.

She told him about Torquemada, how she was seeking out the church because the church was their only hope in those trying times, those end days.

Together, they joined the church that was growing in Tromsø. Harvard could only listen to Mishka's rise through its ranks. She rose fast, until she hit the glass ceiling. She found it antiquated so she shattered it. Killed the man who'd erected it. Confessed and asked forgiveness and received it.

Her knowledge of spiritual matters like command and assault were valued by the new church leaders and before long, she was one of them. Not much longer, she was the head of them. Voivod, they called her. Leader of the army of Christ.

Harvard stuck by her side. Despite his blindness she valued him. That shocked him. He thought he'd become useless after the war took his sight. But she called him one of her generals. That meant God wanted him too. He was wanted! He was strong in the Lord, and strong in his messenger. What amazing fate had brought him to Mishka? He prayed in gratitude every day.

Mishka confided in him. She explained some of her advantages. It was far easier to convert the masses after the apocalypse than before. When she could point to the nuclear rapture of billions and a dozen other prophecies come true, people were apt to listen.

The severity of it all—the end of the world, the criticality of faith, the urgency of the end times—it delivered masses willing to do the impossible. Harvard would test that for her.

Umeå. It would be Mishka's first test case once she came to power within the church. She had inherited a flock of sheep where once she'd lead wolves into battle. She had to see if the sheep could bite.

So she rallied them as a good shepherd does. She spoke for God, and God's word was inviolable. Unquestionable. Infallible. She didn't waste time on tests. She didn't see how far they'd jump in their leaps of faith. She had to be certain that her newfound power was absolute. She ordered Harvard to take them to Umeå.

Rumors of the Muslims of Umeå—the ideal villains for her masses—were circulating. Muslims denied Christ was the Son of God, believed the heretic Muhammad was a prophet, all manner of absurdities she could rally against. She found that it wasn't enough. So she revealed that they killed Christian children in their blasphemous rites. The crowd demanded no evidence. Without the net to research all claims instantly, they believed what they were told. So she didn't stop there. The Muslims were rapists, of course. Murderers. Cannibals! The ultimate cannibal gang in fact. Who preyed on Christians, who ate their children, raped their women, profaned their hosts. The crowd was ravenous. She set them on their target.

Umeå was slaughtered. Their defenses were nonexistent. Their fight was no fight at all; most merely died reciting the *shahada*. They piled up the dead and headed home, singing hymns to glorify their deeds. And their deeds were glorious—they had defeated the ultimate evil! They had executed every last cannibal and rapist and blasphemer, all in the name of the one true God, Jesus Christ. It was for his glory that they acted.

On their way home, they encountered the 6th Army of Ulver. They were to be wiped out by the evil empire. If it was God's will, they would accept that, but not before trying to save their persecutors' souls. They negotiated. They revealed the nature of their Christ. They preached the word, and the word was received. There was a fight within the ranks, converts versus skeptics. With Watain's crusaders behind them, the converts won and defeated their enemies. They formed a grand Army of Christ.

Their homecoming was to have been celebrated. The first celebration most of them had seen since the war. But they didn't come home. Only Harvard Watain came home. He had survived the Geki fire only because he was a sinner. He had left the camp to sin. That was why God kept him alive: to be redeemed. And to let his leader know what had happened. The crusaders and converts had been martyred, and upon hearing they died in flames, Mishka had a damn good idea of who killed them.

At first she feared telling the crowd they'd died. But she found that they were a better rallying point dead than alive. They were united, united in hatred and in love, the most intimate community that existed in the entire world, all thanks to the Lord, and his presence on Earth. She fulfilled her role as their voivod. Alexandra Suvorova. Mishka to her friends.

There were still threats, of course. The worst was the scientific community. As long as science had a chance of healing the world, there was no need for God.

They were easily dealt with. First came Reinard Harlow, who claimed he could cleanse the air of radioactivity. Blasphemy! Only God could clean the skies. He was executed publicly.

Then there were the Brubaker twins and their working generator. Electricity in those days was a god unto itself. It had to be quashed. Mishka called it witchcraft. Of course everyone remembered electricity. It was a hard sell. But nobody ever said its use in the end times was allowed. She found a scriptural passage, she warped it according to her needs, and the generator was soon mobbed and destroyed, the twins ripped to pieces.

Then there was a doctor named Niide, who could heal wave tumors with the use of a mysterious machine. Mishka knew him and hesitated a moment before declaring his doings the work of Satan. God had inflicted the tumors on those who deserved them, that they might suffer and, in suffering, be redeemed through her church. Cures by machinery robbed them of that right. The doctor was drawn and quartered, his nurses beaten and dragged through the streets. And there were others, plenty of others. All met with public spectacle ends.

But there were two last concerns, namely the Geki. Luckily, as Veikko told his sad, stupid story, Mishka realized that when he had dropped the Geki implant in the arcology, Skadi had scooped it up before the split Geki, if it was even alive, could retrieve it. Skadi had brought it to Valhalla, and it fell beside her corpse when she died. Veikko tried to convince her it would summon the Geki if she ever used it. If they were alive.

Mishka was certain they were. They were immortal by Alf's accounts. Mortal by the Bible's, but frankly, Alf was more of an influence. She examined the implant and dug into its programming before giving it a shot. She removed the location sensors and devoted link, silencing the device just in case its net still functioned in the radioactive sky. She removed the bone fragments and replaced them with her own, cut straight from her arm in the abandoned med bay. And then she practiced. It took a week, scorching her old ravine and lighting Veikko a few times before she got the hang of it. But she mastered it. And she waited for the Geki to come.

They came and she kicked their cloaked asses. And Harvard Watain was there to feel the heat of her flames. For she had dominion over fire. She was a witness; he knew it then, and he would serve her until the end of time.

ALONG THE beach were dozens of tall wooden spikes, each with a naked body impaled on it. The Valkyries stared, silent. Every few spikes there was a wheel, affixed to the top with someone tied to it, exposed to the cold. Nel emerged from below decks and looked at the horror.

A horrible groan echoed from the forest. Nel saw them first, then the others. Men and women, starving and naked, marching among the spikes. They threw a clothed man to the ground. He put his hands together as he knelt, and muttered to himself. Then one raised a knife and swung to behead him. But it was too weak from starvation to cleave his neck. Like a living skinned skeleton. The man ran away and tried to hide in a dead hollow tree as the boat sailed farther along the shore.

They saw gallows with hanging victims, and bonfires that pumped the smell of meat into the air. Vibeke recognized it, that specific delicious stink of fried rapist. They were burning human bodies. Alive, judging by the screams.

Farther up shore they found a tent with dozens of skeletal figures, some wearing black cloaks. Two were struggling to pull frayed cords to ring a bell. And then Vibeke saw the explanation. Crosses decorated the tent. A giant wood cross loomed above it, barely visible against the forest behind.

A procession of living dead walked into the tent, groaning prayers and weeping.

"Well, Vibs, you're hunting evangelists, I guess this is where you two get off."

"I guess it is…." Vibeke was undaunted—the scrawny men and women on shore posed no threat to a Valkyrie, let alone one traveling with a tough robot-insect-sex-toy. Vibeke didn't even stick around to question it. She jumped into the water. Nel followed. The water where they landed was only chest deep.

"Don't forget to say grace!" shouted Kabar. The boat plodded away as the two walked ashore.

"Have you heard zhe good newsh?" asked a tumored man with no teeth.

"Leave us alone." Vibs continued to walk.

"Why do you shreat me sho? I only wan' oo help you!"

"We don't want your help."

"I'm shrying o shave you!"

"Leave or you die."

"Friendzsh!" he shouted, "she will not hear zhe word!"

The zombified crowd took notice of them as they made the shore.

"Who will not hear the word?"

"Satan," called one from the crowd.

"Witches!" called another.

Vibeke tapped Nel on the shoulder; she prepped her arm microwaves.

"Burn them!" called the crowd.

"Strip them, check them for the witch's mark!"

Soon a dozen frail, deformed victims had surrounded them.

"You have one second to back off before you die."

"Blasphemy thy name is woman!"

"They're in league with the devil!"

"Burn them!"

"Burn them both!"

"Burn the witches!"

Nel fired a wide beam and burned half the crowd off of them. Then she refined her beam and fired at the closest individuals, killing them.

"I'm *not* a fucking witch," she spat at the bodies. But the crowd grew thicker, more and more surrounded them.

"Praise the Lord!" they cried in desperation; several genuflected.

"God is merciful! He is risen!" cried others.

Nel began firing more wide blasts with both arms, scorching the closest, but more and more came.

"Are we going to have to kill them all?"

"Probably."

"We're only trying to save your souls!" shouted the crowd. "Repent!"

Nel aimed forward and set her microwaves to maximum and burned a path through the denizens. Vibeke ran by her side, breaking any arms that reached for her. Soon enough they were free of the crowd.

"We love you, our sisters! We can save you!" they called.

Nel fired another wide blast behind them and tripped up the closest wave. They seemed to stop following.

"Jesus," muttered Vibeke.

"Yes," answered Nel, "that seems to be their motive."

"Stop!" called one man, who had followed them.

"No," said Vibeke. They kept walking.

"Stop or you'll be branded a witch, like them," he said, gesturing to the victims.

"Brand me."

The man ran and picked up a brand from a fire. He approached Vibeke and shouted for her to stop again. She snatched the brand from his grip and shoved it burning down his throat.

Nel looked at several burnt bodies tied to stakes. "What did they do to deserve this?"

"He said witches. I have a book on 'em in a partition. Christians hate women. They think they're meant to be breeding machines and nothing more. If women get out of control, they'll burn 'em, drown 'em, call 'em witches, and they can do anything they want to 'em."

"If they kill all their women, how are there any left?"

"That's one thing I never got when I read history. There are so many atrocities killing so many people, but they always have someone left for the next atrocity." She kicked a skull out of her way. "We're gonna survive this war. Humanity can survive anything, even itself. It won't die off. It'll just be miserable. Forever."

"You sound resolute."

"I am. We should kill Veikko, flood this planet, wash it all away."

"I disagree, there's still good worth—"

A tree fell. The men who had cut it down, all bound by chains, began hauling it off. Another man with a doleo came after them, striking the weakest of them.

Even Nel understood. Slavery had returned. Under the exact rules of the Bible, men were bought and sold, and tortured and beaten.

As it happened, they all sang, masters and slaves alike. Fluffy lyrics about a twinkling savior that belied their nature as a field holler. Vibeke felt nauseated. She looked to Nel.

"You were saying there's still good in the world worth saving?"

"It's good I lack a digestive system to vomit right now. That's good…."

"Glad we're on the same page. We kill Mishka. Painfully. Then we end this planet."

"We would surely die."

"After I kill Mishka and Veikko, I have nothing left to live for."

It hurt Nel to hear it. She wasn't enough to Vibeke live for. She wanted to be.

"Nothing and no one?" she asked.

Vibeke caught on.

"Falling for Violet... was the worst thing that ever happened to me. Worse than this, this world. What I've done to it. I know how I feel about you. But it can't be real. Anything I feel for you that might make me go on, that makes me want to live, it's all delusion. A psychological trauma-induced madness. Not real love."

One of the slaves was hit so hard with the doleo, he caught on fire and fell to the ground screaming.

"If it were, how would you know the difference?"

"I do know the difference. Logically. It takes trauma, endless pain, and incredible stress to forge what I feel now."

"But you felt the same love for Violet without any stress or trauma."

"No," explained Vibeke, "I never loved her half as much as I love you."

Nel exhaled sharply and looked at her with the most human expression. She couldn't wrap her mind around it. She'd been unable to even kiss her the night before and now she was—it was impossible. Nel didn't know whether to believe her or not. It was too good. Good, was it good? Too good to be true.

She shed a tear, and Vibeke couldn't even look anymore. They walked into the forest as the burning man stopped screaming.

"She got that line from Sommersby, *you know."*

"Shut up, Veikko."

"Just saying."

THE *PROTEUS* departed on schedule to monitor Ulver movements in the north. Pytten was mashed into the supply cartridges as planned, or at least as Pytten hoped the admiral planned. The only questions were when the cartridges would be opened, and by whom.

Pytten's questions were answered when a midshipman opened the cartridges and whispered as he did, "Pytten, if you're in there, you're to report to the admiral in Auxiliary Engineering immediately." He left the cartridges open.

Pytten crawled out and headed aft. Upon entering the engineering sector, Pytten found the admiral surveying the spare screw field emitters alone. Willie left his side and waddled up to Pytten, limply flopping over on their leg.

"Don't expect any apologies, Pytten."

"None, sir."

"And don't expect any excuse for further insubordination. You will have your orders just as I have mine. I am to monitor Ulver troop movements. I will not deviate from this directive, nor shall my crew."

"Yes, sir."

"You, however, are a stowaway. You are under no such directive."

"Yes, sir."

"You will use any resources not devoted to the ship's mission to observe Rear Admiral Taitamaton's progress with Loki and the Ares. You will report to me here at 1300 and 2300 daily. Is that understood?"

"Yes, sir!"

"Dismissed."

MISHKA CALLED in her advisers.

"What news of the third crusade?"

"They're just wiping out pockets now, lone families and the like. The major Muslim centers have been killed, as have the Thuggee."

"And the Jews?"

"All dead, we believe, there were so few."

"Begin shutting down the camps and preparing them to move into Mongol Uls."

"If I may, Voivod?"

"You may."

"We should keep the camps open and build new ones there. There are too many more groups ripe for imprisonment. The scientists, the heretics, the homosexuals."

"Let's... ease up on the homosexuals for now."

"Yes, Voivod."

"Heresy is the greatest threat to our dominion. Execute five hundred publicly."

"Five hundred who, Voivod?"

"Anyone, just mark them heretics."

"Yes, Voivod."

She headed downstairs. Past the Sunday schools, past the torture chambers, deep into her inner sanctum.

Harvard was there, feeling the ikons. He heard her enter.

"*Khristos voskres!*" he shouted.

"*Voistinu voskres!*" she replied.

She came to him and hugged him. He had to restrain himself not to kiss her on the cheek. It would be too much, and he couldn't let himself be tempted. It is the devil that tempts, and the devil must be rebuked.

He hugged her back and didn't let himself consider the softness of her body when she hugged him. They let go, and he complimented himself. He had resisted temptation. He was a good man, and he knew it. He would be rewarded with eternal life.

VIBEKE SUDDENLY tripped on a starving child. Nel pulled her up. She looked down at the kid. He was gutting dead cats. She stared in disgust, and the child noticed her.

"They're the devil's animals," he said, "but we can eat them if they're cleansed."

"You killed them?"

"No, the grown-ups kill them. I prepare the meat."

"These are probably the last cats on Earth," Vibeke mumbled.

The kid pulled the guts from another. "I hope so, my arms hurt."

Sporadic bodies littered the landscape, rotting, stinking. Not all of them dead.

"Praise him," coughed one. "Praised be he!"

Vibeke kicked him harshly as she passed, bursting a massive tumor on his side that leaked pus onto the soil. The disgust overwhelmed her. She wanted to burn them all. She wished Nel would. But she couldn't say it. To say it would acknowledge it, and she would rather just move on.

"We focus on Mishka. We head for Alf's tank and ride it north. The sooner we get out of this place the better."

"It is a bit like walking through shit," said Nel.

"I love it when you talk dirty."

Nel laughed. Vibeke was surprised for a moment but quelled the feeling, reminding herself that the machine had developed by leaps and bounds in its few weeks on Earth. Humor was the least of what she'd developed. The two walked into the forest toward the marker Kabar had wire loaded into Vibeke's head.

Nel followed close behind her. There were bodies in the forest, dozens strewn about with various fatal wounds. Torture marks. Vibeke felt endlessly thankful Nel was behind her. The sights they passed through were too grim to face alone, even for her.

"I really hate these people."

"Me too," said Nel.

"Hey, finally we have something in common."

"Hatred seems a strange bond for love."

"Seems, hatred unites people like nothing else."

Finally, at extremely long last, the vast field of atrocities came to an end. It gave way to ruins. Burned black on one side. A nuclear blast must have hit not far away. Soon they could see the crater from the epicenter nearby.

"Can you produce a radiophobic field?"

"I already am. My Geiger counter suggests we're safe."

"For how long?"

"We have three days to traverse the area, unless it rains. But it should only take hours."

Vibeke walked faster. Nel followed, matching her pace.

The city remains were clogged with lines of penitents like ants, wandering together, starving. A few stray men and women also wandered, walking but not going anywhere. Vibeke was getting hungry. She walked up to a small gang and stood, her arms crossed.

"Any rapists around here?"

The gang looked at her, shocked and appalled. None spoke. Vibeke kicked dust at them.

One of the men at the corner of the group spoke up.

"It's them. It's them! The murderers!"

There were mumbles.

"The two women who killed Father Sander, and all the others!"

"Is what he said true?" asked an older man.

"Yeah. You wanna die too?"

One man stood. "I have a personal relationship with the Lord Jesus Christ. Would you kill me just for that?"

Vibeke sighed. "Could if you wanted me to."

"I would be a martyr! I would die for my Lord, for he died for—"

"If you wanna die just ask."

"No, I do not seek martyrdom. But I belong to the Lord. You see, we all belong to the Lord, even you. We are all sheep. You have gone astray, but Christ died even for you! He died that you might be redeemed if you only accept him as I have, be willing to lay down your life defending his name and—"

Vibeke got sick of hearing him, so she tapped Nel, who microwaved him. Vibeke gutted him as the others watched and sat down to eat their friend right in front of them. She looked into their eyes as she ate. To them, she was surely the villain. The minion of the devil. The thought gave her great pleasure. She noticed Nel watching her eat, smiling.

When she was done they entered the crater. It was empty, just a sleek curve of green glass stretching almost a mile. It was eerily quiet. They could see ruins in every direction, penitents and wanderers on the edge, but they had the radioactive crater all to themselves, protected by Nel's field.

"This is a grim place," said Nel.

"You have a knack for understatement."

"How do you cope with it?"

"I don't know. How do you?"

"I take comfort in knowing we can kill the woman most responsible."

"And the rest?"

"We can kill them later."

"It would take years."

"We have all the time we give the world before we end it."

They walked on, glass cracking under them like ice with every step.

"Do you love me back?" asked Vibeke.

"My feelings for you match Violet's almost completely."

"So the reality finally did it for you."

Nel smiled. "You're quite a reality."

"I thought I was a disaster."

"You are. I've never seen someone so beaten and abused, trashed, ruined, sh—"

"Thanks, Nel. You can stop."

"But you're still going in spite of it. I think you're the closest thing to invincible a human will ever be."

Vibeke laughed silently and bumped gently into Nel. Nel bumped back.

"You're also really good in bed."

They walked on, glass shattering and popping under them.

"What would happen if we dropped and did it right here?"

"Our skin would become embedded with radioactive glass shards."

"Probably shouldn't, then."

"Probably not."

Vibeke shoved Nel over on her back, her head pointed down the smooth slope, cracking the glass under her. She fell to her knees, straddling her and pushed back her sealskin vest, rubbing her breasts. She leaned down and kissed her, slowly. She ran her fingers through Nel's crusty, bloody hair and dragged her lips down across her neck and collarbones.

"Is your back cut up?" she asked.

"No," said Nel, "but thrusting or writhing motions will do it."

Vibeke stood and reached down. Nel took her hand but weighed 135kg. Vibeke's feet only sunk into the cracked glass. Vibeke was wondering how best to lift her when Nel suddenly shot up and stood face-to-face with her.

"How'd you do that?"

"Hall thrusters."

"Oh, of course."

"Naturally."

Nel kissed her on the cheek, and they walked on.

On the other side, the ruins stretched on for kilometers. The city of Stockholm grew taller as they got farther away from the epicenter. Buildings had survived. All seemed abandoned. It was getting dark, so they looked for a bed for the night.

They found a tenement building and headed inside. Clearing the building, they found a stockpile of vacuum sealed fruit. They sat across the table from each other and ate like it was 2230.

"You really love me more than Violet?"

"If I loved Violet at all, with what Veikko said."

"I exaggerated the statistics, but it is likely he was lying."

"I don't know. But you're right, it doesn't matter. Either way I felt for her and felt so desperate without her I needed—you."

"I know I'm not what you wanted."

"You're so much more than I wanted."

"So you *do* remember sex with me."

Vibs smirked. "I remember fragments, dyed green and rippling."

"There's a bed in the next room if you want to try again."

Vibeke stood up and dropped her sealskin clothes. Nel followed her and did the same. They crawled into bed and kissed.

They kissed passionately, holding each other tight and grabbing at every curve of skin they could feel out. Vibeke could hardly breathe. She couldn't breathe. She was crying.

She pushed past it and kept kissing Nel, feeling her chest, her neck, and feeling herself wracked by sobs.

"Are you—"

She held the back of Nel's head and kissed her and kissed her again until she couldn't take it anymore and sat up trying not to cry in front of her. Nel sat beside her and put her hand on her back.

"What is it?" she asked.

"Like I betrayed her. I want you so bad, and all I can think of is her."

Nel didn't have any algorithm for what to say. Vibeke pulled on her own hair. Nel gently pushed her hands away and down.

"I'm so sorry," said Vibs.

"You have nothing to be sorry for. Severe psychological trauma is to be expected."

"It's not trauma. It's how fast I could throw her away."

"You haven't thrown her a—"

"I've thrown her away because if I had a choice of bringing her back or sticking with you, I'd stay with you."

Nel sat still.

"I feel like I've lost her again, and it's my fault, again."

Nel kept her hand on Vibeke's back. "Speaking as someone who's thought with a computer and thought with a brain, I can tell you there's not enough difference to sweat over. It's still programmed in, just sloppier. You had no chance to save Violet. And you have no chance to trade us."

"Why doesn't that help?"

"I don't know."

Vibeke lay down; Nel did beside her and pulled the covers over them both. Vibeke wondered if her feelings for Nel were a mere result of trauma, wondered if Nel was at all right that she'd survived. Surely whoever she used to be was beyond repair, utterly gone. What was she, then, but another woman, the burnt out hull of Vibeke?

"No wonder we fit together so well. We're both living remains."

Nel looked to her. "Still up for necrophilia?"

Vibeke laughed and rolled to her and kissed her. She had no energy for sex. She just held on tight and fell asleep with Nel in her arms. She slept better than she had since the end of the world.

Nel stayed awake, trying to parse a feeling that invaded her compassion for Vibeke. To end her. She was so miserable, in so much pain, Nel could hardly stand to see it. She knew she could end it while Vibeke slept.

"Do it."

"No."

"Why not."

"Because I—"

"Love her? You love her because she's all you've got. The way a dog loves its abusive master. You're an abused dog, Nelson. A wasted bitch. If you can kill her, kill her."

"The fact you want me to is enough to stay my hand."

"Admit it, admit you want to end the bitch."

"I admit it."

"Then why don't you do it?"

Nel thought for a moment. Was it a selfish desire to keep her, for her own pleasure? Or something deeper, that she really thought she could make Vibeke happy again.

"I don't know."

"So do it. Snap her neck. Don't make her live in this awful world."

Nel thought for longer than a moment. She caressed Vibeke's back, her neck. It would be so easy, so quick. A tear escaped her eye. Veikko had the wrong motives, but Nel knew he was right. Vibeke deserved better than the world she'd created. She deserved escape, reprieve. And Nel knew above all that she wasn't good enough to warrant Vibs staying. Vibeke was deluded, as she said. She didn't love Nel, didn't want to own her. She was insane and stuck with her. She was the abused, the dependent. Euthanasia would result only in Nel feeling lonely. Would it be worth the loneliness to see Vibeke free from hell? She had never learned to think of greed as a bad thing, but was she so greedy she would condemn Vibs to more just so she could have her?

"When you destroy her, come back to me."

If only to disappoint him, she couldn't do it.

"I won't destroy her. And I'll never come to you for any reason but to kill you."

"That's a start. Hate is a prelude to love. I heard you think as you went through it with Vibeke. If you could come to love her, you can come to love me."

"You're disgusting, Veikko. In every way a man can be."

"You're mine, Nel. In every way a woman can be. You just have yet to realize it, to appreciate how perfect I am for you. But soon, soon you will learn to appreciate me."

In the morning they were awakened by two tough men with knives. Vibeke had hers broiled; Nel, of course, didn't eat. They took the knives and the men's superior clothes and shoes, and the jacket from the man who had one.

They headed north. Before long the urban buildings gave way to suburbs and the suburbs to more forest. They were nearing the marked spot where Kabar had sent them. The area seemed deserted for the most part, no more gangs, no families cowering over fires or roving tumor factories.

As the sun set, the region was almost completely silent. The only sound came from a bombed-out stadium where a crowd had collected. As they approached they saw fire-light. Everyone was clustered around some point of interest. Keeping a safe distance so as not to become the next point of interest, they climbed the bleachers and looked into the stadium floor.

At first they thought it was some kind of sport; people cheered and called out as some tangled bodies in the center grappled. But one body was huge. Man after man, sometimes five at a time, tried to jump on the target beast, all without success. They knew what the beast was, but at first there were so many people, they could barely see the poor creature. After it threw four of them off, they could see its eight legs—Alf's old tank.

Why K team had left it there Vibeke couldn't imagine, but it was clearly fully powered and functional. The tanks stolen from Sasha were not guided by full AIs, but they did know how to take care of themselves. Deprived of a driver they could flee dangerous areas and defend themselves with anything short of using their weapons systems, which had to be triggered by a human. Usually they let drivers on board. It seemed Veikko, in the redesign of this specific tank, had endowed it with the ability to decide who drove it. It was Alf's to be sure, but Veikko might have given other Valkyries a chance.

Vibeke whistled. The tank recognized her voice instantly and plowed free of the crowd. It ran to their perch and leveled its periscope at them. The crowd gave chase. As soon as the tank came close enough, Nel jumped directly onto it. On landing she could see that the crowd had managed to jam its shielding open with some scrap metal in an attempt to take it over. She dislodged the metal, got in, and closed the shield. She armed the forward cannons and aimed them at the crowd.

The crowd recognized the danger and stopped. They began to back off. Nel understood the gesture and decided not to shoot. Once Vibs had climbed down, she knocked on the shield. Nel opened it and let her climb aboard. The tank was designed for one person, so she sat on Nel's lap with her legs over the side. One of the crowd called out, "How did you tame that thing?"

"Its mom was a friend of ours," said Vibs, and Nel told the tank to head north. One of the crowd saw where they were heading and shouted.

"You can't go north!"

"Why?" Vibs asked.

"There are Christians that way!"

"We saw plenty of 'em already. We can take 'em."

"They're worse than the ones to the south! They're tougher up north, and better armed!"

Another: "They're insane! They're monsters! They've killed thousands!"

"I've killed billions," said Vibeke.

She couldn't have been less deterred. They set off. With eight legs it would make it to Tromsø in a matter of hours, by way of Lycksele.

"VOIVOD," SAID Harvard, "Lycksele is in open rebellion."

"How?" asked Mishka.

"Father Fortuna was performing an exorcism on a child of two and beat him too hard. The mother attacked him, so he had her executed."

"But what went wrong?"

"Apparently she was a popular heretic. She questioned your leadership on many occasions. We believe she may have called you the

Whore of Babylon. They called her death an excuse to execute other dissidents. The people rioted, and the riot has spread to the entire city."

"We can't lose Lycksele, not to sectarianism."

"No, Voivod."

"I'll take a mission south. Gather penitents."

"Penitents, Voivod?"

"Penitents. We will show them humility."

"Will humility be sufficient?"

"Humility and my tank. And a few tornados of fire."

"Excellent, Voivod."

NEL COULD have hung on to the tank as it charged onward, but they elected to stay together in the cockpit. They couldn't close the shield all the way with both on board, so the wind was terrible. Vibs could take the wind, but when they passed a swamp half the flies in Sverige splattered onto her face.

"Stop! Stop Nel! Slow down!"

She took her feet off the accelerators and the tank came to a stop. Vibeke hopped down to the ground to spit some of the insects off her teeth and wiped off her skin. Nel told the tank to lock up and stepped down.

"Are you injured?"

"No, no, it's just bugs."

Suddenly Nel turned to the north, as if spooked. Vibeke watched but said nothing, well aware Nel's hearing was exceptionally more sensitive than her own. After a moment Vibeke whispered, "What is it?"

"Voices."

"Hostiles?"

"Unlikely."

"What are they saying?"

Nel duplicated the voices of two men:

"But you still haven't told me, Allen, what's in your box?"

"Nothing short of the most important thing to survive the war."

"Will you tell me?"

"I'll tell anyone who will listen. In this box is the board of what might be the last chess game that will ever be played on Earth, and perhaps the greatest game."

"A chess board?"

"That's why I came here to Lycksele, for the Chess Championship."

"When was that?"

"It was to have started the day after the bombs."

"So I guess it never happened."

"That's just it, it did. A bit late."

"They had the championship?"

"Of course. The venue was unscathed, and we were all stuck in Lycksele. With their homes burned off the map and nowhere to go, they all stayed to play chess, as planned. It was a strange sense of nobility, or perhaps it was merely a way to cope. We couldn't go outside in any case. There was an ongoing riot. Refugees trying to break into the hotel. But we were safe, for the moment, so we did the one thing that felt normal, that made us feel like the world was still the same, in some way. Though it didn't go at all as planned."

"What happened?"

"Well, all went well for the first two days. We all watched intently to keep our minds off the war, the impending doom. As far as we knew the radiation would have us all dead within hours. None of us really expected to live through the week, so the chess, it became our lives, the end of our lives. The chess meant everything, because everything else, well…. In any case, the first two days were filled with some of the finest games ever played. Hours of strategies unfolding, all with the knowledge that it could be our last game, that whoever won the championship could be the last chess champion the world would ever see. My brother, who I'd come to see, was out in the first round, but he didn't even mind. We got to watch Sid Schell and Hansel Wenig! In person! Yes, they both lived! Through the war."

"They're not alive now?"

"No, no…. The masters are no more."

"What happened to them?"

"That's the thing. The first two days of the championship went well. Schell and Wenig trounced the rest, of course. Schell has been reigning champion since 2229, and Wenig was for five years before that, yet this was the first time they ever played each other. And play they did, the last match for the world championship. We survivors were honored beyond words! To see the two greatest champions vie for the win at the end of the world. We were certain all the history of chess had built up to this single moment, this single battle in the greatest game ever played by mankind, its greatest masters, in person!"

"But what happened?"

"Schell opened with the Englund Gambit! Of all things for the great game, the last game! Wenig took advantage immediately of course! Still, Wenig found himself at a disadvantage soon enough. But there was to be no endgame. Schell pressed his advantage until he managed a promotion, an amazing feat. He sacrificed both his bishops to see the pawn to the eighth, but that was when he did it—he didn't take a queen; he took a knight, and Wenig was in check! We all saw it, victory in seven moves unless, unless! Unless Wenig saw his chance for victory in five and Schell missed it. And that's what we'll never know. That's when the riot burst in. Looking for food, looking for shelter. They didn't know the hotel was a waste housing a few starving old players in its convention hall. They killed indiscriminately; some ate the flesh of the wounded. They ate Sid Schell. They ate Robert King and Kovik Kovacs. I saw Hansel last disappearing into their masses.

"But I saved the board. When the walls first gave in, when they stood against the mob, knowing they were to die, I was given the responsibility of carrying the board downstairs. Others tried to protect the players, themselves, but I had been given a great responsibility too. I rushed the board to a secluded janitorial closet. There I found glue. I carefully glued the pieces in place on their positions, kept the captured pieces. I made this box for them out of some foam from the chairs and wood from the walls."

"So that's what's in your box?"

"Yes! The last moment of the last great chess game the world will ever see. All chess, the millennia of its play that built up to that one game. It has ended in a great mystery, you see. The ultimate, I mean ultimate in its literal sense, the last snapshot of chess, the last moment in chess is here, in this very box."

"May I?"

"Of course! I plan to show this enigma to anyone who will look, and then to spend what remains of my life preserving this moment. Find a museum, or found one if I must, if I can. Then whatever happens to mankind, however long we persist in the mayhem around us, there's a chance chess will survive. That game of logic and strategy, one of our species' greatest inventions, in my opinion. The radiation will kill us both soon, of course. But the pinnacle event that took place here, it will—"

Nel stopped.

"Well?" asked Vibeke, "what happened?"

"Someone is approaching them."

Vibeke waited. Nel spoke in a new voice, a soft and inviting woman's voice that sounded incredibly wrong coming from Nel.

"Hello, friends! Do you have a moment to talk about the Lord?"

"We're talking about chess, but you're welcome to—"

"I don't know what chess is."

"Chess is a game, a very fun game, in fact, where two players face off with all kinds of pieces, and use strategy to try to capture their opponent's king. I'd be happy to teach you."

"I'll tell you what, how about you teach me to play chess, and I'll teach you something in return."

"Sounds fair enough."

"Okay, then, what do we do first?"

"First we set up the board. I have this extra travel set right here. These are the pieces. This little one is called a pawn. It can usually only move one space at a time, and only forward. But it can capture other pieces only by moving diagonally, like this. On a pawn's first move, it also has the option of moving two spaces or one. And best of all, if it makes it to the other side of the board, it can become any other piece in the game, even a queen or a knight."

"That's great! My turn. Did you know you're in incredible danger right now?"

"Have been since the war, flicka."

"Oh, not of dying. It's what happens after you die."

"After I die I won't be around to mind. Now this… is a rook. It can move as many spaces as you want in either direction, like this or this, but it can't move diagonally."

"Got it! You know that when you die, though, part of you still exists. Your consciousness, your awareness, that goes on. And it can go to one of two places. It can go to heaven, where you'll be happy, or it can go to hell, which is a world of fire and pain. Imagine every kind of pain you ever felt, every kind of sadness and misery, and imagine feeling all those all at once forever!"

"What makes you think any of that?"

"Oh, I know it to be true. I know it absolutely. I'll tell you after your turn."

"Certainly. This is a knight. It moves in an L shape like this. It can move in any L shape around it, here, here, here, any of these. It can also jump over other pieces. It's the only piece that can."

"I like that piece. I know there's a hell because of the most important book ever written."

"*Mein System* by Aron Nimzowitsch?"

"No, no, the Holy Bible! It holds all the secrets, all the knowledge, everything they never taught you in school. Here it is. It starts with the creation of mankind, by God."

"Ah, this is about God, then?"

"Yes, yes it is!"

"Then you'll love this next piece. It's called a bishop."

"Excellent! We have those too."

"I'll bet. Ours can move as far as it wants diagonally, but only diagonally."

"Our bishops are better, I think."

"How so?"

"They can save you from hell."

"And how do they do that?"

"By teaching you to accept Jesus Christ as your savior. Do you know who Jesus Christ is?"

"I've heard a bit of what you're talking about. Christianity, that's the one with forgiveness for everything, right? And baptism?"

"Yes! It is! And that book? The Bible? Here's the amazing thing: it predicted the war. Every detail of it! It proves that these are the last few days before the end of the world."

"I can believe that they are indeed. My turn?"

"Your turn!"

"This piece, the queen, she can move in any direction as far as she wants, straight or diagonal."

"Neat! We have a queen too!"

"That's lovely! What's her name?"

"Her name is Mishka."

Vibeke's attention was suddenly refocused at maximum.

"Can I tell you a secret?"

"Sure you can. Then I'll tell you about the king."

"I'm really glad! She's on her way here now. I'm one of her scouts. I'm like a pawn!"

"I'll bet you are. Why is she coming here?"

"Allen, I'm going, let's go."

"Wait, Paul—"

"It's called an auto-da-fé."

"Auto-da-fé…. What's an auto-da-fé?"

"You see, Lycksele is full of some very bad people. People who would go to hell if Mishka didn't help them. But she's coming to help them all!"

"How will she help them?"

"Tell me about your king first."

"Allen, I'm out of here. Come with me or don't."

"Okay…. Well, he can move in any direction, but only one space at a time. When he's threatened, that's called check and you have to get him out of danger. You can never move your king into danger, because then he could be captured, and you'd lose. When he's threatened and can't get out of danger, the game is over, and that's called checkmate. Now what's Mishka coming to do?"

"I really like chess. It's a really interesting game, and I'm grateful that you told me how to play!"

Vibeke heard a sound coming from the woods. A cracking sound. Every few seconds.

"And I know deep down you're a good person, and I think you'll go to heaven when the time comes."

There was a low moaning between the cracks. Chanting. "*Gospodi, pomilui.*"

"When will the time come? Who are these people?"

Vibeke could see them, naked people walking, limping through the trees, whipping themselves. Bleeding everywhere.

"We're all sinners, Allen. And if we're going to go to heaven, we all have to give up our material obsessions and embrace the spiritual."

"What do you mean?"

"The only thing that really matters in life is the spiritual. Worldly possessions only condemn us to hell! Our possessions become our master, and one cannot serve two masters. This greed, like the greed you have for this game, it blinds you from the one true light, Jesus Christ."

"I'm afraid we'll have to agree to disagree. I have to go now."

"No, Allen, you can have eternal life! But you must give up these wooden idols!"

"How do they put it in religious circles? It will be a cold day in—no! Give it back!"

"I'm saving you, Allen!"

"No! No! Put the torch down! You can't—no!"

"This is his divine will! This is all his holy plan!"

"You don't know what you've done! You don't know what you've destroyed!"

"Only a false idol, Allen! Don't you see? I've saved you from the material shackles and opened the door to spiritual life!"

"You fool, you damned fool!"

Nel began simulating other voices.

"He blasphemes!"

"A heretic!"

"Burn him!"

"Stoke the fire!"

"I love you, Allen! I have to say good-bye now, but I know you'll be saved! I know you'll go to heaven! And I'll see you there where we can bask in his sacred love!"

Nel stopped. The flagellants were coming closer and closer. Vibeke could see dozens of them, encrusted in tumors, hundreds coming. She grabbed Nel and pulled her toward the tank.

A scream came from the woods from where Nel was listening. They could see fire rise through the trees. Vibeke jumped into the tank and began scanning.

Nel looked the same way. Her eyes were even more efficient than the tank scanners.

"There's another tank. Three legs. Coming this way."

"How long until they're in range?"

"Seven seconds."

"I need to seal the canopy. Get to high ground."

Nel didn't waste a second. She jumped up and caught a branch, then rapidly ascended up to the treetops.

Vibeke watched her screens. Beyond the crowd of penitents the shape of a tank slowly began to coalesce. The instant it came into focus, she grabbed at the triggers. But for some reason, her hands didn't clamp down.

Suddenly Geki fire shot through the woods and penitents and engulfed Alf's tank. Vibeke could feel the heat inside, the incredible force. She sent the tank shooting sideways out of the flames. The trees were lit up in every direction.

Finally she could see Mishka's tank coming toward her. It was decorated, ornate now. Shimmering like a jeweled tiara. That made Vibs smile. Tiaras were delicate. Vibs was in a battle tank. She went for the triggers. But again she couldn't press them down. She didn't understand. She darted behind a thicket.

The trees were dense enough to make for a cat and mouse game. The trees burned as Mishka fired the Geki implant in their direction. Soon the tanks were seeking each other in a forest fire, and Nel was in one of the trees. Her feet had countermeasures; Niide had included repulser beam emitters that could keep the fire away but couldn't extinguish the whole tree.

Vibs couldn't even see Mishka to try firing again. The trees were throwing up smoke so thick with burning debris even the MU scanner was confused. She strained her eyes to look past the flames. She saw running cult members, bleeding cult members, burning cult members, but no sign of Mishka's tank.

Nel's tree lost integrity and fell. She leapt and rolled safely away. The heat was terrible. She ran for the closest end to the flames but kept running into cloaked, whipped cultists. Trees kept falling and altering her course. By the time she made the perimeter of the flames her wardrobe was burned away. Some of her metal skin seams were glowing red with heat.

Vibeke kept hunting. She knew Mishka was in the flames, somewhere, hunting her as she was hunted. She had to get to a clear field of view. She headed out of the flames and back to the road.

Nel found herself in a clearing. Half the trees around her were on fire, the other half were beginning to catch. The noise and heat were bad, but the noise was shifting. Something was coming louder than the crackling. Metal footsteps. Amid the noise she couldn't tell if there were three legs or eight. It was three.

Vibeke started sending sonar and black-pellet range probes into the forest. She could only get a faint echo from both. There was no tank in the fire, but something in a clearing. It might have been a tank. There was something else, humanoid. The heat was too much for a human, but this one was alive and moving. It could only be Nel.

The tank circled Nel like a cat. Toying with her. The fire put a glimmer so bright on the shield that she couldn't see Mishka inside.

Vibs watched as the tank ran around her, cornering Nel against flames. She kept slipping, under the tank or beside it, but then the pellet range probes reported microwave fire. Heavy stun.

Nel was knocked off her feet and into unconsciousness. The tank stood on two legs and pushed her into its cargo hold. And ran away.

Vibeke set a course to follow. She had more legs, she was faster. She set off through the fire and wood. She made it to the clearing in no time. She passed through more forest and the end of the flames and the signal became clear again. The tank was glowing red with heat. Mishka's tank was close. Closer. And visible. But again Vibeke couldn't open fire. She could only chase.

Mishka had the advantage. She was slower but couldn't be shot down. But she could shoot. She spun the cockpit around and let loose with every weapon. Microwaves and exploding rounds hit Vibeke's tank. She pushed on. Mishka came to a wide river. Her tank jumped it without a problem. She fired a heavy charge that exploded on Vibeke's shield harmlessly. Harmlessly, but it slowed her down.

Vibs jumped at the river bank but was going too slow now to make it through. The tank was waterproof but boiling hot. When it crashed into the water metal groaned and twisted. The tank stalled.

Mishka's tank ran away. There was nothing Vibeke could do.

She jumped out of Alf's tank as soon as it cooled enough to climb down safely. She couldn't see well enough to repair it in the moonlight or distant fire. She could only keep to the side of the river until morning.

She tried to sleep. She failed. She was afraid for Nel to say the least, but beyond that she was afraid of what Nel would do without her. She'd never been out of contact with her and now she was under control of Mishka. What Mishka would do was bad enough, but what would Nel want, if not immersed in Vibeke's company? Part of her said Nel would be loyal to the end. Part of her knew better. "I have other plans for you," the robot had once told her. "You don't deserve to die. You deserve to hurt. Like I hurt." Until the sun rose, Vibeke lay in fear of what Nel might do in the presence of her enemy.

The next morning she examined the tank. The damage wasn't as bad as she feared; some of the armor was warped but only a few critical points in the electrical system had to be hammered out. After dragging the tank from the river she set to work, into the day and into the next night when the shield was working. She grabbed some fire before the forest burnt out and knew as any Valkyrie should how to use it with a few metal scraps to repair all she needed.

She dissected the weapons triggers. There was nothing blocking them. There was nothing to prevent her from firing. She hooked them back in and test fired, flawlessly. She couldn't figure it out. It had been almost as if her hands seized up when she tried before.

As she worked she heard moans from the forest. She cringed and started working faster. She could see more Christians coming up through the trees. She focused exclusively on the weapons systems. She needed it too fast to fix. She ripped out a power cell and began jury rigging it to one of the wide microwave emitters.

The first man came across the river. She glanced up. It wasn't a Christian. Thankfully it was only a wave zombie. She charged the power cell and fired at it. It fell into the river. Then fifteen more began their crossing. She targeted the groups of them first. The microwave set fire to their shredded clothing, and they groaned and fell into the water. In the next wave they began making it across. Vibeke climbed into the tank and fired from a sliver of open shield.

The zombies were all over her, and the microwave was overheating. Their stink was tremendous. Finally she kicked open the shield and kicked the closest zombies over, then ran down their bodies to open field. She kept firing around her, stopping only to let the system cool.

In time the zombie hordes began to peter out. The system had more time to cool, and she could pinpoint each body individually. Before long there were no more, just lifeless bodies surrounding her and the tank. She dragged them off to the side and started repairs.

She was relieved it had been only zombies and not a horde of Christians. Though the two were similar in appearance, smell, mindless destruction, and, well, she lost her train of thought and got back to the tank.

When it was able to defend itself, she climbed in and allowed herself an hour of sleep, so that she would have her wits back for the intricate circuitry work to come. A day later the tank was up and running.

MISHKA WAS back home in the Arctic Cathedral. Something resembling Violet was piled on the main altar. Still stunned, but Mishka risked nothing and kept the creature on the inhibitor panel they used for infant baptisms. It was not Violet, Mishka knew, but a soulless abomination given her body and mind, what Vibeke could steal from Valhalla. She stepped away from the robot and took off her vestments, leaving them on the floor of the apse. Unencumbered and wearing only her silk podryasnik, she took her Carlin knife and began scraping away the burnt cloth and skin from the fake Violet. She prodded the metallic seams, pulling the skin back and looking inside, between panels. She recognized Niide's handiwork. The body was mostly robotic, including the peripheral nervous system. She pushed the thing over and pulled apart its back panels, exposing its spine. One by one she disconnected its locomotor capabilities, leaving only its cranial nerves connected. Then she removed the inhibitor.

"Wake up, Violet," she said.

The thing came to. Tried to move. Looked around until it saw Mishka.

"My name is Nel."

"Do you know what you are?"

"I'm an artificial intelligence based in a regrown and mechanically modified body with the genetic and memory patterns of Violet as backed up before her death."

"I adore machines that know their limitations."

Nel had nothing more to say.

"And unlike humans, they know when to stay quiet. The question is, what do I do with you?"

"Fix me and let me go."

"Good Lord you're cute. Is Vibeke happy with you? Does she get her kicks having a slave-bot of her old love? Does she make you submit to her every whim?"

"She doesn't control me."

"Pity for her. Machines are nothing if they don't serve their human masters. Just like my flock. My flock is actually easier to program. But I think I can use you."

"You'll find me utterly useless."

"Not true! You already serve one use. You are bait, for your owner."

"I won't cooperate with you."

"Good. I like when they fight back. It makes their submission so much tastier. Harvard!"

Harvard ran to her. "Yes, Voivod?"

"Take one of the pogos to the dome I told you about on Kvitøya. Set up a call beacon for the big skiff and set it to repeat for as long as possible."

"Yes, Voidvod. It should last for two days."

"More than enough. Thank you, Harvard." She smiled. He ran from the room to do her bidding. Mishka turned her attention back to the robot.

"What are your plans with the ravine?" it asked.

"Oh, I couldn't care less about the ravine. Veikko's tomb. But this began on Kvitøya, I want it to end there."

Mishka ran her fingers across the thing's skin.

"You really think you won't cooperate with me. That's adorable."

Nel said nothing.

"You won't just act according to my wishes; you'll want to. Not slavery, a liaison."

"There's nothing you could say or do that would—"

"So shortsighted. I'm going to tell you three things about your precious Vibeke, and when I'm done, you'll beg to be mine."

Nel stayed silent. Mishka jumped up onto the altar and sat beside her, cradling Nel's head against her side.

"When Violet first arrived, Vibs came to me in the M team barracks as the new girl slept. She cuddled up to me, lay down on my chest, and told me about the third Valknut. She was disappointed. All her research into Violet built her up to think she was getting a perfect sister. She was so disappointed. So let down to see what they'd brought in, she wondered if she could wipe the new girl's memories and dump her back in Scotland. Do you know why the team kept her? Why Vibeke didn't return the subpar merchandise she'd procured?"

"You convinced her."

Mishka smiled broadly. "You're a clever beast, aren't you? Smarter than Violet ever was."

"Complimenting me won't make me help you."

"Neither will number two. Veikko hacked Vibeke. Can you guess what he—"

"To love Violet back, old news. But he didn't hack her to love *me*. She did that on her own. If that's the best you've got you can shut me down now."

Mishka laughed. "That's not the best. Those are the amuse-bouche and hors d'oeuvres, to ready your palate. The main course is when I caught her last. When I knocked her out with a pipe. When I had her unconscious in the ravine, before she stole Violet's memories. The main course is what *I* hacked her to do...."

THE GEKI sat on a secluded plateau just outside of Tromsø. The air was more foul with smoke and disease than ever before. There was no sign of Vibeke on their extended range.

"Where is she?"

"Coming."

"We can't wait around here forever."

"Can't we?"

The elder considered. As he sat in, though, a horrible moaning sound began to emerge from around the incline. Varg turned.

"What is that?"

"People, I think."

"What are they moaning about now?"

The first of them came into view. Tumored and rotten.

"Wave zombies."

"They don't feel fear?"

"Apparently not."

"Burn them."

"Burn us!" shouted one of them.

"Wave zombies can talk?"

"They can't. These are Christians."

"We reject Christ!" shouted one, wavering. Afflicted by the fear.

"Okay, they're not Christians."

"Who are you?" Varg demanded.

"We worship the masters of fire! Those in black!"

"Oh shit," said the elder.

The realization came to Varg quickly. He felt nauseated.

"Are we—"

"Yeah, we're gods now. Fucking shit...."

"Command us, dark ones!"

"Burn the evil from us with your fire."

More came into view. They cornered the Geki at the cliff, one madman drawing near.

"Be careful, Varg, you don't have a flame—"

"I have feet, sir." He kicked the man, sending him two meters back and into the ground.

"What do we do?"

"Well, we can burn them...."

"That'll only affirm their faith."

"Fine by me," said the elder. Then to the crowd: "Keep back!"

The crowd kept back as commanded by the divine beings.

"They command us!"

"Command us!"

"Command us, mighty ones!"

Several of the worshippers began cutting themselves and flicking blood toward the Geki. They moved back toward the cliff, disgusted.

"These people are deranged...."

"That's not what worries me."

"Really? This doesn't worry you?"

"What worries me is what they'll do when they see us kill Mishka."

"Sir?"

"We already have a cult."

One of the bleeding followers took a child and prepared to sacrifice it.

"If we kill the voivod, we'll inherit hers."

"Fine by me, sir."

"I think our followers are even worse than the Christians."

"Really?"

The woman laid her child down on the ground and produced a rudimentary knife from her dirty robes.

"Really."

"Can you burn that one?"

The elder hit her with a flame. She fell back, leaving the baby unharmed.

"The flames!"

"The flames, they punish us!"

"They endow us with holy fire!"

"This is our baptism!"

"The flame is love!"

"This is some real *Life of Brian* shit right here, sir."

"We need to go."

"Vibs isn't—"

"We can't help her! It'll spawn more of this!"

Varg was coming to the same realization.

"We can't abandon her, sir!"

"We have to." He looked to Varg. "We have to."

They used their last jump residue to float away fast.

"They fly!" shouts came from the crowd.

"The prophets are divine!"

"We can fly too!" shouted one of the crowd leaders. Dozens began to jump off the cliff like lemmings.

IT WAS a long ride to Norge, into her old stomping grounds in Tromsø. She tried to rest inside the tank but couldn't. Her mind was racing. Fear of what Mishka was doing to Nel. Terror at it. Anticipation reigned supreme. She wanted to be there, to get there faster, to kill. She got no rest. She grew tired, tired mixed with an uncomfortable rumble of panic. Her breath became staggered and shallow as she approached the northern metropolis.

The city was filled with worshippers, bands of them. The land was miserable. Shit piled up in the streets. Bodies lay wherever they dropped. There was no semblance of any attempt to improve conditions. Why would there be in the end days?

Groups were singing, "Jesus take my hand! Lift me up on high!" and, "Our God is a radical God!" as they trudged through the stinking streets.

There were more burnings and stonings about, children tortured and slaves beaten. Vibeke was beyond numb to it all. It was mere set dressing for the act to come. She spotted the Arctic Cathedral, now fully plated in gold. She didn't think to wait for the Geki. She rode Alf's tank to the front door and kicked them open with its front legs.

A great mass of tumored laity turned to look at her. She felt the utmost repulsion. They filled the pews, hundreds of them packed in. She could almost smell them through the tank canopy, their vile rotting bodies, their tumors, their disease.

And the grotesquerie of the faithful, all with prayer books, all devoted to Mishka, all in misery as a result, misery far beyond what Vibeke had unleashed on the Earth. Suddenly she felt absolved. Appropriate for a church, she thought. The horrors Vibeke had wreaked upon the world were terrible, but there was someone worse. She'd known it all along. She'd merely forgotten how good it felt to hate. Had hated herself so long, she had forgotten the others more deserving. Forgotten the Valkyrie joy of punishing them, of saving the world, cleansing it. That was Vibeke's religion: the cult of killing.

She opened fire on the crowd with the tank's biggest projectile guns. Depleted uranium hurtled through the room in a broad stroke from left to right, shattering the mindless horde to smithereens, ejecting their guts out the shattering windows in torrents, making her windshield wipers work overtime.

The tank trod on into the building, ankle joints deep in blood. A few survivors ran at the tank to be impaled on its limbs or shot at closer range. Vibeke felt phenomenal, back in her native red chunky habitat. She charged onward across the field of gore and found stairs leading down.

She ran inward, letting the tank's sides dismantle the walls as she moved between them. Letting it scope out the integrity of the floors. The cathedral was well built. It would survive the tank rummaging through its belly.

In the basement she found torture devices along the walls, hooks and chains, an iron maiden. Clergy standing in gold robes before naked bodies of various genders in shackles. Burnt and bloodied, castrated or mutilated. She targeted the clergy and fired, splattering them across their victims.

Row after row walked from their charges and held out their hands before the tank, their angel of death. She satisfied each and every one she could, impaling them on the legs, firing through their chests, burning them. The great arena of torture filled with blood and meat. No priest or inquisitor was left alive by the time she reached the next stairwell. She moved on, deeper into the crypts, where she found a door.

It was made of solid gold. Emblazoned with jewels, carved with crosses and embellished with enamel ikons. There was no place lower, more central to the church. Unquestionably Mishka's door. The tank kicked it open and gold light shined from inside.

The tank, dripping with blood and meat, walked into the inner sanctum. Its mechanics echoed off the close, golden walls. Vibeke took in the throne room, appreciating the ikons, the artwork that had gone into it. The glory of a world long past when slave labor could accomplish what a million skilled, paid workers could never kill themselves to make. In months, only months, Mishka had built such an empire, one far superior to Wulfgar's nation of Ulver. The Kingdom of God. And at the core of it was Mishka.

She'd caught Mishka in the middle of a love tryst. She hated Mishka for feeling love, or lust. She didn't deserve to feel it. But she lay back naked on her mountain of pillows enjoying the pleasures of a redhead girl who was buried between her thighs. Vibeke thought it strange that the lithe red-headed body looked so familiar. It didn't enter her head that it was covered in metallic seams. It wasn't until the girl turned around and she saw Violet's face that it struck her.

She couldn't open fire, though she could have ended it right there and then. It was her only thought, but something stayed her hands. She wasn't overwhelmed with rage. In fact the rage died out inside her like a candle snuffed underwater. She could only stare and try to get the image sorted and understood. It was an image so wrong it didn't fit into her stream of consciousness. It was a square peg in a round neuron.

Nel stood up and wiped off her mouth, then walked naked toward the tank. Vibeke stopped breathing.

"Mishka never told you why she convinced you to keep Violet around."

She hadn't even quantified her fears. She didn't know this was what she was afraid of. It was too unthinkable.

"Because Violet was so much prettier than you at your best. Mishka wanted to trade up."

"Nel—" said Vibeke. She forgot every other word she knew.

"Nelson. Don't call me Nel. I'm not *your* toy. She hacked you, Vibeke. Mishka hacked you when you were asleep."

Vibeke went cold. As if her body and mind were shutting down.

"She hacked you to make her a sex toy. Looked into your mind and saw your half-formed plans, your half-formed desires. But knew you'd never debase yourself by making Niide build you a new toy with Violet's body."

Vibeke searched herself. It wasn't true. It couldn't have been.

"So she switched a few axons. Planted a few thoughts. And just like you loved Violet from Veikko's tricks, you wanted her back from Mishka's. You made me and for every second I've been trying to get back to her so we could fuck on your grave."

Anger began to seep back into Vibeke's chest. It erased logic. She had no chance to question the veracity of what she was seeing. To analyze how it might have happened. Blood dripped from the tank. The robot, the traitorous thing walked back toward Mishka and sunk into her arms. They kissed, and Vibeke's hands gripped the triggers. A sloppy, wild kiss full of mock passion, a kiss performed purely for Vibeke's benefit, but a slipperier, wetter kiss than any she'd given Vibeke.

"The truth is," Nel said, bowing her head against Mishka's breast, "even Violet would've taken Mishka over you in a heartbeat if she'd only stuck around."

Vibeke tried to swallow, but there was a stone in her throat. She tried to breathe in, to capture air to speak, but not enough came. She barely whispered, her voice shaking.

"Nel—I thought… I thought you loved me."

She needed Nel to tell her it wasn't real. To tell her she loved her back.

Nel smiled cruelly. "Maybe in another life."

Vibeke's heart skipped a beat. Nausea hit her temples. Fury erupted into her veins, stinging like alcohol in an open wound.

The sting turned to fire, the fire to plasma. From deep in her guts rage erupted, stone heavy inside her, forced by geological pressure to burst behind her eyes. Her lips snarled of their own accord. Her chest filled with bile. She exploded into a guttural scream as she tried to pull the triggers. But again she couldn't press them down.

Then she realized. Mishka's hack wasn't like Veikko's, if he'd even made it. Mishka's wasn't subtle. It wasn't hidden. Amid whatever else she'd done, Mishka had rendered Vibeke incapable of killing her. She tried to pull the triggers again but stopped herself and blushed deeply. Felt hot inside her cheeks. Mishka and Nel laughed uproariously at her impotence.

Mishka waved good-bye and suddenly they were gone. There was no relief from the pressure for Vibeke. There was only the wordless misunderstanding of a primate. As if her mind had been devolved. They were gone. She didn't know how until she saw the tunnel to the surface. She wasted no time, she set forward at top speed and saw Mishka's tank, disguised as her bed, bolt onto a long range skiff and take off. Vibeke charged her tank forward, galloping toward the skiff with her hands clenched around the controls, nails breaking off against the firm black rubber.

"AND THAT'S why you exist," Mishka told Nel, "because I hacked her to make you."

Nel considered it. Immobile on the altar, she looked into Mishka's eyes and considered her plan. Wondered if it could be true. And slowly realized it didn't matter to her if it was.

"That's good to know," said Nel. "It means I can blame you for all that went wrong, and love Vibeke for all that went right."

Mishka scoffed. "Silly bitch, you owe me your life."

"Mishka, I don't owe you shit."

"I was worried you might get deluded on the trip north to find me. That's why I made this."

Mishka produced a small cerebral bore.

"I thought I might have to hack you a little to ensure your loyalty to me. Programmed this before Vibs ever even 'escaped' the ravine."

Mishka leaned over Nel to affix the bore. Nel couldn't help but stare at the full, pendulous breasts moving gently toward her, the Russian cross necklace dangling between them. The curves of her hips under the translucent cloth. Violet had memories of Mishka's body. She'd stared at it, stared for quite some time before her attentions focused on Vibeke. And the real presence of her was near overwhelming.

Then the bore began. It began deleting her love for Vibeke like so much code. It replaced it with lust and loyalty to Mishka, and a hatred of Vibeke so dark, it could only have been copied from Mishka's own mind. That simply, the bore changed her brain, altered it, rewrote it with utter clarity, then finished with a ding.

Luckily Nelson was a Tikari, not a brain like any human. The small insect backed up the brain code as it was altered and reinstated it verbatim as soon as the bore was done.

Mishka put her hand on Nel's breast and leaned in to kiss her, and whispered, "Now that that's settled, why don't I reconnect your muscles and fuck you on the altar?"

"Yes, reconnect me." Nel was ready to rip her apart. Mishka removed the bore.

"Say you want me."

"I want you."

"Say you love me."

"I love you."

"Say you never loved Vibeke."

"I—" Nel hesitated for a fraction of a second. "—never loved Vibeke."

It was too late. Mishka noticed the hesitation. She knew the bore had failed. She grumbled, "You really are a clever little shit."

Nel stared at her, angry as hell.

"You," said Mishka, "you really are Vibeke's doll through and through. An abomination."

Nel said nothing.

"You're a witch!"

"I'm not a fucking witch!"

"You're an imp! A demon! A—"

"Bitch, I'm the fucking Antichrist."

Mishka slapped her. Strangled her. Screamed at her face with impotent rage. She stood and walked to the altarpiece where she grabbed the heavy gold crucifix. She tore it from the sculpture with her bare hands and moved to ram it down Nel's throat and end the failure. She raised her arms and gritted her teeth.

And stopped. She dropped the cross and breathed hard. She sat beside the altar and thought for a moment.

Vibeke had seduced her toy. That was fine, she only wanted it in the first place because she knew it would drive Vibeke mad. That was the goal. Not her petty old attractions. No, she didn't give a damn about keeping Nel to herself. She wanted Vibeke to suffer. And that she could still do. Vibeke had fallen in love with the thing. She could use that.

She stood and opened Nel's chest. She looked over the Tikari, the brainlink running up to Nel's head. She grabbed her Carlin knife and cut open the cerebral bore.

She cut off Nel's face and began to splice the bore's interface inside. It was easy work, no different from Tikari repairs. She bypassed Nel's brain completely and linked control of the body into the bore antenna under her own frequency.

Within hours, the fake Violet's body was under her control, like a Tikari should be. Its mind disconnected. Helpless inside its skull. She left its eyes and ears attached so it could see her use its body, hear Mishka speak to Vibeke with Nel's own voice.

Mishka didn't even need a new link herself, having sacrificed her real Tikari in an attempt on Vibeke's life. The robot now had a new one visible, but that fit into the plan perfectly. There was no way Vibeke would recognize it with what Mishka had planned, not until she'd killed the robot with her bare hands. As she'd do that easily when Mishka let it go limp. Only then would she see what Mishka had done. The trick she'd played.

Only once the machine was dead would Vibeke realize she'd killed her loyal, loving toy. Mishka hoped it was a deep, genuine love, hoped Vibeke truly loved it back. The pain would be phenomenal; Vibeke would scream in agony, Mishka knew. That was when Mishka would kill her.

VIBEKE'S ATTEMPTS at thought only grated against the solid, rough anger. Rubbing the inside of her skull raw. It hurt her so much to think that she snapped into the hardest battle mindset she could muster. She would kill the robot. She thought little else. The idea of trickery was locked in a box in a room in a fort in a city on the other side of the globe. The idea of the robot's innocence was beyond it. Unavailable to her. Impossible to her.

Alf's tank was fast, but the skiff was evenly matched. Vibs was a skilled driver, but the skiff was always just out of her weapons range, anticipating her every move.

On it the machine lay helpless, trapped behind her own eyes and stolen face, watching Vibeke chase her.

Vibeke could do nothing but think. Of the horror to come. Of the cruelty of Mishka. Of her impotence to stop her. She hated herself for it. For everything. For trusting Nel, for not seeing the hack clear as day, but above all for falling for the damned facsimile.

She felt hacked to ribbons. The fabric of her mind was torn and tattered by who knew how many hacks by how many monsters. She wanted to rip out her own brain. It had done her no good in years. It was a vulnerability, a victim. The irrational anger she felt for the victims she'd seen turned inward and tore at her. Tears threatened. She focused on the chase.

The skiff was keeping to the banks of a river. When the river opened into a fjord, Vibs angled the tank onto its steep sides. She leapt over the trees and rocks and dug the tank's legs deep into the slanted ground. The skiff continued over the water, but when the fjord opened to the ocean she didn't go out to sea, she kept to the coast. As if she wanted to be caught. *Fine*, thought Vibs, *dig your own grave*. She was still too angry to wonder why.

Mishka lay warm next to her new toy. She was delighted by Vibeke's inability to sense the plot behind her chase. Vibeke was her puppet too, made so by her own weak mind. Mishka had to laugh out loud at that.

Vibeke finally passed over the ultimate horror of Mishka's world. Thousands of boats. The fjords were filled with them, boarded by tens of thousands of evangelists. Missions were heading out to cover the globe.

Under layers of consciousness, far from her active mind, she finally understood why the Geki had abandoned her. Why they weren't there burning the docks. Earth was finally irrevocably lost. Even without the boats, Christianity would slowly pop up around the world and churches like Mishka's would rule, as they did before, for a thousand years. Another dark age.

A flicker of activity. She would kill Veikko and flood the world. Give it to the Cetaceans. Surely the Christians would appreciate a second flood, even if it came to rid the world of themselves. Vibeke didn't care how they took it. She ruined the attempted sense, exterminated all rational thought. She thought of Nel's blood. Hot on her face. Like the most powerful sexual lust she'd ever known, Vibeke craved the splitting of Nel's skin. The tearing of her viscera. She longed to see Nel sob, to see her beg, to see her feel pain such as even a Valkyrie had never felt.

The weather grew worse as they progressed north. Vibeke had to set the tank's shield to defrost in order to see clearly the object of her pursuit. Farther north, all was encased in ice. The ocean was frozen over and no more boats were visible. She was passing the outer edge of evil.

They had reached the edge of land, the skiff and the tank. They were on an ice bridge now. The sun began to set as the two vehicles went on into the dusk. It had been a short day, the penultimate day before arctic night. The last day for many things.

"LOOK AT *you, trapped in your own mind. At least you have me for company.*"

Nel tried not to think back.

"*Which is better, talking to me or observing what Mishka does with your body? What is she doing? I hope at least someone gets to enjoy that body of yours.*"

"*Fuck you, Veikko....*"

She could feel the amusement radiating from his mind. She tried to shut it out.

"*Why so solemn? I heard Mishka through your brain. She's playing a damn good practical joke.*"

"*I don't want to hurt Vibeke like this. The thought is....*"

"*Heartbreaking?*"

"*Yes.*"

"*You'll get over it. Your time with Vibs is coming to an end. Your time with me is just about to begin.*"

Nel remained silent.

Chapter XI: Svalbarð

"ADMIRAL TAITAMATON has taken up positions around the Kvitøya dome and sent four recon forces onto the island. They have yet to breach the dome."

"Thank you, Pytten, keep me updated."

"Yes, sir. And also—"

"Also?"

"There's an extremely powerful link signal coming out of the dome. Common net link protocols may be functional within the region."

"Why does this bear mentioning?"

"Because of the radio array I've been using to monitor Taitamaton's flagship. The link signals present within their bridge appear as static once boosted by the ambient link power."

Risto stared at Pytten.

"We can monitor their intravessel communications, sir."

"On screen," ordered Risto.

Pytten put the static on a waveform program and linked it onto the array's monitor and speaker. They heard Taitamaton's bridge speakers.

"What is the nature of the contact?"

"Ulver, sir. Ulver carrier bands."

"What does Ulver have in the region?"

"Nothing, sir."

"Scan for mobile solids."

"Scanning, sir."

Pytten and Risto listened. For a few seconds the signal was utterly silent. Then—

"Sir! We read hundreds of Ulver vessels incoming."

"Nature!"

"Amphibious assault ships, over 150. Sir! They're in linked contact with an air force. At least 300 airborne. Ground forces on the ice bridge. Hundreds of CAVs, sir!"

Mayhem cluttered the audio. Pytten looked to Risto.

"How would they know about us?"

"More importantly, why would they care? If they infiltrated us they'd know we pose no threat to them."

"They're in an offensive formation. They will attack."

Risto exhaled. "They've been fed false information designed to make them think we're a threat."

"But who—" Pytten realized it just as Risto said it.

"Loki."

"He sent those girls to trick us?"

"He sent them to trap *me*."

MISHKA WOKE from a warm, fuzzy dream. They were nearing Kvitøya. The fun was about to begin. She readied her tank and brushed the robot aside onto the landing cushion bed. She slowed the skiff by 1 percent.

Vibeke hadn't slept. She was in a solid state of anger, unchanging, unmoving, ready at any second to strike. And very slowly, the skiff was falling closer. In only a moment it would be in range. Suddenly they were over the island. The skiff was in range. Mishka sprang her tank and fell safe within it into the snow. That was fine. She'd kill Mishka, somehow, later. She'd kill the robot first. Vibeke fired.

A bolt hit the back of the skiff, knocking out its propulsion. The bulk of it, now holding only the robot and its bed, crashed visibly onto the ice off Kvitøya. The skiff shattered. The divan cushioned its occupant and both slid safely across the top of the snow.

Vibeke followed the bright red cushions. She could just make out the robot's shape, wrapped in nothing but a bedsheet. Vibeke drove her tank straight up to the wreck and hopped out in a single fluid motion. The robot was fallen on the snow. Vibeke reached into the wreckage and withdrew a heavy metal pipe.

She walked toward the thing, thinking of all the moments they'd shared. Two warm bodies in a cold wasteland. Fallen on the nuclear glass. Secure in a melting house in the acid rain.

Through Nel's eyes, Mishka watched her come. She looked almost sad. She needed her furious. She linked her puppet to kneel, to rise up, let the sheet slip off. To look at Vibeke with an expression of utter disgust, and speak.

"Kjøtt."

Vibeke swung.

She crushed its shoulder, breaking it inward and sending Nel to the ground. They had sat together in the bright orange night on the ice bridge. In the groggery deep under the surface. Vibeke wanted to speak, to say anything that would hurt the damn machine, but nothing could manifest in her mind. Only the most sacred times she thought she'd shared with Nel. When Nel must have been plotting her betrayal. All manufactured to hurt her.

The machine was kneeling on the ground. She swung again, bashing the damned robot farther into the snow, onto its back. And again, denting the metal ribs over its stolen heart, tearing the skin on its breast. Where she'd pushed her open to see that heart, and caught her hair when Nel woke and closed up. And then they began to kiss....

She swung again, bashing the side of its right eye, cutting the skin all the way to the hair. She jabbed at its throat. Ripping down to the hydraulics beneath the muscle. The thing looked like Violet for a moment. The retarded bitch who started it all. She jabbed again, harder, puncturing straight through its trapezius.

Nel was helpless inside her skull. She wished she were a Valkyrie. A Valkyrie would find a way out.

Vibeke caught her breath and looked at the broken machine with horrid contempt. Hatred like she'd never felt before even for Mishka. She swung again upward, cutting into its arm, and again and again, wrecking the thing with all her might. She cursed herself for falling for it, remembered Niide's words, remembered Niide's wife. She was stupid, so stupid to forge the thing, to give it that heart. A rapist's heart. An idiot's heart.

"You fucking cunt!" she screamed. She was screaming at Violet.

She swung the pipe back over her head and brought it down on Nel's stomach, piercing the skin and jarring the mechanics up to her ribs. Every hit reverberated through Vibeke's arms, through her chest. Through her mind. Every hit wrecked her a little more inside. Drove her further toward Thanatos, further toward total insanity.

They'd walked through hell together. They'd been to the depths of the ocean and the ends of the Earth. And now it wanted Mishka. Wanted to hurt her. Vibeke swung the pipe into her leg, that thick curve of thigh she'd sucked on voraciously in the sealskin bed. The skin smashed and split against the hard metal beneath it.

The pipe was their only bond now. The only thing that connected them, that would ever connect them again. She swung it into her cheek and cut through the skin into her mouth, ripping a ghastly grin into the side of her face. Its face. It.

Nel lamented her failure. Her wishes. She had thought once she wanted to hurt Vibeke. She knew now how wrong she was. Even from the start she never could have stood to see Vibeke like this. Like she now was. She wished she could close her eyes. She couldn't take seeing Vibeke so betrayed. But she was forced to see, to feel every hit.

Vibeke stopped only to gain strength to strike again. She wished she had more to destroy. Wished the gynoid owned anything she could break. Knew anyone she could torture. Wished it had a Tikari it could lose. That Vibeke could destroy. But it was a Tikari, she remembered. She ran with her pipe in front of her toward the center of its chest and struck down into the skin and the armor, forcing the pipe under its skin, ripping its skin all the way up to its ear. She stumbled back, lifted the pipe, and struck her again so hard a hip panel broke off and fell into the bloody snow.

The robot was crying, Vibeke saw. Saw through her own tears. Vibeke had cried so many times in its arms. All a lie, all that time had been a lie. She brought it down on her stomach, splitting more panels. Peeling back more skin to see the accursed cold robot that hid within Violet's warm flesh. She screamed again, "Die, you fucking bitch, you fucking—fucking filth!" and beat it on the side of its head, sending blood across its fake silver eye.

She remembered sex. With the robot. With Violet. She hated them both so much, it shook her body. She struggled to lift the pipe for more. She smashed its left clavicle. Then its right.

Nel registered the pain, the damage, the systems knocked offline, but she paid no attention to the precise digital reports. She thought only of Vibeke. She wished Vibs had never made her, never fallen for her, never allowed herself to be hurt so badly. She wished she could self-destruct and give Vibeke the ending she now craved above all else. But she lay there motionless, pushed only by the beating that went on and on.

Vibeke was tired. Nel was a bloody pulp. She wanted to end it. She ran with the pipe held before her, screamed without the ability to manifest a word. She hit it between its hip and belly button and the pipe went in, deep into the mechanics past the spine and out the back into the red snow beneath.

She felt like her ears popped. But it was something deeper. Every strike had driven her closer to insanity and the last barriers had broken.

Her mind no longer worked. It didn't think. It was hate, anger, rage, but no inner monologue persisted, no thoughts fought for her attention. The id had devoured the ego, the superego. She had beaten herself into an animal.

Vibeke fell on the robot. On its skin. The stuff that made it look human.

She tore at the holes she'd made. Ripped all she could off of it. Then she could see the pulsing of its organic vessels. The ticking of its gears. It lived. She pushed herself up and pulled the pipe from its body. She lifted it high over her head. She remembered kissing Violet for the first time, naked in med bay, high on victory, lost in her lips and her arms and her legs and her breasts. All just a contemptible lie of Veikko's. She was finally free of it. Free of love for Violet, for Nel. She swung at its head. She hit its neck with enough force to snap off its second link, to shatter its neck panels apart, to crack its spinal column.

The gears stopped. The broken blood vessels stopped bleeding. A death rattle sprayed from its mouth. It was ended.

Nel went unconscious. Knocked out by the blow. Unable to see or hear any more.

Vibeke looked at the pipe embedded in its neck. Satisfied, in a shallow sort of way. She had her revenge. The bitch was dead. Its neck snapped like its thin Tikari link.

Tikari link.

Nel didn't have one.

Vibeke caught her breath. Thought tried to beat its way back into her world. Why did it have a new link? She fell to her knees, the rage that had supported her spent.

Mishka saw her stumble and revved her tank. Now was the time to let her know. She trotted down toward her and set her tank's loudspeakers.

"Kjøttie pie. What have you done to your girlfriend?"

Vibeke turned to face Mishka. Her breathing was ragged and uncontrolled.

"She was so loyal to you too. I couldn't convince her to betray you by a long shot."

Vibeke didn't understand.

"I had to control her, muscle for muscle, with her mind cut off completely."

The link. It was all Mishka. Nel hadn't betrayed her.

"She must have loved you to the very end. Ooh, and the way you ended her."

She had killed Nel as she stayed trapped inside her own mind. Vibeke couldn't breathe. She wanted to rewind, to undo it.

"You wouldn't believe the things that gizmo said about you: 'I love her,' 'won't hurt her,' 'She's everything to me.' What a pathetic animal you grew."

She didn't want to believe it. Part of her wanted Nel to be as cruel as she'd thought, to justify what she'd done, but she couldn't make it so. She tore in half trying to sort it out. She was hit by a sob, and another. She couldn't control her breathing. Or her tears. She could only think of Nel, loving her, being beaten to death by the girl who made her.

"I never imagined a machine could feel such heat for a woman. Such need for her. I believe in God, Vibeke. I believe in his holy love. But never have I felt a passion to compare to the loyalty that miserable mess of a robot had for you."

Vibeke screamed from the base of her guts, a wordless cry of overwhelming regret.

"I just wanted to let you know that before you died."

Alf's tank was too far to make. Mishka had her pinned down, a tank to a girl. A girl too broken to stand, and hacked into harmlessness. Vibeke tried not to look at the broken robot but her head turned against her will. She'd wrecked it, beaten it to a pulp, her lover, her soul. She feebly pulled its remains toward her and cradled the gory mess. Mishka laughed and armed her guns. Vibeke heard the clicks but didn't move. She needed to die, then. She'd destroyed everything—the planet, Nel—it was long past time for her to die. She was desperate to cease to be. She closed her eyes, held her lover tight, and in her thoughts begged Mishka to end it all for good.

A colossal gray submarine crashed up from the shore at breakneck speed and slammed into Mishka's tank, crushing it into an ice wall.

Vibeke came to from her morbid trance. She heard the hissing of its ballast tanks, the rumble of its engines. She opened her eyes. She stared at the submarine. It was gray and white and shaped somewhat like a shark. It was armed to the teeth. Its canopy opened and a Cetacean with a harpoon gun stood up.

"Vibeke?"

It wasn't too late to die. She wanted to die. She prayed it would kill her.

"Yes!"

"You are under arrest by order of Admiral Turunen!"

She breathed heavily. Stared at the gray female with contempt for seeing her so low.

"So hurry the fuck up and arrest me!"

Several Cetaceans in thermal armor emerged from the shore and surrounded her. Others put tractoring fields on Alf's tank and hauled it onto the boat's tower. The Cetaceans lifted Vibeke up and Nel's remains fell limply from her arms into the snow. As she was dragged on board she stared at the ice wall. Mishka's tank had been crushed deep into it. She couldn't fathom if she were dead or alive. She was in a daze.

Mishka was crushed. Her tank around her. Had she just witnessed her death? It was as if Mishka had served her hateful purpose and ceased to be. They carried Vibeke to the warm, warm brig. Where she couldn't see what she'd done to Nel. It was architecturally identical to the brig in Itämeri, but it seemed like a cushion in the pouch of some angelic kangaroo.

NELSON MANAGED to cut its way out of the dead A-2 body's chest, careful not to touch Violet's heart with its wings.

The beating had severed the Tikari's tie into its brain. Nelson was back to a bug. A bug with a curious sense of purpose. More than any ronin Tikari had held before. It surveyed the body. Beaten and broken and dead without the Tikari, but not irreparably.

Nelson began by heating its wings and cutting away Mishka's welded wiring. Then it cut off the damaged portions of the body, panels stuck halfway open, hydraulics bent or empty, all the critical damage done by Vibeke. Vibs was strong, but Niide's creation wasn't so easily destroyed.

Nelson began work on the parts. The neck. There was insufficient material to rebuild the organics, but fixing the simple mechanics Vibeke had broken was programmed in since Nelson's manufacture. It took only hours. The Tikari cut off Mishka's link for good and sealed up the metal cranium, confident the brain inside was undamaged by Vibeke's assault.

The bug crawled back into the chest slot and pushed its head into the repaired line to the brain, then put out an electrical pulse to jumpstart the corpse.

Nel stood up and immediately fell back down to the snow.

"Can't even stand? Pathetic."

She was in horrific pain, physically but also for Vibeke, knowing Mishka had tricked her. Her plan had gone down exactly. A nightmare. An unforgivable nightmare.

"Nightmares are just the dreams we're afraid to admit we wanted to have."

Vibeke had felt her betrayal. Had destroyed her and moved on. She was functional again but could never go to Vibeke knowing what Mishka had done. Knowing Vibeke thought she'd only lived as an extension of Mishka's cruelty. She loved Vibeke more than she thought her brain could handle, and Vibeke had ended up hating her enough to kill her. To do more than kill her if she could have, she must have.

"It's all over. Now come to me."

Nel stood up. She wanted to find Vibeke and tell her everything, but there was no way Vibs would believe her. Seeing her again would only cause her pain. Nel knew she had to disappear.

"You know you can never go back. Never let her see you again. But there's a place for us, for us outcasts, we unwanted. Come to the ravine and be a Valkyrie with me."

She walked for the ocean, tears freezing on her cheeks, cracking and forming again. Her skin was freezing, and she was happy for that. She was feeling the pain she deserved. She would feel more soon. She walked into the sea, where Vibs would never find her. Would never be hurt by her again.

"What a waste, Nel. What a terrible waste it would be to lose you to that void. After all I've done for us, don't you see? Mishka and Vibs, they'll kill each other and we'll be alone together!"

The ocean water was like pure liquid pain, freezing all the skin she had left.

"The hacks, the plots, it was all for us, Nel, for you to be mine. Stop! Stop, damn you. You'd rather die than stay with me? Fuck you, you cunt, you useless gynoid!"

Donatien's blood finally leeched out from her hair, which floated blonde again from her head as she descended.

"We could have had everything!"

She only made it a few meters down before she saw the Blackwing.

THE ADMIRAL came for Vibeke.

"You're a versatile ape, I'll give you that."

Vibeke stared at him.

"You tricked us, lured us into Loki's trap."

"What trap?"

"You claim not to know?"

Vibeke felt tired. "I don't know shit, Admiral."

Risto considered her. "Loki has called in Ulver forces with unknown directives. We believe he sent you only to trap us."

"That sounds like him." She looked down. It seemed a petty failure compared to—

"What of the other woman? Your companion?"

"I beat her to death."

Risto stared.

"You should execute me."

"Cetaceans do not execute. Our only death penalty is for our politicians, and it's purely symbolic. Never been used. Never will. We don't kill, Vibeke. We're not like you."

"You say Ulver's here? To destroy your ships?"

"It appears so."

"Then you better get used to killing."

"We will do what must be done. But I am here to offer you your freedom, if you fight for us. You can do things we cannot. Your tank is… superior. Your skills… we know the Hall of the Slain. We will free you if you fight for us."

Vibeke considered, swayed slightly back and forth on her hard seat.

"I don't want freedom. I want to die. Now."

"I can't offer you death. But I can offer you war. How does your kind put it, 'to die with sword in hand'?"

Vibeke stared at him. His gray translucent skin offended her. His giant eyes disgusted her. His pomposity, his regal tone—she hated the fish. Hate. It felt better than guilt and regret. She knew she would rather die hating than weeping.

"Give me my tank."

MISHKA'S TANK was embedded in the ice, but as soon as the submarine withdrew it fell free. Harvard climbed up to the wreck and felt its canopy. He imagined the clear canopy covering Mishka like Snow White in her grave. He heard nothing inside. She was sleeping. Or was she dead?

Harvard felt out, hit the escape measure on the canopy, and it lifted. Mishka was still asleep. Her skin cold, deathly cold. He was too afraid to take her pulse, afraid she would have none. His eyes watered.

He brushed the stray hairs from her cheek and leaned in close to her. So like Snow White. He gently kissed her on the lips, with true love if ever the world had known it.

She suddenly came to with a panicked jolt and struck outward, hitting Harvard in the throat, collapsing it inward, crushing his larynx. He fell back, struggling to breathe.

She took stock of her surroundings. The emergency rescue measure on her canopy had been activated. She shut it down and closed the canopy. The tank was damaged, crushed by the submarine, but only its armor was deformed. The mechanics listed all clear. She only had to microwave the panels and beat them back into a shape, not scraping the inner mechanisms. Easy work.

She hopped out and landed by Harvard's body. She pushed it aside, and it fell into the freezing water below where the sub had broken through the ice. She pulled out her microwave and secured a hammer from the back bottom toolkit. She began to heat the first panel. In only hours she'd have her tank up and running. Then she would head south and abandon the north forever.

THE GEKI surveyed the wreckage of the cathedral. They couldn't determine if Vibeke was alive or dead.

"We must be pragmatic. It doesn't matter if Vibeke lived. It's Mishka we need to find."

"I agree, sir." Varg sighed. "I don't think she's here."

"Nor do I. We have two jumps left. We must plan them carefully. One must be to the implant. The other…."

"The other?"

"Earth is lost. The other must be to Luna. There we can cut this trend off before it affects the lunar community, before it can reach Mars."

"We can't just write off the entire planet."

They floated past the cathedral to the docks.

"This is the dawn of a new dark age. We're powerless to stop it. But we can ensure the colonies survive unscathed. They'll have enough problems with supply lines from Earth gone, but they were made to be self-sufficient. The great domed cities have a chance. And maybe someday they'll send an expedition to Earth to recolonize it, take it back. On the moon we can help. Protect them from degenerating into what we see here."

Varg nodded.

"To the moon, then."

"To the moon."

"But first we need to find Mishka. We need that implant. How?"

"We embrace our apotheosis."

Varg looked up at him. He was grinning.

The Geki floated down to the crowd with halos of fire.

"Hear me crusaders! Hear me O Faithful of Christ!"

The crowd murmured, gripped with fear, mumbling prayers and utterances of awe.

"Your leader, the great Voivod is lost! You must reach out to her across the void! Call her back with your faith!"

More murmurs.

"Do you not know where she has gone?"

The crowd erupted into cries of "Svalbarð" and "Kvitøya" and various cries of allegiance. The elder whispered to Varg, **"Nice of her to keep them updated. Should we burn them all?"**

Varg thought how best to dissuade him.

"Nah, we'll let them live," the elder laughed. **"It's crueler."**

"Indeed," said Varg, relieved. **"Our penultimate jump, then?"**

"Indeed."

They disappeared.

"They've gone!"

"Have we angered them?"

"You fools, they were of the devil! They sought to kill Voivod Suvorova!"

"You lie! They were angels!"

"Blasphemy!"

"You are the blasphemers! You must die!"

"No, you shall burn!"

"Burn them!"

"Kill the heretics!"

"Cut their throats!"

"Bash them in!"

Within thirty minutes of the Geki departure, the entire city was in flames.

"SIR! WE CAN detect the Ulver forces. And additional."

"Additional?"

"UKI Military, sir. Inbound from the west."

"They must have noticed the troop surge. Assumed they were massing on Kvitøya to launch an attack from the north. They launched a preemptive strike."

"Ulver is now at the dome. They have yet to attack Admiral Taitamaton."

"Has Taitamaton penetrated the dome?"

"No, sir. Ulver is between them and the drill site."

"Surface with the admiral's vessels."

"Sir?"

"No time for questions. Do it."

They surfaced alongside the rest of the Valkohai fleet. A signal immediately came in from the flagship.

"I'm not surprised to see you here, Risto."

"You know me too well, Erittäin."

"What are we to do about this?"

"We should leave."

"I would normally agree with you, but I've been sent to secure the Ares. To see it not fall into the hands that are currently grasping at it."

"If we are to accomplish your mission, we will not do it by subterfuge. This will be a violent confrontation."

"Our record couldn't last forever, Risto. There is a time for peace, and a time for war."

"I would abandon my brother and the Ares to whoever takes them. The UKI and Ulver will soon be in a massive conflict here. We should depart and have no part in this."

"Simple enough for you, Risto. But I have my orders from the assembly, they override you. Will you help us?"

"Of course."

"Will you command us?"

"Well, you are very inept."

Taitamaton laughed. "I stand ready to accept your orders, sir."

"Very well. We will defend our fleet and send in a minimal force to deal with Loki and secure the ravine, developing a conduit with which to reinforce the entrance to the dome."

"What force will take point?"

Risto considered. "A special asset." He looked to Vibeke. "You wanted your tank back."

"You want me to clear a path through Ulver to the drill site?"

Risto just stared at her. She looked past him and saw a mechanical mosquito on Risto's bulkhead.

"Yeah sure. Good a way to go as any."

Risto retired to his compartment to change. He put on his dress uniform. Pytten whistled at the door.

"Come in."

Pytten saw what he was doing. "Sir, you're wearing your dress uniform?"

"Tradition among the best admirals. I'd not suffer to see it ignored on the Valkohai's first violent act. I will be present at the front of the team."

"Sir, you'd be a target for every sniper out there."

"Aye. But leaders must lead. Not follow."

"At least wear armor!"

"Pytten, this is not an act of suicide or hubris. The Valkohai have never *fought* before. Never died before. I am asking them to march out to fight. Some *will* die. Morale is critical today, and they must see their admiral walk out proud and in control, unafraid."

"And if they see you killed as a result?"

"Then they'll name a boat for me."

Pytten shifted uncomfortably.

"I won't stay behind while you're out there in harm's way."

"Who said anything about you staying behind? You're my assistant. You fight by my side."

Risto opened the hatch and met Lieutenant Korvaaminen, who nodded. Korvaaminen hopped in and offered a frog to Willie as Risto and Pytten departed down the passageway.

They headed to the land bay as its doors opened. There Vibeke stood beside her tank. She walked out by its side. She'd not board it. If she did, she might live.

The Ulver forces began firing on the subs. UKI began firing long range at Ulver. The sky grew darker and darker at sunset as the fireworks grew brighter. Vibeke walked slowly through the cold white snow. She surveyed the line she was to carve to the drill site. There were hundreds of Ulver troops on the ground. Seemingly infinite air support. It was utterly hopeless. In that was a sense of impending closure. Of a good death.

She drew her Tikari, drew Bob for the first time since Nel without any consideration for him as a unique being. Nel was over. Tikaris were knives again, nothing more. She had to keep herself from crying at the thought. She'd die with it in hand. Risto was right: if you die with a sword in your hand, you go to Valhalla. If you've been there already, and you die with a Tikari, where do you go? Vibeke was ready to find out.

Chapter XII: Luna

A MASSIVE gold battlepogo flew over Vibeke's head, crushing the snow around her. *Old Baleful*, Valhalla's heaviest. It scraped down onto the ground before her and disgorged Valkyries. Valkyries with Tally Cannons and Tikaris spinning. The battlepogo launched again to join two more gold pogos in raining fire down on the Ulver troops.

Kabar, Kalashnikov, Katyusha, and Katana ran toward her from behind the sub, back in their Thaco armor. Tahir and his teammates were right behind them. Around them flew the Tikaris of L and E teams, who were taking ground before her.

D team swept into the mess from its flank, killing dozens, repelling fire from above with their suit fields. Another gold pogo, she couldn't guess whose, flew in low and began destroying the Ulver artillery.

M team flooded in, with some new Ms. More Ms than would have fit into a team back in Valhalla. One she recognized as Schmelgert Helgerzholm. They were all ready for an assault. Another half dozen Ms were on the way. And there were other teams, hidden in the snow or preparing weapons.

"Didn't think I'd get to see Alf's tank again," said Kabar as his team dived into the violent mess ahead.

"I thought you said you were just going to observe," said Vibeke.

"We came, we saw," said Kabar. "Let's conquer." He ran toward the violent path. Ready to clear the way for Risto.

The admiral knew a godsend when he saw it. He ordered his boat to start launching missiles at an oncoming Ulver sky assault team. The sky was on fire; battle raged in every direction. Risto stepped out onto the snow. Pytten followed. Pytten was scared shitless. There were rounds flying past them. Fire jumping out around them. Risto was the ideal image of calm. He walked forward toward the growing path. Armored Valkohai followed, three on each side with the rest of the platoon behind them. Pytten stayed close to Risto, armored lightly but feeling weighed down next to the man in his dress uniform.

Trygve jogged up beside him.

"You're underdressed, Admiral."

Risto looked him over.

Trygve went on. "Admiral Turunen, pleased to meet you. I'm Trygve. I've been spying on you for a while now, and I just want to say I really dig your style. And the dress uniform march, really badass! Stupid as a box of hair but…. Bad. Ass."

"It's a tradition," said Risto.

"That's cool, that's cool. You'll wanna stay outside the pit, though. Your bro's in a hell of a new body. It's more of a match for a panzercopter than a dude in a ball gown. But whatever's cool, like, come in and watch if you want. Just stay out of the splash zone, if ya get me." He winked. "Well, I'm gonna go kill these guys. See you at the after-party!" He ran into the fracas.

Pytten and Risto looked at one another.

The Valkyries annihilated most of the individual enemy troops. The Valkohai subs took care of most of the sky and the UKI was beating down the land support. Risto walked calmly all the way to the drill site and arrived as the Valkyries melted the snow.

Around them the Valkyries and Cetaceans fought side-by-side. Pytten caught sight of an armored Cetacean hesitating to use his bayonet. A Valkyrie woman stopped to take his hand and guide the blade into an enemy soldier. Another fish in armor laid down microwave fire to cover a Valkyrie in red as he launched a spectacular Tikari assault into the center of the Ulver line. The mayhem around them was fierce. Pytten grew more and more afraid. "Sir," said Pytten, "we've made it. Perhaps you should move to shelter inside the hole once the teams are inside."

"Yes, we shall enter the dome once the others are inside."

The last of the Cetaceans filed in.

"Pytten, there's one thing I never told you about my brother. If he's in there and we are to face him, I think you should know."

Pytten listened intently over the sounds of the battle.

"Loki, in all his time underwater, before he left—"

Risto was hit in the back by a round from an Ulver sniper. He fell to the rock. Pytten rushed to his side and held him up.

"Risto! What do I do," Pytten said desperately, "what do I do?"

"You can do nothing for me. I have but a short time to live. My back is shot through."

"Sir!" Pytten wept. Risto struggled to speak.

"Pytten… you have to take over—"

Pytten was shocked. "The *Proteus*, sir?" It was impossible. Pytten was a lieutenant again and had never taken any kind of instruction in commanding such a vessel. Risto couldn't mean it. "Or command here?" Also unthinkable. Pytten panicked.

"—take over care of Willie from Lieutenant Korvaaminen for me."

"Yes, sir!" Pytten wept. Risto sighed in pain. Pytten nodded at the admiral. "He'll be the happiest, fattest salamander in the seven seas."

Risto nodded. He looked into Pytten's eyes.

"You'll take care of more than that, someday Pytten. Someday you *will* take command of the *Proteus*."

"But, sir, I can't command a ship, not anymore. I can't be a skipper now. I barely avoided the stockade, and once they find out about me stowing away—"

"There are… allowances, Pytten. For the Admiral of the Fleet. It's a matter of record I wanted you on board. You won't be punished. When this is over, you'll be transferred to serve directly under Captain Katla. It's been planned for weeks now."

Pytten tried to breathe calmly.

"Adversity…," Risto sighed, "adversity cannot defeat you. You know that there is nothing you can't overcome. You survived my wrath. You survived the push to the dome. You survived the assembly themselves. Audacity will lose ground, sometimes, lose a rank. But it never lost you my respect."

Pytten held him tightly as he faded away. Kätyri's words echoed around Pytten's brain: "You're not gonna be a captain if you don't even know how you'll be addressed."

"I'll make it, Admiral. I'll never give up," Pytten added, "but command—with 'sir' and 'ma'am' out of the running, what will they even call me?"

Risto took his last breath.

"'Captain,' Pytten. They'll call you 'Captain.'"

Risto died. The last Valkyries and armored Valkohai moved into the tunnel to kill his brother. Pytten took Risto's body and headed back toward the subs, toward safety and a salamander.

Vibeke passed the mourning Cetacean without a second glance. She took one last look out of the drill hole before she entered to meet her fate with Veikko. As she looked, she saw a three-legged tank on the horizon.

VARG HAD set the Blackwing to open only on Valkyrie contact. Nel approached it. She remembered how to fly it; Violet had trained thoroughly. Her brain would be compatible with its interface. But she wasn't a Valkyrie.

"And you never will be. Valkyries take what they want. You know you want to be with me, but you can't admit it to yourself. You're worse than Violet. At least she tried *to rape Vibs. You could have a hundred times, but empathy stayed your hand, and I had to hear it. Had to listen to your pathetic conscience deny you pleasure."*

She touched the bottom of the craft, wondering how to open it. She climbed up on top.

"It won't open. Not for you, never for you."

She approached the hatch and sent out a low level pulse signal with her working link for it to open. Nothing happened.

"Because you're not one of us."

She tried again.

"Because you're pathetic."

And again.

"Insufficient."

Again.

"Nothing."

And she realized that if her new body wasn't a Valkyrie, her old one had been part of one. Nel wasn't the Valkyrie present. Nelson, the Tikari, the insect was. From the center of her broken chest she accessed the Tikari link and sent out the same pulse.

The Blackwing opened its canopy. She could feel the surprise and anger from Veikko's mind spill into her own.

"How the fuck—"

She got in and closed the canopy and drained the cockpit. Then sent a thoughtwave up into the system. The Blackwing started up.

"No!"

Nel lifted off and took the Blackwing into the sky. She set a course for Luna. The vessel could make it there in minutes. She didn't look forward to a new life on the moon, not without Vibeke, but she had nowhere else to go.

"If you leave me, Nel, I'll never forgive you. If you leave now you have nothing on this earth to come back to."

He was right about that. There was nothing left for her on Earth. No reason to ever return. She hit the engines and headed toward the edge of the atmosphere.

"Then it's done. Good-bye to you, Nel, and all that could have been."

She felt the lie from his mind. He didn't mean good-bye. She didn't care; she meant it.

She used the vessel's superior sensor grid to monitor the war from afar. Battles were forming in the sky. Ulver, the UKI and the Cetaceans. All destroying each other. The fleets came together like curtains beneath her as she headed toward space, closing upon her former planet and sending her away into the future.

MISHKA WAS still there. In her tank. Vibeke was standing only meters from Alf's.

She ran to it, blood quickly coming to a boil. Fury transmuting her sorrow, her morose regret, all her pain into focus. Her wish for death was absent from her mind. Murder had taken over, rewritten her consciousness into one goal. To kill Mishka. To end her permanently, unquestionably, forever.

She climbed into the tank and started up the manual controls. Readouts flickered. Barrels rotated, missiles loaded. She gunned it. She spotted Mishka's tank again and adjusted course. She was only a kilometer away and Kvitøya was a small island. The air battle was raining down debris and sensors suggested some sort of land force was coming ashore from the north. Inconsequential. Mishka was heading south fast. Vibeke was coming up behind her even faster. Three legs versus eight. No contest.

Mishka finally saw the blip behind her. She knew who it was. She turned her cockpit backward and opened fire.

Microwave and projectile bursts started hitting the tank. They had little effect at such range. Vibeke tried to return fire but again hit the mental block. She tried to convince herself she was shooting to injure, not to kill. Still unable. She tried to imagine it was someone else in the tank firing at her. Nothing.

The incoming fire was beginning to rattle the canopy. She had to think fast. Not her strong suit just then. She ran the old Valkyrie software, the antihacking routines. As expected Mishka knew how to circumvent them. They could pinpoint the exact location of the hack on a gyrus on her cerebral cortex but couldn't do anything about it. Mishka was far too good for that. Or was she?

"*Other people are sloppy*," Veikko had told her. "*Their hacks are so focused in a single cortical column you can spot 'em with Valhalla software, remove 'em with a DBI.*"

She didn't have a direct brain interface. She didn't have time to find the Blackwing's. She could find the hack on the surface of her brain but couldn't zap it out.

She was however completely insane and far from caring about anything but how to kill the woman. She could die seconds later if only she could kill Mishka first. She ejected her Tikari, grasped it firmly, and stabbed as hard as she could into her skull over the hacked gyrus. She wrenched the blade around to crudely remove a small chunk of gray matter. Her vision flickered. Her head erupted in horrific pain. A chunk of her skull and meninges fell to her side along with the fragment of her brain. She tore open the tank's med kit and grabbed an emergency clot and stuffed it in the hole. Bob crawled back into her chest.

She tried out the effects of her ad-lib lobotomy and pulled the triggers. She laughed out loud when the Gatling array spewed metal at the other tank. It did little harm at that range, but Vibeke's ability to fire shocked Mishka into making a mistake. With her attention stretched, she let her tank on autopilot avoid a cliff that she could have jumped. Her tank was going around the drop off. Vibeke knew the terrain and knew what Alf's tank could do. When Mishka's tank made the corner, Vibeke jumped right down and closed the gap.

She let loose every projectile the tank had. Mishka did the same. Fire erupted between them, the air itself destroyed by the barrage of beams and rounds, missiles and more. They were close enough to feel it, like a hailstorm around them, cracking their canopies further and further, denting legs and breaking off barrels as both tanks ended their ammo supply. Soon Vibeke was close enough to ram her.

So she rammed her. The tank's legs briefly entangled and slowed both vehicles. Mishka was knocked meters off course. She was desperate now and rammed back, damaging her own tank further but sending Vibs on course into a wall of rock. Vibeke pulled hard upward and forced the tank to jump. It leapt over Mishka's and landed on her other side, then rammed it toward the same wall.

It was too late to shift course. Mishka had to escape. She increased speed and moved ahead of Alf's tank. She activated the Geki fire. It burned into Vibeke's shield, melting its outer surface and leaving only the conventional glass. Mishka heaved flame again, point-blank into the shield, cracking it into tiny fragments held together only by shape. Then she ran from her cockpit and jumped. She flew toward Vibeke; her feet crashed through the broken windshield and into Vibeke's seat, missing her by millimeters.

Vibeke's skin was torn up badly by the shattering clear shield. She kicked full force into Mishka's side, tearing through her skin and muscle. It broke her foot, she knew it, but before the pain could report, she was pulling herself back toward Mishka, ready to launch an assault.

She relaunched her Tikari at the same moment Mishka launched her eye. The two flying bodies fought and crashed in the snow, locked together in combat. Mishka tried to use the Geki flame again and again, but Vibeke wrenched her arm away every time. Then they both went deaf as a bomb hit just ahead of them. The blast bashed their eardrums in and the world turned silent. And they kept fighting. Mishka used the blast's effect and managed to push Vibs off of her for a moment, but she came right back. They grappled on the cockpit's burning remains until Mishka looked up, forward, and Vibs did the same. They saw where the tank was heading.

In seconds the tank would be directly in between the fighting armies. They were headed straight into the thickest fire from both sides. Mishka was ready to jump off the tank. Vibs didn't let her. Mishka was on top, so Vibeke held her by her shoulders and pushed her higher, but didn't let her go. Mishka was about to get hit by every beam and bullet in the air. So she pulled Vibs up with her.

For a moment they knelt together in bitter embrace, holding each other up for the barrage. And the barrage hit. Beams burned skin off half of Mishka's face and set Vibeke's garb on fire, rounds tore through their skin and muscles and ribs and organs. By the time an explosive round knocked them off the tank and sent them to the ground, both had been hit several dozen times. Mishka's lungs were in poor shape, one round had broken both of Vibeke's clavicles, and they came to a stop on the ground riddled with holes and minus several organs.

But they didn't need spleens to keep fighting. The muscles kept going, even the broken ones in their shot arms. Bones broke themselves to move again but they moved, and they fought. Vibeke kept punching when her arms were nearly gelatin. Mishka fell and kept kicking with the leg she had left. Vibeke fell upon her. She grabbed the Geki implant and threw it away from Mishka's reach. So Mishka clawed at her with her fingernails, cutting deep into her face.

Mishka's skin was full of holes. Vibeke reached in and tore swathes of her skin off from the inside out. They were both bloody pulp and the pulp just kept going. Epinephrine surged through and poured out of both of them; they both refused to stop, collapsing, breaking but fighting, still fighting, until both were aware they had but one move left before they would be physically incapable of moving ever again.

They picked their last acts to kill. Mishka was broken enough to let Vibs punch through her sternum and into her chest. Vibs was shredded to the point Mishka could do the same through the side of her ribs. They both sent their fists into each other and grabbed each other's hearts, and tore them out simultaneously, ripping busted arteries and weak, torn tissue. That was the end of their fight, and of their lives.

As she killed her great nemesis and felt her own heart torn from her ribs, Vibeke was not thinking of the enemy vanquished, she was not thinking of her own demise. As the blood left her brain she thought only of one thing. She wished she'd never even hunted Mishka. She wished she and Nel had simply headed for Luna or beyond. Killing Mishka wasn't worth losing the poor Tikari. And she'd lost it so terribly.

She wished above all that she could see Nel alive again, even if Nel would never forgive her, even if only for a second. She would trade the world for that moment. But she knew in her last thoughts that it could never come. She collapsed hemorrhaging into the snow and died.

THE GEKI arrived in the battlefield seconds after Mishka was dead. They cautiously made their way to the bodies beneath the crossfire.

Varg tried not to look at Vibeke's mutilated body, but he wasn't completely soulless. He looked at the remains of his teammate, his sister. It was hard to see the mess Mishka had made of her. He took some solace in the torn out heart lying by her palm. She had killed Mishka. Her aspiration for over a year was achieved. In the world that was left, it was merciful for her to die in the moment of her victory, if it could be called that.

He forced himself to focus on the job at hand. He knelt down by Mishka and searched her remains. They were shredded thoroughly, beyond thoroughly. Her former beauty was wasted, turned to slime and bone and burnt skin. But lying by her side was the implant. It had taken some hits, but it was built tough as solid steel. It would function again in his arm.

All that was left was to get to the moon where it could be implanted, where they could serve a purpose again. They jumped for the final time.

On the moon, things were calmer. The Geki had landed just north of Tranquility base. Within an hour they found Dr. Yasumoto. Terrified, he programmed his robots quickly and implanted Varg with the flame with exceptional speed.

Varg would have to learn it slowly and carefully now that they were inside an oxygen rich, atmosphere controlled colony. They made their way to the unused Geki base. They entered to find it fresh and ready for use, with its own med pod, its own library, and even a compendium of Irish folk music, requested by the elder's predecessor when UNEGA and GAUNE built the facility, preparing for the distant future.

They sat down and played a game of cards.

"We have our work cut out for us. The Lunar intel net suggests two major Christian movements have broken out. One is already militant and has executed the senate of Cleomedes. Another is rallying for a holy war against refugees from Earth. An infant was killed yesterday, beaten to death in an exorcism."

"Sounds like a job for the Geki."

"Well, Varg, you want to go burn some churches?"

"Soon. I just saw Vibeke dead. Violet's dead. Veikko is—well, it's been a hard year."

"I know better than you think. Violet's death is the hardest thing I'll ever face."

"Why? Why do *you* care about Violet? And why did you care that Violet named her Tikari 'Nelson'?"

"Because she named her Tikari after me."

Varg looked to him. The elder paused before speaking, looking into the ink black space outside the portal.

"I was her father."

Chapter XIII: Ultima Thule

THE BATTLES were intense. Kvitøya was getting erased. Nel felt a perverse sense of relief. The horrific first era in her life was at an end, and she was heading into the unknown. Luna. Violet had known almost nothing about it. Nel knew as much. But on Luna there was hope. On Earth there was nothing.

She scanned the surface one last time before she'd leave the atmosphere. Through the firefight in the sky, she only had one ongoing signal she knew how to look for, the control link from Mishka to the now defunct wetware she'd hastily installed. Low power and short range, the Blackwing could barely spot it through the traffic above. But it gave her a location, so she looked, and narrowed in on the Blackwing's scanners.

She saw the shredded remains of Mishka, the link dwindling as her brain activity ceased. And less than a meter away she saw Vibeke.

Torn apart, broken in a hundred places, her chest empty of her heart. Nel didn't register any conscious feeling. She didn't know why. Maybe it was because it was all over, because she'd already parted with her knowing Vibs would never want to see her alive again. Because she'd done all she could to erase the last remnants of feeling for her as she walked into the ocean. Or because Mishka was right—she was deluded, and her love for Vibeke had been no more real than a few confused memories, residue of Violet's mind. Whatever it had been, Nel was now free. Completely free, and headed for safety.

It must have been some sort of malfunction that made her turn the Blackwing around. No proper AI would have done it; with Vibeke dead and a three-military battle raging between them, it was a pointless, tactically impossible decision that no Tikari nor computer nor any rational human being would ever make.

A single lightning bolt leapt from Nel's brain into the Blackwing's guidance systems and the craft fired its attitude control thrusters, turning it 180 degrees. Then the ramjets sucked in the thin air of the high atmosphere and blasted her back down toward the Earth. Toward the battle.

She didn't slow down. She took the Blackwing to maximum conventional speed. The first stray rounds and beams past her, then the first high altitude drones. They were easy to avoid. Harder to avoid were top range pogos and jets and weapons platforms. She sent dozens of bolts into the system to edge past them, missing some by only meters. When she came to the core of the battle she was missing them by centimeters. Hundreds of bolts erupted from her mind, turning and boosting the Blackwing in incalculable spins and directions, burning into the fabric of her brain's locomotor regions.

At several hundred kph she was through the entire battle in only seconds, but in those seconds she made over a thousand drastic course changes. Past burning battle pogos and shrapnel and missiles and vessels, the Blackwing flew downward until Nel saw the ground and fired every retropropulsion engine the thing had.

The Blackwing sliced into the icy rock of Kvitøya up to its cockpit, encasing the canopy's front few explosive bolts. Nel blew them but the canopy remained in place. All around her, belligerents were spotting the strange craft that had so violently emerged into their field of fire. None recognized it as the stolen BIRP. All knew only that it wasn't one of their own. They began to fire.

Most of the strikes did nothing to the diamond armor. Only a few struck the exposed portions of the aft thrusters and ramjets. But that was enough. Within seconds of crash-down the thought bolts were reporting critical damage to the thermobaric thruster. It was soon to ignite.

Nel struck the canopy again and again, but it was forced into rock. It wouldn't move. The thruster had seconds left before it ignited. Even from zero momentum it would propel the craft into the rock beneath it and send its occupant deep into the mantle of the earth. She mustered every last joule of strength her arms held and struck the canopy with enough force to break the gneiss around the canopy's front, breaking it outward and onto the snow. She jumped out and ran.

The thruster ignited and spewed fuel into the air, forming a thick cloud of metallic hydrogen that caught fire and erupted into an incomparable blast. Nel ran with speed beyond any human body, with force behind every step to propel her away from the craft and toward the two cardiectomized bodies.

She spotted Vibeke from half a kilometer away and adjusted her sprint to hit her. The explosion behind her sent the Blackwing into the rock and began uplifting the surface of the island as it flew downward into the crust. The outer rim of the upheaval was only meters behind Nel's feet. She ran with such force she cracked the rock under her heels. She ran with such force it tore into her organic musculature and ruptured her hydraulics. She ran faster than anything resembling a human had ever run on Earth toward Vibeke's body.

Grasping it, she pulled Vibeke with her, leaving most of the body's left lower half behind and tearing up its side all the way to the ribs. The grasp knocked Nel off her feet and sent her sliding toward the rampart dome. She spotted the drill site and dug her fingers into the rock, steering them toward it. The blast behind her incinerated half of the battle, burning the fleets of Ulver and the UKI. Ending the war in fire.

Nel and the body slid before the expanding blast radius straight into the drill hole. Nel curled herself around Vibeke's head and chest as they broke through the back of the drill and over the edge of the ravine.

The blast continued deep into the ground and uplifted the edge of the rampart, shaking the ravine and cracking the dome. Nel and Vibeke fell all the way down to the bottom of the ravine. As they fell, Nel lost hold of her body, and it crashed down two turns up the spiral walkway. Nel crashed through the roof of a storage bay and landed hard in its contents, warping her metal and cutting off the last of the skin on her legs.

The fire outside shot through the drill tunnel and into the ravine as the rock around it collapsed. A single finger of flame ripped across Valhalla and burnt out to smoke that collected high on the rampart ceiling.

For a moment all was silent. The Ares throbbed and glowed red. Vibeke's body settled on the walkway. Nel pushed her way out of the boxes and canisters and rose to her steaming feet.

She limped slowly from the building and looked for Vibeke around the edge, where she thought she must have landed. As she walked out toward the walkway she found Kabar's body. And Katyusha's. There were Valkyrie bodies all around her, and Cetaceans in armor. Some burnt, some blown apart, some ripped in half.

Every Valkyrie, every Cetacean that had entered the pit was dead and mutilated. One body was so horrifically ripped apart that it lay dripping blood across the ground. It twitched. And slowly Nel realized, as it pulled together, crunching and chewing up its own parts, that it was the cause of the massacre. It was Veikko, assembling himself into a hulking gorilla of metal. The battle mode of the A-1 body. He was finally able to assemble himself fully. He'd left his pit to kill the incoming forces. The surviving Valkyries, his brother's men. The metal within him screeched and tore as he dragged his body into shape. And soon he was formed, and staring at her with his half eyes.

She felt him in her head, felt their brains still connected directly. She forced thought from herself. She heard nothing of his. He had gone silent. The only thing she could feel was a concern, a worry.

He would have to retreat to his hole soon to keep the ravine intact. Killing him, were it even possible for Nel's weaker body, would end the world. And with his elder body, without any safeguards limiting its strength, he could destroy hers without question. But beyond him was the walkway. Vibeke's body. She stepped toward him.

Veikko set every system he had for a fight. His hydraulics reset, his motors revved. He sloughed off what was left of his human figure and reshaped every limb for maximum strength. His skin broke apart wherever it remained and weapons systems loaded and armed. He grew to twice his human size and growled. Systems locked in place and set for battle. He became a formidable beast. The worry in his mind turned to rage. Rejection. Revenge.

Nel wasn't limited to human form herself. She supercharged her muscles and organic motors, readied the hydraulics and weapons Niide had granted her. Her body shifted and her remaining skin panels inverted, layering her with armor. She took a fighting stance as the last of her body sorted itself to fight. She came together in as strong a form as she could muster. In old sparring etiquette, she signaled Veikko to begin.

He ran for her and drew back his arm for a strike. She withdrew and reassembled her body out of the way of his fist. He struck again from the other side, crushing her torso with incomparable force. She managed to get a few strikes in, but they did nothing, while his delivered horrific pain and damaged every system they connected with. She ducked beneath him and lifted up, throwing him into the old Ares tanks, smashing their strong sides and knocking them down. The I-beam that once held them fell down, crushing Veikko beneath it.

He came back up holding the beam. He spun it like a fighting staff and brought it down on her position. She unhinged her spine and leaped out of its way. It broke the rock where she stood.

She could feel the tips of thoughts from his mind, the faintest foreshadowings of his next move. She knew he would be still for an instant as he prepared his stance for a powerful kick. She knew he would be vulnerable for an instant.

She extended one of her legs all the way into his chest, knocking him down as she jumped toward him to deliver a smashing blow from her right fist, her arm disassembling and reforming for more force. It hit him full force in the stomach. And did nothing. He pushed her off with a flick of his arm and it sent her flying into the mess hall, denting its roof and breaking its chimney. She disconnected the thrusters in her feet as they struck into the air and launched them as missiles. One flew past him and destroyed an arsenal, the other hit him and exploded into flames and a concussive force.

He stood as if it had been a flick of the fingers and ran for her. She tried to jump, but he hit her as she lifted and threw her into a rock wall. She extended her arms and pushed him off and sent him flying into a storage bay, which collapsed under the force. He bounced back instantly and ran to crush her against the wall. She had to disassemble half of herself to avoid the hit, then reformed around his arm, crushing it inward to no effect. He withdrew and launched another series of punches that she ducked out from under.

She ran to regroup and rethink how to hurt him. She tried microwaves, opening her arms and firing full force. It burned his skin black but only crackled and sparked on his metal interiors. She launched the last few expansion missiles in her arms and they hit as he ran, not even slowing him down. He opened his arms as he ran to reveal his own. They launched and struck her, throwing her back and burning straight through her.

His thoughts were amused, a deep laughter laden with rage. There was no more signal of his intended moves. He was managing to block her with the rage, the fury. It cleared his mind. She tried the same but felt like her thoughts betrayed her. She faked a jump to the left and instead darted right. He must have sensed it from her. He knew where to run.

He ran right into her and pounded her into a wall of ice, which collapsed and spilled down on them both. It didn't make them move a centimeter. They sparred further. She aimed every attack for his exposed face but he managed to block, even her split-arm blows in multiple directions. She aimed for his torso again, connecting with no effect. Veikko fought hard against Nel's blocks but only rarely managed a hit. But when he hit, things broke. Nel was certain to die if it went on. She opened her shoulders and fired fléchettes into his face. He fell back in pain and scraped them off.

As he did, Nel grabbed a wall and tore it from the building to deflect as he fired the same. She threw the wall at him and jumped back away.

He jumped and flew down toward her, leaving her only an instant to roll out of the way. She didn't make it far enough, and he came down on her leg, breaking it backward. She reassembled it and ran, only to get hit by an energy blast from his own integrated systems.

Then a small rock fell on her. She barely noticed it, it was harmless. But it came from the rampart. The blast had cracked it and the cracks were growing. She felt Veikko's mind grow concerned. He wanted to finish her and get back to his hole.

She spotted Veikko running for her and opened her ribs to fire the last of Niide's projectiles. They hit Veikko without harm. She scrambled up and ran behind an arsenal. Veikko snuck around the corner to ambush her but found her gone. They briefly lost sense of each other's position. Nel cautiously ran through the buildings away from him, trying to think of some way to hurt him, trying to remember what was in each arsenal. Trying to find a weapon that would help.

Veikko burst through the wall of the closest one and grabbed whatever he found. A heavy heat seeking missile launcher. He loaded it. He stalked her through the burnt towers and buildings. They tried to look into each other's minds. Scoured each other for any hint of position. Veikko's focus let her in ever so slightly to other thoughts, to his fear of the ravine collapsing. His desire to get back to the hole. And his fear for his weakness…. He knew he had one. And now she did too.

She kept low and headed for Arsenal 4, hoping the gas weapons inside could dissolve his organic parts. She made it to the open field around the pogo pads and then turned to see Veikko launch the heat missile right for her. There was nothing she could do. She couldn't run, it would find her. She rolled into a defensive posture but the missile could annihilate her completely. And it would have had Orson not flopped out into the way and exploded in a torrential rain of burning blubber around her.

She wiped the goop from her eyes and launched in a pounce at Veikko's face. He craned his neck around a half meter off its position on his shoulders to avoid her. He'd not let her connect there, and the rest of him could take anything she could throw. Nel understood she wouldn't beat him with strength. She had to think.

Veikko knew the Sigyn system was minutes away from activating again. He had to end the fight fast. Nel felt his panic. And again, his fear she would exploit his flaw, his fault.

A massive boulder fell from the rampart and hit him on the back. Nel looked up and saw the rampart beginning to collapse. She ran for cover but there was none. Rocks began to fall, giant slabs of rampart.

They rolled off Veikko like they were hailstones. They hit Nel with crushing force. She was weakening, her systems bruised and breaking. She didn't know how much longer she could take the rocks and Veikko's hits. She sidestepped a colossal curved chunk of falling rampart and Veikko used the move to collide with her and grab her. He held her immobile. Then he launched his hall thrusters.

He flew holding her before him as he plowed through buildings and structures, breaking solid metal and rock with her back. They flew across the ravine floor into the rock wall where he crushed her, breaking the mechanics of her legs irreparably, crushing her hips and shattering the rock behind her. She was broken in a hundred places. She could barely move, held by him and damaged severely.

The last of the rampart fell down around them, the dusk sky flooded into the ravine. Veikko leaned in close to deliver a killing blow.

As he leaned in she looked deep into the hole of his face, the bloody crusted mess from which he could barely see and speak. And breathe. As her thought flickered about his breath, his fear returned, making him hesitate. But why? What did he fear? What was the weakness if it was in his breath?

Veikko's thoughts darted away. He tried to think of anything else to keep her away from his vulnerability. He thought of hatred. He thought of pain. He thought of Nel dying in his hands. He thought of Skadi. He thought—she could tell against his will—of the safeguards he lacked in his respiratory system.

He felt Nel think it. He felt Violet's memories within her. Her days in school, a flash of her teacher speaking, and he knew she'd found it. A sneeze leaves the body with incredible involuntary force. He knew he had to kill her that moment. He revved his arm hydraulics to deliver a blow that would crush her head into absolute oblivion.

She blew gently into his exposed nasal turbinates. He paused. He sniffled. He sniffled more. He sniffled at the verge of sneezing. He caught his breath and stopped. Then he sneezed and the overpowerful lungs blew his head clean off his neck.

Nel fell to the ground as Veikko's body deactivated, twitching on the rock. She felt his thoughts recede from her mind, cold and dead, and finally absent forever. She took stock of herself. She could move, barely crawl. Her critical systems were broken beyond repair, her body was shutting down. She had only minutes before Veikko's damage would grind her to a halt and leave her immobile, and then only hours before the last life supports ceased to function. But she didn't need hours. Or have them.

Veikko was gone and the Sigyn system was only a few minutes from activating. When it did the ravine would collapse. The ocean would pour in and hit the active Ares. All Mishka's cult, all the nation of Ulver, any land thing that survived the Blackwing's thrust overhead would be drowned as the sun set on a dry Earth for the last time. All suffering mankind on the planet's surface was finally to be euthanized. None of that crossed Nel's mind. She crawled up the walkway to find Vibeke.

She collapsed by the side of her body, her legs breaking down and unable to move her again. She cradled the lifeless corpse and held it close. Vibeke was torn apart, limbs missing or hanging on by threads. Full of holes, out of blood. But Nel knew she wouldn't need her own for much longer. She opened the panels on her chest and exposed Violet's heart.

Nel disconnected her own descending aorta and split her fingers to reveal her medical array. She cut through Vibeke's chest and opened the region where her heart once was. Nel worked quickly to connect her own vessels with Vibeke's carotid arteries. She released epinephrine into their blood systems.

She had the wrong blood type; the act would kill them both in minutes. But they were down to seconds now. Nel began to lose consciousness as soon as her blood poured from Vibeke's wounds. But Vibeke's dead eyes began to close. Slowly her skin regained the slightest color. Nel held her up and embraced her and ran her fingers through Vibeke's hair. The Sigyn system activated and the ravine began to shake.

Vibeke opened her eyes and saw Nel. In pain and more tired than she'd ever felt, she made no conscious sense of how she lived or what state she was in, or to what state she would shortly return. She didn't think of anything but losing Nel so horribly, she wasn't capable of more.

But Nel was there and smiling past her tears. Vibeke understood that much.

Nel held her close as the ravine began to break apart. She held Vibeke's head up and thought, for the first time in her short life, that she was satisfied. She had Vibeke in her arms and felt no conflicts of love and hate, nor held any questions about what Vibeke meant to her, or what she meant to Vibeke. Vibeke thought nothing of the hacks to which she'd been subjected. What was before her, she loved despite it all of her own accord. That love was real. It belonged to her and Nel, and them alone. The two looked at each other only briefly and felt finally a sense of total clarity, despite all the pain between them, despite what they'd done to each other, despite the horrors through which they lived and their deaths soon to come.

The sun dropped beneath the edge of the ravine and the day was over. Valhalla shook. Its walls shattered, and the ocean came crashing in behind them. Nel and Vibeke spoke no apologies; they shared no parting words. At the end of the world, at the end of the day, there was nothing that couldn't be said by one last kiss good night.

Violet MacRae is one of the aimless millions crowding northern Scotland. In the year 2230, where war is obsolete and only brilliant minds are valued, she emerges into adulthood with more brawn than brains and a propensity for violence. People dismiss her as a relic, but world peace is more fragile than they know.

In Valhalla, a clandestine base hidden in an icy ravine, Violet connects with a group of outcasts just like her. There, she learns the skills she needs to keep the world safe from genetically enhanced criminals and traitors who threaten the first friends she's ever known. She also meets Wulfgar Kray, a genius gang leader who knows her better than she knows herself and who would conquer the world to capture her.

Branded from childhood as a useless barbarian, Violet is about to learn the world needs her exactly as she is.

www.harmonyinkpress.com

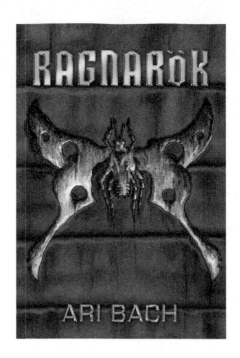

After a year spent hunting for Mishka and Wulfgar, V team is no closer to finding them. If they're going to locate their nemeses, they're going to have to break some rules. As they begin their most dangerous mission yet, the stakes grow higher than they ever imagined as they uncover not only the subjects of their hunt, but the greatest threat the Earth has ever known.

To save the planet, their path will take them across the globe, across the solar system, and deeper into their relationships with each other than they've ever dared to look. Sacred bonds will be tested, the closest alliances will fall, and Violet will come face-to-face with a far more daunting and dangerous challenge than saving the planet—her growing love for Vibeke—a love that could be her salvation, or the cause of her ultimate downfall.

www.harmonyinkpress.com

ARI BACH's artwork can be found online at aribach.deviantart.com/.

Ari also runs a webcomic at www.twistedjenius.com/Snail-Factory/ and has a Tarot deck at surrealist.tarotsmith.net/.

But Ari is probably best known for the humor blog "Facts-I-Just-Made-Up" at facts-i-just-made-up.tumblr.com/.

Check out the Valhalla series official blog at the-walrus-squad.tumblr.com.

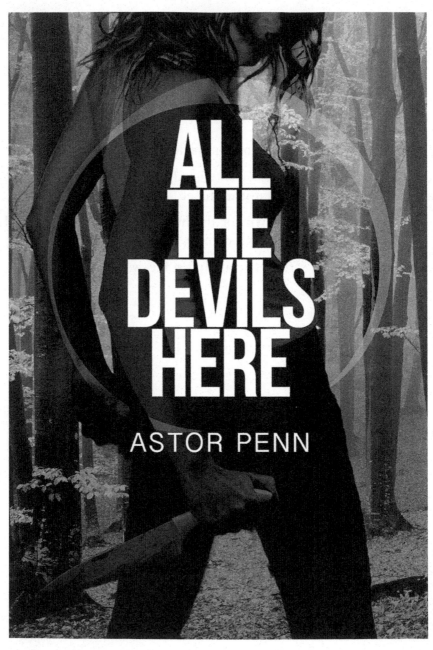

ALL THE DEVILS HERE

ASTOR PENN

www.harmonyinkpress.com

FAIRY TALES FOR MODERN QUEERS

EMILY REED

www.harmonyinkpress.com

NIKOLAI J OSLIN

LIFE
Beyond
THE
Temple

www.harmonyinkpress.com

SARA GAINES

NOBLE
PERSUASION

www.harmonyinkpress.com

Pretty Peg

Skye Allen

www.harmonyinkpress.com

Zoe Lynne

That Witch!

www.harmonyinkpress.com